La
Habana
del Este

MORRO
CASTLE

Casablanca

Ave. de Casa Blanca

NATIONAL
BALLET

PRIBLUDA'S
APARTMENT
Malecón

HAVANA BAY

EMBASSY
APARTMENT

HOTEL
CAPRI

San Lázaro

San Lázaro

Ave. del Puerto

Vedado

San Lázaro

Belascoaín

Centro
Habana

Paseo de Martí

Ave. de Bélgica

La
Habana
Vieja

Desamparado San Pedro

Ave. de los Presidentes

Ave. Menocal (Infanta)

Zanja

Chinatown

Egido

Ave. Simón Bolívar

Máximo Gómez

CENTRO
RUSSO-
CUBANO

PLAZA DE
EVOLUCIÓN

Ave. de la Independencia

Ayestarán

Atares

Ave. del Puerto

Ensenada de Atarés

Ensenada de Guasabacoa

LÓN
METERY

ESE
ETERY

Tulipán

Máximo Gómez

Calzada del Cerro

Luyanó

ógico

INSTITUTO
DE MEDICINA LEGAL

Vía Blanca

Vía Blanca

Carretera Central

Vía Blanca

Calzada de Palatino

Vía Blanca

Ave. Rancho Boyeros

HAVANA BAY

HAVANA BAY

A NOVEL

MARTIN CRUZ SMITH

RANDOM HOUSE NEW YORK

Copyright (c) 1999 by Martin Cruz Smith

All rights reserved under International and Pan-American Copyright
Conventions. Published in the United States by Random House,
Inc., New York, and simultaneously in Canada by Random House of
Canada Limited, Toronto.

Library of Congress Cataloging-in-Publication Data is available
ISBN 0-679-42662-0

Random House and colophon are registered
trademarks of Random House, Inc.

Random House website address: www.atrandom.com

Printed in the United States of America on acid-free paper

98765432   24689753   23456789

First Edition

Book design by Barbara M. Bachman

FOR EM

ACKNOWLEDGMENTS

I would like to thank, in Cuba, the writers José LaTour, Daniel Chavarria and Arnaldo Correa; in Spain, Justo Vasco; in Russia, Konstantin Zhukovski of Tass. They are in no way responsible for any political opinions expressed in this book.

In the United States I was aided by the medical knowledge of Drs. Neil Benowitz, Nelson Branco, Mark Levy and Kenneth Sack, the arson expertise of George Alboff and Larry Williams, the camera of Sam Smith, the lyrics of Regla Miller, the worldly advice of Bill Hanson and the critical reading by Bob Loomis, Nell Branco and Luisa Smith.

Most of all, I owe Knox Burger and Kitty Sprague, who waited for the story.

HAVANA BAY

1.

A police boat directed a light toward tar-covered pilings and water, turning a black scene white. Havana was invisible across the bay, except for a single line of lamps along the seawall. Stars rode high, anchor lights rode low, otherwise the harbor was a still pool in the night.

Soda cans, crab pots, fishing floats, mattresses, Styrofoam bearded with algae shifted as an investigation team of the Policía Nacional de la Revolución took flash shots. Arkady waited in a cashmere overcoat with a Captain Arcos, a barrel-chested little man who looked ironed into military fatigues, and his Sergeant Luna, large, black and angular. Detective Osorio was a small brown woman in PNR blue; she gave Arkady a studied glare.

A Cuban named Rufo was the interpreter from the Russian embassy. "It's very simple," he translated the captain's words. "You see the body, identify the body and then go home."

"Sounds simple." Arkady tried to be agreeable, although Arcos walked off as if any contact with Russians was contamination.

Osorio combined the sharp features of an ingenue with the grave expression of a hangman. She spoke and Rufo explained, "The detective says this is the Cuban method, not the Russian method or the German method. The Cuban method. You will see."

Arkady had seen little so far. He had just arrived at the airport in the dark when he was whisked away by Rufo. They were headed by taxi to the city when Rufo received a call on a cellular phone that diverted them to the bay. Already Arkady had a sense that he was unwelcome and unpopular.

Rufo wore a loose Hawaiian shirt and a faint resemblance to the older, softer Muhammad Ali. "The detective says she hopes you don't mind learning the Cuban method."

"I'm looking forward to it." Arkady was nothing if not a good guest. "Could you ask her when the body was discovered?"

"Two hours ago by the boat."

"The embassy sent me a message yesterday that Pribluda was in trouble. Why did they say that before you found a body?"

"She says ask the embassy. She was certainly not expecting an investigator."

Professional honor seemed to be at stake and Arkady felt badly outclassed on that score. Like Columbus on deck, Captain Arcos scanned the dark impatiently, Luna his hulking shadow. Osorio had sawhorses erected and stretched a tape that read NO PASEO. When a motorcycle policeman in a white helmet and spurs on his boots arrived, she chased him with a shout that could have scored steel. Somehow men in T-shirts appeared along the tape as soon as it was unrolled—what was it about violent death that was better than dreams? Arkady wondered. Most of the onlookers were black; Havana was far more African than Arkady had expected, although the logos on their shirts were American.

Someone along the tape carried a radio that sang, "*La fiesta no es para los feos. Qué feo es, señor. Super feo, amigo mío. No puedes pasar aquí, amigo. La fiesta no es para los feos.*"

"What does that mean?" Arkady asked Rufo.

"The song? It says, 'This party is not for ugly people. Sorry, my friend, you can't come.' "

Yet here I am, Arkady thought.

A vapor trail far overhead showed silver, and ships at anchor started to appear where only lights had hung moments before. Across the bay the seawall and mansions of Havana rose from the water, docks spread and, along the inner bay, loading cranes got to their feet.

"The captain is sensitive," Rufo said, "but whoever was right or wrong about the message, you're here, the body's here."

4

"So it couldn't have worked out better?"

"In a manner of speaking."

Osorio ordered the boat to back off so that its wash wouldn't stir the body. A combination of the boat's light and the freshening sky made her face glow.

Rufo said, "Cubans don't like Russians. It's not you, it's just not a good place for a Russian."

"Where is a good place?"

Rufo shrugged.

This side of the harbor, now that Arkady could see it, was like a village. A hillside of banana palms overhung abandoned houses that fronted what was more a cement curb than a seawall that stretched from a coal dock to a ferry landing. A wooden walkway balanced on a black piling captured whatever floated in. The day was going to be warm. He could tell by the smell.

"Vaya a cambiar su cara, amigo. Feo, feo, feo como horror, señor."

In Moscow, in January, the sun would have crept like a dim lamp behind rice paper. Here it was a rushing torch that turned air and bay into mirrors, first of nickel and then to vibrant, undulating pink. Many things were suddenly apparent. A picturesque ferry that moved toward the landing. Little fishing boats moored almost within reach. Arkady noticed that more than palms grew in the village behind him; the sun found coconuts, hibiscus, red and yellow trees. Water around the pilings began to show the peacock sheen of petroleum.

Detective Osorio's order for the video camera to roll was a signal for onlookers to press against the tape. The ferry landing filled with commuters, every face turned toward the pilings where, in the quickening light floated a body as black and bloated as the inner tube it rested in. Shirt and shorts were split by the body's expansion. Hands and feet trailed in the water; a swim fin dangled casually on one foot. The head was eyeless and inflated like a black balloon.

"A *neumático*," Rufo told Arkady. "A *neumático* is a fisherman who fishes from an inner tube. Actually from a fishing net spread over the tube. Like a hammock. It's very ingenious, very Cuban."

"The inner tube is his boat?"

"Better than a boat. A boat needs gasoline."

Arkady pondered that proposition.

"Much better."

A diver in a wet suit slid off the police boat while an officer in waders dropped over the seawall. They clambered as much as waded across crab pots and mattress springs, mindful of hidden nails and septic water, and cornered the inner tube so that it wouldn't float away. A net was thrown down from the seawall to stretch under the inner tube and lift it and the body up together. So far, Arkady wouldn't have done anything differently. Sometimes events were just a matter of luck.

The diver stepped into a hole and went under. Gasping, he came up out of the water, grabbed onto first the inner tube and then a foot hanging from it. The foot came off. The inner tube pressed against the spear of a mattress spring, popped and started to deflate. As the foot turned to jelly, Detective Osorio shouted for the officer to toss it to shore: a classic confrontation between authority and vulgar death, Arkady thought. All along the tape, onlookers clapped and laughed.

Rufo said, "See, usually, our level of competence is fairly high, but Russians have this effect. The captain will never forgive you."

The camera went on taping the debacle while another detective jumped into the water. Arkady hoped the lens captured the way the rising sun poured into the windows of the ferry. The inner tube was sinking. An arm disengaged. Shouts flew back and forth between Osorio and the police boat. The more desperately the men in the water tried to save the situation the worse it became. Captain Arcos contributed orders to lift the body. As the diver steadied the head, the pressure of his hands liquefied its face and made it slide like a grape skin off the skull, which itself separated cleanly from the neck; it was like trying to lift a man who was perversely disrobing part by part, unembarrassed by the stench of advanced decomposition. A pelican sailed overhead, red as a flamingo.

"I think identification is going to be a little more complicated than the captain imagined," Arkady said.

The diver caught the jaw as it dropped off from the skull and juggled each, while the detectives pushed the other black, swollen limbs pell-mell into the shriveling inner tube.

"Feo, tan feo. No puedes pasar aquí, amigo. Porque la fiesta no es para los feos."

The rhythm was . . . what was the word? Arkady wondered. Unrelenting.

Across the bay a golden dome seemed to burst into flame, and the houses of the Malecón started to express their unlikely colors of lemon, rose, royal purple, aquamarine.

It really was a lovely city, he thought.

Light from the high windows of the autopsy theater of the Instituto de Medicina Legal fell on three stainless-steel tables. On the right-hand table lay the *neumático*'s torso and loose parts arranged like an ancient statue dredged in pieces from the sea. Along the walls were enamel cabinets, scales, X-ray panel, sink, specimen shelves, freezer, refrigerator, pails. Above, at the observation level, Rufo and Arkady had a semicircle of seats to themselves. Arkady hadn't noticed before how scarred Rufo's brows were.

"Captain Luna would rather you watched from here. The examiner is Dr. Blas."

Rufo waited expectantly until Arkady realized he was supposed to react.

"*The* Dr. Blas?"

"The very one."

Blas had a dapper Spanish beard and wore rubber gloves, goggles, green scrubs. Only when he appeared satisfied that he had a reasonably complete body did he measure it and search it meticulously for marks and tattoos, a painstaking task when skin tended to slide wherever touched. An autopsy could take two hours, as much as four. At the left-hand table Detective Osorio and a pair of technicians sorted through the deflated inner tube and fishnet; the body had been left tangled in them for fear of disturbing it any more. Captain Arcos stood to one side, Luna a step behind. It occurred to Arkady that Luna's head was as round and blunt as a black fist with red-rimmed eyes. Already Osorio had found a wet roll of American dollar bills and a ring of keys kept in a leaky plastic bag. Fingerprints wouldn't have survived the bag, and she immediately dispatched the keys with an officer. There was something appealingly energetic and fastidious about Osorio. She hung wet shirt, shorts and underwear on hangers on a rack.

While Blas worked he commented to a microphone clipped to the lapel of his coat.

"Maybe two weeks in the water," Rufo translated. He added, "It's been hot and raining, very humid. Even for here."

"You've seen autopsies before?" Arkady asked.

"No, but I've always been curious. And, of course, I'd heard of Dr. Blas."

Performing an autopsy on a body in an advanced stage of putrefaction was as delicate as dissecting a soft-boiled egg. Sex was obvious but not age, not race, not size when the chest and stomach cavities were distended, not weight when the body sagged with water inside, not fingerprints when hands that had trailed in the water for a week ended in digits nibbled to the bone. Then there was the gaseous pressure of chemical change. When Blas punctured the abdomen a flatulent spray shot loudly up, and when he made the Y incision across the chest and then to groin, a wave of black water and liquefied matter overflowed the table. Using a pail, a technician deftly caught the viscera as they floated out. An expanding pong of rot—as if a shovel had been plunged into swamp gas—took possession of the room, invading everyone's nose and mouth. Arkady was glad he had left his precious coat in the car. After the first trauma of the stench—five minutes, no more—the olfactory nerves were traumatized and numb, but he was already digging deep into his cigarettes.

Rufo said, "That smells disgusting."

"Russian tobacco." Arkady filled his lungs with smoke. "Want one?"

"No, thanks. I boxed in Russia when I was on the national team. I hated Moscow. The food, the bread and, most of all, the cigarettes."

"You don't like Russians, either?"

"I love Russians. Some of my best friends are Russian." Rufo leaned for a better view as Blas spread the chest for the camera.

"The doctor is very good. At the rate they're going you'll have time to make your plane. You won't even have to spend the night."

"Won't the embassy make a fuss about this?"

"The Russians here? No."

Blas slapped the pulpy mass of the heart in a separate tray.

"You don't think they're too indelicate, I hope," Rufo said.

"Oh, no." To be fair, as Arkady remembered, Pribluda used to root through bodies with the enthusiasm of a boar after nuts. "Imagine the poor bastard's surprise," Pribluda would have said. "Floating around, looking up at the stars, and then bang, he's dead."

Arkady lit one cigarette from another and drew the smoke in sharply enough to make his eyes tear. It occurred to him that he was at a point now where he knew more people dead than alive, the wrong side of a certain line.

"I picked up a lot of languages touring with the team," Rufo said. "After boxing, I used to guide groups of singers, musicians, dancers, intellectuals for the embassy. I miss those days."

Detective Osorio methodically laid out supplies that the dead man had taken to sea: thermos, wicker box, and plastic bags of candles, rolls of tape, twine, hooks and extra line.

Usually, an examiner cut at the hairline and peeled the forehead over the face to reach the skull. Since in this case both the forehead and the face had already slipped off and bade adieu in the bay, Blas proceeded directly with a rotary saw to uncover the brain, which proved rotten with worms that reminded Arkady of the macaroni served by Aeroflot. As the nausea rose he had Rufo lead him to a tiny, chain-flush lavatory, where he threw up, so perhaps he wasn't so inured after all, he thought. Maybe he had just reached his limit. Rufo was gone, and walking back to the autopsy theater on his own, Arkady went by a room perfumed by carboys of formaldehyde and decorated with anatomical charts. On a table two feet with yellow toenails stuck out from a sheet. Between the legs lay an oversized syringe connected by a tube to a tub of embalming fluid on the floor, a technique used in the smallest, most primitive Russian villages when electric pumps failed. The needle of the syringe was particularly long and narrow to fit into an artery, which was thinner than a vein. Between the feet were rubber gloves and another syringe in an unopened plastic bag. Arkady slipped the bag into his jacket pocket.

When Arkady returned to his seat, Rufo was waiting with a recuperative Cuban cigarette. By that time, the brain had been weighed and set aside while Dr. Blas fit head and jaw together.

Although Rufo's lighter was the plastic disposable sort, he said it had been refilled twenty times. "The Cuban record is over a hundred."

Arkady bit the cigarette, inhaled. "What kind is this?"

" 'Popular.' Black tobacco. You like it?"

"It's perfect." Arkady let out a plume of smoke as blue as the exhaust of a car in distress.

Rufo's hand kneaded Arkady's shoulder. "Relax. You're down to bones, my friend."

The officer who had taken the keys from Osorio returned. At the other table, after Blas had measured the skull vertically and across the brow, he spread a handkerchief and diligently scrubbed the teeth with a toothbrush. Arkady handed Rufo a dental chart he had brought from Moscow (an investigator's precaution), and the driver trotted the envelope down to Blas, who systematically matched the skull's brightened grin to the chart's numbered circles. When he was done he conferred with Captain Arcos, who grunted with satisfaction and summoned Arkady down to the theater floor.

Rufo interpreted. "The Russian citizen Sergei Sergeevich Pribluda arrived in Havana eleven months ago as an attaché to the Russian embassy. We knew, of course, that he was a colonel in the KGB. Excuse me, the new Federal Security Service, the SVR."

"Same thing," Arkady said.

The captain—and in his wake, Rufo—went on. "A week ago the embassy informed us that Pribluda was missing. We did not expect them to invite a senior investigator from the Moscow prosecutor's office. Perhaps a family member, nothing more."

Arkady had talked to Pribluda's son, who had refused to come to Havana. He managed a pizzeria, a major responsibility.

Rufo went on. "Fortunately, the captain says, the identification performed today before your eyes is simple and conclusive. The captain says that a key found in the effects was taken to the apartment of the missing man where it unlocked the door. From an examination of the body recovered from the bay, Dr. Blas estimates that it is a Caucasoid male approximately fifty to sixty years of age, one hundred sixty-five centimeters in height, ninety kilos in weight, in every regard the same as the missing man. Moreover, the dental chart of the Russian citizen Pribluda you yourself brought shows one lower molar filled. That molar in the recovered jaw is a steel tooth which, in the opinion of Dr. Blas, according to the captain, is typical Russian dental work. Do you agree?"

"From what I saw, yes."

"Dr. Blas says he finds no wounds or broken bones, no signs of violence or foul play. Your friend died of natural causes, perhaps a stroke or aneurysm or heart attack, it would be almost impossible to determine which for a body in this condition. The doctor hopes he did not suffer long."

"That's kind of him." Although the doctor appeared more smug than sympathetic.

"The captain, for his part, asks if you accept the observations of this autopsy?"

"I'd like to think about it."

"Well, you accept the conclusion that the body recovered is that of the Russian citizen Pribluda?"

Arkady turned to the examining table. What had been a bloated cadaver was now split and gutted. Of course, there had been no face or eyes to identify anyway, and finger bones never did yield prints, but someone had lived in that ruined body.

"I think an inner tube in the bay is a strange place to find a Russian citizen."

"The captain says they all think that."

"Then there will be an investigation?"

Rufo said, "It depends."

"On what?"

"On many factors."

"Such as?"

"The captain says your friend was a spy. What he was doing when he died was not innocent. The captain can predict your embassy will ask us to do nothing. We are the ones who could make an international incident of this, but frankly it is not worth the effort. We will investigate in our own time, in our own way, although in this Special Period the Cuban people cannot afford to waste resources on people who have revealed themselves to be our enemy. Now do you understand what I mean?" Rufo paused while Arcos took a second to compose himself. "The captain says an investigation depends on many factors. The position of our friends at the Russian embassy must be taken into account before premature steps are taken. The only issue we have here is an identification of a foreign national who has died on Cuban territory. Do you accept it is the Russian citizen Sergei Pribluda?"

"It could be," Arkady said.

Dr. Blas sighed, Luna took a deep breath and Detective Osorio weighed the keys in her palm. Arkady couldn't help feeling like a difficult actor. "It probably is, but I can't say conclusively that this body is Pribluda. There's no face, no prints and I doubt very much that you will be able to type the blood. All you have is a dental chart and one steel tooth. He could be another Russian. Or one of thousands of Cubans who went to Russia. Or a Cuban who had a tooth pulled by a Cuban dentist who trained in Russia. Probably you're right, but that's not enough. You opened Pribluda's door with a key. Did you look inside?"

Dr. Blas asked in precisely snipped Russian, "Did you bring any other identification from Moscow?"

"Just this. Pribluda sent it a month ago." Arkady dug out of his passport case a snapshot of three men standing on a beach and squinting at the camera. One man was so black he could have been carved from jet. He held up a glistening rainbow of a fish for the admiration of two whites, a shorter man with a compensating tower of steel-wool hair and, partially obscured by the others, Pribluda. Behind them was water, a tip of beach, palms.

Blas studied the photograph and read the scribble on the back. "Havana Yacht Club."

"There is such a yacht club?" Arkady asked.

"There *was* such a club before the Revolution," Blas said. "I think your friend was making a joke."

Rufo said, "Cubans love grandiose titles. A 'drinking society' can be friends in a bar."

"The others don't look Russian to me. You can make copies of the picture and circulate them."

The picture went around to Arcos, who put it back into Arkady's hands as if it were toxic. Rufo said, "The captain says your friend was a spy, that spies come to bad ends, as they deserve. This is typically Russian, pretending to help and then stabbing Cuba in the back. The Russian embassy sends out its spy and, when he's missing, asks us to find him. When we find him, you refuse to identify him. Instead of cooperating, you demand an investigation, as if you were still the master and Cuba was the puppet. Since that is no longer the case, you can take your picture back to Moscow. The whole world knows of the Russian betrayal of the Cuban people and, well, he says some more in that vein."

Arkady gathered as much. The captain looked ready to spit.

Rufo gave Arkady a push. "I think it's time to go."

Detective Osorio, who had been quietly following the conversation, suddenly revealed fluent Russian. "Was there a letter with the picture?"

"Only a postcard saying hello," Arkady said. "I threw it away."

"*Idiota*," Osorio said, which nobody bothered to translate.

"It's lucky you're going home, you don't have many friends here," Rufo said. "The embassy said to put you in an apartment until the plane."

They drove by three-story stone town houses transformed by the revolution into a far more colorful backdrop of ruin and decay, marble colonnades refaced with whatever color was available— green, ultramarine, chartreuse. Not just ordinary green, either, but a vibrant spectrum: sea, lime, palm and verdigris. Houses were as blue as powdered turquoise, pools of water, peeling sky, the upper levels enlivened by balconies of ornate ironwork embellished by canary cages, florid roosters, hanging bicycles. Even dowdy Russian cars wore a wide variety of paint, and if their clothes were drab most of the people had the slow grace and color of big cats. They paused at tables offering guava paste, pastries, tubers and fruits. One girl shaving ices was streaked red and green with syrup, another girl sold sweetmeats from a cheesecloth tent. A locksmith rode a bicycle that powered a key grinder; he wore goggles for the sparks and shavings flying around him as he pedaled in place. The music of a radio hanging in the crook of a pushcart's umbrella floated in the air.

"Is this the way to the airport?" Arkady asked.

"The flight is tomorrow. Usually there's only one Aeroflot flight a week during the winter, so they don't want you to miss it." Rufo rolled the window down. "Phew, I smell worse than fish."

"Autopsies stay with you." Arkady had left his overcoat outside the operating theater and separated the coat now from the paper bag holding Pribluda's effects. "If Dr. Blas and Detective Osorio speak Russian, why were you along?"

"There was a time when it was forbidden to speak English. Now Russian is taboo. Anyway, the embassy wanted someone along when you were with the police, but someone not Russian. You know, I never knew anyone so unpopular so fast as you."

"That's a sort of distinction."

"But now you're here you should enjoy yourself. Would you like to see the city, go to a café, to the Havana Libre? It used to be the Hilton. They have a rooftop restaurant with a fantastic view. And they serve lobster. Only state restaurants are allowed to serve lobster, which are assets of the state."

"No, thanks." The idea of cracking open a lobster after an autopsy didn't sit quite right.

"Or a *paladar*, a private restaurant. They're small, they're only allowed twelve chairs but the food is much superior. No?"

Perhaps Rufo didn't get a chance to dine out often, but Arkady didn't think he could even watch someone eat.

"No. The captain and sergeant were in green uniforms, the detective in gray and blue. Why was that?"

"She's police and they're from the Ministry of the Interior. We just call it Minint. Police are under Minint."

Arkady nodded; in Russia the militia was under the same ministry. "But Arcos and Luna don't usually go out on homicides?"

"I don't think so."

"Why was the captain going on about the Russian embassy?"

14

"He has a point. In the old days Russians acted like lords. Even now, for Cuban police to ask questions at the embassy takes a diplomatic note. Sometimes the embassy cooperates and sometimes it doesn't."

Most of the traffic was Russian Ladas and Moskviches spraying exhaust and then, waddling as ponderously as dinosaurs, American cars from before the Revolution. Rufo and Arkady got out at a two-story house decorated like a blue Egyptian tomb with scarabs, ankhs and lotuses carved in stucco. A car on blocks sat in residence on the porch.

" '57 Chevrolet." Rufo looked inside at the car's gutted interior, straightened and ran his hand over the flecked paint. From the back. "Tail fins." To the front bumper. "And tits."

From the car key in the bag of effects Arkady knew that Pribluda had a Lada. No breasts on a Russian car.

As they went in and climbed the stairs the door to the ground-floor apartment cracked open enough for a woman in a housedress to follow their progress.

"A concierge?" Arkady asked.

"A snoop. Don't worry, at night she watches television and doesn't hear a thing."

"I'm going back tonight."

"That's right." Rufo unlocked the upstairs door. "This is a protocol apartment the embassy uses for visiting dignitaries. Well, lesser dignitaries. I don't think we've had anyone here for a year."

"Is someone from the embassy coming to talk about Pribluda?"

"The only one who wants to talk about Pribluda is you. You like cigars?"

"I've never smoked a cigar."

"We'll talk about it later. I'll be back at midnight to take you to the plane. If you think the flight to Havana was long, wait till you go back to Moscow."

The apartment was furnished with a set of cream-and-gold dining chairs, a sideboard with a coffee service, a nubby sofa, red phone, a bookshelf with titles like *La Amistad Russo-Cubana* and *Fidel y Arte* supported by erotic bookends in mahogany. In a disconnected refrigerator a loaf of Bimbo Bread was spotted with mold. The air conditioner was dead and showed the carbon smudges of an electrical fire. Arkady thought he probably showed some carbon smudges of his own.

He stripped from his clothes and showered in a stall of tiles that poured water from every valve and washed the odor of the autopsy off his skin and from his hair. He dried himself on the scrap of towel provided and stretched out on the bed under his overcoat in the dark of the bedroom and listened to the voices and music that filtered from outside through the closed shutters of the window. He dreamed of floating among the playing fish of Havana Bay. He dreamed of flying back to Moscow and not landing, just circling in the night.

Russian planes did that, sometimes, if they were so old that their instruments failed. Although there could be other factors. If a pilot made a second landing approach he could be charged for the extra fuel expended, so he made only one, good or not. Or they were overloaded or underfueled.

He was both.

Circling sounded good.

2.

Osorio negotiated a white PNR Lada down a potholed street. Like her driving, she talked in a quick, surefooted way, deleting any *s* in the Russian language that she found superfluous. Since Arkady's Spanish consisted of *gracias* and *por favor*, he wasn't inclined to be critical even if she had appeared without warning in the early evening and gathered him in a rush.

She said, "You wanted to see your friend's apartment and so we will."

"That's all I asked."

"No, you asked much more. I think you are refusing to make an identification of your friend because you think you can force us to investigate."

"I assume you want to be sure you're sending the right body to Moscow."

"You think it's impossible for him to be out on the water the way we found him? Like a Cuban?"

"It does strike me as unusual."

"What I find unusual is that when a message comes to you from an embassy in Havana you drop everything to come. That's unusual. That must have been expensive."

The round-trip took half his savings. On the other hand, what was he saving for? Anyway, everything in Havana struck him as unusual, including the detective, although there was something about small size and imperiousness he found endearing. Her features were delicate and sharply cut, dark eyes made darker with suspicion as if she were an apprentice devil handed a tricky soul. He also liked her sporty PNR cap with plastic visor.

"Tell me about this friend of yours," she demanded.

"You're interested?" He got no response to that. Oh well, he was fishing. "Sergei Sergeevich Pribluda. Workers family from Sverdlovsk. Joined the Committee for State Security out of the army. Higher education at Frunze Party School. Stationed eight years at Vladimir, eighteen in Moscow, rising to colonel. Hero Worker, honored for bravery. Wife, dead ten years; one son, a manager in an American fast-food franchise in Moscow. I was unaware of Pribluda's ever being stationed abroad before or studying Spanish. Politically reactionary, a Party member. Interests, Central Army ice-hockey team. Health, vigorous. Hobby, gardening."

"Not drinking?"

"He made flavored vodka, that's part of gardening."

"Not culture, the arts?"

"Pribluda? Hardly."

"You worked together?"

"In a way. He tried to kill me. It was a complicated friendship." Arkady gave her the short version. "There was a murder in Moscow involving politics. As it happened, there was a woman who was a dissident that he suspected. Since I thought she was innocent, I became a suspect and Pribluda was given the job of delivering, as we say, a nine-gram letter in the back of my head. But we had spent time together by then, long enough for me to discover there was something strangely honest about him and for him to decide there was, as you say, something of the *idiota* about me. And when he was given the order to shoot me, he didn't. I don't know whether you could call it a friendship, but our relationship was built on that."

"He disobeyed an order? There's never an excuse for that."

"God knows. He liked to grow his own vegetables. When his wife died, I would go round to his place and drink his vodka and eat his cucumbers and he would remind me that not every guest got to dine with his executioner. Red tomato pickle, green tomato pickle, peppers and dark bread to eat. Lemongrass and buffalo grass to flavor the vodka."

"You said he was a Communist."

"A good Communist. He would have joined the Party coup if it hadn't been led, as he said, by imbeciles. Instead, he drank until it all blew over and then went into a decline. He said we weren't real Russians anymore, only eunuchs, that the last Russian, the last true Communist anywhere was Castro." Which Arkady had taken as drunken ranting at the time, a detail he decided not to share with Osorio. "He said he was looking for a post outside Moscow. I never knew he meant here."

"When was the last time you saw the colonel?"

"More than a year ago."

"But you were friends."

"My wife didn't like him."

"Why not?"

"An old score. Why would the captain turn down the picture of Pribluda and his friends?" Arkady asked.

"He must have his reasons," Osorio said in a tone that suggested she didn't fathom them either.

Jasmine lay like snow over walls, Dumpsters overflowed with the sweet stench of fruit skins.

Binding the ocean was what Osorio called the Malecón, a seawall that protected a six-lane boulevard and an oceanfront line of three-story buildings. The sea was black, and traffic on the boulevard consisted of the running lights of cars a block apart. The buildings were the gaudy group Arkady had seen at daybreak from the other side of the bay; without their colors, dimly lit by lamps, they were occupied wrecks. In the shadow of a long arcade Osorio unlocked a street door and led him up worn stone stairs to a steel door which let them into a living room that could have been delivered complete from Moscow: subdued lamps, stereo, chess set, upholstery on the front door, lace curtains on the balcony doors. Homey Soviet hammer and sickle in silk tacked to a wall. A table and tray of water glasses, dish of salt. Whittled nostalgia—roosters, bears, St. Basil's—on the shelves. Plastic ivy and carnations trimming a kitchenette with a two-burner range, refrigerator, butane tanks. Bottles of Havana Club rum and Stolichnaya stood under the sink.

The only element out of place was a black man in a white shirt with a red bandanna around his head and Reebok basketball shoes on his feet sitting in a corner chair and holding a long, straight walking stick. It took a moment without breathing for Arkady to realize that the figure was a man-sized effigy. The face had a crudely molded brow and nose, mouth and ears, making its glass eyes glitter all the more.

"What is that?"

"Chango."

"Chango?"

"A Santeria spirit."

"Right. And why would Pribluda have it?"

"I don't know. That's not what we came for," Osorio said. What they had come for, apparently, was to see how thoroughly she had dusted the apartment for fingerprints, every door, jamb, knob and pull. Some prints had been lifted, leaving the transfer tracks of tape. But many more prints were visible as brown whorls expertly brushed.

"You did all this?" he asked Osorio.

"Yes."

"Brown powder?" He hadn't seen that before.

"Cuban fingerprint powder. In this Special Period, imported powders are too expensive. We make powder from burned palm fronds."

She hadn't missed any opportunity. Under the lamp was a small turtle, armored and obtuse in a bowl of sand. A perfect pet for a spy, Arkady thought. The shell was branded with a brown fingerprint.

She said, "Pribluda could have had a protocol house, but he rented here illegally from the Cuban who lives below."

"Why do you think he did that?"

For an answer she opened the balcony doors, their curtains lifting like wings with the breeze that rushed in. Arkady stepped out between two aluminum chairs and the balcony's marble rail and looked out on the vault of the night sky and the Malecón, displayed as an elegant curve of boulevard lights. Beyond the seawall was the flash of a lighthouse and deck lights of a freighter and pilot boat entering the bay. As his eyes adjusted he made out the fainter gunwale lamps of fishing boats and, nearer in, a widespread candle glimmer.

"*Neumáticos*," Osorio said.

Arkady imagined them, a flotilla of inner tubes riding black swells.

"Why wasn't there a police seal on the front door?" he asked.

"Because we are not investigating."

"So, what *are* we doing here, then?"

"Putting your mind to rest."

She motioned Arkady inside through the parlor and to a corridor, past a laundry room and into an office that held an ancient wooden desk, computer, printer and bookshelves crammed with binders from the Cuban Ministry of Sugar and photo albums. Under the printer, two briefcases, one of brown leather, the other of extraordinarily ugly green plastic. The walls were covered with maps of Cuba and Havana. Cuba was a big island, Arkady realized, twelve hundred kilometers long, marked with X's on the map. Arkady opened an album to pictures of what looked like green bamboo.

"Sugarcane fields," Osorio said. "Pribluda would have visited them because we foolishly depended on Russia for harvesters."

"I see." Arkady put the album down and moved on to the map of Havana. "Where are we?"

"Here." She pointed to where the Malecón swept east toward the Castillo de San Salvador, where the seawall ended and Havana Vieja and the bay began. West lay neighborhoods called Vedado and Miramar, where Pribluda had scribbled "Russian embassy." "Why do you ask?"

"I like to know where I am."

"You are leaving tonight. It doesn't matter if you know where you are."

"True." He looked to see that the power button of the computer was dusted and prints lifted. Nice. "You're finished here?"

"Yes."

He turned the machine and monitor on and the screen pulsed with an electric, expectant blue. Arkady did not consider himself computer-adept, but in Moscow murderers moved with the times and it had become a requirement of investigators to be able to open the electronic files of suspects and victims. Russians loved E-mail, Windows, spreadsheets; paper documents they burned at once, but incriminating electronic information they left intact under whimsical access codes: the name of a first girlfriend, a favorite actress, a pet dog. When Arkady clicked on the icon for Programs the screen demanded a password.

"Do you know it?" Osorio asked.

"No. A decent spy is supposed to use a random cipher. We could guess forever."

Arkady went through the desk drawers. Inside were a variety of different pens, stationery and cigars, maps and magnifying glasses, pen knives and pencils and brown envelopes with string ties for the diplomatic pouch. No passwords hidden in a matchbox.

"There's a telephone but no fax machine?"

"The telephone lines in this exchange are from before the Revolution. They're not clear enough for fax transmission."

"The telephone lines are fifty years old?"

"Thanks to the American embargo and the Special Period—"

"Caused by Russia, I know."

"Yes." Osorio snapped off the computer and shut the drawer. "Stop. You are not here to investigate. You are here only to verify that it has been examined thoroughly for fingerprints."

Arkady acknowledged the track of prints on doorjambs and desk surfaces, ashtray and telephone. Osorio motioned him to follow her farther down the corridor where there was a bedroom containing a narrow bed, nightstand, lamp, bureau, portable radio, bookcase and, hanging on the walls, a tinted portrait of the deceased Mrs. Pribluda. Beside it was a photograph of the son in an apron looking up at a levitating disk of pizza dough. In the top bureau drawer was an empty frame of snapshot size.

"There was a picture in here?" Arkady asked.

Osorio shrugged. The reading material in the bedroom was Spanish-Russian dictionaries, guidebooks, copies of *Red Star* and *Pravda*, reflecting the interests of a healthy, unreconstructed Communist. The bureau top was clear but showed signs of dusting and collection. In the closet were clothes, an ironing board and an iron dusted for prints. Organized on the floor were rubber sandals, work shoes and a thin, empty suitcase. Arkady stopped for a moment when he heard drumming from the apartment below, tectonic motion with a Latin beat.

Osorio opened the door at the corridor's end to a bathroom of crazed but immaculately clean tiles. A loofah and soap on a rope hung from the shower rod. The corner of the medicine cabinet mirror bore one fingerprint in full bloom, and another peeked from under the flush lever of the toilet.

"You don't miss anything," he told her. "But I wonder why you bothered."

"You will accept that this is Pribluda's apartment?"

"It seems to be."

"And that the prints we find here are Pribluda's?"

"We haven't really checked them, but let's say I do."

"Remember at the autopsy you told Captain Arcos it was a strange way for a Russian to fish."

"In an inner tube at sea? Yes, it was a first for me."

The detective led him back to the laundry room and turned on a hanging bulb and this time he saw, besides a stone basin and clothes line, reels of monofilament and wire and, on rough shelves of orange crate, jars that contained tangles of barbed, ugly hooks graded by size. Each jar was dusted and covered with clear prints. Detective Osorio handed Arkady an index card of lifted fingerprints. Immediately, Arkady saw a large print with a distinctive loop crossed by a scar identical with prints on the bottles. On a jar he found the same, carefully dusted print.

"He was right-handed?" Osorio asked.

"Yes."

"From the angles you can see, when he held the jar, the prints on the jar are his right thumb and index fingers and the prints on the glass are his left thumb and index finger. They're over all the rooms, doors, mirrors, everywhere. So you see, your Russian friend was a Cuban fisherman."

"The body, how long was it dead?"

"According to Dr. Blas, maybe two weeks."

"No one's been here in the meantime?"

"I asked the neighbors. No."

"That must be a hungry turtle."

Arkady returned to the front room, out of habit memorizing the apartment layout as he went: balcony, sitting room, laundry room, office, bathroom, bedroom. Inside the refrigerator were yogurt, greens, eggplant, pickled mushrooms, boiled tongue and a half-dozen boxes of color 35-mm film. He fed dillweed to the turtle and glanced at the black doll that filled the corner chair. "I have to admit these are new aspects to the man I knew. Did you find his car?"

"No."

"Do you know the make?"

"Lada." She shook her head a little for emphasis. "It doesn't matter. Your flight is in four hours. The body is being prepared for the plane. You will accompany it. Agreed?"

"I suppose I will."

Osorio frowned, as if she glimpsed a nuance in the answer.

On the ride back she asked, "Tell me, out of curiosity, as an investigator are you any good?"

"Not particularly."

"Why not?"

"Various reasons. I used to have a fair rate of success, as your captain puts it. But that was when murders in Moscow were amateur affairs with steel pipes and vodka bottles. Now they're professional work with heavy artillery. Also, militia work never paid well but it paid. Now, since the militia has not seen its salary in six months, men don't work with the same zeal. And there's the problem that if you do make progress on a contract homicide, the man who ordered the murder takes the prosecutor to lunch and offers him a condominium in Yalta and the case is dropped, so my success ratio is no longer something to be proud of. And, no doubt, my skills are not what they used to be."

"You had so many questions."

"Habit." Going through the motions, Arkady thought, as if his body were a suit that shuffled to the scene of the crime, any crime, anywhere. He was more irritated with himself than with her. Why had he started snooping? Enough! Osorio was right. He felt her eyes on him. Only for a moment, though. Because they were crossing a power blackout she had to proceed on some streets as carefully as steering a boat in the dark. In Arkady's mind, the syringe beckoned, the needle of a compass.

When they halted for goats wandering over the road the headlights illuminated a wall on which were written "*Venceremos!*" Arkady tried to say it silently but Osorio caught him.

" '*Venceremos!*' means 'We will win!' In spite of America and Russia, we will win!"

"In spite of history, geography, the law of gravity?"

"In spite of everything! You don't have signs like that in Moscow anymore, do you?"

"We have signs. Now they say Nike and Absolut."

He got a glance from Osorio no worse than the flame of a blowtorch. When they reached the embassy apartment the detective told him that a driver would gather him in two hours for the airport. "And you will have your friend to travel with."

"Let's hope it really is the colonel."

Osorio was stung worse than he'd intended. "A live Russian, a dead Russian, it's hard to tell the difference."

"You're right."

Arkady went up alone. A rumba played either in the house or out of the house, he could no longer tell where, all he knew was that constant music made him exhausted.

Unlocking the door, he lit a cigarette, careful not to drop embers on his sleeve. It was a cashmere coat Irina had given him as a wedding present, a soft black wreath of a coat that, she said, made him look like a poet. With the thin Russian shoes and shabby pants that he insisted on wearing he appeared all the more artistic. It was a lucky coat, impervious to bullets. He had walked through a shootout on the Arbat like an armored saint; later, he realized that no one had fired at him precisely because in his miraculous coat he resembled neither gangster nor militia.

More than that, the coat bore the faint lingering perfume of Irina, a secret, tactile sense of her, and when the thought of her became unbearable this scent was a final ally against her loss.

It was odd, Osorio asking whether he was any good. What he hadn't told her was that in Moscow his work suffered from what was officially labeled "inattention." When he went to work at all. He stayed in bed for days, the coat for a coverlet, occasionally rising to boil water for tea. Waiting for night before going out for cigarettes. Ignoring the visits of colleagues at the door. The cracks in the plaster of his Moscow ceiling had a vague outline of West Africa, and staring up he could catch the moment when window light was sideways enough to turn bumps into plaster mountains and turn cracks into a network of rivers and tributaries. Flying a black coat as his flag, his vessel sailed to each port of call.

Inattention was the greatest crime of all. He had seen every sort of victim, from nearly pristine bodies in their beds to the butchered, monstrously altered dead, and he had to say that, in general, they would still be lightly snoring or laughing at a well-told joke if someone had only paid more attention to an approaching knife or shotgun or syringe. All the love in the world could not make up for lack of attention.

Say you were on the deck of a ferry crossing a narrow strait, and although the distance was short, the wind and waves came up and the ship foundered. Into the cold water you go, and the one you love most is in your grasp. All you have to do to save her life is not let go. And then you look and your hand is empty. Inattention. Weakness. Well, the self-condemned lived longer nights than others for good reason. Because they were always trying to reverse time, to return to that receding, fateful moment and not let go. At night, when they could concentrate.

In the dark of the room he saw the polyclinic off the Arbat where he, the solicitous lover, had taken Irina to treat an infection. She had stopped smoking—they both had, together—and out of waiting-room nerves asked him to go to a kiosk for a magazine, *Elle* or *Vogue,* it didn't matter how old. He remembered the fatuous slap of his shoes as he crossed the room and, outside, the flyers of private vendors stapled to the trees—"For Sale! Best Medicines!"—which could have explained why drugs were in short supply in the clinic. Cottonwood seeds lifted into the evening's summer light. Poised smugly on the clinic steps, what had he been thinking? That they had finally achieved a normal life, a blessed bubble above the general mayhem? Meanwhile the nurse led Irina to the examining room. (Since then he had become more tolerant of killers. The carefully planned ambush, colorful wiring, the car packed with Semtex, the trouble they went to. At least they killed deliberately.) Her doctor explained that the clinic was short of Bactrim, the usual treatment. Was she allergic to ampicillin, penicillin? Yes, Irina always made sure the fact was underlined on her chart. At which point, the doctor's pocket beeped, and he stepped into the hall to talk on his cellular phone with his broker about a Romanian fund that promised a three-for-one return. The nurse in the examining room had heard only minutes before that her apartment had been sold by the city to a Swiss corporation for offices. Who was there to complain to? She had caught the word "ampicillin." Since the clinic was out of oral doses, she gave Irina an intravenous injection and left the room. Executions should be as speedy and thorough.

Having bought the magazine, Arkady followed the gauzy stream of seeds drifting back to the clinic, by which time Irina was dead. The nurses tried to keep him from the examining room, a mistake. The doctors tried to bar his way to the sheet covering the table and that was a mistake, too, ending in gurneys being upended, trays scattered, the medical staff's white caps crushed underfoot, finally a call to the militia to remove the madman.

Which was sheer melodrama. Irina herself hated melodrama, the demonic excess of a Russia where the Mafia donned evening clothes with Kevlar vests, where brides wed in see-through lace, where the foremost appeal of public office was immunity to prosecution. Irina loathed it, and she must have been embarrassed to die surrounded by Russian melodrama.

There were five hours until his plane left. Arkady thought the problem with airlines was that they didn't allow passengers to carry handguns. Otherwise he could have brought his and shot himself with a tropical view of dark rooflines rigged with laundry as full as sails and whole new constellations.

What was the final image Irina had in the clinic? The eyes of the nurse widening as she understood the depth of her mistake? Not too deep, only intravenous, but deep enough. They both must have understood. Within seconds, Irina's arm would have displayed a raised, roseate circle and her eyes begun to itch. Arkady was allowed to read their statements later, a professional courtesy. *Irina Asanova Renkova opened the door to the hall, interrupted the doctor's conversation and held up the empty vial.* Already her breath came as a wheeze. While the doctor *called for the emergency cart,* Irina shook and sweat, her heart accelerating to changing rhythms like a kite buffeted by gusts of wind. By the time the cart was located and rolled in, she was in *deep anaphylactic shock,* her windpipe shut and her heart racing, stopping, racing. However, the *Adrenalin supposed to be on the cart,* the shot that could have reset her heart like a clock and eased the constriction of her throat, was misplaced, missing, an innocent error. In a panic, the doctor tried to open the pharmacy cabinet and *snapped off the key in the lock.* Which was the same as a coup de grâce.

When Arkady ripped the sheet off the table at the polyclinic, he was amazed to see all they had done to Irina in the time it had taken him to walk to a kiosk and buy a magazine. Her face lay twisted in the disarray of hair that seemed suddenly so much darker she looked drowned, as if immersed in water for a day. Tangled and unbuttoned to the waist, her dress revealed her chest bruised by pounding. Her own hands were fists of agony, and she was still warm. He closed her eyes, smoothed her hair from her brow and buttoned her dress in spite of the doctor's insistence that he "not disturb the corpus." As an answer, he picked up the doctor and used him to crack a plate glass sold as bulletproof. The impact exploded cabinets, spewed instruments, spilled alcohol that turned the air silvery and aromatic. When the staff was routed and he had command of the examining room he made a pillow of his coat for her head.

He'd never considered himself melancholy, not on a Russian scale. It wasn't as if there was suicide in his family—with the exception of his mother, but she'd always been more dramatic and direct. Well, there was his father, too, but his father had always been a killer. Arkady resisted the idea not out of morality but manners, not wanting to make a mess. And there was the practical question of how. Hanging was unreliable and he didn't want to leave such a sight for anyone to discover. Shooting announced itself with such a boastful bang. The problem was that experts in suicide could teach only by example, and he had seen enough bungled attempts to know how often there was a slip twixt the cup and the lip. Best was simply to vanish. Being in Havana made him feel already half disappeared.

He used to be a better person. He used to care about people. He had always regarded suicides as selfish, leaving their bodies to frighten other people, their mess for other people to clean up. He could always start over, devote himself to a worthy cause, allow himself to heal. The trouble was that he didn't want the memory to fade. While he still remembered her, her breath in her sleep, the warmth of her back, the way she would turn to him in the morning, while he was still insane enough to think he would wake up beside her, or hear her in the next room or see her on the street, now was the time. If it inconvenienced other people, well, he apologized.

From his jacket he took the sterile syringe he had stolen in the embalming room. He'd stolen it on impulse, with no conscious plan, or as if some other part of his brain was seizing opportunities and setting an agenda that he was only learning about as it went. Everyone was well aware that Cuba was hard-pressed for medical supplies and here he was stealing. He broke the bag and laid the contents—a 50-cc embalming syringe and needle—on the table. The needle itself was a 10-cm shaft. He screwed it into the syringe and drew the plunger to fill the chamber with air. His chair had uneven legs, and he had to sit just so in order not to wobble. He pushed the coat and shirt sleeves up his left forearm and slapped the inside of the elbow to raise the vein. It would take about a minute after air was introduced into the bloodstream for the heart to stop. Only a minute, not the five minutes Irina was condemned to live out. There had to be enough air, no mere chain of bubbles but a goodly worm of air because the heart would churn and churn before it gave up. The shutters rattled and swung in. A perfectionist, he rose to push them back, resumed his place at the table. He rubbed the coat a last time on his cheek, the cashmere soft as cat's fur, then pushed the sleeve out of the way, stung his arm again and, as the green cord snapped to attention, eased in the needle deep. Blood budded in the chamber.

Over the pounding steps of his heart he heard someone knocking on the door.

"Renko!" Rufo called.

The plunger had yet to be pushed in, and what Arkady did not want was to make someone hear him drop. What he'd die of was like a deep-sea diver's bends, and convulsions made considerable noise. Like a diver hiding under the surface, he waited for the visitor to go away. When the knocks only became more insistent he shouted, "Go away."

"Open the door, please."

"Go away."

"Let me in. Please, it's important."

Arkady drew out the needle, tied a handkerchief around his arm, let his sleeve fall and dropped the syringe into the pocket of his overcoat before he went to the door and opened it a crack.

"You're early."

"Remember, we talked about cigars." Rufo managed to squeeze his way in, a foot, a leg, an arm at a time. He had changed into a one-piece jogging outfit and carried a box of pale wood sealed with an imposing design of interlocking swords. "Montecristos. Handmade from the finest tobacco leaf in the world. You know, for a cigar smoker this is like the Holy Grail."

"I don't smoke cigars."

"Then sell them. In Miami you could sell this box for one thousand dollars. In Moscow, maybe more. For you, one hundred dollars."

"I'm not interested and I don't have one hundred dollars."

"Fifty dollars. Usually I wouldn't let them go for so little, but . . ." Rufo spread his hands like a millionaire temporarily out of change.

"I'm just not interested."

"Okay, okay." Rufo was disappointed but amenable. "You know, when I was here before, I think I left my cigarette lighter. Did you see it?"

Arkady felt as if he were trying to leap from a plane and people kept dragging him back. There was no lighter in the living room. Arkady searched the bathroom and bedroom, no lighter. When he returned to the front, Rufo was digging through the paper bag of Pribluda's effects.

"There's no lighter there."

"I wanted to make sure you had everything." Rufo held up the lighter. "Found it."

"Good-bye, Rufo."

"A great pleasure. I'll be back in an hour. I won't bother you before." Rufo backpedaled to the door.

"No bother, but good-bye."

Arkady pulled back the coat sleeve from his arm as soon as Rufo went downstairs and with his thumb he found his vein and snapped it with a finger. The urge to be done was so strong now that he stayed at the open door to finish the job. The light on the stairwell below went out. See, now he needed a lighter. Typical socialist collapse, a bulb here, a bulb there. In the light from the room his exposed arm looked like marble. A samba drifted from another apartment. If Cuba sank into the sea, probably the water would percolate with sound. His throat was dry and sore. He leaned on the wall, took the long syringe from his pocket of his coat, tentatively touched his vein with the needle and a red dot appeared and wrapped around his wrist, which he wiped to keep the cashmere clean. But he heard someone climb the steps and, syringe in hand,

31

deciding not to end up as a public spectacle, slipped inside his door and rested against it. Feet stopped at his door.

"Yes?" Arkady asked.

"I forgot the cigars," Rufo said.

"Rufo—"

As soon as Arkady opened the door Rufo carried him past the apartment's cream-and-gold dining chairs and into the far wall's collected works of Fidel, and pressed Arkady by the neck to the cabinet with a forearm. Perhaps Rufo was big but he was quicker on his feet than Arkady had imagined. He pinned Arkady with one arm and pulled the other until Arkady realized that his overcoat was pinned to the cabinet by a knife that Rufo was trying to free for a second thrust. The flapping of Arkady's open coat had misled him. Rufo's other problem was the embalming syringe that stood from his left ear, which meant that six centimeters of steel needle was buried in his brain. Arkady had struck back without thinking because the attack had come so fast. The addition to Rufo's head slowly gained the Cuban's attention, his eyes lifting sideways for a glimpse of the barrel and returning perplexed to Arkady. Rufo stepped back to grope at the syringe like a bear bedeviled by a bee, turning his head and wandering in a circle, leaning sideways lower and lower until he dropped to a knee and pushed with the opposite foot, squeezing his eyes shut until he finally pulled out the needle. Rufo blinked through tears at the long, red shaft and looked up for an explanation.

Arkady said, "All you had to do was wait."

Rufo rolled onto his back, his eyes still turned to the syringe as if it contained his last thought.

3.

Not that she would tell Renko, but Ofelia Osorio had once worked on a Cuban factory ship built by the Russians and complete with Russian advisers, so she was not only practiced in dealing with overbearing "big brothers" from the north but skilled in fending them off with a gutting knife. Earlier, as an idealistic Young Pioneer she had served as a delegate to a World Youth Conference in Moscow and toured Lenin's Tomb, Lumumba University and the subway. She remembered how subway riders drew in their faces at the sight of someone black. Cubans only touched their forearms to indicate someone dark. Russians recoiled as if from a snake. At least, at home. At sea, they were willing enough to experiment.

It wasn't only Russians. Vietnamese investigators came to Havana and Ofelia trained both men and women. When she visited Hanoi she discovered that her best female students had been relegated to typing and that after dinners of international solidarity the plates Ofelia used were washed twice.

What was interesting was that when European and Asian men met Cuban girls in Cuba they were like gluttons in a candy store. Decent family men became animals the moment they landed. Cartoons posted on the streets warned girls to be sure their tourists arrived with condoms. There were vice squads, usually run by detectives putting together their own strings of *jineteras*. A great word, *jinetera*. Jockey, especially descriptive of a girl astride

33

a bouncing pig. In addition to Ofelia's homicide caseload, and with half-hearted official support, she had put together an operation of her own against corrupt police. At any rate, she was mentally armed for a visiting Russian investigator, the worst of all possible combinations.

She lived in a *solar,* an alley of one-room apartments, aptly named for the way it soaked in the heat of the day. In spite of the late hour, Muriel and Marisol, her two daughters, were spread languorously on the cool of the floor intent on a television show about dolphins. The girls were eight and nine with dark hair flocked with gold, and the blue glow of the screen lapped up to their chins like a coverlet. Her mother tipped on the rocking chair pretending to be asleep, a silent reprimand to Ofelia for coming home so late, letting rice and beans simmer on the burners. Two could play at that game. It was a scandal that the mother of a PNR detective would spend the day running errands for everyone in the *solar,* going for cigarettes for one house, standing in line for a pair of shoes for another. "Hustle or starve," the old woman would respond to protests. "With your big pay and our family rations, your daughters will eat two days out of three. You know the joke, 'What are the three achievements of the Revolution? Health, education and sports. What are the three failures? Breakfast, lunch and dinner.' They say Fidel tells that joke. Why?" Ofelia only argued to a certain point because her mother was right. Besides, there were so many other things to argue about with her mother. The week before, Ofelia had come home to find that a portrait of Che had been moved to make way for a picture torn from a magazine of Celia Cruz. Who would displace the greatest martyr of the twentieth century with a fat, old traitor from Florida? Her mother, without a second's hesitation.

Ofelia wrapped her belt around her holster, stripped and folded her uniform neatly on a hanger. As a detective she could go in plain clothes or not, but she enjoyed the reassurance of the blue pants, the gray shirt with PNR shield on the pocket, the cap with its own embossed shield. Also, wearing a uniform saved on her clothes, which were basically two pairs of jeans. She slipped through the curtain into an alcove that served as bathroom, vanity, and shower stall, automatically turning on the Walkman that hung from a string. The radio was a prize found on the Playa del Este on a family trip. She had told her girls to ignore the "love couples" of *jineteras* and their tourists, but after Muriel had stumbled upon something as incredible as a radio the size of a clamshell she and her older sister watched the beach like vultures, ready to search the sand for treasure as soon as any "couple" left.

Water came in lukewarm rivulets, but it was enough. It ran over her forehead and neck and trailed from her hands. She was secretly pleased with her hair, which was cut short and as soft as a cap of Persian lamb. The music was insinuating and percussive. *Your cigar fell down. You told me how good it was and how all the women liked your big cigar. We hardly started smoking and your cigar fell down.* Ofelia let her shoulders relax and roll to the beat. Water ran out the drain between her feet. In the mirror above the sink she saw herself begin to fog. A thirty-year-old woman who still looked like a black cane cutter's daughter. Although she wasn't vain she hated a tan line—better to be the same brown all over. She leaned forward to let water run off her hair like threads of glass.

The detective in her wondered about the dead Russian they found in the water. She would have expected much more interest from his embassy and the fact that they seemed ready to dispose of him like a dog hit on the street was practically proof that he had obviously been up to no good. The bay, after all, was a perfect vantage point for smuggling, infiltration, to spy on shipping. As the Comandante himself said, there was no more vicious enemy than a man you had once called friend.

The new Russian was a bit of a contradiction. The plush coat was a sure sign of corruption, while the poor state of the rest of his clothes indicated a complete disregard for appearance. One moment he seemed a reasonably alert investigator, and the next he disappeared into some private train of thought. He was pale but with eyes deep-set in shadow.

The soap was a sliver her mother had obtained from a friend who worked in a hotel and so luxurious that Ofelia drew out the shower, the most private moment of the day despite the voices from other apartments in the *solar*. One song's worth was what she allowed herself to save the batteries.

Dressed in a pullover and jeans, she ladled rice to Muriel and beans to Marisol and an obscure, deep-fried gristle that her mother refused to identify. From the refrigerator she took a plastic Miranda soda bottle filled with chilled water.

"On the cooking show today they showed how to fry a steak from grapefruit skin," her mother said. "They turned a grapefruit skin into steak. Isn't that amazing? This is a revolution that is more amazing all the time."

"I'm sure it was good," Ofelia said. "Under the circumstances."

"They ate it with gusto. With gusto."

"This is also good," Ofelia sawed into the gristle. "What did you say it was?"

"Mammalian. Did you meet any dangerous men today, someone who might kill you and leave your daughters without a mother?"

"One. A Russian."

It was her mother's turn to be exasperated. "A Russian, worse than a grapefruit skin. Why did you join the police? I still don't understand."

"To help the people."

"The people here hate you. You don't see anyone from Havana who joins the police. Only outsiders. We were happy in Hershey."

"It's a sugar-mill town."

"In Cuba, what a surprise!"

"You can't move to Havana without a permit. I'm an expert in police work. They want me here and I want to be here and so do the girls."

This was one issue where Ofelia could always count on her daughters' support.

"We want to be here."

"Nobody wants to be in Hershey. That's a sugar-mill town."

Her mother said, "Havana is full of girls from sugar-mill towns without official permits, and they're all making dollars on their backs. The day is going to come when I'm looking for condoms for my granddaughters."

"Grandmother!"

Her mother relented, and they all quietly sawed the meat on their plates until the old woman asked, "So what does this Russian look like?"

It struck Ofelia. "Once in Hershey you pointed out a priest who was defrocked for falling in love with a woman."

"I'm surprised you remember, you were so little. Yes, she was a beautiful woman, very religious, and it was a sad story all around."

"He looks like that."

Her mother mulled it over. "I can't believe you remembered that."

Just when Ofelia thought that family tension had subsided enough for a pleasant evening meal, however late, the phone rang. Theirs was the only phone in the solar, and she suspected her mother of using it to run the neighborhood lottery. The illegal Cuban lottery was rigged to the legal Venezuelan lottery, and the bet takers with phones had a great advantage. Ofelia rose and moved slowly around the girls' chairs toward the phone on the wall to let her mother know she wasn't going to run for anyone's nefarious business. Her mother maintained an expression of innocence until Ofelia hung up.

"What was it?"

"It's about the Russian," Ofelia said. "He killed someone."

"Ah, you were meant for each other."

When she arrived at the apartment, Captain Arcos was slamming down the phone and telling Renko, "Your embassy cannot provide you protection. There will be expressions of anger from the Cuban people to those who have sold them out. To those who plant the Judas kiss on us for thirty pieces of silver. If it were up to me, I would not let a single Russian on the street. I could not guarantee the safety of a Russian, not even in the safest capital in the world, because Cuban anger is so deep. You crawl to the camp of the enemy and you warn Cubans we better do the same. That history has left us behind. No! Cuba is master of history. Cuba has more history to make and we do not need instruction from any former comrades. That's what I told your embassy."

Arcos had worked himself into such a rage his face balled like a fist. His black sergeant Luna stood by, slouching, ominous and bored at the same time. Renko sat calmly wrapped in his coat. Rufo sprawled in his silvery running suit, his gaze aimed at a syringe clasped in his left hand. What amazed Ofelia was the lack of technicians. Where was the normal bustle of video and light operators, the forensics experts and detectives? Although she didn't question the authority of the two men from the ministry, she made a point of loudly snapping on surgical gloves.

"The captain speaks Russian, too," Renko told Ofelia. "It's a night of surprises."

Arcos was in his forties, Ofelia thought, exactly the generation who had wasted their youth in learning Russian, and been bitter ever since. Not an insight she'd share with Renko.

"He has a point, though," Renko told her. "My embassy does not seem inclined to help me."

"This is the unbelievable statement he gives us," Arcos said. "That Rufo Pinero, a man with no criminal record, an honored Cuban sportsman, a driver and interpreter for Renko's own embassy, approached him with the intent to sell cigars, was told 'no' and, anyway, returned to this apartment here and, without warning or provocation, attacked Renko with two weapons, a knife and a syringe, and in a fight accidentally drove a needle through his own head."

"Are there any witnesses?" asked Ofelia.

"Not yet," Arcos said, as if he might dig one up still.

Ofelia had not worked with the captain before but she recognized the type, better at vigilance than competence and promoted well beyond his natural abilities. She couldn't expect any help from Luna; the sergeant seemed to regard everyone, including Arcos, with the same dark disregard.

She unzipped Rufo's running suit and found that under it he was still completely dressed in the shirt and pants he had been wearing at the ILM. In warm weather that made very little sense.

In his shirt pocket was a plastic case and passport-sized ID that read: *"Rufo Pérez Pinero; Fecha de nacimiento: 2/6/56; Profesión: traductor; Casado: no; Numero de habitacion: 155 Esperanza, La Habana; Status Militar: reserva; Hemotipo: B."* Glued in a corner was a photo of a younger, leaner Rufo. In the same case was a ration card with columns for months and rows for rice, meat, beans. She emptied Rufo's pockets of dollars, pesos, house and car keys, handling everything by the edge. She thought she remembered his having a cigarette lighter, too. Cubans noticed that. For some reason she also had the conviction that the Russian had already gone through Rufo's pockets, that she wasn't going to find anything that he hadn't already.

"Has the investigation started now?" Renko asked.

"There will be an investigation," Arcos promised, "but of *what* is the question. Everything you do is suspicious: your attitude to Cuban authority, reluctance to identify the body of a Russian colleague, now this attack on Rufo Pinero."

"My attack on Rufo?"

"Rufo's the one who is dead," Arcos insisted.

"The captain thinks I came from Moscow to attack Rufo?" Renko asked Ofelia. "First Pribluda and now me. Murder and assault. If you don't investigate that, what exactly do you people investigate?"

Ofelia was unhappy because basic protocol was to work a crime scene as soon as possible and Luna had done nothing. She stepped back for a wider view and saw a knife lodged chest-high in the side panel of a wooden cabinet yet not a book in it disturbed, not even *Fidel y Arte,* which was a heavy presentation book with valuable plates. Neither a chair broken nor a bruise on Renko, as if the confrontation had been over in an instant.

"Your friend is a spy and you are a murderer," Luna laid into Renko. "This is intolerable!"

Without dislodging it, Ofelia examined the knife in the cabinet. The weapon was Brazilian manufacture, spring-loaded with an ivory handle and silver butt, the blade double-edged and sharp as a razor. Driven into the wood was a black thread.

Arcos said, "I told the embassy, Renko is like any other visitor, he enjoys no diplomatic protection. This apartment is like any Cuban apartment, it does not enjoy extraterritorial protection. This is a Cuban matter, completely up to us."

"Good," said Renko. "It was a Cuban that tried to kill me."

"Don't be difficult. Since the facts of this matter are so cloudy and you are alive and no harm done, you should consider yourself lucky if you are allowed to leave Havana."

"You mean leave Havana alive. Well, I missed tonight's flight."

"There will be another in a week. In the meantime, we will continue to investigate."

The Russian asked Ofelia, "Would you consider this an investigation?"

She hesitated because she had found in the lapel of his black coat a narrow cut the wrong place for a buttonhole. Her pause incensed Arcos.

"This is my investigation, run as I see fit, considering many factors, such as whether you surprised Rufo, stabbed him with the needle and, when he was dead, placed it in his hand. It could still have your prints."

"Do you think so?"

"Rigor mortis has not set in. We'll look."

Before Ofelia could stop him, the captain knelt and tried to bend Rufo's fingers off the syringe. Rufo held tight, the way dead men sometimes did. Luna shook his head and smiled.

Renko told Ofelia, "Inform the captain it's a death spasm, not rigor mortis, but now he'll have to wait for the rigor to come and go. Depending on how much he wants to wrestle with Rufo, of course."

Which only made Arcos pull harder.

She took Renko back to Pribluda's flat on the Malecón for lack of a better place for him to stay. He didn't have the money for a hotel, the embassy's apartment was now a crime scene, and until he officially identified Pribluda he would only be staying in the flat of an absent friend.

For a minute she and Renko stood on the balcony to watch a solitary car sweep along the boulevard and waves lap against the breast of the seawall. Out on the water lamplights spilled from fishing boats and *neumáticos*.

"You've been on the ocean before?" Ofelia asked.

"The Bering Sea. It's not the same thing."

"You don't have to be sorry for me," she said abruptly. "The captain knows what he's doing."

Which sounded hollow even to her, but Renko relented, "You're right." He was wrapped in his black coat, like a shipwrecked man happy with the only article he'd rescued. She felt a conspiracy of sorts between the two of them because he hadn't mentioned to Arcos and Luna the earlier visit to Pribluda's flat.

"The captain doesn't usually investigate homicides, does he?"

"No."

"I remember newsreels of Castro's first trip to Russia. He was a dashing revolutionary hunting bear in a beret and green fatigues while our Kremlin Politburo stumbled through the snow after him like a pack of fat, old, love-smitten tarts. It was a romance meant to last forever. It's hard to believe that Russians are now hunted in Havana."

"I think you are in a confused state. Your friend dies and now you are attacked. This could give you a very distorted view of Cuban life."

"It could."

"And be upsetting."

"Certainly distracting."

She didn't know what he could mean by that.

"There were no other witnesses?"

"No."

"You answered the door and Rufo attacked you without warning."

"That's right."

"With two weapons?"

41

"Yes."

"That sounds implausible."

"That's because you're a good detective. But do you know what I've found?"

"What have you found?"

"I have found from my own experience that—in the absence of other witnesses—a simple, resolutely maintained lie is wonderfully difficult to break."

4.

As soon as Arkady was alone in Pribluda's flat he went to the office and opened the computer, which immediately demanded the password. An access code that combined up to twelve letters and numbers was virtually unbreakable, but a code also had to be remembered, and this was where the humans Arkady knew tended to use their birthday or address. Arkady tried the names of the colonel's wife, son, saint (although Pribluda was an atheist, he had always enjoyed a bottle on his saint's name day), favorite writers (Sholokhov and Gorky), favorite teams (Dynamo and Central Army). Arkady tried 06111968 for the date of Pribluda's Party membership, a chemical $C12H22011$ for sugar, a homesick 55-45-37-37 for the coordinates (latitude and longitude, minutes and seconds) of Moscow. He tried words written and transposed into numbers (even though the correct order of the Russian alphabet was a matter of controversy heading into the twenty-first century). The computer fan would buzz for a moment, then purr along. He tried until he traded the glow of the machine for the dark of the balcony, where he took solace in the steady sweep of the lighthouse beam and the deep insomnia of the night.

Arkady discovered he fostered a killer's calculation that even if his story was implausible, the truth was no more plausible. He was also a little bemused by his own reaction to the attack. He had defended himself instinctively, the way a man about to dive resists being pushed.

He had no idea why he had been attacked except that it had to do with his friend Pribluda. Not that Pribluda was a friend in the ordinary sense. They shared no tastes, interests, politics. In fact, truth be told, Pribluda was in many ways a terrible man.

Arkady could imagine him now bringing out the vodka and saying, "Renko, old pal, you're fucked. You are in a crazy country, in a foreign land where you know nothing, including the language." Pribluda would hunch forward to touch glasses and grin that ghastly smile of his. He had the habit of loosening a button, a collar, a cuff with each glassful, as if drinking was serious work. "All you can be sure of is that you know nothing. No one will help you because of your brown eyes. Everyone who steps forward as a friend will be an enemy. Everyone who offers to help is hiding a knife behind his back. Cheers!" The colonel would make a grand gesture of throwing the vodka's cap into the sea. That was his idea of panache. "Do you appreciate logic?"

"I love logic," Arkady might say.

"This is logic: Rufo had no reason to kill you. Rufo tried to kill you. Ergo, someone sent Rufo. Ergo, that someone will send someone else."

"A nice thought. Was that a present to take home?" Arkady would nod in the direction of the man-sized doll brooding in the corner. The way its shadow shifted when the breeze pushed the lamp was a bit unnerving. "Charming." He fished from his coat a piece of notepaper on which he had written Rufo's address and the house key he had lifted off the body before Luna arrived.

"What I think you should do," Pribluda would steamroll on, "is lock yourself with a gun and oranges, bread and water in a room at the embassy, maybe a bucket for personal needs, and don't open the door until you go to the airport."

In his mind, Arkady asked, "Spending a week in Havana hiding in a room, wouldn't that be a little perverse?"

"No. Killing Rufo when you were going to kill yourself, *that's* perverse."

Arkady went down the hall to the office and returned with a map of the city that he spread under a lamp.

"You're leaving?" Pribluda was always horrified when Arkady quit before the bottom of the bottle.

Arkady searched for a street called Esperanza and wrote down Rufo's address on a piece of paper. He thought, I'm not just going to sit and wait. I also have your car key. If you want to help, tell me where the car is. Or give me your code.

Pribluda's ghost, insulted, disappeared. Arkady, on the other hand, was wide awake.

Stepping onto the street in a foreign city in the middle of the night was diving into a dark pool without knowing how deep the water was. An arcade of columns ran the length of the block, and he didn't emerge into faint, gassy light until he reached the lamp at the corner. He continued along the boulevard because its long curve against the sea simplified the problem of orientation.

Although he listened for the stir of a car or a footfall, all he heard was his own echo and the surge of the ocean on the other side of empty traffic lanes. On the way he passed a mural of Castro painted up the side of a three-story building. The figure appeared to be a giant walking through his city, his head obscured in the dark above streetlamp level, wearing his characteristic military fatigues, legs in mid-stride, right hand tossing a salute toward an unseen someone vowing "*A Sus Ordenes, Comandante!*" Well, Arkady thought, the Comandante and he made a strange pair of insomniacs, a furtive Russian and a sleepless giant on patrol.

Six blocks on was a dark hotel front and a taxi, the driver's head cradled on the steering wheel. Arkady shook the man and, when one eye squinted open, held up Rufo's address and a five-dollar bill.

Arkady sat up front as the taxi flew like a bat through the blackout, the driver yawning the entire way as if nothing short of a collision was worth waking up for, slowing only when mounds of urban rubble loomed in the headlights. Rufo's address was stenciled on the front of a low, windowless house on a narrow street.

The cab fumbled away while, with Rufo's lighter, Arkady found the right key; when he had taken the house key off the dead man before calling the PNR Arkady noticed how like his own house key Rufo's was, a Russian design with a star stamped on the grip, no doubt a souvenir of socialist commerce. It did occur to him that if Detective Osorio had tried to enter with the keys he had left on Rufo she was frustrated and annoyed.

The door opened to a room narrow enough to make claustrophobia creep up his back. He walked the lighter flame between an unmade daybed and a low table with a ceramic ashtray-and-nude and a stack of TV and stereo, tape deck and VCR. A minibar looked ripped out of a hotel suite. A pedestal sink was lined with minoxidil, vitamins and aspirin. An armoire held, besides clothes, boxes of Nike and New Balance running shoes, cigar boxes, a library of videotapes and copies of Windows '95, a regular emporium. He opened a door to glimpse a filthy toilet, ducked back into the room and moved more slowly. Tacked to the walls were newspaper articles headlined GRAN EXITO DE EQUIPO CUBANO and, over a photo of a young world-beating Rufo raising his boxing gloves, PINERO TRIUNFA EN USSR! Framed pictures showed groups of men in team jackets in Red Square, at Big Ben, the Eiffel Tower. Arkady turned the photos and copied names he found on the back. Names and numbers were also scribbled on the wall by the bed.

```
Daysi 32-2007
Susy 30-4031
Vi. Aflt. 2300
Kid Choc. 5/1
Vi. HYC 2200 Angola
```

The only sense Arkady could make of the list was that he had been the visitor arriving on Aeroflot at 2300 hours, eleven at night, and that there seemed to be another visitor from Angola due at almost the same late hour. Anyway, the list was a lot of phone numbers for a room with no phone or phone jack. Arkady remembered that Rufo had had a cell phone when they met at the airport, although when Arkady had searched Rufo's body later, the phone was gone.

On a hook hung an elegant, ivory-colored straw hat with "Made in Panama" and the initials RPP stamped on the sweatband. He searched the bureau, felt under the pillow and mattress, flipped through videos that all seemed to be boxing films or porn for more personal labels. The minibar held airline nuts and healthful bottles of Evian. There was no sign of any visit by Luna or Osorio, no fingerprint dust of burned palm fronds.

Most important, he found no reason for Rufo to try to kill him. Rufo had put some planning into the attack. The running suit made sense for the same reason painters wore coveralls, and he felt that the same thought had registered with Osorio. But why bother killing someone who would be gone from the scene in a matter of hours? Was Rufo after something or was it simply open season on Russians in Havana?

As he stepped outside, the light of dawn showed next to the apartment a scarred wall in bullfight red that said GIMNASIO ATARES. At the curb in a PNR sedan was Detective Osorio. She fixed her eyes on Arkady long enough to make him squirm before she put out her hand. "The key."

"Sorry." Arkady fished in his pocket and gave her the key to his apartment in Moscow. He could always break into his own home if need be.

"Get in the car," Osorio said. "I would like to lock you into a cell but Dr. Blas wants to talk to you."

With his trimmed beard and whiff of carbolic soap, Dr. Blas was the Pluto of a personal, genial underworld, welcoming Arkady back to the Instituto de Medicina Legal and praising Osorio.

"Our Ofelia is very intelligent. If Hamlet had an Ofelia half as smart he would have solved the murder of his father the king in short order. Of course, they wouldn't have had much of a play." Two young women in snug IML T-shirts walked by in the corridor;

the doctor's eyes approved. "We were trained by the FBI in Washington and Quantico until the Revolution, then by the Russians and Germans. But I like to think we have our own style. Your problem, Renko, is that you have no confidence in us. I noticed that the first time you were here."

"Is that it?" Arkady asked.

He thought his problem was that Rufo had tried to kill him, but the director seemed to have a bigger picture. They walked by a glass case with two head shots of men with slack mouths and closed eyes.

"Missing persons and unidentified dead. For the public to see." Blas picked up his thread. "When you think of Cuba you think of a Caribbean island, a place like Haiti, a country like Nicaragua. When we say, for example, we have identified a body as a Russian, you wonder how good is that identification, how qualified are these people who are telling me to accept this body and take it home? When you see a body retrieved from the water the way dogs play with bones, you question how careful the police work is. That is why you stole Rufo's key and went to his room on your own. I go to international conferences all the time and I meet people who don't know Cuba and have the same misgivings. So, let me tell you something about myself. I have a medical degree from the University of Havana with a specialty in pathology. I have studied at the Superior School of Investigation in Volgograd, in Leipzig and Berlin. Last year I lectured at Interpol conferences in Toronto and Mexico City. So, you have not been dropped off the end of the earth. Some enemies of Cuba want to isolate us, but we are not isolated. The international aspect of crime does not allow us to be isolated. I will not allow it."

They passed a handcuffed man in a chair. He lifted a face of old scars and fresh bruises.

"Waiting for his psychological evaluation," Blas explained. "We have other experts in forensic biology, dentistry, toxicology, immunology. A Russian might find this hard to believe. You used to be the teacher and we used to be the students. Now we are the teachers in Africa, Central America, Asia. Our Ofelia"—Blas nodded to Osorio, who had been gliding along modestly—"has taught in Vietnam. There is no ignorance here. I will not allow it. As a result, I am pleased to say that Havana has the lowest rate of unsolved homicides of any capital city in the world. So when I say who a body is, that's who he is. But Detective Osorio tells me that you are again hesitant about the identification of Colonel Pribluda."

"He is reacting to the attack on himself," she said.

"My reaction has probably been colored by that," Arkady conceded. "Or finding Pribluda dead. Or jet lag."

Blas said, "You have a week more here. You will adjust. It was very enterprising of you to go to Rufo's. Ofelia said you might. She's intuitive, I think."

"I think so, too," Arkady said.

"If what you say is true, Rufo inadvertently killed himself by his own hand during a brief, violent struggle?"

"Accidental suicide."

"Very much so. But that does not answer the question of *why* Rufo attacked you. I find this very troubling."

"Between us, I'm troubled too."

Blas stopped at the head of a stairway from which rose a sour coolness like the odor of spoiled milk. "The nature of the attack with a knife *and* a syringe is so peculiar. There was an embalming syringe stolen here yesterday, although I don't understand when Rufo could have taken it. You were with him the whole time, weren't you?"

"I went to the rest room once. He could have taken it then."

"Yes, you're right. Well, it was probably that syringe, although I don't understand why a murderer would choose to use it when he already had a better weapon. Do you?"

Arkady gave the matter some thought. "Did Rufo have any record of violence?"

"I know the opinion of Captain Arcos in this matter, but I have to be honest. Better to say that Rufo had a record of not being caught. He was a *jinetero,* a hustler. The kind who hangs around tourists and finds someone a girl, changes their money, gets them cigars. Supposedly very successful with German and Swedish women, secretaries on vacation. May I be direct?"

"Please."

"It is said that he would advertise to foreign women that he had a *pinga* like a locomotive."

"What is a *pinga*?" Arkady asked.

"Well, I'm no psychiatrist, but a man who has a *pinga* like a locomotive doesn't use a syringe to kill someone."

"More likely a machete," Osorio spoke up.

"You can't see many of those. How many people would have machetes in the city?"

"Every Cuban has a machete," Blas said. "I have three in my own closet."

"I have one," Osorio said.

Arkady stood corrected.

Blas asked, "You can't shed any light on this syringe?"

"No."

"Understand I am not a detective, I am not the PNR, I am only a forensic pathologist, but I was trained by my Russian instructors of long ago to think in an analytical fashion. I believe we are not so different, so I will show you something to build your confidence in us. And you may even learn something from us."

"Such as?"

Blas rubbed his hands like a host with a program. "We will start where you came in."

The morgue had six drawers, a freezer and a glass-faced cooler, all with broken handles beaded with condensation. Blas said, "The refrigerators still work. We had an American pilot from the invasion at the Bay of Pigs. He crashed and died, and for nineteen years the CIA said they never heard of him. Finally his family came and got him. But he was in good condition in his own humidor right here. We called him the Cigar."

Blas rolled out a drawer. Inside, the purple body identified as Pribluda was rearranged: skull, jaw and right foot between the legs, a plastic sack of organs where the head should be. Left open, the stomach cavity released a zoo-like bouquet that made Arkady's eyes smart, and the whole body had been placed in a zinc tub to keep the liquefying flesh from overflowing. Arkady lit a cigarette and inhaled deeply. That was reason to smoke right there. So far, Arkady's confidence was not rising.

"We did have funding promised from our Russian friends for a new refrigeration system. You can understand how important refrigeration is in Havana. Then the Russians said we had to buy it." Blas turned his head this way and that to study the corpse. "Are you aware of any characteristics of Pribluda that are different from this body?"

"No, but I think that after a week in the water and having body parts switched, most people look alike."

"I was instructed by Captain Arcos not to perform biopsies. However, I think I am still the director here and so I did. The brain and organs show no evidence of drugs or toxins. That is not conclusive because the body was in the water such a long time, but there was another aspect. The heart muscle displayed definite signs of necrosis, which is a strong indicator of heart attack."

"A heart attack while floating in the water?"

"A heart attack after a lifetime of eating and drinking like a Russian, an attack so massive and so quick he had no time even to thrash, which was why all the fishing gear was still on board. Did you know that life expectancy is twenty years less in Russia than in Cuba? I will give you samples of the tissue. Show them to any doctor in Moscow and they will say the same."

"Have you ever seen *neumáticos* die of a heart attack before?"

"No, mostly shark attacks. But this is the first time I've heard of a Russian *neumático*."

"Don't you think that's worth an investigation?"

"You must understand our situation. We have no crime scene and no witnesses, which makes an investigation very discouraging, very expensive. And no crime. Worse, he's Russian and the embassy refuses to cooperate. They say no one worked with Pribluda, no one knew him and that he was merely an innocent student of the sugar industry. For us even to visit the embassy requires a diplomatic note. All the same we asked for a photograph of Pribluda, and since we didn't receive that, we have matched him and the body to the best possible certainty. There is nothing more we can do. We must consider him identified and you must take him home. We will have no more 'cigars' here."

"Why ask the embassy for a photograph? I showed you one."

"Yours wasn't good enough."

"You can't match anything to the way he looks now."

Blas let a smile win his face. He rolled the body drawer shut. "I have a surprise for you. I want you to return home with the right idea of Cuba."

On the second floor Blas led Arkady and Osorio into an office with the faded title ANTROPOLOGÍA on the door.

Arkady's first impression was of a catacomb, the remains of martyrs assiduously sorted by shelves of skulls, pelvises, thigh bones, metacarpals lying hand in hand, spines tangled like snakes. Dust swam around a lampshade, the light reflected by case after case of neatly pinned tropical beetles iridescent as opals. A fer-de-lance with open fangs coiled within a specimen jar topped by a tarantula on tiptoe. What looked like dominoes were burned bones in gradations from white to charcoal black. On the wall the baroque jaws of a shark outgrinned a jawbone of human teeth filed to points. The cord for the ceiling fan was the braided hair of a shrunken head. No catacomb, Arkady changed his mind, more a jungle trading post. A sheet covered something humming on a desk, and if it were a great ape going philosophical Arkady wouldn't have been surprised.

"This is our anthropological laboratory," said Blas. "Not a large one, but here we determine by bones and teeth the age, race and sex of a victim. And different poisonous or violent agents."

"The Caribbean has a number you won't see in Moscow," Osorio said.

"We are deficient in sharks," Arkady said.

"And," Blas said, "by insect activity how long the victim has been dead. In other climates, different insects start at different times. Here in Cuba, they all start at once, but at different rates of progress."

"Fascinating."

"Fascinating but perhaps not what a investigator from Moscow would call a serious forensic laboratory?"

"There are different laboratories for different places."

"Exactly!" Blas picked up the jawbone of pointed teeth. "Our population is, let's say, unique. A number of African tribes practiced scarification and sharpening teeth. The Abakua, for example, was a secret leopard society from the Congo. They were brought here as slaves to work on the docks and in a short time controlled all the smuggling in Havana Bay. It took the Comandante to turn them into a folkloric society." He set down the teeth and directed Arkady's attention to an exhibit of a skull and two-edged ax spattered in dried blood. "This skull might look to you like evidence of trauma."

"It conceivably might."

"But to a Cuban a skull and an ax covered in animal blood may be a religious shrine. The detective can tell you all about it if you want." Osorio squirmed at the suggestion and Blas went on. "So when we make a psychological analysis of a person we use the Minnesota profile, of course, but we also take into consideration whether a person is a devotee of Santeria."

"Oh." Not that Arkady had ever used the Minnesota profile.

"Nevertheless"—Blas lifted the cloth—"let me prove that, in spite of superstitions, Cuba is still abreast of the world."

Unveiled on a desk was a 486 computer hooked up to a scanner and printer, each running, and an 8-mm video camera mounted lens down above a stand. Resting in a ring on the stand and tilted up to the camera was a skull with a hole in the center of the forehead. The cranium was wired together. Missing teeth made for a gaping cartoon smile.

Arkady had only read about a system like this. "This is a German identification technique."

"No," said Blas, "this is a Cuban technique. The German system, including software, costs over fifty thousand dollars. Ours costs a tenth as much by adapting an orthopedic program. In this case, for example, we found a head with teeth hammered out." Blas touched the keyboard, and on the screen appeared a color picture of a Dumpster stuffed with palm fronds topped by a decapitated head. At a keystroke the police and Dumpster were replaced by four photographs of different men, one getting married, another dancing energetically at a party, a third holding a basketball, the last slouching on a swaybacked horse. "Four missing men. Which could it be? A murderer might have been confident once in believing a face in advanced decay with no teeth could not be matched to any photograph or records. After all, here in Cuba nature is a very efficient undertaker. Now, however, all we need is a clear photograph and a clean skull. You are our guest, you choose."

Arkady chose the bridegroom, and at once the man's image filled the screen, eyes popping from nervousness, hair as carefully arranged as the frills on his shirt. Dragging a mouse on the pad, Dr. Blas outlined the groom's head, hit a key and erased his shirt and shoulders. At the tap of a key, the head floated to the left of the screen, and on the right appeared the skull as it stared up at the videocamera like a patient waiting for the dentist's drill. Blas repositioned the skull so that it gazed up at the camera lens at precisely the same angle as the face. He enlarged the face to the same size, enhanced the shadows so that flesh melted and eyes sank into hollows, placed white darts on the skull at jaw and crown of the skull, at the outside points of the brow, within the orbital and nasal cavities, across the cheekbones and the corners of the mandible. In comparison to the laborious reconstruction of faces from skulls that Arkady knew in Moscow, the tedious application of plastique to plaster bone, this was manipulation at the speed of light. Blas added arrows at the same points of the photograph and, with a tap, brought up between each pair of corresponding markers their distance measured in pixels, the screen's many thousand phosphors of light. A final keystroke merged the two heads into a single out-of-focus image with an overlay of numbers between the arrows.

"The numbers are discrepancies in measurement between the missing man and the skull when they are exactly matched. So we prove, scientifically, they could not possibly be the same man."

Blas started over again, this time with photo no. 3, a boy smiling proudly in a Chicago Bulls shirt, one hand weighing a basketball. Blas sliced off, enlarged and enhanced the boy's head, then brought up and positioned the skull on the screen. The distances between marker darts came up virtually the same, and when Blas merged the two images the numbers ratcheted down to zero and a single face that was both dead and alive looked out from the screen. If ever there was a picture of a ghost this was it.

"Now our missing man is not missing anymore and you see that even if things are supposed to be impossible in Cuba we do them anyway."

"That's why you wanted a photograph of Pribluda?"

"To make a match to the body we took from the bay, yes. But the photograph you brought was insufficient and the Russian embassy refuses to provide another."

There was an expectant wait until Arkady picked up the cue.

"I don't need a diplomatic note to go to the embassy."

Blas acted as if the thought had never occurred to him. "If you want to. The Revolution always needs volunteers. I can write the embassy address, and any car on the street will probably take you there for two dollars. If you have American dollars this is the best transportation system in the world."

Arkady was awed by the doctor's ability to put a good gloss on anything. His attention returned to the screen. "What was the head cut off with?"

"In the Dumpster?" said Blas. "A machete. The machete cut is a distinct wound. No sawing."

"Did you identify the murderer?"

Osorio said, "Not yet. We will, though."

"How many homicides a year did you say?"

"In Cuba? About two hundred," Blas said.

"How many in the heat of passion?"

"Overall, a hundred."

"Of the rest, how many for revenge?"

"Maybe fifty."

"Robbery?"

"Maybe forty."

"Drugs?"

"Five."

"Leaving five. How would you characterize them?"

"Organized crime, without a doubt. Paid murders."

"How organized? What were the weapons in those cases?"

"Occasionally a handgun. The Taurus from Brazil is popular, but usually machetes, strangling, knives. We have no real gangs here, nothing like the Mafia."

"Machetes?" To Arkady's ear, that did not have the ring of modern homicide. True, he remembered when any Russian murderer who wiped his knife after slicing a victim's throat was rated a smooth operator, back in the curiously innocent days before the worldwide spread of money transfers and remote control bombs. Which left Cuba in terms of criminal evolution the equivalent of the Galápagos Islands. Suddenly, the Instituto de Medicina Legal was put in perspective.

"We have a ninety-eight percent homicide solution rate," Blas said. "The best in the world."

"Enjoy it," Arkady said.

5.

The Russian embassy was a thirty-story tower with an architectural suggestion of squared chest and armored head looming like a monster of stone that had crossed continents, waded through oceans and finally stopped dead in its tracks ankle-deep among the green palm trees of Havana. Plate glass shone on its face, but overall the building stood in its own shroud of shadow and stillness. Inside, office after office was stripped to bare walls and phone jacks. Ghosts lingered in the bald spots and stains of hallway runners, in the hazy, unwashed bottles standing along the walls, in a ventilation system that spread an ancient reek of cigarettes. From the office of Vice Consul Vitaly Bugai, Arkady looked down at a world of white-colonnaded mansions, embassies French, Italian and Vietnamese, their roofs strung with elaborate radio dipoles and antennae, satellite dishes framed by gardens of pink hibiscus.

Bugai was a young man with small features squeezed into the center of a soft face. He wore a silk robe and Chinese sandals and floated in a liquid atmosphere of air-conditioning, moving, it seemed to Arkady, by contradictory impulses, relief that another Russian national was not dead and irritation that he would have to deal with the survivor for another week. He was also, perhaps, a little surprised that any vestige of Russian authority had been able to defend itself.

"Those houses were all from before the Revolution." Bugai joined Arkady at the window. "They were rich people. The biggest Cadillac dealership in the world was in Havana. When the Revolution came, the road to the airport was lined with Cadillacs and Chryslers left behind. Imagine being a rebel in a free Cadillac."

"I think I've seen some of those cars."

"Still, this is not a Black Hole. A Black Hole would be a posting in Guyana or Suriname. There's the music, the beaches, shopping in the Bahamas an hour away." Bugai flashed a golden Rolex on his wrist. "Havana's sea level and for me that's important. Of course, it's no Buenos Aires."

"It's not like the old days, either?" Arkady asked.

"Not at all. Between technicians and military support we had twelve thousand Russians here and a diplomatic staff of another thousand in attachés, deputies, cultural liaisons, KGB, secretaries, clerks, communications, couriers, security. We had Soviet housing, Soviet schools and camps for Russian children. Why not? We put thirty billion rubles into Cuba. Cuba got from Russia more foreign aid per person than any other country in the world. You have to ask yourself, who did more to bring down the Soviet Union than Fidel?" Bugai caught Arkady's glance. "Oh, the walls have ears. The Cubans are excellent at electronic surveillance. We trained them. The only really safe lines are at the embassy. You just have to stop worrying. Anyway, now we have a diplomatic staff of twenty people. This is a ghost ship. Never mind that we drove ourselves into bankruptcy to pay for this floating circus, that our entire system came crumbling down while they danced the salsa. The point is, relations between us and the Cubans have never been worse and now you tell me that you can't identify Pribluda's body?"

"Not conclusively."

"It was conclusive enough for the Cubans. I've talked to a Captain Arcos and he seemed very reasonable, considering he pulled a Russian out of Havana Harbor."

"A dead Russian."

"As I understand it, death was caused by a heart attack. A tragic but natural event."

"There's nothing natural about Pribluda floating in the bay."

"With spies these things happen."

"Officially, he was a sugar attaché."

"Right. Well, all he had to do was drive around the island and visit some cane fields and see the Cubans won't make their sugar quota, because they never have. As for secret intelligence, the Cuban army is now moving missiles with oxen instead of trucks, that's all you need to know about that. The faster we get this little episode behind us the better."

"There is the other little episode of Rufo and me."

"Well, who knows what you are? We've lost a driver and an apartment thanks to you."

"I'll stay at Pribluda's. It's empty."

Bugai pursed his lips. "That's not the worst solution. I intend to keep this problem as far from the embassy as possible."

Arkady discovered that talking to Bugai was much like trying to catch a jellyfish; every time he groped for an answer the vice consul floated out of reach.

"Before the Cubans even found the body someone here at the embassy knew that Pribluda was in trouble and sent me a fax. It was unsigned. Who could that be?"

"I wish I knew."

"You can't find out?"

"I don't have enough staff to investigate my staff."

"Who assigned Rufo to me?"

"The Cuban Ministry of the Interior assigned Rufo to *us*. Rufo was their man, not ours. There was no one else on hand when you arrived in the middle of the night. I didn't know exactly who you were and I still don't know exactly who you are. Of course, I've called Moscow, and perhaps they've heard of you but what you're really involved in I don't know. Crime is not my specialty."

"What I'm involved in is identifying Pribluda. The Cubans asked for photographs of him and wanted to come to the embassy. You refused."

"Well, this is my field. First, we had no photographs. Second, the Cubans always use any opportunity to gain access to the embassy and poke around sensitive areas. It's a state of siege. We were the comrades, now we're the criminals. Punctured tires in the middle of the night. Being pulled over for shakedowns when the police see Russian license plates."

"Like Moscow."

"But in Moscow the government has no control, that's the difference. I have to say we never had any trouble with Rufo until you."

"Where's the ambassador?"

"We're between ambassadors."

Arkady reached for a notepad from the desk and wrote, "Where is the resident intelligence agent Pribluda reported to?"

"It's no big secret," Bugai said. "The chief of guards is here, he's just muscle. But the chief of security has been in Moscow for the past month interviewing for a position in hotel management, and he made very clear to me that while he was gone he wanted 'no red flags.' And as for me, I do not intend to be recalled to Moscow over a spy who had a heart attack floating around in the dark."

"When Pribluda communicated with Moscow he used a secure line?"

"We send encrypted E-mail on a hooded machine that wipes clean, not even a ghost on the hard drive once you delete. But not that many messages are encrypted. The usual faxes, calls and E-mail are plain text on ordinary machines, and I would love a shredder that actually worked." Arkady produced the photograph of the Havana Yacht Club to ask about Pribluda's Cuban friends, but the vice consul barely glanced. "We have no Cuban friends. It used to be an event when a Russian artist visited Havana. People just watch American films on television anyway. Fidel steals them and shows them. It costs him nothing. Some people have satellite dishes and pick up Miami. And there's Santeria. He's willing to promote voodoo to entertain the masses. African superstitions. The longer I'm here the more African these people get."

Arkady put the Yacht Club away. "The Cubans need a better picture of Pribluda. The embassy must have a security photograph of him."

"That would be up to our friend in Moscow. We'll have to wait until he returns from his job search, and that could be another month."

"A month?"

"Or more."

Bugai had kept retreating and Arkady had kept advancing until he stepped on a pencil that broke with a sharp crack. The vice consul jumped and looked not as cool as jellyfish anymore, more like an egg yolk at the sight of a fork. His nervousness reminded Arkady that he had killed a man; whether in self-defense or not, killing someone was a violent act and not likely to attract new friends.

"What was Pribluda, your sugar attaché, working on?"

"I can't possibly tell you that."

"What was he working on?" Arkady asked more slowly.

"I don't think you have the authority," Bugai began, and amended as Arkady started around the desk. "Very well, but this is under protest. There's a problem with the sugar protocol, a commercial thing you wouldn't understand. Basically they send us sugar they can't sell anywhere else, and we send them oil and machinery we can't unload anywhere else."

"That sounds normal."

"There was a misunderstanding. Last year the Cubans demanded negotiations of agreements already signed. With such bad feelings between the two countries we let them bring in a third party, a Panamanian sugar trader called AzuPanama. Everything was resolved. I don't know why Pribluda was looking into that."

"Pribluda, the sugar expert?"

"Yes."

"And a photograph of Pribluda?"

"Let me look," Bugai said before Arkady took another step. He backed to the bookshelves and retrieved a leather album, which he opened on the desk, flipping through ring-bound pages of mounted photographs. "Guests and social events. May Day. Mexican Cinco de Mayo. I told you Pribluda didn't come to these things. Fourth of July with the Americans. The Americans don't have an embassy, only a so-called Interests Section bigger than an embassy. October, Cuban Independence Day. Did you know that Fidel's father was a Spanish soldier who fought against Cuba? December. Maybe there's one. We used to have a traditional New Year's party with a Grandfather Frost for Russian children, a major affair. Now we have only a few children, but they demand Santa Claus and a Christmas party."

In the photograph two girls with bows in their hair sat on the lap of a bearded man in a plush red suit, a round figure with cheeks rouged to a cheery glow. Presents ringed a tinsel tree. Behind the children spread a buffet line of adults balancing plates of cheeses and Christmas cakes and glasses of sweet champagne. At the far end someone who might have been Sergei Pribluda shoved his whole hand into his mouth.

"The heat in that suit was unbelievable."

"You wore it?" Arkady took a closer look at the picture. "You don't look well."

"Congestive heart failure. A bad valve." Kneading his arm, Bugai went around his desk and rooted through drawers. "Pictures. I'll make a list of possible names and addresses. Mostovoi is the embassy photographer, then there is Olga."

"You should be in Moscow."

"No, I angled for Cuba. They may not have enough drugs here but they have excellent doctors, more doctors per person than anywhere else in the world, and they'll operate on anyone, a general, a farmer, some little man who rolls cigars, it doesn't matter. Moscow? Unless you're a millionaire you wait two years at least. I'd be dead." Bugai blinked through a film of sweat. "I can't leave Cuba."

Elmar Mostovoi had a monkey's round mug and curved fingernails and a hairpiece of frizzled orange that sat on his head like a souvenir. He was in his mid-fifties, Arkady guessed, but still in good shape, the sort who did push-ups on his fingertips, wore his shirt open and rolled up his pants to show off a shaved chest and shins as smooth as tubes. He lived in Miramar, the same area as the embassy, in an oceanfront hotel named the Sierra Maestra, which offered many of the features of a sinking freighter: listing balconies, rusted railings, a view of the water. The furnishings of Mostovoi's apartment were quite plush, however, with a sofa and chairs covered in vanilla leather sitting on a deep shag rug.

"They put Poles, Germans and Russians here. They call it the Sierra Maestra, I call it Central Europe." Mostovoi inserted a Marlboro into an ivory cigarette holder. "Did you see the popcorn machine in the lobby? Very Hollywood."

Mostovoi's apartment was decorated with movie posters (*Lolita*, *East of Eden*), the photographs of an expatriate (Paris bistro, sailing, someone waving at the Tower of London), books (Graham Greene, Lewis Carroll, Nabokov), souvenirs (dusty campaign cap, bronze bells, ivory phalluses in ascending size).

"Are you interested in photographs?" Mostovoi asked.

"Yes."

"An appreciator?"

"In my way."

"Do you like nature?" It was very natural. Mostovoi had boxes of eight-by-ten black-and-white photographs of young female nudes half hidden by fronds, romping through waves, peeking through bamboo. "A cross between Lewis Carroll and Helmut Newton."

"Do you have any photographs of your colleagues at the embassy?"

"Bugai is always after me to take pictures of his so-called cultural events. I can't be bothered. You can't get Russians to pose like this. You can't even get them to take their clothes off."

"The climate, perhaps."

"No, even here." Mostovoi pondered the photograph of a Cuban girl lightly breaded in sand. "Somehow, the people here manage to balance socialism with naiveté. And by mixing with the Cubans I don't live with the paranoia that has gripped the rest of our dwindling community."

63

"What paranoia is that?"

"Ignorant paranoia. When an intelligence agent like Pribluda floats around the harbor in the middle of the night, what is he doing but spying? We never change. It's disgusting. It's what happens to Europeans in Paradise, we kill ourselves and blame the natives. I hoped Pribluda had more sense. You know, the KGB used to produce very civilized people. I said something in French to Pribluda once and he looked at me as if I were speaking Chinese."

Mostovoi opened another box. On top, a girl squeezed a volleyball. "My sports series."

"More of that dramatic angle."

The next shot was of a light-colored nude cradling a skull on her lap. The girl directed a sultry glower through a mane of curls that only half covered her breasts. Around her were molten candles, drums, bottles of rum.

"Wrong box," Mostovoi said. "My rainy-day series. We shot in here and I had to use the props at hand."

The skull was a rough facsimile, lacking detail around the nasal orifice and teeth, although Arkady was impressed by the number of artifacts a serious photographer had to have ready for a rainy day. In the next picture another girl wore a beret to model clay.

"Very artistic."

"That's kind of you. There's talk of a show at the embassy. Bugai strings me along. I don't care. I only hope I'm there with my camera when he has his heart attack."

She was buxom with fine hair fading from blond to gray and an oval face with small eyes a little damp with recollection. Although her air-conditioning had failed, Olga Petrovna's flat was a little corner of Russia with an Oriental rug on the wall, geraniums thriving in pots and a canary bright as a lemon trilling in a cage. Brown bread, bean salad, sardines, cole slaw with pomegranate seeds and three types of pickles were laid on the table. By an electric samovar sat a pot of jam and tea glasses in silver holders. She sorted through photograph albums for Arkady and, in a ladylike fashion, plucked at her dress where it adhered.

"They go back twenty-five years. It was such a life. Our own schools with the best teachers, good Russian food. It was a real community. No one spoke Spanish. The children had their Pioneer camps, all in Russian, with archery and mountain climbing and volleyball. None of this baseball idiocy of the Cubans. Our own beaches, our own clubs and, of course, there were always birthdays and weddings, real family events. It made you proud to be Russian, to know you were here protecting socialism on this island far from home in the teeth of the Americans. It seems hard to believe we were so strong, so sure."

"You are an unofficial historian of the embassy?"

"The embassy mother. I've been there longer than anyone else. I came very young. My husband is dead and my daughter married a Cuban. The truth is, I'm hostage to a granddaughter. If it weren't for me she wouldn't speak Russian at all. Who can imagine such a thing? Her name is Carmen. This is a name for a Russian girl?" She poured tea and added jam with a conspiratorial smile. "Who needs sugar?"

"Thank you. Did your granddaughter go to the embassy Christmas party?"

"Here she is." Olga Petrovna opened to the first picture of what appeared to be the most recent album and pointed to a curly-haired girl in a white dress that made her look like a walking wedding cake.

"Very cute."

"Do you think so?"

"Completely."

"Actually, it's an interesting mix, Russian and Cuban. Very precocious, a little of the exhibitionist. Carmen insisted—all the children insisted—on an American Santa Claus. That comes from watching television."

From snapshot to snapshot Arkady followed the little girl's progress to Santa's lap, a whisper in his ear and her retreat along the buffet. He pointed to a broad back at the table. "Isn't that Sergei Pribluda?"

"How could you tell? It was Carmen who dragged him to the party. He is such a hard worker."

Olga Petrovna had the highest esteem for Pribluda, a strong individual with a real worker's background, patriotic, never drunk though never shy, quiet but profound, obviously an agent but not the sort to act mysterious. Certainly not a weakling like Vice Consul Bugai.

"Remember the word 'comrade'?" asked Olga Petrovna.

"All too well."

"That's what I would call Sergei Sergeevich in the best sense of the word. And cultured."

"Really?" That was such a new perception of Pribluda that Arkady wondered whether they were speaking of the same person. Unfortunately, despite her respect for the colonel, she had no other pictures of him. Then, with great delight, "Oh, here she is." A girl of about eight in an outgrown school jumper of dull maroon stood at the threshold of the room. She glowered at Arkady from under a vee of brows. "Carmen, this is our friend Citizen Renko."

The girl advanced in three deliberate steps, shouted "Hai!" and delivered a kick a millimeter short of contact with his chest. "Uncle Sergei knows karate."

"He does?" Arkady had always thought of Pribluda as more a kidney-punch devotee.

"He carries a black belt in his briefcase."

"Did you ever see it?"

"No, but I'm sure." She administered a karate chop to the air and Arkady stepped back. "Did you see? Fists of fear."

"That's quite enough," Olga Petrovna said. "I know you have homework."

"If he's a friend of Uncle Sergei's he'll want to see it."

"That is enough, young lady."

"Stupid coat," Carmen looked Arkady up and down.

Olga Petrovna clapped her hands until the girl tucked in her chin and marched to the next room. "I'm sorry, that's children now."

"When was the last time you saw Sergei Sergeevich?"

"A Friday after work. I had taken Carmen for an ice cream on the Malecón when we ran into him talking to a Cuban. I remember Carmen said that she heard something roar, and Sergei Sergeevich said his neighbor kept a lion that ate little girls. She became so irritable we had to hurry home. Usually they did get on wonderfully." When Arkady had her show him on a map she pointed to the Malecón in front of Pribluda's flat. "Sergei Sergeevich wore a captain's cap and the Cuban was carrying one of those enormous inner tubes they fish from. A black man is all I remember."

"Did you hear a roar?"

"Something, maybe." As she put the albums away she asked, "Do you think there's any truth to this story that Sergei Sergeevich is dead?"

"I'm afraid there might be. Some of the Cuban investigators are very competent."

"Dead of what?"

"A heart attack, they say."

"But you have some doubts?"

"I just like to be sure."

Olga Petrovna sighed. Even in her time in Havana the city had become another Haiti. And Moscow was overrun by Chechens and gangs. Where could a person go?

Arkady took a taxi back to the Malecón and walked the last few blocks to Pribluda's apartment past boys demanding Chiclets and men offering *mulatas,* and beyond conversation starters of *"Amigo, qué hora es? De qué país? Momentico, amigo."* Overhead hung balconies, arabesques of wrought-iron spikes and potted plants, women in housedresses and men stripped to their underwear and cigars, music shifting from window to window. Decay everywhere, heat everywhere, faded colors trying to hold together disintegrating plaster and salt-eaten beams.

He thought for a moment he had caught sight of a man keeping pace behind him in the dark of the arcade. Was he being followed? He couldn't tell. It was hard to single out a shadow when everyone knew which way the streets ran except you, when everyone looked in place but you, with the sea on one side and on the other a maze of demolition piles, cars hauled onto sidewalks, lines of people waiting for ice cream, a bus, bread, water.

So he plunged on in his coat, drawing glances as if he were a monk wandered off the Via Dolorosa.

6.

Ofelia was Arkady and Dr. Blas played Rufo. They posi-tioned the tables and taped the floor of the IML conference room to indicate the perimeters of the walls, bookshelves and doors of the embassy flat so that they could—for their own information—"reconstruct the facts" of Rufo Pinero's death.

"Reconstruction of the facts" distinguished Cuban forensic medicine from the American, Russian, German. In Cuban laboratories, in Nicaraguan rain forests, in the dusty fields of Angola, Blas had re-created homicides to the amazement not only of judges but of the criminals themselves. A reconstruction of the facts surrounding the death of the Russian *neumático* might be impossible because of the drifting and deterioration of the body. Rufo's death, however, took place in an apartment, not open water, and left certain irrefutable facts: Rufo's body with an oversized arterial syringe in hand, a knife with Rufo's prints stuck into a bookcase, no bruises on the dead man's body, no disheveled clothes, no signs that pointed to anything but a swift, fatal confrontation.

Nevertheless, the doctor was stymied and breathing hard. They took into account that Rufo Pinero was a former athlete, taller and heavier than Renko by twenty kilos, maybe more. The Russian was exhausted by travel, confused, clearly not athletic, though not totally obtuse. Blas thought that described Renko well enough.

They staged the attack various ways. Rufo rising from a chair, waiting in the room, entering the door. No matter, wielding scissors and a pencil as a knife and syringe, Blas didn't come close to efficiently or rapidly dispatching Ofelia. Part of the problem was that she was so fast afoot. Ofelia had run the hundred-meter dash at school and hardly gained a kilo since then. She had a habit of shifting her weight from foot to foot that Blas found annoying.

Another problem was that the attack spoke of surprise. Yet using both a "knife" and a "syringe" made Blas slow and unwieldy. The simple act of bringing out not one but two weapons gave a victim time to react. Rufo would have been led laps around the room and table and chairs would have flown in all directions had Ofelia been the intended victim.

"Maybe it was a spontaneous attack," Blas said.

"Rufo wore a body-length jumpsuit of waterproof material over his shirt and pants. There's nothing spontaneous about that. He knew what he was going to do."

"Renko does not look quite so elusive."

"Maybe if he was threatened with a weapon."

"Two weapons."

"No," Ofelia decided, "Rufo had one weapon, the knife. The needle was the surprise for him." She hurried because she was a mere detective and Blas was a pathologist renowned for the rigor of his methodology. However, she could almost see the fight take place. "You know how the Russian always wears that ridiculous coat. I believe the knife pinned the coat to the bookcase. There is a tear in the lapel of the coat and there was a coat fiber on the knife. I think that was when Rufo was killed."

"With the syringe?"

"In self-defense."

Blas took Ofelia's hand, which was slim on the soap-scented meat of his palm. "What is wonderful about you is your sympathy for the most unlikely people. Only, this is not an investigation. You and I are merely satisfying our professional curiosity about the physical facts of a death."

"But don't you wonder?"

"No." Blas's expression said he wasn't a sexist, but that women often lost focus. "You're concerned about the syringe. Very well, we lost one in the lab. Either Renko or Rufo could have stolen it. But why would Renko? For drugs? I found no drugs in the syringe. He stole it as a weapon? If he had any fear for his life he wouldn't have come to Havana. We must be more sophisticated. For example, consider character. Rufo was a hustler, an opportunist. He saw the syringe and took it. Renko is a phlegmatic Russian. Everything for him is a mental debate, I guarantee you. And there is the matter of physical force. Ask yourself if Renko thought he could subdue someone as strong as Rufo. Even in self-defense."

"Maybe he didn't think, maybe he reacted."

"With a syringe already in his hand? A syringe for which he had no use? A syringe that ended in Rufo's grip?"

She withdrew her hand. "Rufo pulled it out of his head. I would."

"Maybe? Would? You are speculating. Truth reveals itself more to logic than to inspiration." Blas had caught his breath. "We'll try the reconstruction again. Only, this time move a little slower. You forget that Renko is a smoker, probably a drinker, certainly out of condition. You, on the other hand, are most definitely in shape, younger, more alert. I don't see how he could start to defend himself. Maybe Rufo slipped. Ready?"

Rufo was not the sort who slipped, Ofelia thought.

She had had a good friend named María at the university. Some years later, María married a poet who declared himself an observer for human rights in Havana.

Soon Ofelia saw on television that he had been sentenced to twenty years for assault and that María had been arrested for prostitution. When Ofelia visited her in jail María told a different story. She said that she had just come out of her house in the morning when a man grabbed her and started to pull her clothes off at her own front door. When her husband ran out to protect her, the man knocked him to the ground and kicked in his teeth. Only then did a police car appear, driven by a single officer who took only a statement from the man, who claimed that María had propositioned

71

him and, when he turned her down, that her husband had assaulted him. Maria remembered two other items: that the backseat of the car was already covered in a plastic sheet and that when the man who beat her husband got into the front of the patrol car he picked up two aluminum cigar tubes from the seat and slipped them into his shirt pocket. The cigars were his, laid aside for safekeeping. The poet and María hanged themselves in different prisons on the same day. Out of sheer curiosity Ofelia went back and read their arrest report, which declared that the good citizen who had come wandering by their door was Rufo Pinero.

Rufo hardly needed one weapon, let alone two.

If the issue of the syringe bothered her and the death of María upset her, the Russian infuriated her. The arrogance to steal Rufo's key, as if he would even know what he was looking at in a Cuban's room. To think that he could stand in front of a map of Havana in Pribluda's office and see more than a piece of paper.

For Ofelia every street, every corner on the map was a memory. For example, her first school trip to Havana when she was running hurdles at what used to be the greyhound track in Miramar, where she returned at night with Tolomeo Durán and lost her virginity on the high-jump mat. That was Miramar to her. Or the theater in Chinatown where her uncle Cucho was knifed to death in the middle of a pornographic movie. Or the Coppelia ice-cream parlor on La Rampa where she met her first husband, Humberto, while they waited three hours for a spoonful to eat. Or the Floridita bar in Havana Vieja where she caught Humberto with a Mexican woman. More than one marriage had ended because tourists came prowling for Cuban men. Divorce was easy in Cuba. She had friends who had been divorced four or five times. What would a Russian know about that?

Blas gasped, "Still too fast."

7.

Havana had sunk into evening shadow, the sea scal-
loped black, swallows darting through the arcade when Arkady
reached the Malecón. As he went up the stairs he heard the
ground-floor neighbor's radio and not quite a lion's roar but a definite reverberation.

Slotted light spread from shutters across the walls of Pribluda's
sitting room to the black doll sitting in the corner, its head tucked
away. Perhaps it was the low angle of sun off the water but the flat
seemed subtly altered: a lower ceiling, wider table, a chair turned
a different direction. Since a kid, Arkady always turned chairs
slightly out from a table as if they carried on a silent conversation.
A childish habit, but there it was.

Apart from the door the only access to the apartment was the
balcony and an air shaft midway down the corridor. Even as
Arkady turned on lights a power brownout reduced them to candles. He hung up his coat in the bedroom closet and stuck his
passport in a shoe while he opened his bag. The shirts were perhaps folded a little differently.

If there were snoops they hadn't taken any food—the Russian
stockpile in the refrigerator was still complete. Arkady poured chilled
water from a jar. Dim light crept from the refrigerator to the glasses
on the table, the turtle's bowl, the glass eyes of the rag doll. Black
paint gave Chango not only color but a rough kind of vigor. Arkady
lifted the red bandanna to touch the face, which was papier-mâché

molded into crude features, half-formed mouth about to speak, half-formed nose about to breathe, half-formed hand about to push off its walking stick and rise. Dolls should be more insubstantial, not quite so conscious or as watchful, Arkady thought. Sweat located his spine. He was going to have to stop wearing a coat in Havana.

The noise from below reminded him that he had meant to try in at least one language or another to interview the ground-floor neighbor. According to Detective Osorio, this was the person who had illegally rented Pribluda the second-floor rooms. The illegal part appealed to Arkady. Also, he wondered why the neighbor didn't want both floors himself. The cacophony could have been even more stereophonic.

When the noise stopped it was interesting how like a seashell a shuttered apartment could sound. The barely audible sweep of cars, stirring of water along the seawall, the pounding of the heart. Maybe he was wrong about the chairs and bag, he thought. Nothing else seemed out of place. The din started downstairs again, and he took his glass to Pribluda's office phone and studied the list of numbers he had copied off Rufo's wall.

```
Daysi 32-2007
Susy 30-4031
Vi. Aflt. 2300
Kid Choc. 5/1
Vi. HYC 2200 Angola
```

Now that he thought about it, why had he assumed that *Vi.* stood for visitor? Granted, he was a visitor arriving on Aeroflot, but was the word for visitor the same in Spanish and English? Rufo knew he was coming. Wouldn't it be more important to know what day of the week? He looked up the word for Friday in Pribluda's Spanish-Russian dictionary. "Viernes." *Vi.* stood for Friday. Which suggested that on another Friday at 10:00 P.M. with a person or at a place with the initials *HYC* something would happen concerning *Angola*. Was that vague enough?

Arkady tried the names on the list and got an answer on the first ring.

"Dígame."

Arkady, in Russian, "Hello, is this Daysi?"

"Dígame."

"Is this Daysi?"

"Oye, quién es?"

In English. "Is this Daysi?"

"Sí, es Daysi."

"Do you speak English?"

"Un poco, sí."

"Are you a friend of Rufo?"

"Muy poco."

"You know Rufo Pinero?"

"Rufo, sí."

"Could we meet and talk?"

"Qué?"

"Talk?"

"Qué?"

"Do you know someone who speaks English?"

"Muy poco."

"Thanks."

He hung up and tried Susy.

"Hi."

"Hello. You speak English."

"Hi."

"Could you tell me where I could find Rufo Pinero?"

"El coño Rufo? Es amigo suyo? Es cabrón and comemierda. Oye, hombre, singate y singa a tu madre también."

"I didn't catch that."

"Y singa tu perro. Cuando veas a Rufo, pregúntale, dónde está el dinero de Susy? O mi regalito de QVC?"

"Let's say, you know Rufo. Do you know anyone who speaks English or Russian?"

"Y dígale, chupa mis nalgas hermosas!"

While he was trying to find *chupa* in the dictionary, Susy hung up.

A noise drew him to the parlor, although he found no one but Chango glowering from his chair. The doll had slumped a little, still surly, top-heavy. Had its head turned since he had been in the room last, raised its eyes to steal a sideways glance? For some reason he was reminded of the giant Comandante he had seen painted on a wall the night before, the way the figure seemed to loom above the lamps like an all-knowing, all-seeing specter, or the way a director hovered in the dark at the back of a theater. Arkady had felt exceedingly small and uninformed.

He refilled his glass and wandered back to the office and the map of Havana over the desk. Facing it, Arkady could see the full scope of his ignorance. Neighborhoods called Havana Vieja, Vedado, Miramar? They sounded beautiful, but he could have been staring at hieroglyphics for all he understood. At the same time, it was a relief to be far from Moscow, where every street suggested Irina or a journalist's café she'd favored, the shortcut to the puppet theater, the ice rink where she'd goaded him into skating again. At every corner he'd expected her to appear, walking full tilt as she always did, scarf and long hair snapping like flags. He had even returned to the clinic, retraced his steps like a man trying to find that single step, that pivotal error he could correct and turn everything back. But his futility mounted as the days rolled in like waves, one black crest after another, and the distance between him and the last time he saw her only grew.

In fact, his very work was a reminder that time was a one-way proposition. A homicide meant, by definition, that someone was too late. Of course, investigating a crime that had already happened was relatively simple. Investigating a crime that hadn't yet occurred, to see the lines before they connected, that might demand skill.

At a creak of wood Arkady noticed Sergeant Luna standing in the office door. It wasn't just the sound, Arkady thought, more like an entire force field crossing the threshold. He didn't recognize Luna immediately because the sergeant was in jeans, sweatshirt and a cap that said "Go Gators." Air Jordans graced his feet and his muscular hands flexed around a long metal club as if he were trying to squeeze it in half. The man was a natural athlete just by the bounce in his feet. Dirt covered his arms and shirt as if he'd come directly from a game. The barrel of the club said "Emerson."

"Sergeant Luna, I didn't hear you come in."

"Because I walk quiet and I have a key." Luna held a key up to illustrate and put it in a pocket. He had a voice like wet cement being turned by a shovel. The narrow cap emphasized his round head and the way muscles played on his forehead and jaw. The whites of his eyes were slightly fried. His biceps balled with anger.

"You speak Russian, too."

"I picked it up. I thought we could have a talk without the captain or the detective, with no one else."

"I'd like to talk." Luna had been so silent around Captain Arcos, Arkady was happy to hear the sergeant out. The bat bothered him. "Let me get you something to drink."

"No, just talk. I want to know what you're doing."

Arkady always tried honesty first.

"I'm not sure myself. I just didn't think the identification of the body was certain enough. Since Rufo attacked me, I think maybe there is more to find out."

"You think that was stupid of Rufo?"

"Maybe."

"Who are you?" Luna poked him with the fat end of the bat.

"You know who I am."

"No, I mean who are you?" Luna poked him again in the ribs.

"I'm a prosecutor's investigator. I wish you'd stop doing that."

"No, you can't be an investigator here. You can be a tourist here, but you can't be an investigator here. Understand? *Comprendes?*" Luna walked around him. For Arkady it was like talking to a shark.

"I understand perfectly."

"I wouldn't go to Moscow and tell you how to do things. It shows a lack of respect. And you killed a Cuban citizen."

"I'm sorry about Rufo." Within limits, Arkady thought.

"It seems to me you're very difficult."

"Where is Captain Arcos? Did he send you?"

"Don't you worry about Captain Arcos." The sergeant gave him another poke of the bat.

"You're going to have to stop that."

"Are you going to lose your temper? Are you going to attack a sergeant of the Ministry of the Interior? I think that would be a bad idea."

"What do you think would be a good idea?" Arkady tried to emphasize the positive.

"It would be a good idea if you understood you are not Cuban."

"I swear I don't think I'm Cuban."

"You don't know anything here."

"I couldn't agree more."

"You do nothing."

"That's pretty much what I'm doing."

"Then we can be friendly."

"Friendly is good."

For his part, Arkady felt he was being agreeable, soft as a pat of butter, but Luna still circled him.

"Is that a baseball bat?" Arkady asked.

"Baseball is our national sport. Want to see it?" Luna offered the bat to him handle first. "Take a swing."

"That's all right."

"Take it."

"No."

"Then I'll take it," Luna said and swung the bat into Arkady's left leg above the knee. Arkady dropped to the floor and Luna moved behind him. "See, you have to step into it to drive the ball. Did you feel that?"

"Yes."

"You have to turn into the ball. You're from Moscow?"

"Yes."

"I'll tell you something I should have told you before. I am from the Oriente, the east of Cuba." When Arkady tried to rise, Luna took a judicious chop into the back of the other knee and Arkady fell backward into the hall and started to crawl toward the parlor to lead the sergeant away from the list of phone numbers. Always thinking, Arkady told himself. Luna followed. "Men from the Oriente are Cuban, but more so. They like you or they don't. If they like you, you have a friend for life. If they don't, you have a problem. You're fucked." Luna kicked Arkady forward onto his face. "Your problem is I don't like Russians. I don't like the way they talk, I don't like their smell, I don't like the way they look. I don't *like* them." The hall was too narrow for a full swing of the bat, but Luna jabbed Arkady's ribs to emphasize his points. "When they stabbed Cuba in the back, we threw them *out*. Hundreds of Russians flew from Havana every *day*. The night before the KGB was thrown out someone punctured the tires of all the embassy cars so that they would have to *walk* to the airport. It's *true*. The fuckers had to find cars at the last second. Otherwise, *think* of the embarrassment, Russians walking twenty kilometers to the air*port*."

Arkady called for help, all too aware he was shouting in the wrong language and that with the banging from below no one would hear him anyway. Once in the parlor he pushed himself up against a wall and, standing on legs that went every which way, actually landed a blow that made the bigger man grunt acknowledgment. As the two men scuffled around the table the turtle bowl rolled off. Finally the sergeant got free enough to swing the bat again and Arkady found himself on the rug, blinking through blood, aware he'd lost a few seconds of memory and a brain cell or two. He felt a foot across his neck as Luna bent close to feel Arkady's shirt pocket and pants. All Arkady could see was the rug and Chango in his chair staring back. No mercy there.

"Where is the picture?"

"What picture?"

The foot pressed on Arkady's windpipe. Well, it was a dumb answer, Arkady admitted. There was only one picture. The Havana Yacht Club.

"Where?" Luna eased up to give him another chance.

"First you didn't want it, now you do?" As Arkady felt his windpipe close he said, "At the embassy. I gave it to them."

"Who?"

"Zoshchenko." Zoshchenko was Arkady's favorite comic writer. He felt the situation needed humor. He hoped there was no poor Zoshchenko at the embassy. He heard a contemplative slap of the bat in Luna's hand.

"Do you want me to fuck you up?"

"No."

"Do you want me to seriously fuck you up?"

"No."

"Because you will stay fucked."

Although Arkady was pinned like an insect he did his best to nod.

"If you don't want me to mess with you, you stay here. From now on you're a tourist, but you will do all your touring in this room. I'll send some food every day. You don't leave. Stay here. Sunday you go home. A quiet trip."

That sounded quiet, Arkady got that.

Satisfied, Luna removed his foot from Arkady's neck, lifted Arkady's head by the hair and clubbed him one more time as if dispatching a dog.

When Arkady was conscious again it was dark, and he was stuck to the carpet. He ripped his head off and rolled to the wall to look and listen before he dared move any more. New blood oozed around one eye. The furniture was a mass of shadows. Sounds of work had stopped below, replaced by the unctuous strains of a bolero. Luna was gone. Altogether, Arkady thought, a hell of a vacation. And certainly the worst suicide he had ever attended.

Just standing proved to be a feat of balance, as if the sergeant's baseball bat had driven all the fluid from one inner ear to the other, but he managed to drag a chair to prop against the door.

With the blood washed off, the head in the bathroom mirror wasn't so bad, one gash at the hairline he had to shave around and pull back together with butterfly tapes from the medicine chest, otherwise just a new topological feature at the back of the skull. A little broader bridge of his nose, a knot on his forehead, a lasting impression of the rug on his cheek, some difficulty swallowing, but all teeth accounted for. His legs felt broken, but on the other hand, they worked. Luna had done a fairly good job of limiting the damage to bruises and indignities.

He hobbled to the bedroom closet and found the pockets of his coat turned out, but his passport with the photograph of the Havana Yacht Club still rested in the shoe where he had put them. Light-headedness and nausea rose, signs of a concussion.

Muddy blood stained the parlor rug. Like any party, he thought, cleaning up was the hard part. He'd do it later. First things first. In a kitchen drawer he found a whetstone and a narrow bladed boning knife that he honed to a fine edge. On the seat of the chair propped against the door he balanced a bag of empty cans as an alarm and perhaps a little fun underfoot, and he unscrewed all the lightbulbs in the parlor and hall so that if Luna returned he would enter the dark and be silhouetted by the light. The best Arkady could do for the air-shaft window was ram it shut with a stick. The best he could do for his head was stay flat. Which he was about to do when he passed out.

He didn't feel refreshed. What time it was he couldn't tell, the room was dark. What room he was in he wouldn't have known except for the rough bristles of the parlor rug on his face. Like a drunk, he wasn't positive which way was up.

His body had set in a position of least pain, all things being relative, and in the manner of a broken chair it had no intention of sitting up again. He did anyway because a little circulation was probably good for bruised limbs. The turtle crawled by, practically trotting. Arkady followed on all fours to the refrigerator, pulled out the water jar and luxuriated in the soft, unthreatening nimbus of the appliance light.

On a purely objective basis it was interesting how much worse he felt. Drinking water was painful. Touching his head with a damp cloth combined agony and relief.

Irina liked to say, "Be careful what you wish for." Meaning, of course, her. Having lost her, what he'd wished for was an end to his guilt, but he really hadn't meant being *beaten* to death. In Moscow you were left alone to kill yourself. In Havana there wasn't a moment's peace.

The phone cord was ripped from the wall, although Arkady wasn't sure whom to call anyway. The embassy, so they could cringe again at the trouble one of their nationals was causing?

The dark was so quiet he could almost hear the sweep of the lighthouse beam over the bay and feel the brush of light across the shutters.

Don't leave, Luna had said.

Arkady didn't plan to. He laid his head in the refrigerator and went to sleep.

When he woke again morning light streamed into the flat. Arkady lifted his head as carefully as a cracked egg. The Malecón's backfires and shouts sounded loud and hot, amplified by the sun.

He staggered down the hall to the bathroom mirror. The nose was no better and his forehead had the dark hue of a storm cloud. He dropped his pants to see the stripes of bruises on his legs.

Rest and water, he told himself. He ate a handful of aspirin, but didn't dare shower for fear of slipping, for fear of not hearing the front door, for fear of hurting.

Two steps and he was dizzy, but he reached the office. He had crawled from it when Luna began demonstrating his baseball skills to lead the sergeant away from the miserable list of Rufo's phone numbers. Oddly enough, the list was where Arkady had left it, in the Spanish-Russian dictionary, meaning that Luna either didn't know how to search or that he had come only for the picture of the Havana Yacht Club.

Since he had a little time now, Arkady thought that a real investigator would use this opportunity to learn Spanish and phone repair and try Daysi and Susy again. Instead, he slid down the wall to a seated position with the knife in his hand. He wasn't aware of sleeping until a backfire from the street jolted him awake.

Not that he was scared.

. . .

Two young uniformed policemen, one white, one black, patrolled the seawall. Although they carried radios, handguns and batons, their orders seemed entirely in the negative: don't lean against the wall, don't listen to music, don't fraternize with girls. Although they seemed to pay no special attention to the house, Arkady thought it would be a little wiser to escape in the evening.

He cleaned the carpet because it was too depressing to look at his own dried blood. The music below had changed to a work-theme salsa accompanied by a power drill; Arkady wasn't sure whether he was above a flat or a factory. Not all the blood came out of the rug; enough remained to suggest a mottled rose.

Luna could scrub the bat and Arkady was sure that the entire ball team was willing to swear the sergeant had been gamboling on a field with them. How many players were there on a side in baseball? Ten, twenty? More than enough witnesses. Bugai wouldn't lodge a protest. Even if he did find the nerve, to whom would he complain but Arcos and Luna? The only communication that Arkady could expect between the embassy and Luna was the question "Do you have a Zoshchenko working there? No? Thank you very much."

Arkady shaved for morale's sake, working around the damage on his face, and tried to comb his hair over the repair on his brow. When the nausea let up he celebrated by changing into a clean shirt and pants, so that he looked like a well-groomed victim of a violent crime. He also tied another knife to a broom to use as a spear and, giddy with achievement, peeked through the balcony shutters.

A PNR patrol car appeared about every forty minutes. In between, the patrolmen fought their own war against boredom, sneaking a cigarette, staring at the sea, watching Havana girls in their variety strut by in shorts and platform shoes.

. . .

In the late afternoon Arkady woke with an enormous thirst and a headache aggravated by the noise below. He had aspirin and water while he admired Pribluda's variety of pickled garlic heads and mushrooms. He just didn't feel like food at the moment, and when he turned away from the refrigerator he realized that Chango had disappeared. The doll that had sat in the corner was gone.

When? During Luna's lecture on the finer points of baseball? With the sergeant or of Chango's own volition? The missing doll was reminder enough that a patrol car was due in a minute and that Luna was overdue. Through the shutters he saw two black girls dressed in matching pedal pushers of citrus yellow teasing the PNRs.

Some vacations stretched and some seemed to fly by in a moment, not even time for a tan. Arkady decided that when man-sized dolls started walking around it was time for him to go, too, and camp at the embassy whether he was welcome or not. Or the airport. Moscow's airports, for instance, were full of people going absolutely nowhere.

Arkady put on his precious coat with the phone list and picture in one pocket and keys and knife in the other, and cleared the chair and bag of cans from the door. He still had Pribluda's car key. Who knew, he might be able to drive. As he tottered down, the stairs pulsated underfoot.

From the street door he saw the girls and the two PNRs bantering and posturing. Behind them the Cuban sky was gold edged in blue, more mixed day and night than a simple sunset. As a car limped by, my God, a two-seater Zaporozhets belching black smoke, Arkady slipped out into the long shadow of the arcade.

8.

Wearing a cherry-red halter and denim shorts with a Minnie Mouse patch on a back pocket, Ofelia sat in an aquamarine '55 DeSoto outside the Casa de Amor and asked herself: Was it cigar fumes? Something in the rum? The two spoonfuls of sugar in *café cubano* that made men crazy? If she saw one more young Cuban girl on the arm of one more fat, balding, lisping Spanish tourist, Ofelia would kill.

She'd pulled enough of them in. Some were family men who had never before been unfaithful but suddenly found it unnatural to spend a week in Havana without a *chica*. More were the sort of human slugs who came for Cuban girls, as before they had traveled to Bangkok or Manila. It wasn't white slavery anymore, it was sex tourism. More efficient. And it wasn't white, anyway. What tourists in Cuba wanted were *mulatas* or *negritas*. The more northern the European, the more guaranteed that he was after the experience of a black girl.

The Casa de Amor was originally a motel, ten units with patios and sliding aluminum doors around a swimming pool. A heavyset woman in a housedress read a paperback in a metal chair on a lawn that had been paved over and painted green. In the office was a register and selections of condoms, beer, rum, Tropicola. The tip-off that something wrong was going on was that the pool water was clean. That was for tourists.

Traffic went in and out. At this point Ofelia was expert at telling a German (pink) from an Englishman (sallow) from a Frenchman (safari shorts), but what she was waiting for was a Cuban uniform. The law was useless. Cuban law excused a man for making sexual advances, assuming it was a masculine given, and put the burden of proof on Ofelia to prove that the girl initiated the approach. Now, any Cuban female over the age of ten knew how to incite a male into making the first overt proposal. A Cuban girl could make Saint Jerome make the first advance.

The police were worse than useless, they preyed on the girls, demanding money for letting them into hotel lobbies, for wandering around the marina, for allowing them to take tourists to places like the Casa de Amor, which was supposed to be for conjugal activities between Cuban couples who couldn't find sufficient privacy at home. Well, *jineteras* had the same problem and could pay more.

Traffic went in and out the office, the girls steering in their clients like little tugboats. Ofelia let them go. Someone in authority had arranged matters at the Casa de Amor, and what Ofelia wanted more than anything else was for some sleazy PNR commander to check his operation, see her in the car and invite her to join his string. A badge and gun rested in her straw bag. The look on his face when she brought them out? *Vaya.*

Sometimes Ofelia felt it was her against the world. This one feeble little campaign of hers against an industry that was nearly official. The Ministry of Tourism discouraged any real crackdown on *jineteras* as a threat to Cuba's economic future. If they deplored prostitution, why did they always add that Cuba's were the most beautiful, healthiest prostitutes in the world?

The week before, she had picked up a twelve-year-old *jinetera* in the Plaza de Armas. One year older than Muriel. That was the future?

She hadn't given Renko a lot of thought until she gave up surveillance at the end of the day and visited the IML to check whether the dead Russian was tagged for transport and, when she found the body wasn't, looked for Blas. She found the director working at a laboratory counter.

"I'm looking into something," Blas said. "I am not investigating, but you made such a point about the syringe I think you especially will be interested."

His instrument was a camcorder modified to fit onto a microscope. The microscope eyepiece had been removed so that the camera could focus directly on a grayish paste spread on a specimen slide. A cable led from the camcorder to a video monitor. On its screen was a magnified version of the paste with gradations in color that ran from tarry black to chalk white. In front of the monitor was an embalming syringe.

"Rufo's needle?" Ofelia asked.

"Yes, the syringe stolen from here, from my own laboratory, and found in the hand of Rufo Pinero. Embarrassing but also informative because the tissue packed into a needle shaft, you know, is a core sample as good as a biopsy."

"You squeezed it out?"

"For curiosity's sake. Because we are scientists," Blas said as he moved the slide in minute increments under the camera. "Working backward: brain tissue, blood corresponding to Rufo's blood type, bone, cocheal material from the inner ear, skin and more blood and skin. What's interesting is the last blood, which actually would have been the first blood in the needle shaft. Tell me what you see."

The screen was a stew of cells, larger ones solid red, the smaller cells with white centers.

"Blood cells."

"Look again."

With Blas you always learned, she thought. On the second look, many of the red cells seemed crushed or exploded like overripe pomegranates. "There is something wrong with them. A disease?"

"No. What you see," he told her, "is a battlefront, a battlefront of whole blood cells, fragments of blood cells and clumps of antibodies. This blood is hemolyzed, it is at war."

"With itself?"

"No, this is a war that only occurs when two different blood types come into contact. Pinero's and . . . ?"

"Renko's?"

"Most likely. I'd love to have a sample from the Russian."

"He says he wasn't touched."

"I say otherwise." He was definite, and she knew that when Blas was definite he was almost always right.

"Will you test for drugs?" she asked.

"No need. You weren't at the autopsy, but I can tell you that on Rufo's arm are the tracks of old injections. Do you know how much a new syringe is worth to a user? This proves Rufo had two weapons."

"But Renko is alive and Rufo is dead."

"I admit that is the baffling part."

Ofelia thought of the cut in Renko's coat. That was from the knife. Why wouldn't the Russian mention a wound from the needle?

Blas had registered the fact that she was still in her shorts and halter, black curls shining, a glow on her brown skin. "You know, there is a meeting next month in Madrid I have to attend. I could use someone to help with the projector and charts. Have you ever been to Spain?"

The doctor was popular with the women on his staff. In fact, an invitation to accompany him to an international conference on pathology was one of the prizes of the institute. He was admired, sometimes awe-inspiring, connected to the highest government elite, and all Ofelia could really say against him was that his lower lip, nested in his trim beard, was always wet. Somehow that was enough.

"It sounds nice but I have to help take care of my mother."

"Detective Osorio, I've asked you to two conferences now. Both important, both in fascinating places. You always say you have to take care of your mother."

"She's *so* frail."

"Well, I hope she gets well."

"*Thank* you."

"If you can't go, you can't go." Blas pushed aside the microscope and camera as if they were dinner gone cold. Ofelia's eyes, however, were fixed to the monitor, to a magnified terrain of warring blood cells where she saw a new answer.

9.

There were more PNRs stationed on the Malecón than Arkady had expected. Taking the first street from the water, then avoiding a patrol car at the next corner, he found himself behind the block he had just left and at an alley with a flat-faced, vintage American Jeep in house-paint red. Behind it were two more Jeeps, green and white, each with new roll bars and upholstery. They shone under lamps strung out from a humming generator set inside open garage doors where a man in coveralls inspected an inner tube he held in a tub of water. He raised a white, amiable face and carried the tube to an air hose.

"Needs air," he said in Russian.

"I suppose so," Arkady said.

Inside, under a caged bulb hanging on a cord, a Jeep sat on ramps over a mechanic working on his back. As the engine revved a rubber hose taped to the exhaust pipe funneled white smoke to the alley. There were other signs of the garage's makeshift nature, the lack of work pits and hydraulic lifts. An engine hung on chains from an I beam above garage disorder, tanks, tool cabinets, oil-cans, ammeters, tires, tire lever and well, a folding chair behind a worktable of mallets, a board of car rings on hooks, vises and clamps and greasy rags everywhere, a beaded curtain marking off a personal area, and Arkady realized that he was directly below Pribluda's parlor. A boom box vied for volume next to the Jeep.

Since the hood was open, Arkady could see a transplanted Lada engine resonating like a pea in a can. A knit cap, smudged face and dirty beard rolled out from under the car to study Arkady from an upside-down angle.

"Russian?"

"Yes. Everyone can tell?"

"It's not so hard. Have an accident?"

"Kind of."

"In a car?"

"No."

The mechanic looked up at the object of his labor.

"If you need a car you could do worse than this. A '48 Jeep. Try to get parts for a '48 Jeep. The best I can do is a Lada 2101. I had to eliminate the differential and adapt the brakes. It's just the seals and valves now that are driving me crazy." His eyes strained to watch something he was reaching for under the car. The engine raced and he winced. "What a shit rain." He rolled back under and shouted, "See any tape?"

Arkady found wrenches, goggles, welding gauntlets, buckets of sand, but reported no tape.

"Mongo isn't there?"

"What is a Mongo?" Arkady wasn't sure he heard right because of the music.

"Mongo is a black man in coveralls and a green baseball cap."

"No Mongo."

"Tico? Man working on a tire?"

"He's there."

"He's looking for a leak. He'll be looking all day." After what Arkady had to assume were strong words in Spanish the mechanic said, "Very well, we'll perform heart surgery by going in through the ass. Find me a hammer and a screwdriver and get a pan ready."

Arkady handed him the tools. "You like Jeeps?"

The mechanic rolled under the car. "I specialize in Jeeps. Other American cars are too heavy. You have to put in Volga engines and Volgas are hard to find. I like a tough little Jeep with a little Lada heart that goes *takatakataka*. Are you sure you don't want a car?"

"No."

"Don't be put off by appearances. This island is like a Court of Miracles, like in medieval Paris, where the lame could walk and the blind could see because all these cars are still running after fifty years. The reason is that the Cuban mechanic is, by necessity, the best in the world. Could you turn the radio up?"

Unbelievably, the volume had another notch. Maybe this was a Cuban-made radio, Arkady thought. Meanwhile, the violent whacks from under the Jeep made his head throb.

"So you sell cars?" Arkady shouted.

"Yes and no. An old car from before the Revolution, yes. To buy a new car requires approval from the highest level, the very highest. The beauty of the system is that no car in Cuba is abandoned. It may look abandoned, but it's not." One more whack. "The pan, the pan, the pan!"

Arkady heard a glutinous gush. In a single move, the mechanic swung the pan under the Jeep in his place and shot out on his cart, rolling across the floor until he backhanded a column of tires and swung to a stop and sat up, grinning. He was a robust specimen with the smirk of near disaster, and looked so much like a test pilot after an interesting landing that it took Arkady a moment to notice that the mechanic's coverall legs ended at leather pads at the knees. When he wiped his face and removed his cap his hair rose into a salt-and-pepper mane too unique for Arkady not to recognize the short man from Pribluda's photograph of the Havana Yacht Club, simply far shorter than Arkady had expected.

"Erasmo Aleman," he introduced himself. "You're Sergei's friend?"

"Yes."

"I've been waiting for you."

Erasmo pushed his cart with wooden blocks edged in tire tread to maneuver around his garage at full speed, washing at a cut-down sink, wiping his hands at a barrel of rags. The radio was down to half throat.

"I saw a policewoman take you upstairs a couple of nights ago. You look . . . different."

"Someone tried to teach me baseball."

"It's not your sport." Erasmo's eyes went to the bruise on Arkady's cheek to the Band-Aid on his head.

"Is this Sergei?" Arkady produced the snapshot of Pribluda with the Yacht Club.

"Yes."

"And?" Arkady pointed to the black fisherman.

"Mongo," Erasmo said, as if it were self-evident.

"And you."

Erasmo admired the picture. "I look very handsome."

"The Havana Yacht Club," Arkady read the back.

"It was a joke. If we'd had a sailboat we would have called ourselves a navy. Anyway, I heard about the body they found across the bay. Frankly, I don't think it's Sergei. He's too pigheaded and tough. I haven't seen him for weeks, but he could come back tomorrow with some story about driving into a pothole. There are potholes in Cuba you can see from the moon."

"Do you know where his car is?"

"No, but if it were around here I'd recognize it."

Erasmo explained that diplomatic license plates were black on white and Pribluda's was 060 016; 060 for the Russian embassy and 016 for Pribluda's rank. Cuban plates were tan for state-owned cars, red for privately owned.

"Let me put it this way," Erasmo said, "there are state-owned cars that will never move so that private cars can run. A Lada arrives here like a medical donor so that Willy's Jeeps will never die. Excuse me." He turned down a salsa that threatened to get out of hand. "The reason for the radio is so the police can say they don't hear me, because you're really not supposed to make a garage out of your apartment. Anyway, Tico likes it loud."

Arkady thought he understood Erasmo, the type of engineer who labors happily below the deck of a sinking ship, lubricating the pistons, pumping out the water, somehow keeping the vessel moving while it settles in the waves.

"Your neighbors don't complain about the noise?"

"There's Sergei and a dancer in this building, both out all the time. On one side is a private restaurant, they don't want the police visiting because it costs them a free dinner at the least. On the other side lives a *santero* and the police certainly don't want to bother him. His apartment is like a nuclear missile silo of African spirits."

"A *santero?*"

"As in Santeria."

"He's a friend?"

"On this island a *santero* is a good friend to have."

Arkady studied the picture of the Havana Yacht Club. There still was some message in it that he didn't understand. If he was going to be beaten over the head he wanted to know why.

"Who took the picture?"

"Someone passing by. You know," Erasmo said, "the first time I met Sergei, Mongo and I saw him standing next to his car on the side of the road, smoke pouring from the hood. Nobody stops for anyone with Russian plates, but I have a weak spot for old comrades, no? *Pues*, we repaired the car, only a matter of a new clamp on a hose, and as we talked I discovered how little of Cuba this man had seen. Cane fields, tractors, combines, yes. But no music, no dancing, no fun. He was like the walking dead. Frankly, I thought I'd never see him again. The very next day, though, I was on First Avenue in Miramar and I was fishing with a kite."

"With a kite?"

"A most beautiful way to fish. And I became aware that this Russian, this human bear from the day before, was standing on the sidewalk and watching. So I showed him how. I have to tell you that we never saw Russians alone, they always moved in groups, watching each other. Sergei was different. In our conversation he mentioned how much he wanted a place on the Malecón. I had the rooms upstairs I certainly wasn't using and one thing led to another." For a disabled man, Erasmo was constantly in motion. He rolled backward to a refrigerator and returned with two cold beers. "'51 Kelvinator, the Cadillac of refrigerators."

"Thanks."

"To Sergei," Erasmo proposed. They drank and his eyes tabulated the damage on Arkady, "That must have been a long flight of stairs. Nice coat. A little warm, no?"

"It's January in Moscow."

"That explains it."

"Your Russian is very good."

"I was in Cuban army demolitions in Africa assigned to work with Russians. I can say in ten different ways in Russian, 'Don't step on that fucking land mine.' But Russian boys are always stubborn, so he blew himself into very small pieces and I lost both legs. As a living symbol of internationalist duty and in place of my limbs I was honored with my very own Lada. From that Lada came two Jeeps and, voilà, I had a garage. I have Him to thank."

"God?"

"El Comandante." Erasmo gestured as if stroking his beard.

"Fidel?"

"You're getting it. Cuba is a big family with a wonderful, caring, paranoid papa. Maybe that describes God, too, who knows? Where did you serve?"

"Germany. Berlin." For two years Arkady had monitored Allied radio transmissions from the roof of the Adlon Hotel.

"The rampart of socialism."

"The crumbling dike."

"Crumbled. Dust. Leaving nothing standing but poor Cuba, like a woman naked to the world."

They drank to that, the first food Arkady had in a day, the beer's alcohol a mild anesthetic. He thought of the black fisherman that Olga Petrovna had seen with Pribluda. There was time to go to the embassy later and hide away.

"I'd like to meet Mongo."

"Can't you hear him?" Erasmo turned the radio off and Arkady heard what could have been a rolling of stones in surf if stones shifted to a beat.

Walking in the *santero's* door, Arkady was unprepared. When Russians were taught about Cuba, all they read about was white men like Che and Fidel. What Russians learned about blacks were the Western crimes of imperialism and slavery. The only blacks they encountered in Moscow were the miserably cold African students imported to Patrice Lumumba University. The musicians in the *santero*'s front room were different. They were black men with lined faces, dark glass and blackness wrapped around them, with little accent marks like white golf caps or dreadlocks or Mongo's green baseball cap, but with a mantle of shadow vibrant in the candlelight. The entire room floated in the watery light of forty or fifty candles placed on a side table and along the wainscoting. No more than settling in, a drummer lazily slapped the wooden boxes he sat on, two others cocked their heads to listen to tall, narrow drums as they tapped the heads and Mongo shook a gourd draped in seashells. Bells, sticks, rattles lay at his feet. He put the gourd down to pick up a metal plate that he hit with a steel rod to produce notes so fine and bright it took Arkady a while to recognize the instrument as the blade of a hoe. A tablecloth hung over a mirror. When Arkady tried to approach Mongo, a fat man in a cloud of cigar smoke chased him and Erasmo away.

"The *santero*," Erasmo told Arkady. "Don't worry, they're just warming up."

The mechanic had changed from his coveralls to a pleated white shirt he called a guayabera, "the very height of Cuban formality," but with telltale grease on his hands and his beard he looked like a corsair in a wheelchair. He pressed on through a kitchen and hallway until he led Arkady to a backyard where, under two spindly coconut palms crossed like an X, an old black woman in a white skirt and a Michael Jordan pullover stirred a cauldron simmering on coals. Her hair was gray and cropped as short as cotton.

Erasmo said, "This is Abuelita. Abuelita is not only everyone's grandmother, she is also the CDR for our block. The Committee for the Defense of the Revolution. Informers usually, but we are blessed with Abuelita, who dutifully watches from her window from six in the morning and sees nothing all day long."

"Did she ever see Pribluda?"

"Ask her yourself, she speaks English."

"From before the Revolution." Her voice was young and whispery. "There were a lot of Americans and I was a very sinful girl."

"Did you ever see the Russian here?"

"No. If I saw him, then I would have to report him for renting from a Cuban, which is against the law. But he was a nice man."

A pig's head bobbed in the stew. A bottle came Erasmo's way; he took a long drink and shared it with Abuelita, who drank daintily and passed it to Arkady.

"What is it?" he asked her.

"Fighting rum." Her eyes took in the tape on his head. "You need it, no?"

Arkady had expected that by now he would be safely tucked away in the embassy basement with maybe a cup of tea. This was only a minor detour. He drank and coughed.

"What's *in* it?"

"Rum, chilies, garlic, turtle testicles."

More people arrived every minute, as many white as black. Arkady was used to the hushed assembly of the Russian Orthodox church. Cubans pushed into the yard as if they were joining a party, a few with the somber devotion of worshipers, most with the bright anticipation of theatergoers. The only arrival without any expression was a pale, black-haired girl in jeans and a shirt that said "Tournée de Ballet." She was followed by a light-brown Cuban man with blue eyes, hair silver at the temples, in a formal, short-sleeved shirt.

"George Washington Walls," Erasmo introduced him. "Arkady."

Not Cuban. In fact, an American name that rang a bell. Behind Walls came a tourist with a maple-leaf pin and the last man Arkady wanted to see, Sergeant Luna. This was nightlife Luna, a splendid Luna in linen pants, white shoes and tank shirt that showed off the slabbed muscles of a triangular upper body. Arkady felt himself automatically cringe.

"My good friend, my very good friend, I didn't know you were feeling so good." Luna put one bare arm around Arkady and the other around a girl whose skin and mass of hair were the same amber color. She dazzled in spandex pants, halter, scarlet finger-nails, and squirmed so much in Luna's grip Arkady wouldn't have been surprised if a ruby popped from her navel. "Hedy. *Mujer mia.*" The sergeant leaned confidentially on Arkady's shoulder. "I want to tell you something."

"Please."

"There's no Zoshchenko at the Russian embassy."

"I lied. I'm sorry."

"But you did lie and you left the apartment, where I told you to stay, understand? Now you have a good time tonight. I don't want to see you spoil anybody's fun. Then you and I will have a talk about how you're going to the airport." Luna scratched his chin with a short ice pick. Arkady understood the sergeant's dilemma. Half of Luna wanted to be a good host, half of him wanted to plunge the ice pick into someone's face.

"I don't mind walking," Arkady said.

Hedy laughed as if Arkady had said something clever, which Luna didn't like, and he said something to her in Spanish that chased the color from her cheeks before turning his attention back to Arkady. Luna had a smile with broad white teeth and lots of pink gums.

"You don't mind walking?"

"No. I've seen so little of Cuba."

"You want to see more?"

"It seems a beautiful island."

"You're crazy."

"That could be."

The girl in the Tournée de Ballet shirt was named Isabel and she spoke excellent Russian. She asked Arkady whether it was true he was staying in Pribluda's apartment. "I live above him. Sergei was receiving a letter for me from Moscow. Did it come?"

Arkady was so disconcerted by Luna it took him a second to respond. "Not that I know of."

The sergeant seemed to have other duties. After consulting with Luna, Walls told his friend with the maple-leaf pin, "The real thing starts in a minute."

"I wish I spoke Spanish."

"You're Canadian, you don't need to. Investors don't need to," Walls assured him. "And all the investors are coming here. Canadians, Italians, Spanish, Germans, Swedes, even Mexicans. Everyone but Americans. This is the next big economic explosion on earth. Healthy, well-educated people. Technological base. Latin is hot. Get in while you can."

"He's been selling me for two days," the Canadian said.

"He sounds persuasive," Arkady said.

"Tonight," said Walls, "we've organized something folkloric for my friend from Toronto."

"I detest this," Isabel told Arkady.

"Isabel, we're speaking English for our friend now," Walls pleaded in the good-natured way of a man who actually means it. "I gave you English lessons. Even Luna can speak English. Can you speak a little English?"

"He says he'll take me to America," Isabel said. "He can't even take himself back to America."

"I think the show's about to begin." Walls ushered people back into the house as drumming hit a new intensity. "Arkady, I missed something. What are you doing here?"

"Just trying to fit in."

"Good job." Walls gave him a thumbs-up.

Each drum was different—a tall *tumba*, hourglass *bata*, twin *congas*—and each called to a different spirit of Santeria or Abakua, a *maraca* to rouse Chango, a bronze bell for Oshun, it was all mixed up, like mixing drinks, a little dangerous, yes, Erasmo asked even as he explained. Mongo, eyes shining from wells of perspiration, beat on his blade, his call in a language that was not Spanish answered simultaneously by the drummers and their drums, as if each man possessed two voices. Everyone had crowded into the room and pressed against the walls. Erasmo rocked in his chair as if he could lift it up by the sheer power of his arms to tell Arkady this was the wealth of Cuba, its history of

Spanish *bolero* and French *quadrille* colliding with the whole continent of Africa, creating a tectonic explosion. The boxes on which they sat and drummed proved the Cuban genius. In Africa the secretive Abakua had "talking drums," Erasmo said. When they arrived in chains to work on the docks of Havana and the slave masters here took their drums away, they simply beat on boxes, and presto! Havana was full of drums. The Cuban musician, like the Cuban fisherman, could not be stopped! All Arkady knew was that in Moscow he had heard a little Cuban music on tape; this was the difference between seeing a picture of the sea and standing knee-deep in the water. As Mongo's deep voice called in a language that was not Spanish, the rest of the room swayed and answered, congas carrying the rhythm, hands on boxes syncopating off the beat. Luna smiled and nodded, arms folded by the door. Arkady tried to plot an escape route to slither through, but Luna was always between him and the exit.

"You know that man?" Erasmo asked.

"We've met. He's a sergeant in the Ministry of the Interior. How can he be involved in a show like this?"

"Why not? Everybody does two things, they have to, there's nothing unusual about that."

"Arranging Santeria?"

Erasmo shrugged. "That's Cuba today. Anyway, it's not really Santeria, it's more Abakua. Abakua's different. When my mother heard there were Abakua in the neighborhood, she'd pull me off the street because she thought they were collecting little white children to sacrifice. Now she lives in Miami and she still thinks so."

"But this is a *santero*'s house, you said."

"You don't do Santeria at night," Erasmo said as if it were self-evident, "that's when the dead are out."

"The dead are out right now?"

"It's a crowded island at night." Erasmo smiled at the idea. "Anyway, Luna must have connections with the Abakua. Everyone is into Santeria or Abakua or something."

"His friend, George Washington Walls. Why is that name familiar?"

"He was famous once. The radical, the hijacker."

Very famous once, Arkady realized. He remembered a newspaper picture of a young American in an Afro and bell-bottom trousers burning a small flag at the top of an airplane ramp.

"What kind of investments can Walls offer in Cuba? When the dead aren't walking?"

"Good question."

Arkady had missed the point when the rhythm had changed and Luna and his golden friend, Hedy, had taken center stage, dancing not so much separately as skin to skin, hips rolling, the sergeant's large hands sliding around her back as she arched, eyes and lips bright, slipping away only to invite him even closer. Arkady did not know if this was religious or not; he did know that if it took place in a Russian church the icons would have fallen to the floor. As everyone else joined in Walls maneuvered Hedy away from Luna and toward the Canadian, who danced as if he were playing ice hockey without a stick. Now it was even harder to reach the door.

Erasmo pushed Arkady. "Get out there."

"I don't dance." He was doing well just standing, Arkady thought.

"Everyone dances." The rum seemed to hit Erasmo all at once. He rocked back and forth in his wheelchair to the beat until he locked his chair, slid off the seat and danced with Abuelita like a man wading energetically through heavy surf. He said to Arkady, "No legs and I still move better than you."

Embarrassing but true, Arkady thought. It was also true that, in his condition, Arkady found the drumming and darkness and mixed smells of smoke, rum and sweat as overwhelming as an overstoked fire. The drums spoke together, apart, together again, breathless, syncopated, off the beat. As Mongo shook the gourd the shells strung across its belly rippled like a snake. The chant went from call and response to Mongo in his dark glasses, his voice volcanically deep. He swayed, hands a blur. The rhythm spread, divided, split again like rolling lava. Maybe it was the effect of fighting rum on an empty stomach. Arkady slipped into the hall and found that Isabel followed.

"I didn't study classical dance for this," she told Arkady.

"It's not the Bolshoi, but I don't think the Bolshoi does this sort of thing very well."

"Do you think I'm a whore?"

"No." He was taken aback. The girl looked more like a candlelit saint.

"I'm with Walls because he can help me, I admit. If I were a real whore, though, I'd learn Italian. Russian is no use at all."

"Maybe you're a little hard on yourself."

"If I were hard on myself, I'd cut my throat."

"Don't do that."

"Why not?"

"I've noticed that few people are good at cutting their own throat."

"Interesting. A Cuban man would have said, 'Oh, but it's such a pretty throat.' Everything with them leads to sex, even suicide. That's why I like Russians, because with them suicide is suicide."

"Our talent."

Isabel looked thoughtfully aside. She had the emaciated allure of a Picasso, he thought. Blue Period. Wonderful, the two most depressed people in the house had connected like magnets. He caught Walls's anxious glances in their direction. At the same time he noticed that Luna remained by the door.

"How long are you going to be in Havana?" Isabel asked.

"A week, then back to Moscow."

"Is it snowing there now?" She rubbed her arms as if imagining them cool.

"I'm sure it is. Your Russian is extraordinarily good."

"Yes? Well, in my family Moscow was like Rome to Catholics, and, before the Special Period, to speak Russian was useful. Are you a spy like Sergei?"

"It seems to have been a great secret. No."

"*Claro*, he isn't a very good spy. He says if they needed a good agent in Havana they never would have sent him. He was going to help me get to Moscow and from there, of course, I could go anywhere. Maybe you can help me." She scribbled an address on a piece of paper and gave it to him. "We will talk tomorrow morning. Can you come just at that time?"

Before Arkady could beg off, Walls joined them. "You're missing everything," he told Isabel.

"I wish I could," she said. "We were talking about Sergei."

"Were you?" he asked Arkady. "Where is the good comrade?"

"A good question."

Shouts erupted in the living room, and a moment later Hedy rushed past them through the hall. The *santero* and the Canadian followed.

"Oh, no," Walls said. "I didn't mean this real."

"What do you mean?" Arkady asked.

"She's possessed."

Isabel was unfazed. "It happens all the time. This whole island is possessed."

The backyard was dark, but Hedy had kicked over the soup cauldron and spun on the coals as sparks nested in her hair. She swung out of the fire, her spandex dulled by ashes, golden hair pulled into tufts, while the *santero* ran after, trying to pull something invisible from her body. The Canadian looked ready to retreat to someplace tame and far away. As Luna burst into the yard the *santero* spread his arms helplessly and put Hedy between himself and Luna.

Erasmo squeezed his chair through and told Arkady, "Luna says he is going to kill the *santero* if he doesn't get the spirit out of Hedy. The *santero* says he can't."

"Maybe he should try again." Arkady saw the ice pick in Luna's hand.

As Luna yanked Hedy aside, her halter strap broke and one breast spilled out like a loose eye. Luna seized the *santero* by the neck and bent him belly-up between the trees. The Canadian bolted through the crowd as it poured into the yard and pushed Arkady forward. No one else moved except Abuelita, who shoveled her hands into the fire, rose to her toes and poured a bright stream of live coals over Luna's back. As Luna wheeled on her Arkady caught the sergeant's wrist, which was like grabbing the iron wheel of a locomotive, bent it back and up in the "come along" grip as taught to the Moscow militia and ran Luna headfirst into the wall. Luna bounced off, leaving a pink imprint on the cement. Blood ruby-spotted his white shoes.

Arkady decided he had not swung the sergeant hard enough.

"Now you're fucked *de verdad*." Luna wasn't even breathing hard, he'd barely started.

"*Parate*." A small woman with a needle-sharp voice stepped in between. Since she was in a skimpy top and shorts and not a PNR uniform, it took Arkady a moment to recognize his new colleague, Detective Osorio. Where she had come from and how long she had been taking in the scene with her grim little gaze he didn't know. A straw bag hung from one hand and in the other was a Makarov 9-mm, he recognized the gun right away. She didn't raise it or aim it, but it was there. Luna recognized the gun, too. He lifted his hands to signify not surrender or shyness but an awareness of growing complications, his own duties as an officer, and that he was done only for the time being.

"Truly fucked," Luna told Arkady on his way out.

"You okay?" Walls asked Arkady. "I'm sorry about this. Typical Cuban party. Too many spirits in one place. Now you'll have to excuse me, my investor has a head start."

Abuelita dusted ashes from her palms. In the middle of the yard Hedy looked down at her torn halter and the dirt on her shiny shorts and burst into tears. Arkady went into the house to look for Mongo and the drummers, but they had all left. Osorio followed him with an expression that said fools were multiplying.

10.

While he and Osorio put Erasmo to bed Arkady looked
around at what the mechanic afforded himself for living quarters:
a small space enlarged by the fact that his cot, counter, table and
chairs were all cut to half height. On a pillow of gold African cloth
was a collection of military medals and campaign ribbons. The
photographs on the wall reflected more glory than Erasmo had let
on. A hospital-bed scene of Erasmo being visited by two men in
military fatigues—a tall, swarthy man in aviator glasses who
would have passed as Armenian in Russia, the other older with a
full gray beard and wiry brows, unique and unmistakable, the
Comandante himself. Neither man wore officer's insignia on his
cap or shoulders; this was, after all, an egalitarian army. Castro
was as puffed with pride as a father. The second visitor seemed to
focus more ruefully on Erasmo's shortness of limb.

"The Cuban general in Angola," Osorio said.

Another picture showed the same distinguished friends on the
deck of a fishing boat, this time with Erasmo strapped into the fighting chair. Family pictures displayed friendly, affluent men and
women at swimming pools, bridge tables, dancing. Or children on
baseball fields, bicycles, ponies. And the entire family in formal suits
and ballroom gowns at champagne receptions and Christmas parties. In one wide photomontage they and hundreds more like them
spread up and down the grand double stairway of a white mansion.

"He'll sleep a long time," Osorio said.

" 'Unconscious' is the word."

Just as Luna had been the last man Arkady wanted to encounter, the last place he'd expected to see again was Pribluda's apartment, but at Osorio's insistence he climbed the steps with her. Although he thought he had tidied up fairly well, as soon as he turned on the light the detective noticed a difference.

"Dried blood on the carpet. What happened here?"

"You don't know? You work with Luna and Arcos."

"Only for this case because Russians are involved."

"You weren't surprised to see the sergeant come after me with an ice pick?"

"All I saw was you throwing him into a wall."

"It's a tense relationship. After all, he did beat me with a baseball bat. I think it was a baseball bat, he said it was."

"He hit you?"

"You know nothing about that?"

"This is a serious charge."

"Other places, not here. Here, my experience is, not much is investigated."

"As a matter of fact," Osorio said, "I did ask your friend, Erasmo, before he passed out, what happened to you? He said you told him you fell down the stairs." See, Arkady thought, that was the penalty of ever telling less than the truth. Osorio's eye fell on the empty corner chair. "What did you do with Chango?"

"What did I do with Chango?" Arkady asked. "The doll? Only in Cuba would this question come up. I don't know. Either Luna took him or Chango left on his own. How did you find me?"

"I was looking for you. You weren't here, so I followed the drums."

"Naturally." Arkady touched the cut on his hairline to feel if it had split open.

Osorio set her bag on the parlor table. "Let me see your head. You cleaned up all the other evidence of this so-called attack."

"Detective, I've been here three days and I've seen the PNR excuse itself from two violent deaths. I don't think you're going to investigate mere assault."

She pulled his head down, brusquely turned it one way and then the other and ran her fingers over his scalp. "What do you claim Luna said?"

"The captain mentioned that he'd prefer I stayed off the street."

"Well, you didn't."

He winced as she parted the hair around a cut. "I didn't get far."

"What else?"

"Nothing." Arkady wasn't about to strip and show her the bruises on his back and legs and he wasn't going to hand over the yacht club picture so it could be delivered straight to the sergeant. That he still had it was the luck of tossing his passport with the picture inside a shoe.

Osorio released his head. "You should see a doctor."

"Thanks, that's helpful."

"Don't be insulting. Listen, I'm only saying that since there's no evidence here that you haven't compromised and your story has changed already once and since officers of the Ministry of the Interior do not beat visitors from other countries, even from Russia, another explanation is more likely. Considering the blows you took to your head, you may not be responsible for what you say."

He wondered why Osorio had insisted on coming to the apartment. He also wondered why she was dressed like a vamp with platform shoes and carrying a big straw bag. "Detective, what are you here for?"

"Because I want you to go home alive."

While he tried to come up with an answer to that the lights in the room faded and went dark. He stepped out to the balcony and saw that the problem wasn't only in the apartment, an entire arc of buildings along the Malecón had gone black.

Arkady fed Pribluda's turtle by the illumination of Rufo's lighter and then lit a cigarette and inhaled wonderful, pain-soothing fumes. Osorio sat in the dark at the table.

"A power outage," Osorio said.

"I know the feeling."

"You should stop smoking."

"That's my biggest problem?" He found candles above the sink, lit the fattest one and joined the detective.

"Besides Sergeant Luna and your friend downstairs, who else did you know at the *santero's*?"

"No one," Arkady said. "I'd heard of Walls."

"Everyone in Cuba knows George Washington Walls."

"Luna arranged the show for him. I think Luna's going to arrange a show for me. You may not be safe here." Arkady had not intended to stay in the flat himself. She reached into her bag and laid out a Makarov 9-mm, the same police issue as in Moscow. "Would you have used that on Luna?"

"He knows I have the bullets. The patrolmen you see on the street, they have guns but they don't have bullets."

"There's a comfort." He saw her lay a toiletry kit by the gun. "What is that for?"

"I'm staying the night."

"I appreciate the gesture, detective, but you must have some place to be. A home, a family, a beloved pet."

"Are you offended to have a woman protect you? Is that it? Do Russians suffer from machismo?"

"Not me. But why do it if you don't believe me about Luna?"

"Luna is not the one I worry about. Dr. Blas examined the syringe that you say Rufo attacked you with. The doctor wasn't supposed to, but he did, to look for signs of drugs."

"Were there?"

"No, only blood and brain tissue of Rufo's and traces of a different blood type altogether."

"Maybe he stabbed someone else."

"Did he? Where did Rufo get the syringe?"

"Dr. Blas said he stole it at the institute."

"Yes, that's what the doctor said. I have a different answer. Wasn't that Rufo's lighter you used?"

"Yes, I suppose it is."

"Light it."

He did as she asked and the flame became a resonating circle between them. Osorio reached into the light and pushed his coat and shirt sleeve up his forearm to show two dark bruises on the artery.

"That's why I came back."

Arkady regarded the marks with the expression of a man surprised to find himself tattooed.

"Rufo must have scratched me when we were struggling."

She ran her finger lightly along the vein. "These are punctures, not scratches. Why did you come to Havana?"

"I was asked, remember?"

He blew out the flame, but he felt her eyes still intent on him. He no longer knew why he had answered a summons he could have easily ignored, but exhuming the reason was more than he cared to do for the Policía Nacional de la Revolución. All the same, control of the situation had clearly passed to the hands of the detective.

Because of the heat they camped on the balcony in metal chairs. Streetlamps were still lit, and the balcony was a vantage point to see Luna if he returned on the ocean side of the Malecón. Osorio seemed to have a different concern, following Arkady's every move, as if he might suddenly execute a dive to the pavement. Perhaps candy-colored top and shorts were *jinetera* fashion—she'd given him a brief account of the surveillance—but as they only accentuated how fine-boned she was, with hair in rows of black curls and her eyes set under extravagant lashes, it was like being tended by a child. Why he was with her rather than pounding at the door of the Russian embassy for asylum he didn't know.

A wave collapsed along the wall, and he wondered whether the fishing lights farther out rode ebb or flow. He couldn't see the village of Casablanca across the bay, but the lighthouse cast and retrieved its beam. Osorio nudged him and he saw sitting on the seawall the girl who had been possessed at the *santero's*. Hedy appeared freshly cleaned and shined and had engaged the attention of a late-night stroller wearing the elegantly blousy shirt of a European male on vacation.

"Italian is the official language of *jineteras*," Ofelia dropped her voice.

"So I've heard. It's Hedy, the girl from the *santero*'s. At least she's on her feet again."

"Not for long." Osorio laid down the words like a bet.

There were times when Arkady thought Osorio spoke with the satisfaction of a hangman. "So, just what happened to her? She was possessed but the *santero* couldn't help her?"

"The drummers were Abakua."

"So?"

"Abakua is from the Congo and she was possessed by a Congo spirit. *Santeros* don't deal with Congo spirits."

"Is that so? That sounds awfully . . . departmental."

Osorio narrowed her eyes on him. "We can believe in Santeria, Palo Monte, Abakua or Catholic. Or any combination. You think that's impossible?"

"No. It's amazing the things I believe in: evolution, gamma rays, vitamins, the poetry of Akhmatova, the speed of light. Most of which I take on faith."

"What did Pribluda believe in?"

Arkady thought for a moment because he liked the question. "He was hard as a barrel and did a hundred sit-ups every day, but he thought the key to health was garlic, black tea and Bulgarian tobacco. He distrusted redheads and people who were left-handed. He liked long train trips so he could wear pajamas day and night. He never picked a bad mushroom. He still called Lenin 'Ilyich.' He warned you never to say the devil's name because he might come. In the bathhouse he washed first, then steamed, which is more polite. He said vodka was water for the soul."

Hedy and her new friend walked out of view. Osorio stretched her feet out onto the balcony rail, ostensibly getting comfortable, though there was little comfort in deck chairs. Arkady noticed that the soles of her feet were a delicate pink.

Arkady said, "I know that Dr. Blas has determined that Pribluda had a heart attack and he has a point about the fishing gear seeming to be intact. But maybe there was more than fishing gear. If you told me Pribluda keeled over trying to run a marathon, I might believe it. Basking in the water, no. Let me ask, how well do you know Dr. Blas? Can you depend on his honesty?"

She took a moment to answer. "Blas is too vain to be wrong. If he says a heart attack, it was a heart attack. Have the body examined in Russia if you want, they'll tell you the same thing."

"There are other questions that can only be answered here."

"There will be no investigation," Osorio said.

"An investigation of Rufo?"

"No."

"Of Luna?"

"No."

"Of anything?"

"No." Her disdain would have flattened a man of any sensitivity.

A black swell moved under the beam of the lighthouse. There were times when he could almost feel the sea reach out to him like a wonderful, dreamless sleep. The balcony faced north toward familiar constellations. The truth was that he didn't believe in an expanding universe anymore, he believed in an imploding universe, a furious rushing together of everything down a celestial drain to a single point of absolute nothing. He sensed Osorio's eyes watching him.

"I have two daughters, Muriel and Marisol," she said. "Do you have children?"

"No."

"You're married?"

"No."

"Married to your work? Dedicated? Che was like that. He was married and had children, but he gave himself to the revolution."

"More like divorced from my work. Not like Che, no."

"Because you have the same . . ."

"Same what?"

"Nothing." After a space, she asked, "You like Cuban music? Everyone likes Cuban music."

"It has a certain beat."

"It has a *beat?*"

"Primarily."

There was a longer pause.

"You play chess, then?" Osorio tried.

Arkady lit a cigarette. "No."

"Sports?"

"No."

"Cuba invented baseball."

"What?"

"Cuba invented baseball. The Indians who lived here, the ones Columbus found, they used to play a game here with a ball and a bat."

"Oh."

"You never read that?"

"No, what I read in Moscow was that Russia invented baseball. There is an old Russian game with a ball and bat. The article said that Russian emigrants to the United States took the game with them."

"I'm sure one of us is right."

"The only difference is that Sergeant Luna used a steel bat."

"Aluminum."

"I stand corrected."

Osorio recrossed her legs. Arkady leaned back to release a long plume of smoke.

"If there were an investigation," she finally said, "what would you do?"

"Start with a chronology. Pribluda was seen first at eight in the morning by a neighbor, a dancer. He was seen last by a co-worker at the embassy between four and six in the afternoon. She said he was talking on the street here to a *neumático*, a black man. If I could speak Spanish I'd go up and down the Malecón with this picture until I found everyone who saw him that day."

"I suppose we can talk to the block CDR."

"I know who that is."

"Okay, we'll do that."

"And take another look where the body was found."

"But we found it across the bay in Casablanca. You were there."

"Not in the daylight."

"This is not an investigation."

"No, absolutely not."

"You're not afraid of being attacked again?"

"I'll be with you."

Her eyes seemed get even darker. *"Qué idiota."*

That seemed to be her name for him.

Finally, he fell asleep in the chair, although he was aware of her perfume, a faint scent of vanilla that tinged the air like ink in water.

11.

Predawn lent the Malecón an underwater light, as if the sea had covered the city overnight. Arkady and Osorio followed the faint glow of Abuelita having a morning cigar at her windowsill. She invited them into an apartment with walls as worn as old clothes, with layers of color, offered them *café cubano* in dark, heavy glasses and seated them by a statue of the Virgin that had a peacock feather at its back and at its feet a copper crown stuffed with sandalwood and dollars. Arkady felt fine, virtually rejuvenated by the fact that Luna had not returned in the middle of the night with a baseball bat or pick. Detective Osorio was back in her blue uniform and dark mood. Abuelita showed no burns from having juggled live coals the night before. In fact, she had the manner of a young girl only pretending to be old and at once was flirting with Arkady, thanking him for coming to her aid the night before, allowing him to relight her cigar, and although the smoke, the scent and golden hues were disorienting, he managed to explain to her that while there was no official investigation into Pribluda's death, there was curiosity about his life and asked whether she as a vigilant member of the Committee for the Defense of the Revolution could describe his routine.

"Boring. Sometimes your friend would be gone for weeks, *claro,* but when he was here it was always the same. He would leave at seven with his briefcase and come back about seven at night.

Except Thursdays. Thursdays he would be back in the middle of the afternoon and out again and back again. Saturdays, he shopped at the Diplomercado, because he always found a little something for me. Chocolates or gin. A kind man. Sundays, he went fishing with Mongo off the seawall or tied inner tubes to the car to drive somewhere else."

"You're very observant."

"Is my duty. I am the CDR."

"Thursday was his busy day?"

"Oh, yes." Her eyes and her smile widened.

He was aware of missing an insinuation but he pressed on.

"Besides his extra trip, did anything else make his Thursdays different?"

"Well, he took the other briefcase."

" 'Other'?"

"The nasty green plastic one. Cuban."

"Just that day?"

"Yes."

"When was the last time you saw him?"

"I'd have to think. *Hijo,* let me think."

Arkady may have been confused but he was not stupid. "What is the money in the crown for?"

"Offerings from people who want spiritual advice, to cast the shells or read cards."

"I need advice about Pribluda." He added five dollars to the crown. "It doesn't have to be spiritual."

Abuelita concentrated. "Now that I think about it, maybe two Fridays ago was the last time? Yes. He left a little later than usual and came back a little earlier, around four."

"Four in the afternoon?"

"In the afternoon. Then he left again around six. I remember because he changed into shorts. He always wore shorts when he went out with Mongo on the bay. But Mongo wasn't with him."

Osorio was unable to contain herself. "See, everything points to Pribluda being the body."

"So far."

114

Arkady was pleased, too, because everybody had something. He had a version of Pribluda's final day. Osorio had her moment of triumph. Abuelita had five dollars.

Outside the day approached more as distinguishable shadow than as light. As Arkady and Osorio walked up the Malecón a huddled mass proved to be four PNRs stealing smokes. They approached Arkady out of curiosity until they registered Osorio's uniform and the detective gave them a heavy-lidded look that sent them stumbling in retreat. In her uniform and cap, heavy belt and holster, she constituted a small armored column, Arkady thought. Or a little tank with laser eyes.

In the entire harbor the only craft in motion was the Casablanca ferry approaching its Havana landing. The windows of the ferry burst into flame, and then, as the sun slid off, faces of morning commuters squinted through the glass. Churning through backwash the boat rubbed against a pier fendered in tires, and the instant a gangway was laid passengers emerged, some equipped with briefcases for a day at the office, others pushing bikes laden with sacks of coconuts and bananas, by a sign that asked DISTINGUISHED USERS not to bring firearms on board and into the warming, yellowing day.

A countersurge of new riders pushed onto the boat, carrying Arkady and Osorio with them. The interior was set at pre-swelter, seats along the sides, bike riders to the rear, bars to hang from crisscrossing the ceiling. Arkady's coat drew stares. He didn't care.

"Do you love boats as much as I do?"

"No," Osorio said.

"Sailboats, fishing boats, rowboats?"

"No."

"Maybe it's a male characteristic. I think the appeal is the apparent irresponsibility of boats, the sense of floating anywhere, while the opposite is true. You have to work like a dog to keep from sinking." Osorio gave him no response. "What is it? What's bothering you?"

"It is contrary to revolutionary law for a tourist to rent rooms. Abuelita should have reported him. He was hiding among the people because he was a spy."

"If it's any comfort, I doubt that Pribluda ever passed as a Cuban. He wanted a view of the water. I can understand that."

The more Arkady saw of the harbor the more impressed he was by both its size and inactivity, a panorama of torpor: Havana's docks and cargo offices on one side and on the other Casablanca's verdant bluff with a pink weather station and a white statue of Christ. On the inner bay Arkady saw a few isolated freighters, a motionless herd of cargo cranes and the raw torch and smoke of refineries. Heading to sea was a black Cuban torpedo boat of humpback Russian design with automatic cannon on the rear deck. He noticed Osorio studying his head.

"How do I look?"

"Ripe. Your embassy should lock you up."

"I'm safe with you."

"The only reason I'm with you is because you want to go to Casablanca and you don't speak a word of Spanish. *Viejo*, I have other things to do."

"Well, I'm certainly enjoying myself."

The village of Casablanca looked as if it had started at the top of its hill at Christ's feet and then rolled down to the water's edge, piling shanties of cinder block and sheet steel on top of more dignified colonial houses. Scarlet bougainvillea tumbled over walls and the air warmed with the sticky smell of jasmine. From the ferry landing, Arkady and Osorio climbed up to a depot for trolleys equipped with cow catchers for rural duty. They walked a main street with shutters closed against the morning heat, including the closed door and boarded-up windows of a tiny PNR station, and down the remains of a circular stairway to a park of weeds, a cement curb, a panorama of the bay and the tar-black water and pilings, refuse and cans where the *neumático* had been found three days before.

The scene was different in the daytime, without klieg lights, a crowd, music and Captain Arcos shouting urgent misdirections. The sun picked out the details of a waterfront row of elegant houses so gutted they looked like Greek temples gone to ruin, and defined just how flimsy was the dock that reached over the water to a half-dozen fishing boats. The craft all had long poles raised like antennae and "Casablanca" bravely painted on the stern in case they set out for the larger world.

"This is where he ended up, not where he started. There's nothing to find," Osorio said.

The dock disappeared behind a barricade to a shack Arkady hadn't noticed at all on his first visit. He went around to a back gate that opened to a yard that could have been on Devil's Island. An indiscriminate variety of wrecks and boats with patchwork hulls sat hauled up amid sleeping cats. A dog barked from a deck. Two men stripped to the waist straightened a propeller shaft while at their feet hens scratched for corn. Here was self-reliance, a boatyard that could run up a stout little vessel out of flotsam and supply eggs, besides. The two men kept their faces turned away, but maybe that was the effect of Osorio's cast-iron glare, Arkady thought. The Noah of this yard emerged from the dark of the shack. His name was Andrés; he wore a captain's cap tipped confidently forward, and he produced what sounded like florid explanations before they were trimmed by Osorio.

The boat being repaired, he said, was built in Spain, used as an auxiliary of a freighter, declared technologically obsolete and sold to Cuba for scrap. That was twenty years ago. Arkady suspected that suggestions of smuggling and storms at sea were lost in the translation. Osorio was different from other Cubans, who registered every emotion with a sweeping emotional needle. Osorio's needle never budged.

"Has Andrés heard about the body found here?"

"He says that's all they talk about. He wonders why we came back."

"Did they find anything else in the water where the *neumático* was found?"

"He says no."

"Does he have a chart of the bay?" Arkady picked his way to the dock around mounds of cans and bottles salvaged from the water and stinking of slime.

"I told you before, the body just floated here. We don't have anything like a scene of the crime."

"Actually, what I think we have is a very large scene of the crime."

Andrés returned with a chart that revealed Havana Bay as a channel that flowed between Havana the city and Morro Castle and fed three separate inner bays: Atares, west and nearest to downtown Havana, Guanabacoa in the middle and Casablanca east. Arkady followed with his finger the tracery of shipping lanes, ferry routes, depths, buoys, the very few hazards, and understood why the bay of Havana had been the great marshaling yard of Spain's American possessions. But it was all one "bag bay" to Andrés.

"What floats in can float out, he says. Depending on the tide: in during high, out during low. Depending on the wind: northwest in, southeast out. Depending on the season: in winter winds were generally stronger, in summer hurricanes drew water out to sea. If everything is equal a body can spin forever in the middle of the bay, but usually the wind is steady from the northwest and drives bodies right to his boatyard, which was why you find live *neumáticos* in Havana and dead *neumáticos* in Casablanca."

Arkady tested the spindly dock and for some reason felt promise. Andrés's own boat, *El Pingüino*, was a coquettish blue with room for two if they could shift around an engine box, floats, buckets, gaff and tiller. Forward, a sail was furled between outrigged fishing poles. Aft, rope and wire lay on a transom crosshatched from braining fish. No satellite uplink, sonar, fish finder, radar or radio.

Osorio followed. "Looks are deceiving, Andrés says. It's enough boat, he claims, to reach Key West and get arrested for taking American marlin." As a note of her own she added, "In Havana the first Hemingway deep-sea fishing tournament was won by Fidel."

"Why am I not surprised?"

Drawn to the boat, Arkady crossed planks spaced widely enough for him to follow his reflection in the water. What he didn't understand were the floats, each numbered and skewered so that at least three meters of orange pole would stand free above the water.

"This," Andrés explained through Osorio, "is the Cuban system." The fisherman turned the chart over and, with a pencil stub, drew a wavy surface of the water and then, at regular intervals, the poles floating upright. A "mother line" connected them in a long string of poles. "The problem with fish is that they swim at different depths at different times. At night with a full moon, the tuna feed deeper. At the same time, red snapper or grunts feed closer to the surface. And turtles, too, though you can only catch them while they're copulating, a season that only lasts a month. Of course, they're illegal, so he never would. But with the Cuban system you can fish for them all by hanging hooks from different sections of the mother line at different depths: forty meters, thirty meters, ten. Everybody sets out different lines and this way they comb the whole sea."

"Ask him about a current that would have carried a drifting *neumático* from the Malecón into the bay."

"He says that is where boats concentrate because that's where fish are found, in the current. Boats don't fish the entire bay, just that corridor with mother lines and a gamut of hooks."

"Now ask him what they found, not here at the dock but out on the water. I don't mean fish."

Andrés stopped for breath like a man outrun by his mouth. A Cuban who poached in Florida, after all, Arkady thought, was a man given to overreaching.

"He asks, something snagged in the bay? Around the time that poor man was found at the dock?" As if to aid recollection Andrés glanced back toward the two men who had been working on the propeller shaft but his friends had vanished. "Trash maybe, hooked accidentally?"

"Exactly."

By now Osorio understood the drift, and when Andrés retreated to his shack she went with him. They returned with a plastic bag and perhaps fifty sheets of what looked like lottery tickets that had obviously been soaked through and then set out to dry. In green on white, a barely legible pattern said *Montecristo, Habana Puro, Fabrica a Mano* over and over again.

"These are official state seals before they're gummed and cut for cigar boxes," Osorio said. "With these, ordinary cigars could have been labeled expensive Montecristos. This is very serious." Andrés became a torrent of explications. "He says the seals snagged on someone's line, he can't remember whose, a week or more before the body was found. The bag had leaked, the seals were ruined, besides that was when the weather changed, no one came to their boats and the seals were forgotten. He dried them but just to read them and see if they were worth reporting. He was about to himself."

Arkady was entertained by the idea of such valuable cigars. Sugar and cigars, the diamonds and gold of Cuba.

"Could you ask exactly where the bag was found?"

Andrés marked the chart five hundred meters off the Malecón between the Hotel Riviera and Pribluda's flat. "He says only a lunatic would steal government seals, but he thinks a *neumático* is desperate to begin with. To sail on a ring of rubber and air? At night? The tide goes out or a current carries him to sea? One little puncture? Sharks? A man like that makes all fishermen look bad."

Osorio was disgusted with Casablanca. In the village's PNR station, so dark that a portrait of Che was an undusted ghost, the officers stirred just enough to take a signed statement from Andrés and give a receipt for the seals to her.

Arkady was content, having done something remotely professional, and on the ferry ride back bought a paper flute of peanuts roasted in sugar that he induced Osorio to share.

Her attitude had changed a little. "That man Andrés only showed us the cigar seals he found because he looked into your eyes. You knew he was hiding something. How did you do that?"

It was true that from the moment Arkady walked into the boatyard he felt guided to the flimsy dock and the spear-shaped floats of the "mother line." He could say it was the way the workmen avoided Osorio, but no, it was as if *El Pingüino* had called his name.

"A moment of clarity."

"More than that. You saw through him."

"I'm highly trained in suspicion. It's the Russian method."

Osorio gave him an opaque, humorless gaze. He had yet to figure the detective out. The fact that Luna had backed off when Osorio arrived in the *santero*'s yard suggested as much that they were working together as on opposite sides. She could just be a smaller version of the man who had beaten Arkady with a bat. Yet there were moments when Arkady would spy an entirely different, unrevealed person stirring within her. The ferry engines reversed and threw the deck into vibrations as it coasted to the dock.

"Now we should go to a doctor," Osorio said. "I know a good one."

"Thanks, but I finally have a mission. Your Dr. Blas needs a better photograph of Sergei Pribluda. I volunteered to find it. At least, to try."

The address Isabel had given him the night before was an old town house that, like a dowager in a once fine but tattered dress, maintained an illusion of European culture. Wrought-iron railings guarded marble steps. Lunettes of stained glass cast red and blue light onto the floor of a reception room staffed with women sitting in white housecoats.

Arkady followed strains of Tchaikovsky, bright and brittle notes from a badly tuned piano, into a sun-filled courtyard, where, through an open window, he saw a class in progress, dancers who balanced the upper bodies of starving waifs on a powerful musculature that started at the small of their backs, sculpted the haunches and flowed down through the legs. While Russian ballerinas tended to be doe-like and softly blond, however, Cubans had whippet-thin faces trimmed in black hair and eyes and lit with the arrogance of flamenco dancers. In their leotards they combined poverty and chic, moving on point in stiffly elegant, birdlike steps in taped toe shoes across a wooden floor patched with squares of linoleum.

As a Russian, he took a moment to adjust. He had been brought up with the attitude that great dancers—Nijinsky, Nureyev, Makarova, Baryshnikov—were, per se, Russian, that they graduated from schools like the Vaganova Academy in St. Petersburg and that they danced with the Kirov or Bolshoi until they escaped. Even now, although they were free agents like ice-hockey players, the tradition was still Russian. Yet here was a room of dancers as exotic as hothouse orchids. Especially Isabel, who had the classic line, who made every move seem effortless, whose arabesques were infinitely smooth, whose grace even from the last row stole the eye until the mistress clapped her hands and dismissed the class, at which point Isabel gathered her sweatshirt and bag, joined Arkady and demanded in Russian, "Give me a cigarette."

They took a table in a corner of the courtyard, Isabel inhaling fiercely, looking Arkady up and down. "Eighty degrees and you're still in your coat. That's class."

"It's a style. I noticed that you're very good."

"It doesn't matter. I will never be more than corps de ballet no matter how good I am. If I weren't the best I wouldn't be in the company at all."

Arkady was struck again by the melancholy of her voice and the long line of her neck, with its nape of feathery black curls on milk-white skin. Also by her fingernails, which were bitten to the quick. She drew on her cigarette hungrily, as if it served for food. "I like that you're thin."

"There's that." Arkady lit a cigarette himself, celebrating an attribute he had been unaware of.

"You can see the conditions in which we have to work," Isabel said.

"It doesn't seem to stop you. Dancers dance no matter what, don't they?"

"They dance to eat. The ballet feeds us better than most Cubans see. Then there's the chance some infatuated Spaniard from Bilbao will set us up in an apartment in Miramar, and all we have to do is drop our pants whenever he's in town. The rest of the girls would say, 'Oh, Gloria, you're so lucky.' I would slit my throat rather than live like that. The others at least get to travel from Cuba and be seen while I rot here. Sergei was going to help."

"A ballerina who defects *to* Russia?"

"You're laughing?"

"It's a change. I was never aware of Pribluda's interest in the ballet."

"He was interested in me."

"That's different," Arkady conceded. Her self-absorption was so complete she had yet to notice any scuff marks on him. "You were close?"

"On my part, strictly friends."

"He wanted to be closer?"

"I suppose so."

"Did he have any photographs of you?" Arkady thought of the frame in Pribluda's bureau, of Isabel's willowy pose in class.

"I believe so."

"Do you have any photographs of him?"

"No." She appeared to find the question ridiculous.

"Or the two of you together?"

"Please."

"Only asking."

"Sergei wanted a different relationship but he was so old, not the most handsome man in the world and not very cultured."

"He didn't know a plié from a . . . whatever?"

"Exactly."

"But he was doing something for you."

"Sergei was communicating with Moscow for me, I told you. You're sure there was no E-mail or letter?"

"About what?"

"Getting out of this wretched country."

Arkady had the sensation that he was talking to a fairy-tale princess imprisoned in a tower.

"When did you last see Sergei?"

"Two weeks ago. It was the day of the first night of *Cinderella*. One of the principal dancers was ill, I was filling in as one of the ugly stepsisters and there was a problem with my wig, because here in Cuba the ugly stepsisters are blond. So it was a Friday."

"What time?"

"In the morning, maybe eight. I knocked on his door on the way down. He came to the door with Gordo."

"Gordo?"

"His turtle. I named him. It means 'fat boy.' "

Arkady could see Pribluda opening the door. Had the colonel imagined himself a knight errant rescuing Isabel from her island prison?

"You lived right above Pribluda," Arkady said, "did you ever notice who visited him?"

"Who would visit a Russian if they knew his home was watched?"

"Who is watching?"

She touched her chin as if such a delicate feature could sprout a beard. "*He* watches. *He* watches everything."

"The last time you saw Pribluda, did he mention what he was going to do that day?"

"No. He didn't boast like George, who always has big plans. But Sergei brought you."

"He didn't send for me, I just came." Arkady tried to get the conversation back on track. "Did you ever see Pribluda with a Sergeant Luna from the Ministry of the Interior?"

"I know who you mean. No." Isabel awarded him a smile. "You stood up to Luna last night. I saw you."

"In a feeble way." What Arkady remembered of the encounter was being saved by Detective Osorio's arrival.

"And you are going to save me." She placed her cool hand on his and said as if they'd reached an understanding, "When the letter comes from Moscow I will immediately need an invitation to Russia. *Pues,* that you must organize through some cultural entity, a dance company, a theater, anything. Do you see where Cubans are dancing now? New York, Paris, London. It doesn't have to be the Bolshoi at the start for me, if only I can get out."

Over Isabel's shoulder Arkady saw George Washington Walls almost trip and recover as he entered the courtyard from the street. His light complexion was even lighter for a moment before he regained momentum, the street stroll of an American slowed to a Cuban pace and an actor's self-consciously casual style: pressed blue jeans and a fastidiously white pullover over brown biceps. The man had to be fifty, Arkady thought, and Walls could almost play himself as a young man if there was a movie. Why not? As Arkady remembered, there had been the war protests, the march on Washington, the plane. As he crossed the courtyard he distributed a pat on the shoulder here, a smile there. The only one impervious to his charm was Isabel, who recoiled from a kiss. He sat and told Arkady, "Oh, oh, I am on the outs. Arkady, you seem to be the new boy in town."

"*Comemierda*," she leaned across the table to say, then twisted out her cigarette and marched back to the rehearsal room.

"Do you want me to translate that?" Walls asked Arkady.

"No."

"Good. She is as mean as she is lovely and she is a lovely lady." Walls sat and gave Arkady his full attention. "Are you interested in ballet? I contribute to the cause here, but I'm actually more of a fight fan myself. I go all the time. You?"

"Not too much."

"But sometimes." Walls eyed the repair work on Arkady's head. "So, what happened to you anyway?"

"I think it was baseball."

"Some game. Look, I wanted to thank you for stopping Luna last night."

"I think you helped."

"No, you did it and it was the right thing. The sergeant was out of line. These things happen in Cuba. Do you know who I am?"

"George Washington Walls."

"Yeah, that says it all, doesn't it? Here I am like a kid checking out everyone Isabel talks to. You surprised me, I admit it. Last night I didn't come on too well, either. The problem is, I'm the elder statesman of radicals on the run in Cuba but I'm like a kid when it comes to Isabel."

"That's all right." Arkady changed the subject, "What was it like to be 'on the run'?"

"Not bad. In East Germany, the old Democratic Republic, the blond Hildas and Ilses used to line up to serve under the black commander. I thought I was a god. Here I am trying to wring one little smile from Isabel's lips."

"You've been here a while."

"I've been here forever. I don't know what the fuck I had in mind. The truth is, I always let my mouth get away from me. My mouth said, 'I'm not going to war, I'm not going to let you push around my black brothers in the South, I'm hijacking this fucking plane.' And the rest of me's going, 'Jesus Christ, I didn't mean that, please don't hit me again.' I didn't really think they'd take me to Havana. But my eyes were popping, I was totally dosed on speed and waving a big cowboy gun in the cockpit, they must've thought I was one fucking dangerous dude. I got out of the plane here and one of the stewardesses hands me a little American flag. What was going on in her head? I don't know. Fuck, I burned it. What else? That picture was everywhere. Drove the FBI straight up the wall. They made me a Most Wanted and, at the same time, a hero to half the world. So that's what I've been for twenty-five years, a hero. At least, they tried. They thought they had a hardened revolutionary and they sent me to camps with Palestinians, Irish, Khmer Rouge, the scariest men on earth, and it turned out that I was really just a loudmouthed boy from Athens, Georgia, who could spout a lot of Mao and play a little ball and probably would have ended up with a Rhodes Scholarship at Oxford if I hadn't come to Cuba instead. Those guys were scary. Eat-the-snake scary. Know the type?"

"I'm trying to imagine."

"Don't. They finally gave up and brought me back to Havana and gave me a cushy job translating Spanish to English. It was a comedown, but I was still full of revolutionary zeal and I would translate thirty pages a day until my Cuban colleagues took me aside and said, 'Jorge, what the fuck is the matter with you? We're each translating three pages a day. You're upsetting the quota.' I think the day I heard those words I understood what Cuba was all about. The light dawned. Karl Marx had hit the beach and all the

126

mother wanted was a cold daiquiri and a good cigar. You know, when the Soviet Union was paying, it was kind of a party here. The problem is, the party's over."

"Still . . ." Arkady tried to align the images of the world-shaker and investment hustler.

Walls caught the look. "I know, I was *somebody*. Look, so was Eldridge Cleaver and Stokely Carmichael. Brother Cleaver crawled back to the States to do time, and Stokely ended up in Africa mad as a bedbug, dressed up in his uniform and gun in Kissidougou waiting for the revolution to come knocking on his door. So tell me, did Isabel ask you to get her out of Cuba?"

"Yes."

"Well, she obsesses on this, she obsesses on men she thinks can help. And she's right, they'll never let her be a prima ballerina here and they'll never let her out. Do you love her?"

"I just met her."

"But I saw you two together. Men fall in love with her very fast, especially when they see her dance. Sometimes they fall all over themselves to offer to help."

"I would help if I could."

"Ah, that means you have no idea of the situation."

"I'm sure of that," Arkady admitted. "Do you know Sergei Pribluda?"

"I did. I heard they found him in the bay. Are you a spy too?"

"Prosecutor's investigator."

"But Sergei's friend?"

"Yes."

"Let's talk outside." Walls led Arkady past the reception desk and through the fronds of a small yard to the street where a sleekly molded white American convertible with a red leather interior sat at the curb. On rounded tail fins were silver rings and on the lid of the trunk the mere suggestion of a spare tire. As if he were introducing a person, Walls said, "'57 Chrysler Imperial. Three hundred twenty-five horsepower V-8, TorqueFlite transmission, Torsion Aire suspension. Ernest Hemingway's car."

"You mean, like Hemingway's car?"

Walls caressed the fender. "No, I mean Hemingway's car. It was Papa Hemingway's, now it's mine. What I wanted to talk about is this letter coming from Russia for Isabel. Did she tell you about her family?"

"A little."

"Her father?"

"No."

Walls dropped his voice. "I love Cubans, but they do trim the truth. Look, these people bankrupted Russia. At a certain point Russia was bound to say, 'Let's get somebody sane in charge.' "

Why? Arkady wondered. Russia never had anyone sane in charge. Why pick on Cuba? "What are you talking about?"

"Lazaro Lindo was number two in the Cuban Party, posted in Moscow, a logical choice. It was supposed to be a quiet coup, just a swift transfer of power and a comfortable house arrest for Fidel. Lindo came back from Moscow on a black plane and all the way he was told about troops mobilizing and tanks revving. You can imagine the scene when the poor son of a bitch gets off the plane and there's Fidel waiting at the bottom of the ramp. The same night the embassy in Moscow bundles Mrs. Lindo and Isabel, who's two years old, onto another plane for Havana."

"Fidel knew?"

"From the start. He let the plot roll to see who'd sign on. There's a reason the Comandante has survived this long."

"What happened to Isabel?"

"Her mother went crazy and fell under a bus. Isabel was raised by her aunt under another name, which was the only reason she was picked for dance school. Cuban ballet is like Cuban sports, a miracle until you find out how it's done. They search the country for little prospects and she was a star at twelve. The uproar when they figured out she was Lazaro Lindo's little girl? Now, they point to her and say, 'See how we let the children of enemies of the people rejoin society.' What they're not going to do is promote the name Isabel Lindo on the bill as a prima ballerina, and they're never going to let her tour."

"Is her father still alive?"

"Died in jail. Somebody dropped a rock on him. What I'm saying is, this is no ordinary message Isabel wants from Russia. It might have all sorts of names and accusations and the messenger may be very sorry that he helped stir things up. She won't tell you that, but I will."

"I appreciate it."

"She's difficult, I know. You can help."

"How?"

"Don't get her hopes up."

"Did Pribluda get her hopes up?"

"Sergei was going to work for me."

"As what?"

"Security."

"Security? What kind of security can a Russian offer in Cuba? Is the Russian Mafia here?"

"Close. In Antigua, the Caymans, Miami. Not in Havana, not yet. Actually, what I worry about now is Luna. Have you seen the sergeant today?"

"Not yet. Luna said I would see him again, and I don't think he's a man of idle threats. I doubt Sergeant Luna knows what an idle threat is."

Walls went around to the passenger side and opened the dashboard. Nested on chamois cloth was a huge handgun with a slot trigger. "A Colt .45 automatic, a classic, Fidel's favorite. Luna has been useful. He has a lot of interesting connections. But you saw last night how he's just getting out of control. I have to disengage and it might be easier with someone watching my back. Maybe you'd be interested."

Arkady had to smile. Not much had amused him lately, but this offer did. "Right now I'm watching my own back."

"You don't look it. You have a 'fuck you' quality in an understated way. You could do general security, too."

"I don't speak Spanish."

"You'd learn."

"Actually, I prefer safer work."

"It's absolutely safe. The truth is, Arkady, I live in this tropical paradise on sufferance. There are people who would seize any opportunity, any embarrassment and say, 'Screw George Washington Walls, he's yesterday's news; if the Americans still want him, send him back.' In my situation, the quieter the better."

"Well, that's interesting, but I'm only in Cuba a few days."

"People say that. People say they're just coming through Havana, but you'd be surprised how often they stay. Someone comes around the world to a place like this, it's not pure chance. There's a reason."

12.

Arkady expected that any minute Luna would drop from a street sign or pop up from a manhole cover and make good on his promise to "fuck him up." Fucking up and killing were close but not the same. There was that added sexual charge, the suggestion of rough mating, as if a missing eye or ear were a reasonable token of intercourse. Killing was clean. Fucking up sounded messy.

Strangely enough, though, Arkady felt revitalized. Not exactly happy, but fueled by the search for the photograph and the small license it gave him to ask questions about Pribluda. Amused also, in a time of depression, by the implausible offer of employment providing security for an American radical like George Washington Walls. Perhaps because Havana was so unreal to him Arkady felt slightly invulnerable, like a man aware he is only having a nightmare. Luna was a nightmare figure. Luna was perfect.

When he got back to Pribluda's flat he propped the front door shut and carried a bottle of chilled water to the office, where he turned on the computer and, when the machine demanded a password, entered GORDO. The machine chirped and the screen blinked and offered icons: PROGRAMS, STARTUP, ACCESSORIES, MAIN, PRINTER. Twenty-five years in the KGB and an agent used a turtle's name as his password. Lenin wept.

Still interested in Pribluda's last day, Arkady went through ACCESSORIES to CALENDAR. Hours, days, months rolled backward without appointments, but what curious comfort to take, he thought. He couldn't speak Spanish, but he could navigate the universal PC desktop. CUMIN was the Cuban Ministry of Sugar and charts, RUSMIN the Russian Ministry of Trade, SUGFUT the futures prices of Cuban, Brazilian and Indian sugar as they competed in commodities pits. Meanwhile, a downstairs din of drums and maracas suggested that Erasmo the car mechanic was at work. Arkady intended to talk to Mongo and find a photograph of Pribluda, but first things first, while he had the inspiration.

He opened SUGHAB, which divided Havana into 150 sugar mills. The last file saved was COMCFUEG.

```
Commune Camilo Cienfuegos is the former Hershey sugar
mill east of Havana. Visits to the field uncover poor
Cuban maintenance of antiquated equipment. However, we
must also frankly acknowledge that Russian ships carrying
spare parts have failed to materialize, the latest being a
freighter which was expected to make Havana by last week.
It is suspected that the ship's captain has diverted it to
another port along the South American coast and sold its
cargo for a better price. Regrettably, this makes negotia-
tions with the Ministry of Sugar more difficult.
```

Arkady supposed the Cubans would be testy about that. He started a search for the Havana Yacht Club. Nothing. Rufo Pinero. Nothing. Sergeant Luna and, for good measure, Captain Arcos. Nothing. Opened the E-mail outbox and inbox. Empty.

A document labeled AZUPANAMA caught his eye because Vice Consul Bugai had mentioned successful negotiations between Russia and Cuba thanks to a Panamanian sugar broker of that name, and Arkady thought it might be interesting to see what role the commercial attaché Sergei Pribluda had played in that. He hit RETRIEVE, and from its grave sprang a short, one-sided correspondence.

serk@dit.com/IntelWeb/ru Wed Aug 5 1996
A.I. Serkov, Manager
Diamond International Trading
1123 Smolenskaya Ploshad, Rm. 167
Moscow

Dear Serkov,
Greetings from the land of mambo kings. I am just now
getting used to sending mail through the internet so I
hope you are all well, etc. The weather is agreeable,
thank you. Let me know if this reaches you safely.
Yours,
S.S. Pribluda

It was like watching someone learn to ride a bicycle.

A.I. Serkov
Diamond International Trading
Dear Serkov,
Progress.
Yours,
S.S. Pribluda

Arkady liked the sound of that. Progress! Russian and to the
point. Also interesting in that it had no E-mail address or time
sent, suggesting that it was a note for a real message to be sent
from an encrypted machine at the embassy.

serk@dir.com/IntelWeb/ru Mon Oct 1 1996
Serkov,
The Chinese contact has borne fruit. I think you will see
that the fox is flushed! A fox and a wolf!
Pribluda

What a wordsmith. Pribluda had obviously been flushed with
victory. "Success!" was all an agent need say. "Chinese contact"

133

seemed far too much, not that Arkady was aware of any part of China abutting Havana.

According to the spreadsheet, Pribluda's finances were straightforward, so much allotted each month for food, laundry, personal items, gasoline and car repair. The only unexplained expenditure was a hundred dollars paid every Thursday. If the item was sex, Arkady thought, Pribluda would have hidden it; as an unreconstructed Communist, Pribluda had a skewed but iron-bound morality. No, the item could be for his Chinese contact. Or karate lessons. According to little Carmen, Pribluda did carry a black belt in his briefcase.

The more immediate fact was that the colonel had much more money than was found with the body in the inner tube. Arkady shut down the computer and searched the apartment again, more his line of work. This time he emptied everything, including shoes and hatbands. In pants hanging in the closet he found two red ticket stubs. In the medicine cabinet he found, rolled with white pasteboard inside a white aspirin bottle, a couple of pills left for sound effects and $2,500 American.

Which didn't tell him much. All the same, Arkady was satisfied with finding anything. He picked up a knife in the kitchen and let the blue of the sea draw him to a balcony chair. One moment he was full of nervous energy, the next barely able to move his feet. Was it the six-hour time difference from Moscow? Fear? The breeze was soft, the weight of the knife across his stomach was reassuring and he fell asleep, cooled by the sweat on his face.

He awoke to the rising pitch of sirens. The sun had moved to the far end of the Malecón, and coming up the seawall boulevard was a high-speed vanguard of four motorcycles, their way cleared in advance by PNRs who had suddenly appeared ahead at every intersection to stop all other traffic and chase bikers and pedicabs out of the way. Behind the bikes came a smooth, silent convoy, and as it flashed by people on the sidewalk paused in midstep, eyes darting to each vehicle as it flew past, from boxy Land Rover to wide Humvee, to a little Minint Lada that ran like a lapdog in front of two black Mercedes 280s with tinted glass and the sway-ing ride of heavy armor, from radio van to ambulance, from trailing Land Rover to a rear guard of four more cycles, an energetic whirlwind that made the entire Malecón come to a stop like a population in a trance and then, with its passing, released them.

Arkady's name was being shouted, and down on the pavement he saw Erasmo tilted backward in his wheelchair.

"*Bolo*, did you see him?" Erasmo touched his beard to signify *El Líder, El Comandante*, Fidel himself.

"That was him?"

"In one of the Mercedes. Or his double. No one knows and the where or when of the presidential cavalcade is never announced ahead of time. In fact, it's the only surprise in Cuba." Erasmo grinned and swung the chair back and forth. "You said you wanted to talk to Mongo when he came to work. Well, he didn't come."

"Has he got a phone?"

"Very funny. Come down and we'll find him. Besides, it's too beautiful to be inside. I'll give you the Cuban perspective."

Arkady thought that unless a person had an armored car and entourage it might be beautiful outside, but with Luna outside it was probably safer in.

"Look," Erasmo admitted, "I need a driver."

Driving a Jeep with the radio pounding and Erasmo half over the car door, calling to friends on the Malecón was a different view of life. To begin with, the mechanic gave the PNRs a rude salute.

"Professional *hijos de puta*," he explained to Arkady. "I'm a *capitalino*, someone from Havana. We despise police, who are all rubes from the countryside, and they don't like us. It's war."

"Okay."

Some houses were Spanish castles carved from pink limestone, office buildings showed ranks of shutters with cockeyed slats and the sun itself disintegrated into light. While Arkady watched for Luna, Erasmo identified oncoming traffic. "'50 Chevy Styleline, '52 Buick Roadmaster, '58 Plymouth Savoy, '57 Cadillac Fleetwood. You're a lucky man to see one of those." He also had Arkady slow by every girl thumbing a ride. In their bright Lycra pedal pushers, halters and hair clips each girl resembled Madonna, the singer not the mother of God.

"Isn't it dangerous for girls to hitch rides?" asked Arkady. In Moscow the only females who dared were either prostitutes or women so old they were bulletproof.

"If buses aren't running, women must find rides some other way. Besides, Cuban men may be macho but they have a sense of honor." All the girls Arkady saw were fullbore pubescent, with bare midriffs or body suits painted on, their thumbs out ostensibly for eunuchs. Erasmo spotted a hitchhiker in hot orange. "When you see a girl like that, you should at least honk."

"Did Pribluda honk?"

"No. Russians know nothing about women."

"You think so?"

"Describe a woman to me."

"Intelligent, humorous, artistic."

"Is this your grandmother? I mean a woman. Like the kinds here. *Criolla*: very Spanish, very white. Like the dancer Isabel. *Negra*: African, black, which can be very forbidding or very sexy. In the middle, *mulata*: a caramel color, skin soft as cocoa, eyes like a gazelle. Like your friend the police detective."

"You saw her?"

"I noticed her."

"Why do men always describe women in edible terms?"

"Why not? And the best to most Cuban men, *china*: *mulata* with just a hint of Chinese, of the exotic. Now describe a woman."

"A knife in the heart."

They drove for a while.

"That's not bad," Erasmo said.

"When you called me on the street, you said 'Bolo.' What does that mean?"

"Bowling ball. That's what we call Russians. *Bolos.*"

"For our . . . ?"

"Physical grace." Erasmo unveiled a vicious grin. The mechanic had a broad, vigorous face, huge shoulders. Arkady realized that with legs the man would have been a Hercules.

"Speaking of Chinese," Arkady said, "are there Chinese events on Thursdays around Havana?"

"Chinese events? Wrong city, my friend."

Undeniably, Arkady thought.

They went past high rises that had the dinginess of fingered postcards, until the Malecón was swallowed by a tunnel. Emerging in Miramar, Erasmo directed Arkady along the water on a dreary, sun-washed street called First Avenue. They passed the Sierra Maestra, the apartment house, where Arkady had interviewed the photographer Mostovoi. Erasmo pointed out a film theater called the Teatro Karl Marx that had been the Teatro Charlie Chaplin, and if there was a better example of socialist humor Arkady couldn't think of it. Beyond was a line of beach houses in pastels (peeling), family crests (defaced) and patios with (new) cinder-block benches, where Erasmo had Arkady steer the Jeep up on the sidewalk and stop as if that were safer than the street.

"For the tires, at least," Erasmo said. "This is an island of cannibals. Remember *Alive?* The plane crash? Fidel is our pilot, but he would call a crash a Special Period."

Erasmo's wheelchair was a folding model with bicycle tires and once it was pulled from the back of the car and he was seated, he let Arkady know not to even offer a push. He tacked recklessly around broken bottles to a series of pool-sized basins filled with brackish water and, only a step below them, a shelf of pocked coral and seawater of restless green. Concrete blocks like the stones of a pyramid had been set out as a breakwater and snorkelers floated between them and the coral.

"They're spearfishing for octopus," Erasmo said when Arkady caught up. "Before the Revolution you could swim here in a freshwater pool, a saltwater pool or the ocean. Parties all the time, American friends learning the mambo." He lifted his chin toward a house with a wooden pergola on the second floor where sheets billowed like eager sails. "My grandmother's. She wore a sable jacket and used a lorgnette instead of eyeglasses, women of a certain class did. I used to tear up and down here on a Schwinn tricycle with streamers on the handlebars. I suppose in a way I still do."

"Do you still have family here?"

"They left long ago. Flew out, sailed out, paddled out. And, of course, if you leave, you're officially a traitor, a *gusano,* a worm. You can't just disagree with Fidel, you are *against* Fidel, *against* the Revolution, a criminal, a faggot or a pimp. That way there's no one against Fidel except scum."

Arkady looked at the house. It was quite grand. Erasmo's hair and beard had gone a little wild in the breeze.

"You didn't want to live here?"

"I used to. I traded for rooms where a garage wouldn't be so obvious. Mongo lives here now."

"You're old friends?"

"Old friends. You know, he often misses work but up to now he always let me know."

They backed the chair up the steps and through a progression of dining room, sitting room, courtyard, second parlor all turned into separate apartments, the larger rooms divided by plywood and sheets into two apartments, so that the house was a *pueblecito,* as Erasmo called it, a little city. He knocked at a door in the rear. When there was no answer, he told Arkady to feel over the doorframe for a key.

"This was my bedroom whenever I slept here. Some things stay the same. I loved it. Here I was Captain Kidd."

The room afforded such a sweeping view of the water it had to be a theater of fantasy for a boy brought up on pirate tales of the Caribbean, Arkady thought. The accommodations were tight: cot, sea chest, desk and shelf of adventures like *Don Quixote, Ivanhoe* and *Treasure Island,* with the overlay of a CD player, a mirror trimmed in red velvet, coconuts and seashells on the windowsill, a plastic saint surrounded by paper flowers. A truck-sized inner tube suspended from the ceiling made a bumper and chandelier in one. Hung in fishnet bags around the walls were flippers, reels, candles, sticks, jars of hooks by size. Under the bed were a toolbox, cans of motor oil, drums and gourds. On a hook over the bed was what looked like a crossbow without the bow, a long wooden muzzle with a pistol grip and trigger and three round bands of heavy rubber hanging from the front end.

138

"Speargun," Erasmo said. He had Arkady take it down and showed him how to place the elongated back end against a hip to pull the bands with both hands to a cocked position. The spear itself was a steel bolt with, instead of barbs, two folding wings held down by a sliding collar behind the tip. "The Cuban fisherman meets his prey on all fronts."

Arkady was more interested in pictures of boxers on the wall.

"Kid Chocolate, Kid Gavilan, Téofilio Stevenson. Mongo's heroes," Erasmo said.

Under a newspaper photo of Fidel in a sparring pose with a tall, spindly fighter the caption read, "*El Jefe con el joven pugilista Ramón Bartelemy.*"

"You said his name is Mongo."

Erasmo shrugged as if it were self-evident. "Ramón, Mongo, same thing."

The picture of Cuban boxers in front of the Eiffel Tower was identical with the one Arkady had seen in Rufo's room, except now Arkady saw that next to Rufo was Ramón "Mongo" Bartelemy.

"If he's not here, where do you think he is?"

"I don't know. His tube is here. Arkady, do you mind if I ask about the PNR? There were two stationed across the street until the show at the *santero*'s. I know they don't like Russians, but is there anything you want to tell me? After all, it's where I live too."

Arkady thought that was a reasonable request. "Sergeant Luna might have something to do with them."

"Luna. That Luna, the dark phase of the moon, unseen but there. Yes, a bad man to cross and a very bad man to embarrass before his friends. An exquisite choice of enemy. And now the PNRs are gone. You may want them in case he's coming back."

"That's occurred to me."

"You're so intent on finding Sergei?"

"Or what happened to him."

"You should start thinking about what's going to happen to you. You have no authority and you don't even pretend to speak the language, which is a relief. You can't investigate, all you can do is get involved."

"In what?"

"Cuba, which is very complicated. But simply, if you don't want your head in a bucket, stay away from Luna. I tell you that because I feel a little responsible for last night. I don't need any more regrets."

Arkady opened the shutter wider. Under a low sun, waves pressed against an offshore breeze and two *neumáticos* came into view riding the crown of a swell, each in turn sliding up the incoming brow, sinking from sight and reappearing the next slope of water like riders on submerged horses. "So, if Mongo's tube is here, where is he?"

"He can still fish."

By the time Arkady and Erasmo returned outside the *neumáticos* were using short paddles to maneuver around the breakwater. Green aerated waves churned between the breakwater and rock. The fishermen had to come in on one rush as much as possible and the boulders struck Arkady as an excellent place to crack a head.

"When does Mongo go out?"

"You never know. *Neumáticos* go out day or night. They fish one stretch of the bay and then another. I think you have to call fishing from an inner tube a feat of improvisation. They can stay close to shore or go miles out, where the charter boats are hooking marlin. The boats don't like that, having a couple of poor Cubans mess with their tourists."

"The *neumáticos* try to catch marlin?"

"They could. They're like buoys, they just drag behind until a fish gets tired. A fish could tow them to Florida, who knows? But they've got to get the fish back, no? Would you like to land a marlin in an inner tube? No. Another problem is barracuda because they'll bite on anything. A barracuda on your lap isn't so much fun either. So, they take smaller fish. They do well, especially at night, but then you have to take flashlights and lamps, and at night the inner tubes attract sharks, that's the part I wouldn't like. That's why *neumáticos* go in pairs, for safety."

"Always in pairs?"

"Absolutely, in case one gets sick or loses his fins. Especially at night."

"Do they have radios?"

"No."

"And what exactly could a *neumático* do while his friend was being eaten by a shark?"

Erasmo let his eyebrows rise. "Well, we have a lot of religions in Cuba to choose from."

What appealed to Arkady was the marginal aspect of the fishermen, the way they folded into the motion of the sea, rose on the horizon and then slid from sight, their vanishing act. Lying back in their tubes, they removed their flippers and sat up, paddles lifted. A still space was followed by a trough sucking sand and then a set of three waves gathering strength. Both men chose the same climactic surge and stroked in deep pulls to ride it around the breakwater and up the rocks. The nearer spilled, clutching his tube with one hand and rocks with the other until he could scramble up on his belly. The second was an older man in a straw hat, and he timed his landing to let the wave's momentum smoothly lift him standing onto the coral, the brim of his hat trembling raggedly in the breeze, shirt and pants bleached, black shanks ending in feet gray with calluses. He found a tide pool in which to deposit his catch while he tucked his gear between the tube and the net that constituted his one-man craft. Despite the weight and dripping of the inner tube balanced on his head, he found a match to light the stub of a cigar in his mouth.

Arkady dug out the photograph of the Havana Yacht Club for Erasmo to show him. The fisherman put his finger on Mongo and pointed to the sky.

"*Pe'cando con cometa. Con cometa.*"

"It's what I thought." Erasmo pointed out to Arkady a dot in the sky. "You see that kite? The old man says maybe he saw Mongo fishing over there. Even from the air the industrious Cuban finds his fish."

Arkady thought of Pribluda's heart attack. "Could you ask him if he ever fishes in the rain?"

"He says, 'Sure.' "

"When there's lightning?"

A solemn shake of the head. "No."

"When was the last time there was lightning on the bay?"

"He says, a month."

They took the Jeep. Since the kite was too far over the water to keep track of from the street, Arkady stopped for another look. From a bathing stairway he saw about two hundred meters farther on a thin figure in a cap standing on steps and playing out a string rising with a delicate curve that disappeared into the air. Perhaps three hundred meters over the water a kite rode the offshore wind. The Jeep honked.

"Sorry, but you should have seen them," Erasmo explained when Arkady returned to the car. Arkady swiveled and saw a pair of long-legged blondes rollerblading away. "*Jineteras* on wheels, a mechanic's fantasy."

"We're looking for Mongo."

"Right. To fish with a kite you actually need two lines," Erasmo said when they started driving again. "One to the kite, one to the hook. The first line takes the second one out, and when the kite is far enough to reach the kind of fish you want, you jerk the second line and it falls into the water."

"What about the charter boats below?"

"Richly amusing. They're playing Hemingway and here's a hook dropping down from some poor Cuban bastard on the beach."

Even though Mongo was not in view of the street, once they were close the kite string led them to two lime-green beach houses attached like Siamese twins at the second floor. The windows were boarded and weeds grew on the roof. Arkady helped Erasmo into his chair, and they moved through the walkway that ran between the houses to rocks sparkling with fish scales. A long shovel stood, inserted by the blade between cement stairs that had split. Reels of kite and hook cord spun on the wooden shaft, feeding themselves so fast to the outbound kite that they hummed. A green baseball cap fluttered on the handle. Whether he had seen Mongo or the shovel, Arkady wasn't sure. The car horn hadn't helped.

"How could he disappear so quickly?" Arkady asked.

"He can be elusive. That's what they called him when he was in the ring, the Elusive Mongo."

"Why would he run?"

"You'd have to ask him, but people stay away from police investigations if they can."

"Would you know his cap?"

"Of course."

As Arkady reached for the cap a breeze flipped the cap onto the water, where it floated in and out until an undertow dragged it under. At the same time, the spools on the shaft ran out and kite and hook cords flew into the air and could have been strings to the sun for all the chance of retrieving them.

It was January. In Moscow, the water would have been frozen and he could have walked out and picked up the hat, Arkady told himself. In Moscow, kites didn't carry hooks, black dolls didn't run from house to house and people might fall under wheels but they didn't turn into shovels, that was another difference.

13.

Ofelia found Renko at the Malecón apartment. After he placed a chair against the door he led her down the hall to the office, where the computer monitor told a tale that was sad but true.

American attempts on the life of the Cuban Head of State
have included the use of exploding cigars, exploding sea
shells, poison pens, poison pills, poison diving suits,
poison sugar, poison cigars, midget submarines, snipers,
bounties. They have employed Cubans, Cuban-Americans,
Venezuelans, Chileans, Angolans, American gangsters.
Cuban Security has investigated 600 plots against the
President's life. The CIA has tried to introduce hallu-
cinogenic sprays into television studios where the President was broadcasting and depilatory powders to make his
beard fall out. For these reasons, the President contin-
ues to make use of a number of secure residences and
never announces his schedule in advance.

"You found Pribluda's password."

"Wasn't that brilliant of me?" he said. "This was entered January 5, the next to last file Pribluda entered, and I have to ask myself, what has this got to do with sugar?"

"It's nothing that any Cuban doesn't know. The life of the Comandante is always at risk."

"The day before he disappears, maybe the day before he dies, Sergei Pribluda gets the urge to write a short history of assassination attempts?"

"Apparently. He was a spy. Why are you interested?"

"I'm fishing with the Cuban method, setting hooks everywhere."

Ofelia had showered at home and come in jeans, a shirt tied at the midriff, sensible sandals, floppy straw bag over her shoulder, but she maintained a professional attitude. "Did you find a photograph of Pribluda for Dr. Blas?"

"No."

"But you have been busy." New and old maps of Havana printed by the Ministry of Tourism, Rand McNally and Texaco covered the desk.

"A cultural visit to the ballet, a pleasant drive on the Malecón. You?"

"I have other cases, no?" She regarded Pribluda's computer. "This machine is on Cuban territory."

"Ah, but the memory of this machine, that is purely Russian." Like a virtuoso of the keyboard, he exited the file, shut off the computer and, as screen and room went dark, said, "Useless without the code."

"You don't have the authority, the language or background to investigate here."

"I'd hardly call what I'm doing investigating. But then, you're not either."

It was not easy to control her temper around this man. She opened the bag and brought out a screwdriver, screws and slide bolt. The screwdriver was hers, but it had taken her an hour at the flea market outside the Central Train Station to find the bolt and screws.

"I brought you this for the door."

"Thank you, that's very thoughtful. Let me pay."

"A gift from the Cuban people." She thrust them into his hands.

"I insist."

"I insist more."

"Then, thank you. I will sleep like a babe. Better than a babe, a bivalve."

Whatever that meant, she thought.

After screwing in the bolt and latch, Renko celebrated what he called his "heightened sense of security" by opening a bottle of Pribluda's rum and taking a tray of Pribluda's pickles, mushrooms and other Russian indigestibles on a tray out to the balcony. Sitting in an aluminum chair, she scanned the street for danger while he basked in a half-moon that balanced at the end of a silver path across the water. The beam from Morro Castle swept the air, and the occasional Lada rattled by like a drum set being delivered. *Jineteras* in all hues of spandex cruised the seawall. An old man sold carrots from a briefcase that Renko pointed out looked identical with Pribluda's plastic briefcase and Ofelia said was of Cuban manufacture. A *neumático* out for night fishing carried a huge, inflated inner tube, making his way like a two-legged snail bearing his shell. Bikers raced on the pavement, and she saw a boy swoop by a tourist and snatch the woman's handbag off her shoulder so neatly that she spun around searching the ground while he crossed the boulevard and darted up a side street. PNRs arrived to play out the drama, the tourist turned, disillusioned, to her hotel, and the equilibrium of the Malecón reestablished itself. Night divers climbed up the rocks, flashlights in one hand and squid in the other. Small dogs fought over the carcasses of gulls. Men drank from paper bags. Couples tucked into the night shadows of the pillars of the wall.

From the portal below came a slow country *son*, a poem by Guillén adapted to a six-stringed guitar. *"María Belén, María Belén, María Belén, watching your hips roll and sway from Camagüey to Santiago, from Santiago to Camagüey."*

Renko lit a cigarette. "Actually, Sergeant Luna seems to have forgotten about me. He didn't seem the forgetful type. Good rum."

"Cuba is known for its rum. Did you know the computer password the first time I brought you here?"

"No."

146

Ofelia hadn't thought so, which meant that he had found it since he had moved into the apartment, although she herself had looked everywhere when she dusted the place for prints. She controlled the impulse to glance back at the apartment and was aware of him watching her do just that.

"I've been thinking. Maybe it would be safer if you went to the embassy and stayed there under guard."

"Ruin my Caribbean vacation? Oh, no."

Even in poor light she saw the scab and bandage at his hairline. She felt unaccountably responsible for his state of health and infuriated, as usual, by the way he twisted a conversation.

"But you still claim that the sergeant attacked you? You think there is a conspiracy against you?"

"Oh, no, that would be crazy. I would say, however, after Rufo *and* Luna, a hint of animosity."

"Rufo is one thing," she maintained. "The accusation that an officer would attack you is an effort to paint Cuba a backward country."

"Why? It could certainly happen in Russia. The Russian senate is full of Mafia. They regularly assault each other with clubs, chairs, guns."

"Not in Cuba. I think you imagined Luna."

"I imagined the captain wears Air Jordans?"

"Then why hasn't he come back?"

"I don't know. Maybe because of you."

She wasn't sure how to take that.

Renko said, "You told me Dr. Blas was honest, and if he said the heart muscle of the man you pulled from the bay shows signs of cardiac arrest, the doctor is telling the truth?"

"If he says so."

"Let's say I do believe him. What I don't believe is that a healthy man has a heart attack for no reason. If he was out on the water and hit by lightning, that would be a different matter. Shouldn't Blas examine the body for signs of a bolt?"

"Anything else?" She meant to be sarcastic.

"You could find who Rufo talked to between the time he let me off and when he came back to kill me. Check his telephone records."

"Rufo didn't have a telephone."

"He had a cell phone when he picked me up at the airport."

"He didn't when I searched him. In any case, there is no investigation."

The Cuban guitar was the sweetest guitar on earth, with notes that flickered the way light dappled the water. She watched him light another cigarette from the ember of the first.

"Have you ever stopped smoking?"

"Certainly." He inhaled. "But I know a doctor who says the optimum time to start smoking is in a person's forties, when a person can really use nicotine's effect to focus the mind and forestall senility. He says it generally takes about twenty years for the consequences—cancer, coronary problems, emphysema—to develop, and then you are ready to go anyway. Of course, he's a Russian doctor."

Although she regarded it as a filthy habit, Ofelia heard herself say, "There were times I wished I smoked. My mother smokes cigars and watches Mexican *telenovelas* and shouts to the characters, 'Don't believe her, don't believe that bitch!' "

"Really?"

"My mother is light-skinned from a family of tobacco growers, and even though she married a black cane cutter, my father, she always maintains the cultural superiority of tobacco workers. 'When they roll cigars in the factory, there's someone reading aloud the great stories. *Madame Bovary, Don Quixote.* You think in the middle of the cane field there's someone reading *Madame Bovary?*' "

"I imagine not."

Ofelia opened her bag, laid the Makarov on her knees and placed a necklace of white and yellow beads around her neck.

"Very pretty," Renko said.

Blas would have disapproved. Yellow was for Oshun, the goddess of fresh water and sweet things, the color of honey and gold and Oshun's *mulata* glow. Ofelia was comfortable wearing it around the Russian because he was ignorant.

"Just beads," she said. "Does the music bother you?"

A song lingered in the arcade under the balcony. Havana being so crowded, there was a problem of privacy. Sometimes lovers

148

chose the dark of the Malecón portal to consummate what they couldn't find room for anywhere else. The song said, *"Eros, blind man, let me show you the way. I crave your strong hands, your body hot as flames, spreading me like the petals of a rose."*

"No," Arkady said.

"You don't understand any Spanish?"

"Honey and absinthe pour from your veins, into my burning furrow and making me insane." Along with the song came murmuring and rustling from below. Couples on the seawall moved closer.

"Not a word."

"You know," Ofelia said, "there are differences between rumba, mambo, son, songo, salsa."

"I'm sure."

"But everything is based on drums, for dancing."

"Well, I'm not much of a dancer."

Not everyone had to be a dancer, Ofelia thought. Not that she found him attractive. As her mother would say, will he live through the day? Ofelia's first husband, Humberto, was black as a domino, a baseball player, a fantastic dancer. The second, a musician, was the sort everyone called *chino*, not only because he was such a handsome mix but because everybody liked him. He played bongos, which demanded an outgoing personality. Until he finally went out completely. But an even better dancer than Humberto. Her mother despised them both and simply called them Primero and Segundo, leaving lots of room for additions. Compared with them, wrapped in his black coat in spite of the heat, Renko looked like an invalid.

"That's how spirits communicate," she explained. "They're in the drums. Unless you dance the spirits can't come out."

"Like they came out for Hedy?"

"Yes."

"Then it's safer not to dance."

"Then you're already dead."

"Good point. Abakua is a version of Santeria?"

"They couldn't be more different. Santeria is from Nigeria, Abakua is from the Congo." It was like confusing Germany and Sicily.

"Blas said they used to run smuggling."

Ofelia was starting to learn how Renko hid behind the most innocent expressions ready to pounce. She wasn't going to get into the fact there were two Abakuas, a public one with sincere devotees who could be university professors or Party members and a secret criminal Abakua that had risen from its grave. This second Abakua was, needless to say, for men only and had a thieves' morality. Murder of an outsider was allowed, while informing on another Abakua was the ultimate sin. And Cubans believed the Abakua could reach anywhere. Ofelia knew an informer who got himself assigned to a post in Finland to escape Havana. He died falling through the ice and people said, "Abakua!" The police had not penetrated the Abakua. In fact, more police—black and white—were becoming members. Anyway, the last thing she needed was this sort of conversation with a Russian.

"We don't have to talk about it," Arkady said.

"It was the way you asked."

"I sounded smug? It's just my ignorance. I apologize."

"We will not talk about religions."

"God knows."

From the radio in the portal rose the deep beat of a drum that Ofelia knew had to be a tall *iya* with a dark red center on the skin, accompanied by the grinding rhythm of a belly-shaped gourd. A single horn insinuated itself, the way a man asked a woman to dance.

"Anyway, it's not a bad thing to be possessed," Ofelia said.

"Well, I have an unimaginative Russian mind, I don't think it's going to happen to me. What is it like?"

"Theoretically?" She watched him for the slightest hint of condescension.

"Theoretically."

"As a child, you must have spread your arms and put your head back and danced in the rain. You are drenched and clean and dizzy. If you are possessed, it's like that."

"Afterward?"

"Your mind still spins."

An *abwe*, the poor man's triangle, joined in from below. It was nothing more than a hoe blade played with a stick of iron, but an *abwe* could sound like the ticking in the mind when a man's strong hand reached around your waist. As the saxophone tried to wrap around it, the gourd trembled, the drum stopped and started like a heart. These were the snares set for silly girls who lingered in shadows. Not Ofelia. She visualized a clear mind.

She looked toward his arm, the one she had found the bruises on. "You're sounding better. You were not in a healthy mood when you came here."

"I am now. I'm curious about Pribluda and Rufo and Luna. I have a new purpose in life, so to speak."

"But why did you want to hurt yourself?"

She half expected contemptuous dismissal, but Renko said, "You have it backwards."

Ofelia sensed the next question so strongly she asked before she checked herself, "Did you lose someone? Not here. In Moscow?"

"I lose people all the time." He lit one cigarette from the other. "Most boats that go on the rocks really don't intend to go there. It's not a mood, it's just exhaustion. Exhaustion from self-pity." He added, "You're with someone and for some reason with them you feel more alive, on another level. Taste has taste and color has color. You both think the same thing at the same time and you're doubly alive. And if you manage to lose them in some gruesomely irrevocable way, then strange things happen. You wander around looking for a car to hit you so you won't have to go home in the evening. So this incident with Rufo is interesting to me because I don't mind a car hitting me, but I do mind a driver *trying* to hit me. A fine distinction, but there you are."

In the night Ofelia awoke to find lovers gone, the moon becalmed. In the very lack of breeze she detected a faint scent, a perfume she traced to Renko's soft black coat, to the sleeve of a man who claimed he'd never been possessed.

Osorio left before dawn, and as soon as she was gone
Arkady expected Luna to climb up the front of the building or
crawl through the air shaft. It wasn't so much that Arkady didn't
trust Osorio as that he didn't understand her. Why she would
spend the night in a metal chair with the island's least popular
Russian was a mystery to him, unless she was working with Luna
and only insinuating herself into the apartment. If that was the
case, all the locks in the world wouldn't help.

By eight o'clock the Malecón stretched like a floodlit stage.
Boys crouched in the blue shadow of the seawall to spool loose
fishing line. Men opened cases of homemade hooks and weights
for sale. Bikes rolled by with a father on the pedals, a boy on the
handlebars, mother and baby on a plank over the rear wheel, an
entire family rolling by. Still no Sergeant Luna.

Arkady went downstairs, but instead of going out on the street
he knocked on Erasmo's door, deliberately pounding out of rhythm
with the music from the garage's radio until Tico answered and let
him into Erasmo's private area with the cut-down bed and table.

"Erasmo's not here." Tico was in his coveralls, with an inner
tube over his shoulder and a Tropicola can in his hand.

Arkady shouted over the radio. "You speak Russian."

"I speak Russian." Tico sounded as if he'd just realized it. He was the same age as his friend Erasmo, but time seemed to have left his hair dark and thick as fur, no wrinkles or lines of care to mark his smooth, trusting visage, a boy's face on a middle-aged man.

"Do you mind if I go out through the garage?"

"I don't mind. You can go but you can't come back. The garage is closed."

Arkady pushed through the beaded curtain. Tico told the truth. The doors of the garage were closed, the Jeeps inside, parked bumper to bumper.

Tico said, "The garage is closed because Erasmo doesn't want me selling any cars while he's gone."

"I won't bother you, I just want to go out the back way." And avoid any eyes out front, Arkady thought.

"Erasmo's with the Chinese. He's with the Chinese."

"He is? What Chinese?"

"The dead Chinese. But he'll be there all day and I'm not supposed to sell any cars. He said, 'Radio silence!' I'm not supposed to talk to anyone."

"Where are the dead Chinese?"

"Radio silence!"

"Ah."

"I wasn't supposed to answer the door."

"No, you were being polite." Arkady dug a pencil from his coat and spread a piece of paper over a hood. "Can you write it?"

"I can write as well as anyone."

"Don't tell me, but write where I can find Erasmo and the Chinese."

"They're dead, that's a clue."

"Good." As Tico bent over the paper and printed in block letters, Arkady threw in, on the off-chance, "Do you know where Mongo is?"

"No."

"Do you know what happened to Sergei?"

"No." Tico returned the pencil with an anxious expression. "Are you going to see Erasmo now? If you see him right away he'll know it was me."

"Not right away."

Tico brightened. "Where are you going?"

"The Havana Yacht Club."

"Where is that?"

Arkady held up a map. "In the past."

He went out the garage doors and walked the back street half a dozen blocks before returning to the Malecón. The boulevard had become familiar in a matter of days, the coughing of trucks, boys casting nets from the seawall, scruffy dogs chewing on a flattened carcass of a gull. A PNR at a corner gave all his attention to a bicycle cart weighted with teenage girls. No Luna at all.

In Arkady's hand was Sergei Pribluda's forty-year-old Texaco map, a foldout map that located the Presidential Palace and American embassy, Cuban-American Jockey Club and racetrack, Woolworth's and Biltmore Country Club of a vanished Havana. Not that the city wasn't still surreal. Houses on the Malecón were fantasies: Greek pediments on Moorish columns and crumbling walls with fleurs-de-lis in faded pinks and blues. Venice had merely the threat of sinking. Havana looked sunken and raised.

What surprised Arkady was how much Havana was the same as on a forty-year-old map. He walked by the colossal Hotel Nacional and the angled glass tower of the Hotel Riviera, both "popular with vacationing Americans" according to the key of the map. *Neumáticos* filled inner tubes with air at a former Texaco gas station "with Fire Chief service!"

It took Arkady ninety minutes to walk the Malecón, cross the Almendares River with its small boatyards and sewer stench, and stroll westward the length of Miramar, past Erasmo's family house and the steps where Mongo disappeared. He could have taken a taxi at any point, and he knew by now that half the cars on the road were happy to be flagged down to earn a few American dollars. He didn't want to drive into the past, he wanted to sink into it step by step.

At Miramar's very end he approached a traffic circle with an at-one-time Texaco station, a stadium that had been the Havana grey-hound track and, according to Pribluda's map, the Havana Yacht Club.

It wasn't the sort of place people just stumbled onto. There were no other pedestrians. Cars hurtled around the circle and spun away. Only someone looking for it would have noticed a driveway curving along a screen of royal palms and around a lawn to a classical mansion in white with heavy columns, twin grand staircases and broad colonnades. Over it lay the ghostly silence of a colonial governor's palace abandoned in a coup, occupants decamped, the first signs of decay visible in the split reflection of a broken window and a red tile missing from the hip of the roof. Carved above the pediment of a central porch was the design of a ship's wheel on a pennant. In the entire scene there was no move-ment at all except for the sway of palm fronds. It was easy to imag-ine Havana's social elite posing on the steps because he'd already seen it, in the photograph of Erasmo's family.

He climbed a stairway and walked through open mahogany doors into a hall of white walls and limestone floors. Under a wrought-iron chandelier an elderly black woman in an aluminum chair stared up at him through thick glasses as if he'd dropped from a spaceship. A red telephone sat at her side, and the sight of a visitor prompted her to call and talk to someone in slurred Spanish while Arkady went on through tall French doors to an empty hall. A line of reception rooms connected like a bright and airy tomb, and the sound of his footsteps preceded him in the direction of a bar with a dark, curving counter stripped of stools, chairs, bottles. A portrait of Che hung by an empty glass case that must at one time have displayed race trophies, sailing ladders, models. All that was left of a nautical theme were wall medallions of a ship's wheel. The bar opened to an outdoor area with a stage ready for a Cuban band that could teach even Americans the mambo.

He returned inside and climbed to the second floor. At the top of the stairway was a tall admiral's chair of black mahogany. Everything else had been carted away and nothing added except more metal chairs of the Revolution. He stepped out onto a porch facing the ocean for a view of a private cove.

A brick promenade as large as a city plaza spread out to a row of thatched umbrellas and fan-shaped palms that led on to white sand and shallow water embraced by broad piers and, beyond, enough anchorage in bright blue water for a regatta. The only craft Arkady saw now were *neumáticos,* dots on the horizon, and the only figures on the beach were a dozen boys kicking a soccer ball back and forth.

Arkady couldn't resist the temptation. After he went back down the stairs he removed his shoes and socks to walk onto the beach and feel the warm fine-grained sand underfoot. The boys ignored him. He climbed the steps of a wide cement pier and walked fifty meters to its end. Havana had disappeared. The club dominated a hundred meters of waterfront, joined on the western side by the old dog track and toward the east by a white minaret rising over palms. Not a single person was on the beach before the Moorish tower, and although the sand ran to a point of wild scrub that could have been a desert island, it was familiar. From his shirt pocket Arkady brought out the photograph of Pribluda, Mongo and Erasmo with those same trees at the same size and angle in the background. He was standing where the picture had been taken. At the Havana Yacht Club.

The boys on the beach of the club waved, Arkady thought, at him and then he turned to the clapping of an inboard powerboat sweeping around a breakwater. It skimmed the waves, shooting rays off its windshield, then slowed with a skater's turns until Arkady could make out George Washington Walls in short sleeves and sunglasses. He swung the boat about and approached parallel to the pier, dropping the engine to a silken idle and keeping a safe distance from the pilings. The boat was low, long and angular, its hull and deck of gleaming, black mahogany, its bow sheathed in brass. In the cabin, black curtains were drawn. The dash had the glinting brightwork and deep patina that came only from age and infinite care. Fluttering from the transom pole was a pirate's pennant with crossed sabers.

"Hemingway's boat?" Arkady asked.

Walls shook his head. "Maybe Al Capone's. A seaplane tender turned rumrunner."

"Capone was here?"

"He had a place."

Once again, Arkady was impressed. "How did you know I was here?"

"The basic form of communication on this island is old women with phones. Why are you here?"

"Curiosity. I wanted to see the yacht club."

"Doesn't exist."

"I've always wanted to see someplace that didn't exist."

"Cuba's the place." Walls admitted. He looked at the club and back at Arkady and the shoes in Arkady's hand. "Yeah, you look like you're settling in. Do you have a couple of minutes? How would you like a cup of coffee with *two* men who have been on the FBI's Most Wanted List?"

"That sounds irresistible." Arkady hesitated. "Has Luna been invited, too?"

"Not to this party. No drums, no dancing, no Luna. Hop in."

Walls reversed and swung the stern to present the transom with the name "Gavilan" on the stern. Arkady jumped without breaking a leg, and as he slipped into a leather seat the boat scooped him up and moved away from the dock.

The ride was brief, smoothly skimming the waves out of the cove to deeper, bluer water until Walls slowed as smoothly as a limousine driver to a stop, the sharp nose of the boat headed to the wind. Giving Arkady a sign to wait, he ducked down into the cabin and returned with a tray table that locked into the cockpit deck, ducked down and returned with a brass tray carrying a basket of sweet rolls, a pot of coffee and three china demitasses with "Gavilan" written on the side. The cabin doors opened again for a small, silver-haired man in black pajamas and slippers, who climbed the steps and sat himself across from Arkady. He wore the smile of a man who was both magician and the rabbit in the hat.

Walls said, "John, I want you to meet Arkady Renko. Arkady, John O'Brien."

"A great pleasure." O'Brien took Arkady's hand with both of his. He caught Arkady's glance at the pajamas. "Well, it's my boat and I dress as I please. Winston Churchill, you know, used to wander around in the altogether. I'll spare you that. And you wear this somewhat astonishing coat, George told me about that. I apologize for not coming up sooner, but when George winds up the *Gavilan* I stay below. Falling overboard would be fatal for my dignity. You like *café cubano*, I hope?"

Walls poured. O'Brien might have been close to seventy, Arkady guessed, but he had a youthful voice, engaging eyes and an oval face as lightly freckled as a shorebird's egg. He wore a wedding band on his hand, a silver Breitling on the wrist.

"How do you like Havana?" he asked Arkady.

"Beautiful, interesting, warm."

"The women are unbelievable. My friend George here is smitten. I can't afford to fall in love because I still have family in New York, on Long Island, a very different island. I happen to be a faithful man and someday, God willing, I'll be home."

"There are problems now?" Arkady broached the subject delicately.

O'Brien brushed a crumb from the table. "A legal hurdle or two. George and I have been fortunate enough to find a home away from home here in Cuba. By the way, I am sorry to hear about your friend Pribluda. The police think he's dead?"

"They do. Did you know him?"

"Of course, he was going to do some security work for us. A simple man, I would say. Not a very good spy, I'm afraid."

"I'm not a judge of spies."

"No, just a humble investigator, to be sure." O'Brien added a touch of Irish brogue. He clapped his hands. "What a day! If you're going to be a fugitive from justice, where would you rather be?"

"Are you the only fugitives in Cuba?"

"Hardly. How many of us are there?" O'Brien cast a doting eye on Walls.

"Eighty-four."

"Eighty-four Americans on the lam. Well, it's better than a life in a federal minimum-security prison, where you get lawyers, congressmen, dope dealers, the usual cross section of America. Here you get genuine firebrands like George. For a businessman like me, it's an opportunity to meet entirely new people. I never would have had the chance to become so close to George in the States."

"So you try to keep busy?"

"We try to stay alive," O'Brien said. "Useful. Tell me, Arkady, what are you doing here?"

"The same."

"By visiting the Havana Yacht Club? Explain to me, what has it got to do with a dead Russian?"

"A missing man at the place that doesn't exist anymore? That sounds perfect to me."

"He's sort of careful," Walls said to O'Brien.

"No, he's right," O'Brien said and patted Arkady's knee. "Arkady's a man who's just sat down to play cards and doesn't know the rules of the game and doesn't know the value of his chips." O'Brien's black pajamas had pockets. He took out a large cigar that he rolled between his fingertips. "You know the great Cuban chess champion Capablanca? He was a genius, thinking ten, eleven moves ahead. He smoked Cuban cigars, of course, while he played. One title match his opponent extracted a promise from Capablanca that he wouldn't smoke. All the same, Capablanca brought out his cigar, squeezed it, licked it, savored it, and his opponent went nuts, lost the match and said that not knowing *if* Capablanca was going to light up was even worse than him smoking. I love Cuban cigars, too, although the joke's on me because the doctor says I'm not allowed to smoke anymore. Just tease myself, that's all. Anyway, what led you to the club, that's your cigar. We'll just have to wait for you to light it up. For the time being, we'll simply say you were curious."

"Or amazed."

"By what?" asked Walls.

"That the club survived the Revolution."

"You're talking about the Havana Yacht Club now," O'Brien said. "The French, you know, they beheaded Louis, but they didn't burn Versailles. What Fidel did was give the club, the grandest, most valuable single property in the entire country, to a construction union and charge Cubans, black or white, one peso to use the beach. Very democratic, communistic, admirable."

Walls pointed toward the Moorish tower. "La Concha, the casino on one side of the cove, they gave to the caterers' union and the greyhound track they turned into track and field."

"God knows, I respect idealism," O'Brien said, "but let me put it this way, as a result these properties have not been developed to their maximum. There's an opportunity here to create something of enormous value for the Cuban people."

"Is that where you come in?"

"I hope so. Arkady, I was a developer. Still am. George can tell you I'm not sneaky. Disney's sneaky. When they start buying up land they form a little corporation that sounds like your neighbors trying a little preservation, buying an acre here, an acre there and then you wake up one morning and there's a two-hundred-foot mouse outside your window. I'm up front. Every developer wants one great landmark development, his own Eiffel Tower or Disneyland. I want to make the Havana Yacht Club once again the center of the Caribbean, bigger and better than ever."

Walls took over. "See, the government developed Varadero Beach and Cayo Largo because they wanted to keep tourists as far from Cubans as possible. But tourists want Havana. They want the girls at the Tropicana and strolling in Havana Vieja and dancing all night at the Palacio de la Salsa. The government's finally getting the right idea, restoring the Malecón, rebuilding old hotels, because what tourists want is style. Fortunately, by a miracle, the Havana Yacht Club is in great condition."

"Its upkeep drains the state of half a million pesos a year. George, tell him it could be making the state thirty million dollars a year."

"It could," Walls said.

O'Brien pointed to the club and beach. "That's conference center, restaurant, nightclub, twenty suites, twenty rooms, time shares or condo that can be explored. Plus spa, berthing for boats, you want luxury cruisers. What I'm describing to you, Arkady, is a gold mine waiting for someone to pick up a shovel."

Arkady couldn't help wondering why two well-placed American fugitives would share their aspirations with him, although he sensed that O'Brien was the sort of salesman who enjoyed his own performance, like an actor who could deliver the most outrageous lines while he winked at the audience. Since Arkady's construction experience had been in Siberia, he felt at a loss at luxury cost projections. "To make the club into a hotel might be expensive."

"Twenty million," Walls took over. "We'd find the money and the Cuban government wouldn't put up a single peso or dollar."

"A lot of people," O'Brien said modestly, "would call that a gift."

"And what do you want in return?" Arkady asked.

O'Brien said, "Guess."

"I don't have the faintest idea."

O'Brien leaned forward as if sharing a secret. "Last year an Indian casino in Connecticut, in the—excuse my language—fucking north woods, with no sex, no style, no sun, cleared one hundred million dollars. What do you think a casino set among palm trees and cruise ships and million-dollar yachts and the famous, reborn Havana Yacht Club might possibly take in? I don't know, but I'd love to find out."

"We're asking for a twenty-five-year lease of the old La Concha casino and an even split of profits with the Cuban government," Walls said. "It's a no-risk situation for them, but there's a political problem in that they made such a big deal about closing casinos after the Revolution."

"Closing casinos and closing the Mafia," O'Brien said. "Which was why, with the CIA, the Mafia tried to kill the President."

"Castro, he means," Walls said. "And it's not easy to get Cubans to reverse direction. It would stop us cold if there was even a hint any Mafia, American or Russian, was involved. Our casino has to be absolutely clean."

"Any project at an early point," said O'Brien, "is like a bubble, anything can burst it. Your friend Pribluda was going to be our protection from the sort of Russians who are, I assure you, swarming into the Caribbean like the Visigoths. The wrong people showing up at the wrong time can burst the bubble. Which is why I told George we should take the boat and get a certain Russian investigator off the yacht-club dock before anyone else heard you were there."

"And brings us back to the question," Walls reminded Arkady. "Why were you at the club?"

Arkady felt like a can between two expert can openers. The photograph of the Havana Yacht Club was in his pocket. However, he wasn't in the mood to offer to strangers what he had kept at some cost in blood from the sergeant.

"In four more days I'll be back in Moscow and it won't matter why I went to the club."

"Why go back?" O'Brien asked. "Stay here."

Walls said, "Pribluda's gone. I hate to put it this way, but there is an opening now."

Arkady took a moment to understand the new direction of the conversation. "An opening for me?"

"Maybe," O'Brien stressed. "You don't mind if we got to know you a little better before we offered you a position?"

"A position?" Arkady asked. "That sounds even better than work. You don't know me at all."

"Oh, I don't?" O'Brien said. "Let me guess. In your forties, right? Disappointed in your work. It's evident you're bright but you're still just an investigator? A little reckless, working too close to the edge, inviting disaster. Except for the coat, cheap clothes, cheap shoes, signs of an honest man. But the way things are in Moscow now you must feel like a fool. And personal life? I'm taking a stab in the dark, but I'd say you don't have one. No wife, maybe not even kids. Zero, dead end. And that's what you can't wait to get back to in only four more days? I'm not trying to suck you into a criminal endeavor, I'm opening you a door on the ground floor of the biggest project in the Caribbean Basin. Maybe you'd rather soak up vodka and freeze to some fucking miserable death in Moscow, I don't know. All I can do is offer you an opportunity for a second chance at life."

"Not a bad guess."

O'Brien smiled in a not unkind way. "Ask yourself this, Arkady, will you be missed in Moscow? Is there anyone you can't say good-bye to on the phone? Is there anyone you'll miss?"

"Yes," Arkady said, a second late.

"Sure. Let me tell you about the saddest picture in the world. The saddest picture in the world is in the Prado Museum in Spain, it was painted by Goya and it's a picture of a dog in the water. You just see its head and muddy water swirling around and the dog's big eyes looking up. The dog could be taking a swim, except that the title Goya gave it is *Drowning Dog*. I look at you and I see those eyes. You're drowning, and I'm trying to give you a hand out of the water. Have you got the nerve to take it?"

"And the money?" Arkady asked, just to play the fantasy out.

"Forget the money. Yes, you'd be rich, have a Cuban villa, car, boat, girls, whatever, that's not the point. The point is you'd have a life and you'd be enjoying it."

"How would I do that?"

"Your visa can be changed," Walls took over. "We have friends who can extend your visa and you can stay as long as you like."

"You wouldn't worry then about me being at the Havana Yacht Club?"

"Not if you were on the team," Walls said.

"We're not offering a free ride," O'Brien said, "but you'd be part of something big, something to be proud of. All we're asking in return is one miserable token of trust from you. Why were you at the Havana Yacht Club? How did you get the idea?"

Before Arkady could answer, the boat was surrounded by upwelling light. He looked over the side, and in the water a thousand spoons reflected the sun.

"Bonito," O'Brien said.

"They always go east to west?" Arkady asked.

"Against the current," Walls said. "Tuna go against the current, so do the marlin, and eventually the boats do, too."

"A strong current?"

"The Gulf Stream, sure."

"Going towards the bay?"

"Yes."

First one and then by the dozens the fish exploded from the water. Iridescent, glassy arcs surrounded the *Gavilan* and salt spray rained. In seconds the entire school had scattered, replaced by a long dark shape with blue pectoral wings.

"Marlin," Walls said.

Without apparent effort the big fish kept pace within the shadow of the boat, a faint veil of pink trailing behind him.

"He's taking his time," Arkady said.

"Hiding," said Walls. "He's an assassin, that's the way he operates. He'll slice up a whole school of tuna and then come back to feed."

"Do you fish?"

"Spearfish. Evens the odds."

"Do you?" Arkady asked O'Brien.

"Hardly."

From above, the marlin's sword was thin as a draftsman's line, unsheathed yet almost invisible. The men were transfixed until the marlin sank into deeper water, blue into blue.

They took Arkady not back to the Yacht Club but through fishing boats along the western shore. On the outer dock of the Marina Hemingway a trio of Frontier Guards in fatigues lazily waved the boat in. The *Gavilan* steered to the inner dock, where a hook for weighing fish stood among the thatched parasols of a cantina and disco stage, the smell of grilled chicken and blare of amplified Beatles. An empty swimming area was defined by floats, but snorkelers had gathered along the canal where Walls started veering toward an open berth. Not Hemingway, but an old man in a hat with a band of miniature beer cans waved Walls away and shouted angrily at swimmers, *"Peligroso! Peligroso!"*

Steering wide of the snorkelers, Walls continued down the canal to a turnaround. Fishing boats with rod racks and flying bridges slid by, speedboats as low and colorful as sun visors, and power yachts with sun lounges and Jet Ski launches, oceangoing palaces of affluence and indolence sculpted in white fiberglass. The shouts from a volleyball court were pure American.

"Texans," Walls said. "Cruising people from the Gulf, they leave their boats here year round."

Along the canal people washed out lockers, carried baskets of food and plastic bags of laundry, pushed trucks of bottled gas. Walls eased to a stop at the inner end of the canal, where a market sold CopperTone and Johnnie Walker Red. Outside, a Cuban girl in a Nike shirt sat with a blond boy. His shirt had a portrait of Che.

O'Brien shook Arkady's hand again in an enthusiastic double grasp. "You're staying next to the *santero*, I understand. We'll talk tomorrow."

"About a 'position'? I don't think I'm qualified. I know nothing about casinos."

"The way you handled Sergeant Luna you sound eminently qualified to me. As for casinos, we'll give you the grand tour of all the famous sin spots of Havana. Right, George?"

Walls said, "You could have your own boat right here, Arkady. Girls come at night, knock on the side of the boats. They'll cook and clean, too, just to stay on board."

Arkady glanced around at his putative yachting neighbors. "What are the Americans like?"

Walls tried half a smile. "Some are free spirits and some are the same rednecks I tried to leave thirty years ago. One son of a bitch from Alabama wanted me to autograph my wanted poster. He said it was a collectible. I was ready to slice and collect his fucking nuts."

"Ah, well," O'Brien said, "to be a souvenir, that has to be a form of death. Arkady, you'll consider the offer?"

"It's an unbelievable offer."

"Seriously, think about it," O'Brien said. "I understand, it's tough to leap even from a sinking ship."

There was death and death. Leaving by the marina's traffic gate, Arkady encountered a fisherman staggering under the weight

165

of a marlin mounted on an enormous wooden plaque. The fish was caught in midflight, dorsal fin fanned, spear challenging the sky, the entire animal a metallic blue so unreal it could have been a small submarine, and Arkady remembered once walking with Pribluda in Moscow, following the river to the Church of the Redeemer. It was spring, and where the river sluiced in turgid, rubbery folds under the Alexander Bridge men fished with long, whiplike poles. Pribluda asked, "What man in his right mind would eat a fish caught in Moscow. Such a fish would have to be tougher than a boot. Renko, if you ever see me with a fishing pole in the middle of Moscow, do me a favor. Shoot me."

15.

Ofelia reached the pool at the Casa de Amor and heard Los Van Van on the radio in a room overhead singing *"Muevete!"*— Move it!—and it was as if wooden claves were dancing down her spine and she thought, not for the first time, how she distrusted music. So it had been a shock for her to put her fingers on the Russian's vein and feel the rhythm of his pulse. "Don't mess unless you want to be messed with" was one of her mother's favorite sayings. Along with "Don't move your ass unless you're advertising." Sometimes she thought, Moving your ass, that was the Cuban Method. That was why life was such a mess, because at the worst times and with the worst of men some signal would trickle down from her brain and say, *"Muevete!"* On the street in the shade of ceiba tree sat a '57 Dodge Coronet with private plates she had been allotted for surveillance work. Its front bumper hung on wires from too many collisions. She knew the feeling.

Since the shore on this stretch of Miramar was stone flats and coral rubble, the Casa de Amor was built around a pool area, empty except for two boys playing table tennis. Early afternoon was the time when most *jineteras* and their new friends from abroad would be riding rickshas around Old Havana, sipping *mojitos* in the Bodeguita del Medio or listening to romantic music in the Plaza de la Catedral. Later, boutique hopping and dinner in a *paladar*, where a plate of rice and beans could cost a Cuban's weekly salary, back to the Casa de Amor for a little sex and then the long evening out at the dance clubs.

When Cuban couples came to the Casa de Amor to consummate their passion, no rooms were ever available. But for "love couples" of *jineteras* and tourists, yes, there was always a room with fresh sheets, towels and a vase with a long-stemmed rose. Ofelia had discovered that complaints to the police had gone nowhere, which merely meant that the police themselves were protecting the motel. At the room rate of $90 a night, the cost of first-class accommodations at the Hotel Nacional, there was reason to protect such a gold mine, even if the gold was mined with the sweat of Cuban girls.

A heavyset woman in coveralls swept the street with a branch besom at a steady six strokes a minute. Ofelia stationed herself by an ice machine under the stairs to the second floor and listened to the music and occasional footfall from the rooms overhead. Only the middle two units were occupied—just as well, since her manpower and time were so limited. The boys at the Ping-Pong table finished one game and started another.

The Russian, she had decided, was a disaster to be avoided. Just the light in his eyes was like the ember of a banked fire warning, "Don't stir." It was bad enough he was a danger to himself; his story about Luna was insanity. Here was a man who threw Luna halfway up a wall and then acted modestly surprised when the sergeant's head split open. How Renko had banged up his head, she didn't know. Maybe there was something to his story about the bat. In her opinion, though, Renko was a goat whose brilliant idea of catching a tiger was to stake himself down. He would bring the tiger, might bring all the tigers in the jungle, what then? Which was a shame because he wasn't a bad investigator. To return with him to Casablanca and watch him draw out the fisherman Andrés was an instruction in police work. He wasn't dumb, just crazy, and at this point she was afraid to be with him and afraid to leave him on his own.

The street sweeper dropped her broom in a can. Over Ofelia's head a door closed, and two pairs of footsteps made their way the length of the balcony, Ofelia keeping pace below. She placed herself under the stairs as they came down. It wasn't until the couple stepped down to pool level that they were aware of the convergence on them of Ofelia, holding herself as tall as she could in her PNR gray and blue, and the street sweeper, who dropped her broom to show her own uniform and gun.

The tourist was a redheaded man in a shirt, shorts, sandals, a Prada bag around his thick neck, his arm draped like a freckled sausage over the girl's shoulder. He said, "*Scheisse.*"

Ofelia recognized Teresa Guiteras. The girl was black, smaller than Ofelia with a mop of curls and a yellow dress that barely reached her thighs. Teresa protested, "This time it's love."

During a public-works frenzy in the thirties, Cuba had built police stations in the style of Sahara forts. The one on the west end of the Malecón was particularly sun-blasted, white paint peeling off battlements, a radio mast on the roof, a guard sheltering in the shade of the door. Air-conditioning had never been introduced and the interior stifled, with historic scents of piss and blood. The police regularly mounted campaigns against *jineteras,* cleaning up the Malecón and Plaza de Armas. The next night the same girls would be back, but paying a little more to the police for protection. Because Ofelia's minor operation was directed at corrupt officers of the PNR rather than at the girls, she was not popular with the other detectives, all male, who shared her office. When she returned with the girl, she found the wall behind her desk newly decorated with a poster of Sharon Stone straddling a chair, and taped in the center of the poster the regulations concerning premature discharge of a weapon. Ofelia stuffed the poster into a wastebasket and set a tape machine with two radio-style microphones on the desk. The third person in the room was Dora, the patrol sergeant who had been the watch by the pool, an older woman with a face mournful from experience.

Teresa Guiteras Marín was fourteen, a tenth-grade student from the country town of Ciego de Avila, although she had already been warned before by Ofelia about soliciting tourists near the Marina Hemingway. Ofelia asked how and where Teresa had met her friend (by chance on the Malecón), what money or rewards had been offered or given (none except for a Swatch, a friendship token), whose idea was the Casa de Amor (his), who paid at the reception desk and how much (he did, she didn't know how much, but he also bought her a rose that she would like to go back to the room for). Finally, Ofelia asked whether she had seen or paid or communicated in any fashion with any member of the PNR. No, Teresa swore she hadn't.

"You understand that if you do not cooperate, you will be fined a hundred pesos and entered in the register of prostitutes. At fourteen."

Teresa slipped her feet from her platform sandals and drew her legs up onto the chair. She had all the mannerisms of a child, the pouty lip and downcast eyes.

"I'm not a prostitute."

"You are. He paid you two hundred dollars to be with him for a week."

"A hundred and fifty."

"You sell yourself too cheaply."

"At least I can sell myself." Teresa played with a curl, wrapping it around a finger. "That's more than you ever see."

"Maybe. But you had to buy false residence papers to stay in Havana. You had to pay a room illegally to sleep in, then pay the Casa de Amor to screw in. Most of all, you have to pay the police."

"No." Teresa seemed definite about that.

"You have a boyfriend who takes care of that?"

"Maybe."

This was a doublethink that drove Ofelia crazy. Teresa didn't consider herself a prostitute, no. *Jineteras* were students, teachers, secretaries merely making extra money. Some parents were proud of how their little Teresas helped to support the family; in fact, some regular visitors to Cuba didn't dare arrive without presents for their favorite *chica*'s mother, father, little brother. The problem was AIDS, which was like throwing young girls into the maws of a dragon. Only you didn't have to throw them, they lined up to dive.

"So now you work two places," Ofelia said. "Days you're at the Casa de Amor, nights you're at the boats. Is that the kind of life you want to lead?"

Teresa's eyes shone through her hair. "It's better than school."

"Better than the hospital? Did you check this German friend of yours?"

"He was clean."

"Oh, you have a laboratory?"

It was like arguing with children. They would never be infected, they took vitamins, anise, vinegar. The men refused to wear condoms because they hadn't come around the world to smoke half a cigar.

"*Hija,* listen. Unless you give me the name of police who take money from you I will enter your name in the register of prostitutes. Whenever there is a sweep of prostitutes you will be dragged away. And if you are ever caught again you will be sent to a reeducation farm for two years minimum. That's a nice place to grow up."

Teresa pulled up her knees and glowered. Her pout was exactly like Muriel's. She was three years older.

Herr Lohmann had been waiting in an interrogation room. He folded his arms and tilted back in his chair as Ofelia examined his visa. He spoke lederhose Spanish. "So I have one room at the Hotel Capri and another at the Casa de Amor? I paid for both. Twice the money for Cuba."

"How did you even know about the Casa de Amor?"

"The girl told me. She's not exactly a virgin, you know."

"To be clear," Ofelia said. "You are forty-nine. You are having sex with a fourteen-year-old girl, a student. You did this regardless of the laws of Cuba for the protection of children. Are you aware that you could be spending six years in a Cuban jail?"

"I doubt that very much."

"So you are not afraid."

"No."

She opened his passport and flipped through stamped pages. "You travel quite a lot."

"I have business to attend to."

"In Thailand, the Philippines?"

"I'm a salesman."

"Based?"

"In Hamburg."

His passport photo was a head and shoulders of a respectable burgher in dark suit and tie.

"Married?"

"Yes."

"Children?"

No answer.

"Here for?"

"Business."

"Not for pleasure?"

"No. Although I enjoy other cultures." He had teeth like a horse. "I was at the bar at the Hotel Riviera and this girl asked if I could buy her a cola."

"To enter the lobby of the Riviera she had to be with a man. Who was it?"

"I don't know. In Havana I am approached by a lot of men who want to know do I need a car, a cigar, whatever?"

"Were there any police in the lobby?"

"I don't know."

"You are aware that it is against Cuban law for Cuban citizens to visit a hotel room."

"Is that so? Sometimes I stay at hotels in the countryside run by the Cuban army. When I bring a girl I just pay double. You're the first one to make a fuss."

"You left the Riviera and went to the Casa de Amor, you and Teresa. According to the guest register at the Casa de Amor you signed in as her husband, Sr. Guiteras."

"Teresa took care of that. I never went in the office."

Ofelia looked at notes she had taken of a phone call. "According to the Riviera, you arrived there at the beginning of your visit with a friend, an Italian."

"A male friend."

"Named Mossa. He took the room next to you?"

"So?"

"Wasn't he also in the room next to you at the Casa de Amor?"

"So?"

"The two of you met Teresa and her friend together?"

"Wrong. I found Teresa and he connected on his own."

"You found her?"

"Or she found me. It makes no fucking difference. Girls develop faster here." He smoothed his hair back. "Look, I have always been a supporter of the Cuban Revolution. You can't arrest me for being attracted to Cuban girls. They're very attractive."

"Did you use a condom?"

"I think so."

"We looked in the wastebaskets."

"Okay, no."

"I think for your own sake we will have you examined by doctors and send a medical report to your embassy."

His smile sealed. As he pressed against the table his shirt opened to a gold chain, body heat, the smell of stale cologne. He whispered, "You know, you're even better-looking than Teresa."

At that moment Ofelia suffered the fantasy that Renko was with her and that he picked up the German the way he had picked up Luna and rammed the German into the wall.

"The doctor will make a thorough examination," Ofelia said and left the room.

The detective room wasn't as empty when she went back. The Sharon Stone poster was back on the wall, and Teresa looked sideways at the plainclothes detectives, Soto and Tey, sharply dressed men who bent over the paperwork on their desks and exchanged smirks. If Ofelia had any other place to question the girl she would have used it.

Teresa announced, "*Singa tu madre.* I'm not saying anything against my friends."

"Good girl," Soto said. "With the right friends you don't have to say nothing."

"Osorio has confused sex and crime," said Tey. "She's against both."

"It's been so long, right?" said Soto.

"I'd be happy to help her remember," offered Tey.

"You can't touch me," Teresa told Ofelia. "I don't have to tell you nothing."

"Don't listen to them." Ofelia felt her neck get hot.

"Don't listen to *them*? They're not on my ass, you are. You're the bitch, not them. I make ten times what you make. Why would I listen to you?"

"Congratulations, I am putting you on the official list of whores. You will be examined by a doctor and sent out of Havana."

"You can't."

"It's done."

But when she went into the hall with Dora, all Ofelia could think of were her own daughters and she didn't have the heart to order Teresa's name onto the register.

"Tell her I did, though," she said. "And have the doctor look at her. And have the doctor examine our tourist all over and draw some blood and make it painful."

"So what is the point of what we're doing if we let her go?" Dora was sick of sweeping streets.

"I'm not after girls, I am after corrupt police."

"Then you're after men, and in the PNR there are a couple of us and thousands of them. From the top down, everybody winks. They think you're a fanatic and you know what the real problem is? You're not."

Ofelia returned to the Casa de Amor because although she might have lost Teresa it was just possible that Lohmann's Italian friend and his girl hadn't yet left the motel. This time, she decided, she would question them right in the room, not even go close to the station house. If that was against procedure, well, procedure guaranteed humiliation and failure. She didn't need Dora along, she didn't need anyone. This was on her own.

When Ofelia was angry she took steps two at a time. The rooms were set back between dividers for privacy's sake and hanging on the doorknob of the unit next to Lohmann's was a plastic tag that said DO NOT DISTURB. The two boys were playing their endless table tennis, but otherwise no one was around. Maybe she was in luck. Maybe she was stupid. She certainly wasn't going to be appreciated, not if the girl was anything like Teresa. What poor Cuban girl wouldn't think she was in heaven at a motel like this? Then shopping at a boutique for a swimsuit that would show off her cute bottom? Or trying on cat-eyed Ray-Bans or a Gucci scarf?

She knocked on the door. "Housekeeping."

The radio still played. The pool was a blue lens. The boys played, the sound popping off their paddles. A breeze tugged on the lazy fronds. Ofelia took a deep breath and caught the faint smells of barnyard and butcher. There was no answer to her knock.

"Police," she said.

The door was unlocked but blocked and she had to use all her strength to enter, and since someone had turned the air conditioner off and the temperature was in the eighties, it was like gaining admission to an oven of ripe smells of blood and body waste. In opening the door she had rolled a body to the side, and she tried to pick her way across a floor covered with a fallen chair, emptied bureau drawers, clothes and sheets to the drapes on the other side. She drew them open and all the light in the world flooded in.

The body she had stepped over was a naked male, a dark-haired European with arms, back, flanks and scalp slashed. Ofelia had once seen the body of a man who had fallen into the blades of a combine, been chewed and spat out, which was what this man looked like, except that the wounds' individual length and curve were the unmistakable work of a machete. Lying on the bed was a naked female, arms and legs splayed, her head twisted like a dummy's and half sliced off. Bed and carpet were dark red as if someone had poured blood by the pail. A corona of blood spattered the wall above the headboard. But there was no broken furniture, no bloody smears of struggle on the walls.

To be first at an undisturbed homicide, Dr. Blas always lectured, was a gift. If you were not a willing investigator, if you could not take advantage of the unique opportunity of being first on the scene, if you were not able to engage sensorially and intelligently, if your eyes or your mind closed even a little to the fading, ineffable shadow of a murderer, then you should not open the door. You should raise children, drive a bus, roll tobacco leaves, anything but steal that gift from men and women with the discipline and stomach for the job.

Both bodies were hard with rigor mortis, four hours dead at least in Havana heat. The man's wounds looked defensive, administered while he crawled across the floor. If he was conscious enough to do that, why hadn't he cried out? Who had died first? Blood outlined the girl's legs. The hair of her head and pubis were the same honey color, and although her face was angled into the pillow, Ofelia recognized her as a smudged version of Hedy, the beautiful girl who had been possessed and danced through coals.

Having done as much as she could without rubber gloves, Ofelia went to the bathroom, stepping around blood scuffs on the floor, and threw up in the toilet bowl. When she flushed the water swirled and backed up, a rising gorge of vomit on pink water. Before it overflowed she thrust her hand into the toilet throat as far as she could reach and freed a blood-soaked ball of toilet paper from the trap. Between dry heaves she laid what she found on a towel: a wadded Italian passport for a Franco Leo Mossa, 43, of Milan, and Cuban papers for a Hedy Dolores Infante, 25, of Havana. Also half of a photograph torn badly. The picture must have been taken on impulse at an airport curb amid a blur of taxis and suitcases and harried Russian faces. The subject was Renko, wearing a rueful smile and his black coat. Ofelia didn't know why, but her instinct was to put the photograph in her pocket before she staggered out to the bedroom, to the fresh air of the oceanside balcony and a view of *neumáticos* plying the sea.

16.

A pair of Chihuahuas led Arkady down the path, rolling soulful eyes at him, prancing around a poinsettia here, sniffing a headstone there, like a pair of tiny landlords until they led him under the hanging pods of a tamarind tree where three Chinese, stripped to the waist, were scrubbing a marble lid they had lifted off a sarcophagus. Erasmo perched inside the tomb with a sack of tools.

"There aren't a lot of jobs where having no legs is an advantage," Erasmo said. "Working in a coffin happens to be one. You don't look happy."

Arkady said, "I've just come from the Havana Yacht Club. You told me the Havana Yacht Club was a joke, just a few fishermen, you, Mongo and Pribluda. But the picture was taken at the yacht club and you never mentioned that the club actually existed."

Erasmo frowned, dug his hand into his beard and scratched. "It does and it doesn't. The building is there, the beach is there, but it's hardly a club anymore. It's complicated."

"Like Cuba?"

"Like you. Why didn't you tell me you killed Rufo Pinero? I had to hear it on the street."

"It was an accident."

"An accident?"

"Of a sort."

"Yes, that's like saying Russian roulette is a game of a sort. So we do the same things in different ways. Anyway, I didn't lie to you. We did call ourselves the Havana Yacht Club as a joke. It was funny at the time."

"Some club. Pribluda may be dead, Mongo may be missing and you may be the last living member."

"I admit, it's not funny when you say it."

"Unless there are others. Are there any other members you haven't told me about?"

"No."

"Rufo?"

"No."

"Luna?"

"No. The three of us, that's all. You know, you're pissing me off and you're making my friends very uneasy."

The Chinese followed the conversation with an anxiety matched by their lack of comprehension. Erasmo coolly introduced Arkady to them, brothers named Liu with spiky black hair and cigarettes gripped between their teeth. Arkady took in the cemetery's quiet anarchy, a marble cross leaning on a Buddhist altar, tablets inscribed with Chinese characters and wrapped in morning glory, headstone photographs of the departed that peered through scummy ovals of glass. A nice place to die, Arkady thought, quiet, cool, picturesque.

"So this is the Chinese Cemetery?"

"Yes, it is," Erasmo said. "I told the Lius you were an expert on fighting crime. That's why you're so angry. It makes them feel much better."

"There's a lot of crime in a cemetery?"

"In this one, yes."

Now that Arkady noticed, many of the tombs were cracked and reinforced with cement seams and steel bands. Some of the disrepair had occurred over time and under the pressure of spreading roots, but there were also signs of vandalism, marble replaced by cinder blocks or a padlock on a vault's brass door, probably not to keep the dead in, Arkady realized.

"Cubans don't like the Chinese?"

"Cubans love the Chinese, that's the problem. And some Cubans need lucky bones."

"For what?"

"Ceremonies. If they want money they dig up the bones of a banker, if they want to get well they dig up the bones of a doctor."

"That makes sense."

"Unfortunately for the Chinese, their bones are supposed to be the luckiest. So this is where certain people come with their crowbars and shovels, which is very upsetting to Chinese families that revere their ancestors. Dead or alive, they want granddad in one piece. Little did I know that demolition expertise would prove so useful in civilian life. How did you know where to find me?"

"Tico maintained radio silence but I got him to write it out." Arkady looked down at the coffin, where Erasmo had laid a drill, bell, welder's goggles and surgical mask on a towel. From an athletic bag Erasmo took a vial of something fine-grained and black. "Gunpowder?"

"Just a touch. Life would be boring without it."

Taking a break, the brothers Liu sliced up a papaya and sat down between tombstones to eat. The Chihuahuas curled up with the lions. Was this the "Chinese contact" that Pribluda had been talking about, a place to come for lucky bones?

The problem was that he seemed to be going in reverse, knowing less all the time rather than more. He didn't know how or where Pribluda died, let alone why. The circle of Pribluda's acquaintances constantly expanded, but none of them had anything to do with the price of sugar, supposedly what the colonel had been investigating. Arkady had never before encountered such a variety of pristinely unrelated people and events: men in inner tubes, Americans on the run, a madman from Oriente, a ballerina, now Chinese bones and Chihuahuas. The truth was, Arkady thought, that apart from grave-robbing there was no suggestion of any crime at all, except for the attacks on him, and that was an error in timing, all they'd had to do was wait. Now? His head was clearing, the bruises on his legs had passed from blue to hopeful green, and the very shapelessness of evidence was interesting. He needed it to be interesting because while he was engaged he was like a man walking on deep black water. He needed to keep going.

Erasmo pulled the mask over his nose and goggles over his eyes before lifting a can with a plastic lid.

"More gunpowder?" Arkady asked.

"A different explosive." Erasmo lifted the lid and shut it at once, as if taking a peek at plutonium. "Ground habaneros, the hottest chilies on earth. I defused all sorts of bombs in Africa. Bombs that looked like doorknobs, alarm clocks, toilet seats, toy planes, dolls. You have to be creative." He upended the empty can between his thighs and drilled through its bottom. Erasmo poured in gunpowder and tamped it down.

"In your room I saw some pictures of you with . . ." Arkady tried out the gesture of the make-believe beard for the Name That Could Not Be Uttered just to feel Cuban.

"Fidel," Erasmo said warily.

"And another officer in glasses."

"Our commander in Angola."

"You won a lot of military decorations."

"The ribbons? Oh, yes. Well, what would I rather have, the ribbons or my legs? I'll let you guess. I used to be so proud. Fidel said we would go to Africa and I saluted and said, 'At your orders, Comandante!' I didn't know he would be giving orders after we got there. Fidel was here in Havana looking at a map of Angola. We were in hills and rivers that didn't exist on Fidel's map, but it didn't matter, he gave orders to set up our forces wherever his finger landed. Sometimes we had to ignore him. When he found out he was furious. There was one little village, a speck that must have been on his map. He said we had to take it and use it as a battalion command post. We said it was just a couple of huts, a garage and a well. We could go around it and come back whenever we wanted, but Fidel said that unless the village was taken in twenty-four hours every battalion officer would be charged with treason. So, Tico and Luna and a boy named Richard and I went in to clear the way. Maybe this is a boring story?"

"No."

"Very well. The village was strung like a Christmas tree. Little plastic mines to pop through your foot. Bouncing Betties to cut you off at the waist. Claymores with trip wires to something as insignificant as an empty can you'd kick out of your way. There was a car in the garage, not with the key, that would have been too obvious. A '54 Ford station wagon with real wooden panels. You can't imagine how valuable a vehicle was in country like that. But just stepping into the garage meant digging up a whole daisy chain of little mines. Then to look underneath the car first with a mirror and then on your back. To pop the hood with a wire from a distance, to inspect the engine and make sure every wire's automotive, open the glove compartment, the trunk, power windows, seats, hubcaps. It was in beautiful condition. We cleared everyone else out of the garage so I could cross the wires. It started right off. It ran out of gas right away, but the battery was good and everything seemed fine until Richard kicked a tire. That was one place I hadn't looked, in the tire." Erasmo pushed a cardboard disk over the gunpowder. "That was the end of Richard. Plus, the bumper flew off spinning like a helicopter rotor and caught Tico. We radioed for the ambulance. On the way it hit a hole where we had dug out a mine and drove right into the minefield. Somehow it didn't touch a mine but that's where the ambulance was stuck while Tico was bleeding to death until Luna picked him up and ran right through the mines to the ambulance. And that's how we liberated a pisshole in Angola on special orders from the Comandante."

"And how Tico became careful about tires."

"He's *very* careful about tires."

Erasmo dropped the can and Arkady retrieved it.

"Can I help?"

"No, thanks," Erasmo said. "Do you know the largest minefield in the world? The American base here at Guantánamo, thanks to the U.S. Marines and, especially, our Russian friends, who designed our side of the minefield and then took the plans home. No more help, please." He opened the can of chilies and poured them into the larger can. "Aha! When a grave robber opens this, there will be a deadly cloud awaiting him. Coughing, crying, sneezing, temporary blindness is, I think, a very humane way of dealing with grave robbers. *Así*, a Cuban solution to a Cuban problem."

"Luna saving Tico is a different picture of the sergeant."

"No, it's not. It's just the other side. People here have two sides, what you see and the opposite."

"It's complicated?"

"It's real. You don't understand. Cuba was something. We had idealism, and we stood up to the most powerful, most vindictive country on earth. Fidel was great. But Cuba isn't a big enough country for him, and the rest of us can't be heroes forever. Stop asking questions, Arkady. For your own sake, go home."

The Lius looked up expectantly; they may not have understood the words but they could tell when a conversation had wound to an end. The Chihuahuas blinked their marble-sized eyes, then tore after a lizard. They chased it up a bougainvillea vine to the peak of a waist-high pagoda and when the youngest Liu laughed and performed a karate kick, Arkady was reminded of something else.

"Are there any martial arts dojos in Havana?"

Erasmo said, "Chinatown."

You had to block things out, Ofelia thought. She ignored the technicians collecting their small evidence first—clots, hairs, night bag, glasses, bottles of Havana Club—working their way up to plastic bags for bedsheets and clothes. She paid no attention to the photographers working around the female sprawled in bed like a *Naked Maja*. All her focus was on Dr. Blas. His hands in waxy rubber gloves, he bent over the body by the door to show her why, although the male was painted in his own blood and the track on the carpet showed his agonizing, futile progress to the door, the dying man didn't cry for help.

"The radio was on. People who take these rooms, as you told me, tend to make noise, and who knows how much alcohol they consumed? His carotid and peroneal arteries were both cut—however, he was alive enough to try to cover up while he was hacked by the machete. He was alive enough to make it to the door, probably after his assailant left. But he never called out. Why? It wasn't because of the radio." With the tip of a pencil he probed a dark spot under the dead man's Adam's apple and slid the pencil halfway in. "A hole in the trachea. With a hole in your windpipe you cannot say a word. There is no such wound on the neck of the female, she had her throat cut pure and simple. But the first blow to the male, I am sure, was this puncture."

"Not made by a machete."

"No, the wound is perfectly round. Still, this sort of mess is typical of the 'crime of passion.' You did well to keep the hotel calm, and you were lucky to find the documents the way you did."

Which was Blas's sly way of saying he knew she had been ill in the toilet. The doctor was at ease with death in a way she, it was becoming clear, never would be. A body that had been cut up was a flower in bloom, releasing a smell that lodged like beads of blood in the sinuses and a taste that coated the tongue. All the same, she had made a sketch and notes to hand over to whomever the Ministry of the Interior sent over; this was no longer a case of prostitution, and the ministry didn't generally leave violent crimes involving foreign visitors to mere detectives of the PNR.

Blas said, "I'll examine the sexual aspect, too. She was a prostitute."

Ofelia looked at the bed. For a girl with her head half sliced off Hedy looked remarkably serene, neatly edged in blood, sheets hardly rumpled. "The killer didn't have sex with her."

"You kill a girl in bed, that's sexual to me."

A little insight *there,* Ofelia thought.

"I saw the female last night at a Santeria ceremony."

"What is the matter with you? You have so much potential, why do you indulge in such mumbo jumbo?"

"The girl was possessed."

"Ridiculous."

"You've never been possessed?"

Blas wiped his pencil. "Of course not."

"It happened to me once. They had to tell me later." The entire night had remained a blank to her.

"Was this Italian at the ceremony?"

"No."

"Fine. Then she came somewhere else later and picked him up here. If I were you I wouldn't get into Santeria unless there is a very good reason. We are at a hotel that, wrongly or rightly, specializes in tourists. Should we tell everyone there are religious fanatics going from room to room killing people?"

"What do you think the Russian will say?"

"Renko? Why should he say anything?"

"He was at the ceremony last night. He saw the girl."

"He'll still say nothing because we won't tell him. Do you think the Russians would inform us of every murder?" Blas ran the waxy fingers of his gloved hand down the back of the Italian's legs, hamstrung so that the dead man had to drag them as he crawled. "Renko is not our colleague. We don't know really what he is. The fact that an investigator would come to Havana is a sign of something else going on. A better photograph of Pribluda is all I want from him."

The photograph of Renko at the airport resided in her pocket. With all the confusion in the room there was still time to rediscover it.

She asked, "Did Sergeant Luna ever show you a picture of Renko?"

"No." Blas ran his hand up the dead man's arms. "Right-handed by the musculature. Lovely fingernails."

A chevron of deep cuts down the dead man's back indicated that the attacker had stood over him and hacked right and left. Ofelia considered mentioning the two round bruises she'd found on Renko's arm, but it seemed somehow a breach of trust.

"Perhaps we should reexamine the dead Russian. Is it possible he was struck by lightning? It did rain that week."

"Only there was no lightning on the bay. I'm ahead of you. I checked the meteorological record for lightning and the body for burns. Don't worry about Renko." Blas pinched the arm for stiffness. "I have dealt with Russians. Every one, including women with whom I was intimate, was a spy. Each was the exact opposite of what he or she claimed to be." He tucked a smile into his beard, and at that moment looked to Ofelia like a man too fond of his memories. "What does Renko claim to be?"

"A fool."

"His case may be an exception."

Blas turned the body onto its back. Loss of blood ended in stupefaction, and although his hair twisted in matted strips, the expression on the Italian's face was of someone yielding to sleep. Ofelia brushed hair from an oblong scab at the hairline.

"It looks like he bumped his head a few days ago," Blas said. "The least of his problems now."

"Who does he remind you of?"

"No one."

"How would you describe him?"

Blas cocked his head like a carpenter delivering an estimate. "European, forty to fifty, medium height, hair black, eyes brown, high forehead, incipient widow's peak."

"Renko?"

"Now that you mention it."

They had to shift the body from the door as an investigating team from the ministry arrived, led by Captain Arcos and Sergeant Luna. Arcos gawked at the body on the floor. Luna went to the foot of the bed and stared down at Hedy. His skin went gray, and as his lips spread he breathed through his teeth while Ofelia delivered her statement. She wanted to ask, Where is your ice pick? Instead she slipped away while Blas took over.

The Casa de Amor had emptied. At the sight of PNR Ladas and an IML forensics van with scales of justice painted on the door the Casa's guests returned just long enough to grab their overnight bags and run. At the bottom of the stairs Ofelia found a hose and washed first the soles of her shoes and then her face and hands.

The criminal laboratory of the Ministry of the Interior was in the Antiguo Hotel Via Blanca, a nineteenth-century brownstone palace erected in an erroneous burst of Spain's imperial confidence just before the first Cuban Revolution. A somber Iberian mood still resided in the building's dark walls and narrow windows.

While Blas's Instituto de Medicina Legal carried out autopsies the laboratories of Minint analyzed drugs and arson, ballistics and explosives, fingerprints, documents and currency. The work was done for the PNR, but the uniform was military fatigues.

"Fidel loves uniforms," her mother always claimed. "Put someone in uniform and you've created an idiot who watches his neighbors and says, 'How did he get that dollar? How did she get those chickens?' " Her mother would laugh so hard she'd have to waddle to the water closet. " 'Socialismo o Muerte?' Please inform Fidel it's not 'either-or.' "

In the evidence room, weapons were labeled and kept on shelving that on the underside still bore stencils of the FBI. The rifles were farmers' shotguns; anything military was recirculated back to the army or militia. Enough machetes to clear a cane field, axes and knives and homemade curiosities: a mortar barrel made from bamboo, sugarcane shaved into spears. On opposite shelves lay incidental evidence: bagged clothes, envelopes of rings and earrings, centavos in jars, shoes, sandals, a freshly tagged black swimming flipper and an inner tube.

Someone had rinsed the flipper, and when Ofelia held it to the light she saw the faintest charring inside the strap, which could have been her imagination or Renko's influence. She replaced the flipper carefully, as if putting off a question.

She went to the records room, where a haze of paper dander hung under fluorescent lights. The two working computers at the table were being used, but in a carrel behind stacks of volumes tied with faded ribbon she found a third, where she pulled up the file on her friend María.

María Luz Romero Holmes, age: 22, address: Vapor 224, Vedado, La Habana, charged with solicitation outside that address. José Romero Gómez, 22, same address, charged with assault. There was more: marital and educational status, employment, and the statement of the witness.

I was walking up Vapor to the university when this woman
(indicating María Romero) came out her door and asked the
time. Then she asked where I was going and placed her
hand on my member. I said, to the university. When she
tried to arouse me I said no, I wasn't interested, I
didn't have the time. That's when she began screaming and
this man (indicating José Romero) rushed out of the
house, cursing and swinging a lead pipe at me. I defended
myself until the police came along.
Signed,
Rufo Pinero Pérez

It was Rufo Pinero's name that had prodded her memory. A
former boxer innocently headed to the university. For a lecture on
poetry? Ofelia wondered. Nuclear science?

The police photograph of María showed her wet with tears but
defiant. In his photograph her husband's eyes were dark slits, his
nose split, his jaw swollen large as a gourd.

The statements of the witness is corroborated by this
arresting officer, who was also threatened and assaulted
by the Romero couple in the course of his duty.
Signed,
Sergeant Facundo Luna, PNR

Ofelia remembered how María had said a plastic sheet had
been placed over the rear seat of the police car because Luna
knew he would be transporting people covered in blood, and how
Rufo had taken cigars out of the police car's glove compartment,
cigars he had put in beforehand so they wouldn't be damaged during the scuffle. Luna and Rufo planned ahead.

She thought she knew what had happened at the Casa de
Amor. Blas had suggested a crime of passion, a Cuban boyfriend
who killed the Italian and the Cuban girl in a fit of uncontrollable
anger. But what Ofelia saw in her mind was Franco Mossa and
Hedy drinking in the dark, dancing to the radio, laughing. It
wasn't likely Hedy spoke much Italian, but how much did she

need? She retired to the bathroom, emerged undressed, a busty honey-colored girl. She slipped into bed, and as he took his turn in the bathroom she slipped right out again and opened the balcony door for a friend. The Italian turned off the bathroom light and, half blind, walked into the darkened bedroom. Hedy couldn't have seen much. She'd have heard the sucking sound of the ice pick as it was pulled from the Italian's neck, though. What had Hedy thought they were up to? Extortion was the usual game with tourists. She would have been silent and surprised when the machete whistled out of the dark and cut her head half off her shoulders. The killer must have been as bloody as a slaughterhouse wall when he was done. The question was, Why the photograph of the Russian? Who had carried it, Hedy or her friend? Was there a moment when he turned on the bathroom light and saw to his own surprise that he had butchered an Italian named Franco, not a Russian named Renko?

Since she was on the machine already, she ran a search for other connections between Rufo Pinero and Facundo Luna. Besides María's case, two files showed up. Four years earlier a group of criminals had gathered to distribute drugs under the pretense of organizing a political opposition. When members of the community became aware of this plan, they burst into the ringleader's house and demanded he surrender the drugs. In a scuffle provoked by the ringleader and his family, two patriots who had to defend themselves were Rufo Pinero and Facundo Luna. More recently a cell of so-called democrats had staged a rally with the true intent of releasing infectious diseases, only to be physically barred by vigilant citizens, including the alert Luna and Pinero.

Ofelia felt that Cubans should be allowed to fight their enemies because the gangsters in Miami would stop at nothing: assassination, bombing, propaganda. For Cuba to even exist took vigilance. However, the role of Rufo and Facundo in these cases made Ofelia uneasy. She turned off the computer half wishing she hadn't turned it on in the first place.

On her way out, she discovered the officers who had been working at the table were gone. Sitting alone was Sergeant Luna.

She was surprised he had left the Casa de Amor already. His arms were crossed, stretching his shirt across his chest. His face hung in the shadow of his cap as he worked his jaw from side to side. His chair was turned, half blocking the way to the door.

Suddenly she was back in Hershey, in the cattle fields where the egrets came from their roosts along the river. The birds were as white as shavings of soap, and as they crossed the carbon-black smoke that lifted from the chimneys of the sugar mill her anxiety was for the egrets' purity. Nevertheless they would float in and stalk the cattle fields, impervious to dirt. She was so busy watching them that she didn't notice that the bull had been let into the field, and the person who had led the bull in hadn't seen her. The bull saw her, though.

The bull was the largest animal she'd ever seen. Milky white with downward twisting horns, creamy curls between the horns, shoulders bloated with muscle, a pink sac down to his knees, eyes red with the indolent torpor of a violent king. Not dumb, however, not in this situation. Because he ruled. And he waited for her to make her move.

But something distracted it. Ofelia turned her head and saw a figure in black that had jumped the fence and was waving and hopping from foot to foot. It was the town priest, a pale man who had always seemed so sad. His cassock flapped around him as he laughed and goaded the bull, ran in a circle around it and threw clods until it charged. Lifting his cassock, the priest took the longest strides Ofelia had ever seen. He dived over the fence ahead of the bull, which drove a deep-rooted post half over and went on savaging the wood in frustration while Ofelia raced to the part of the fence nearest her. She remembered her first gulp of air from the safety of the other side and how she didn't stop running until she was home.

Luna said, "Captain Arcos asked if you gave us all the evidence you found in the motel?"

"Yes."

Luna shifted so that his bulk blocked her even more and let his thick arm hang slack.

"Everything?"

"Yes."

"You told us everything you know about this?"

"Yes."

The sergeant looked toward the carrel.

"What were you looking for?"

"Nothing."

"Maybe something I can help you with?"

"No."

The sergeant didn't move. He made her press by his arm as if it were a line that would define just where she stood.

17.

Arkady's route to Chinatown passed by the aquarium
stillness of deserted department stores, a *perfumeria* window with
nothing to display but a can of mosquito repellent, the staff of a jew-
elry store with elbows glued to empty cases, but around the corner
of Calle Rayo, life: red lanterns, a roasted whole pig, fried plantain
and fried batter, mounds of oranges, lemons, coral peppers, black
tubers cut to white flesh, green tomatoes in papery cowls, avocados
and tropical fruit for which Arkady had no name, although he
understood by the dollar signs that this market in the very center of
Central Havana was for private vendors. Flies spun dizzily in sweet
smells of ripening pineapple and banana. Salsa from a hanging
radio vied with tapes of wistful Cantonese five-tone scale and customers with obscured but still-discernible Chinese features drilled
vendors with Cuban Spanish. At a corner stall a butcher chopped a
cow skull open, and a cotton-candy vendor with her hair festooned
in blue, sugary wisps that rose from a tub read Arkady's note and
pointed to a walk-up with the sign KARATE CUBANO.

Arkady had come in a rush. He had gone from the Chinese
Cemetery to Pribluda's flat and from there to Chinatown because
his mind was finally functioning. Abuelita, the eyes of the CDR,
had said that on Thursday afternoons Pribluda left the Malecón
with his ugly plastic Cuban briefcase. The girl Carmen had
claimed that Thursdays were when Uncle Sergei practiced karate.

According to his own spreadsheet, Thursday was the day of Pribluda's unexplained hundred-dollar expenditure. Didn't it all fit together? Wasn't it possible that every Thursday, carrying in a common Cuban briefcase not a black belt but an envelope stuffed with money, the spy Sergei Pribluda had met his "Chinese contact" at a karate dojo in Havana's Chinatown? Most likely the colonel kept a sweatsuit or karate gear in a dojo locker, reason enough for him to stop in the changing room, where, as Arkady imagined it, not a word to the contact had to be said, not if he had a similar briefcase. The two briefcases could be switched in a moment, and the anonymous contact would be headed down the stairs before Pribluda untied his shoes to practice those deadly kicks he showed to Carmen. The entire business would be swift, silent and professional. Arkady had the briefcase and this was Thursday.

The only problem was that when Arkady ran gasping up the stairs the door where the dojo was supposed to be now read EVITA—EL SALÓN NUEVO DE BELLEZA. Inside, two women wearing masks of blue mud reposed in barber chairs even as workmen bolted a third chair to the floor. Arkady retreated to the market and went through the process with the same piece of paper and received the same misinformation.

At a Chinese restaurant where no one was Chinese and egg rolls came with a dab of ketchup Arkady found a waiter who spoke enough English to say that there were no more dojos in Chinatown, although there were maybe twenty in the city. Four more days. He should call Pribluda's son in case the boy wanted to meet the plane, assuming the boy could leave his pizza ovens for a few hours. Then Arkady had no plans. He had run out. He had the clear eye of a man who had no plans at all.

Well, there was the picture of Pribluda he was supposed to be finding, but for a moment Arkady had thought he'd caught sight of Pribluda's ghost slipping between bright mounds of exotic fruit. The walls of the restaurant were bordello red and had the usual picture of Che Guevara looking so much like Christ in a beret it was unearthly. Arkady had noticed simply while walking through the streets and passing open windows that people hung more portraits of Che than of Fidel, although Che's very martyrdom seemed

to validate Fidel. But martyrs had the advantage of staying romantically young, whereas Fidel, the survivor, came framed in two ages:
the passionate revolutionary with index finger stabbing each ora-
torical point and the graybeard lost in haunted reflection.

Arkady felt haunted by stupidity. It had been exciting for a
moment to believe in his revived powers of deduction, like finding
an old steam engine in a derelict factory and thinking that a match
held under the boiler would bring the pistons back to life. No
churning pistons here, he thought. Thank God, Detective Osorio
hadn't been around to witness the fiasco.

On his way from the restaurant he pushed through the market
and skirted a group of boys pummeling one another outside a theater. It was a shabby corner cinema painted Chinese red with
pagoda-style eaves and a poster that showed a karate master in
midair. The title of the film was in Chinese and Spanish, and in
parentheses at the bottom of the poster in English, "Fists of
Fear!". Arkady remembered the ticket stub in Pribluda's pants.
That was what Carmen had been trying to ask him, not "Did you
see? Fists of fear!" but "Did you see *Fists of Fear!?*" He joined the
line at the box office, paid four pesos for a ticket and climbed
the red steps into the dark.

The interior was aromatic of cigarettes, joss sticks, beer. The
seats were bald and taped. Arkady sat in the last row, the better to
see the rest of the audience, rows of heads that bobbed and
howled appreciatively for a film that had already started and
seemed to involve a studious young monk defending his sister
from Hong Kong gangsters. The dialogue was Chinese with subti-
tles in another form of Chinese, not even Spanish; the laughing of
the actors was hideous, and every kick sounded like a melon being
split. Arkady had barely stood the briefcase on his lap before he
was joined in the next seat by a small, sharp-nosed man with
glasses and a similar briefcase.

A whisper in Russian. "Are you from Sergei?"

"Yes."

"Where have you been? Where has he been? I was here all day
last week and I've seen this film once already today."

"How long has this film been playing here?"

"A month."

"Sorry."

"I would think so. I'm the one who's taking all the chances. And this film is for cretins. It's bad enough I'm doing this, but to treat me this way."

"It's not right."

"It's debasing. You can pass that on to Sergei."

"Whose idea was it?"

"To meet here? It was my idea, but I didn't intend to pass whole days here. They must think I'm a pervert." On the screen the gangster chief pulled on a glove equipped with a power drill and demonstrated it on a luckless henchman. "Actually, in the old days this was the best porno theater in Havana."

"What happened when they switched to karate films?"

"We brought our girlfriends and screwed. The Chinese never paid attention to what we did."

It was dark, and Arkady didn't want to examine his companion too obviously, but what he could see sideways was a bureaucrat in his sixties with a gray mustache, eyes bright as a bird's.

"So you have spent a lot of time here."

"I suffer from a certain personal history. Surprised to see Chinese in Cuba?"

"Yes."

"Brought in when the slave trade closed. There's no smoking," the man said to explain why he was cupping his cigarette. He switched briefcases and, using the cigarette as a little lamp, dipped his head into the one he'd taken from Arkady to count the money, the same hundred-dollar expenditure Pribluda had paid every week. "You understand, I am under extraordinary pressure. If I had known what buying a car would entail, I never would have agreed to any of this."

"You can buy a car?"

"Used, of course. '55 Chevrolet. Original leather." On the screen, gangsters marched into a studio where the girl had just finished sculpting a dove in white marble. As they broke off the statue's wings her brother flew through the studio window on a motor scooter. "Where is Sergei?"

194

"Not feeling well," Arkady said, "but I'll tell him you wished him a quick recovery."

The monk was a whirlwind, dispatching hoodlums with a variety of leaps and kicks. With every blood-spraying kick Arkady's head throbbed, and when the gangster chief pulled on his glove Arkady stood.

"Aren't you staying?" his friend said. "This is the good part."

Ofelia was late for the meeting with Muriel's teacher.

She rushed because she was convinced that the Italian with Hedy was slaughtered simply because he resembled Renko. She had gone to the medical clinic in time to find Lohmann, the salesman from Hamburg, still being examined and he truculently answered yes, his friend Franco had bumped his head a few days earlier on one of those stupid low doorways in Havana Vieja. Poor Hedy had not been too bright to begin with, and place, time, looks, names, a simple scrape on the Italian's head, everything had conspired against her.

Also Ofelia wanted to shower. She felt death lying like a film on her skin. If other people couldn't smell it, she could.

A footbridge led from the Quinta de Molina to the school, modern and airy with pastel walls covered with self-portraits of students in their maroon uniforms, skirts for girls and shorts for boys, and murals on the theme of "Resistance!" featuring children with rifles downing hapless American jets.

Muriel's class had recently visited a banana plantation, and the classroom walls were decorated with paper bananas. Ofelia wondered where they got the paper. The school had one book for every three students, no new books in the library for three years, no chemicals for chemistry. "They learn in the abstract," as her mother put it caustically; nevertheless the school was clean and orderly. Ofelia made profuse apologies to Miss García, Muriel's teacher, an older woman with eyebrows as thin as spider legs.

"I'd almost given up on you." The brows lifted to indicate exasperation.

"I'm so sorry." Was there anything more self-abased than a parent meeting with a teacher? Ofelia wondered. "Is there something special you wanted to talk about?"

"Of course. Why would I have asked you in?"

"There's a problem, no?"

"Yes. A great problem."

"Muriel has not been turning in homework?"

"She turns in her homework."

"It's good?"

"Adequate."

"She misbehaves in school?"

"She behaves normally. That was the reason she was allowed to go on the trip. But deep in her, in the soul of this little girl, is something rotten."

"Rotten?"

"Festering."

"She hit someone, she lied?"

"No, no, no, no. Don't try to get off easy. Deep in her heart is a worm."

"What did she do?"

"She violated my trust. I took only my best students to the farm. To learn of the struggle in the countryside. Instead, she revealed herself as an anti-revolutionary and a thief." Miss García set a paper bag on her desk. "On the way back on the bus this fell out of her shirt. I heard it fall."

Ofelia looked inside the bag. "A banana."

"Stolen goods. Stolen by a daughter of an officer of the PNR. This is not going to end here."

"Actually, a banana skin, no?" Ofelia lifted it from the bag by its unpeeled end. The skin was brown and blotchy, ripeness on the edge of rotting.

"Banana or banana skin, it makes no difference."

"She had eaten it or not?"

"That doesn't matter."

"You heard it fall. It's not likely you would hear an empty banana skin fall on a moving bus."

196

"That's not the point."

"Whose custody has it been in? There could be more than one person involved, there might be a whole ring involved with this banana. I will test it for fingerprints inside and out. We can do that. I'm glad you brought this to my attention. Don't worry, we'll get them all, each and every one. Do you want me to?"

"Well." Miss García sat back, and her tongue dabbed at the corner of her mouth. "It was in my custody, of course. I don't know how it got eaten."

"We can investigate. We can make sure the perpetrators never show their faces in this school again. Is that what you want?"

Miss García looked aside, the eyebrows settled, and she said in an entirely different voice, "I suppose I was hungry."

Now Ofelia felt even worse. There was no pleasure to be had in cowing a teacher who didn't even recognize she was slowly starving. Miss García's problem was her revolutionary purity; she had to be the only person Ofelia knew who didn't have some small enterprise on the side. Next the poor woman would start hallucinating and see Che wandering the halls. Ofelia was so ashamed she couldn't wait to get her hands on Muriel.

Arkady opened the briefcase and laid the contents on Pribluda's desk, photocopies that were in Spanish, naturally, every word. If he'd only studied Spanish at school instead of English and German, which were only good for sciences, medicine, philosophy, international business, Shakespeare and Goethe. For sugar, Spanish seemed to be the key. Arkady tried anyway:

A document with the title "Negociación Russo-Cubano" with
   lists of names, Russian for the "Ministerio de Commercio
   Exterior de Rusia" (Bykov, Plotnikov, Chenigovskii), Cubans
   for the Cuban "Ministerio de Azúcar" (Mesa, Herrera, Suárez)
   and a third of Panamanian mediators from AzuPanama
   (Ramos, Pico, Arenas).

A "Certificado del Registro Público Panameño" for AzuPanamá, S.A., including a list of "directores" with the same names as the mediators, Sres. Ramos, Pico, Arenas.

A "Referencia Bancaria" for AzuPanama from the Bank for Creative Investments, S.A., "Zona Libre de Colón," signed by the bank's "Director General," John O'Brien.

Face pages of Cuban passports for Ramos, Pico and Arenas.

Cubana airline tickets from Havana to Panama for Ramos, Pico and Arenas.

Room vouchers for Ramos, Pico and Arenas from the Hotel Lincoln, Zona Libre, Colón, billed to the Cuban Ministry of Sugar.

A long list of Russian commitments in funds and cash equivalents totaling $252 million for Cuban sugar.

A revised list after mediation by AzuPanama for $272 million.

A deposit slip of $5,000 in the name of Vitaly Bugai at the Bank for Creative Investments, S.A., Zona Libre, Colón, República de Panamá.

In other words, the mediators Ramos, Pico and Arenas were Cuban, and the neutral AzuPanama was a creation of the Cuban Ministry of Sugar and the Bank for Creative Investment. Arkady's Spanish was nonexistent, but his math was fair. He understood that Cuba had defrauded Russia of an extra $20 million, one beggar stealing from the other. He also understood that the Cubans' silent partner in crime was the pirate who owned Capone's boat.

Close up, Muriel's dark eyes had irises like solar flares, frightening glimpses of the eleven-year-old soul. Her interrogation was brief because she admitted to worse than her teacher claimed. She had bought the banana.

"The workers at the farm were selling them. I had a dollar from Grandmother. We bought a bunch."

"A bunch? Miss García found only one banana."

"Everyone in class hid a banana. She only found mine."

Ofelia's mother ticked on her rocker. "We got all the others, don't worry."

"That's not the point," Ofelia said. "You've turned my daughters into profiteers."

"A lesson in capitalism."

"They're not supposed to sell bananas at a state farm like that."

"A lesson in communism."

Marisol, the younger sister, said, "My class is going to see baseballs made. I can get baseballs."

Ofelia's mother said, "Good, maybe we can cook them."

In her mind Ofelia saw the militant Miss García looming over her two beautiful daughters, and her mother defending them like a hen in a housedress, the family universe embattled within and without.

"I'm taking a shower."

"Then what?" her mother asked.

"I have to go out."

"To see that man?"

"He's not a man, he's a Russian."

Arkady found that he had been expecting the detective, with her inquisitor's glare, informal shorts and pullover, straw bag and gun. All the AzuPanama documents were out of sight, and Osorio could swing her gaze all she wanted.

"Did you find a picture of Pribluda today?"

"No."

"Well, I found a picture of you." It was plain she relished the surprise. "Do you remember Hedy?"

"How could I forget Hedy?"

Osorio told him about the two bodies at the Casa de Amor, Hedy Guzman and an Italian national named Franco Leo Mossa. She described the condition of the room, positions of the bodies, nature of the wounds, time of death.

"Machetes?" Arkady asked.

"How did you guess?"

"Statistics. There was no outcry?"

"No. The murderer also used something round and sharp to puncture the Italian's throat so he couldn't call out."

"Like an ice pick?"

"Yes. At first, I thought of an extortion turned violent. Sometimes a *jinetera* goes with a tourist and when his pants are down a so-called boyfriend shows up and they rob him."

"We know who her boyfriend is."

"Then I thought the dead man looked like you."

"There's a compliment you don't get every day. Was he the man we saw her with on the street the other night?"

"I'm pretty sure. Did you dance with Hedy?"

"No. We were only introduced. By Sergeant Luna."

"You talked to her?"

"Not really. She wasn't completely sober, and later, of course, she was—possessed."

"After the *santero*'s, Hedy cleaned herself up and returned here. We saw her, you and I. At the time I wondered why. I mean, everything was over. The sergeant was gone and this was not the usual place she picked up tourists. I think the reason she was here was you."

"I'd only met her."

"Maybe she wanted to meet you again."

"She would have known the difference between a well-dressed Italian and me. Why even think of me?"

"This was in the room." She showed him the picture.

A camera had the photographer's eye and it was always odd to see yourself as others imagined you. If they were dead, Arkady thought, that lent a certain finality to what had been a simple snapshot. Arkady saw cars, baggage, heavy coats, a Russian herd at Sheremetyevo Airport. Only he was in focus. He had delivered the colonel a farewell smile but no embrace sprinkled with vodka and tears, their history was too complicated for that. Perhaps what Pribluda wanted, finally, Arkady thought, was someone who knew him that well and would still see him off. The photograph reminded him of the empty frame he had found in Pribluda's bureau drawer.

"Pribluda took this when I dropped him off at the airport. He said he'd use it for target practice for old times' sake. This was in the room?"

"Hedy was not a mental giant. She was probably still in a daze from the *santero's*. I think maybe someone gave her that to help her pick you out."

"You think the man in this picture could pass as Italian?"

"In the dark some people are hard to tell apart. Did I tell you that the dead man's name was Franco?"

"Yes."

"If a European called Franco looked like Renko, his name sounded like Renko, she met him outside Renko's apartment and his head had a cut the same as Renko's, he was probably Renko enough for Hedy. I think it's possible the murder of this Italian was a second attempt on your life."

"This happened two nights ago?"

"Yes."

Luna had said he would be back to fuck him up, Arkady remembered, and the libidinous Franco Mossa sounded as thoroughly fucked as a man could get.

"Does Sergeant Luna know about the correct identification of the body?"

"He does now. He and Arcos took over the investigation."

Luna would be back again. The days of grace were over.

Arkady asked, "Why kill Hedy?"

"I don't know."

"Why leave the photograph on her?"

"He didn't, he flushed it down the toilet."

"Then how did you get it?"

"The picture was trapped with toilet paper." She described the deeply petaled slashes, the blood-smeared sheets and blood-soaked air that had been baking in the sun for a day and a half, and confessed to her nausea. "It was unprofessional of me."

"No, it's an occupational disease," Arkady said. "The reason I left the autopsy was to be sick. See, we share a common weakness. I feel like smoking just hearing about it."

"Dr. Blas has never been sick."

"I'm sure."

"Dr. Blas says we should welcome smell as information. A body's fruity bouquet might indicate amyl nitrate. The hint of garlic can be arsenic."

"He'd be a delightful man to have dinner with."

"Anyway, I've showered."

"Showered and took the time to paint your toenails. A lot of detectives wouldn't bother to do that. You took a chance."

More than taken a chance, he thought; by removing the picture the detective had altered the crime scene, tacitly admitting that she suspected Luna as much as he did. Sharing the picture was the first real step forward on her part, painted toes and all. Now it was his turn, that was the etiquette. He could hold on to his scraps of information until he was safely back in Moscow, where the contents of the briefcase he had picked up at the Chinese theater might mean the hook for Bugai and an exchange of red-faced accusations between the Russian Ministry for Foreign Trade and the Cuban Ministry of Sugar. Over money, of course. Once back in Moscow, though, he'd never find out what happened to Pribluda.

"Have you ever heard of a Panamanian sugar company called AzuPanama?"

"I've read about it." Her eyes cooled. "In *Granma,* the Party newspaper. There's a problem with the Russians over the sugar contract and AzuPanama is supposed to help."

"Mediate?"

"So I understand."

"Because AzuPanama is neutral."

"Yes."

"Panamanian?"

"Of course."

He led her to the office, opened the green briefcase and emptied its contents item by item on the desk.

"Copies of participants' lists from Russia, Cuba and AzuPanama. A list of company directors for AzuPanama and, for those same names, Cuban passports, Cubana tickets and hotel receipts. Plus a Panamanian bank reference from John O'Brien, residing in

Cuba, and a deposit slip from the bank for Vice Consul Bugai, also here."

It seemed to be going well, Arkady thought. Next he could introduce the concept of O'Brien and George Washington Walls, then their involvement with Luna and Pribluda. Osorio cleared her throat and sorted the items more neatly, touching them the way a person did when handling fire.

"I thought you were getting a picture of Pribluda for Dr. Blas," she said.

"Oh, I am. I happened to come across these first."

"Where did they come from?"

"Why don't you look to see what they are?"

A slight hiss developed in Osorio's Russian. "I can see what they are. What they are is very evident. Documents manufactured to embarrass Cuba."

"You can see by comparing names on this certificate of registration with the passports that AzuPanama isn't really Panamanian at all. AzuPanama was set up in Panama by Cuba with the help of a bank controlled by the American fugitive O'Brien. That's what Pribluda was after when he died. So far, AzuPanama has cost Russia an extra $20 million. Men have died for less."

"Of a heart attack?"

"No."

"Dr. Blas says so."

"Anyway," Arkady went on, "we can make a positive match of the names from AzuPanama with a roster from the Ministry of Sugar. That's what Pribluda would have done next."

"*We* are not doing anything." Osorio stepped back. "You lied to me."

"Here are the documents."

"I'm looking at you. What I see is a man who claims to look for a picture of his dead friend while he gathers all sorts of anti-Cuban materials. I come to help you and you throw these papers, which you don't tell me where they came from, in my face. I won't touch them."

This was not going the way Arkady hoped.

"You can check them."

"I'm not helping you. I don't really know anything about you. It's your word and a picture that you're Pribluda's friend, that's all I know. Just your word."

"No, that's not true." Her words crystallized what had been vague before. What had bothered Arkady was how his picture got from Pribluda's flat to Hedy. "Did you give Pribluda's picture of me to Luna?"

"How can you ask a question like that?"

"Because it makes sense. Let me guess. After the autopsy you came here to dust for fingerprints and found the picture of this miserable Russian who had just arrived. You naturally called Luna, who told you to bring the picture to him."

"Never."

"Who gave it to poor Hedy. Have you been helping Luna all along?"

"Not in that way."

"Do all Cuban police carry an ice pick and a baseball bat?"

"When you see Luna with a machete, *bolo*, that's the time to be afraid. You should have stayed in Moscow. If you had, more people would be alive."

"There you're right."

Osorio snatched up her bag. She was out the door before he could consider whether he had really handled the issue of Azu-Panama as well as possible. But why would a Cuban be impressed by mere evidence? This was Havana, after all, a place where sugar attachés floated in the dark, where a Havana Yacht Club did, didn't, might exist, where a girl could lose her head two nights in a row. Osorio's lie about the picture had simply been one absurdity too many. All the same there had been a nasty edge to his words that he regretted.

When she reached the street, Ofelia realized that, apart from a bolt on his door, Renko had no protection if Luna came back. What she had not told the Russian was how Luna looked when he stood over Hedy's body at the love motel, how his eyes reddened and the muscles of his face worked like a twitching fist. Or how the sergeant had later sat in the archive room, and how simply moving by him was like walking in the shadow of a volcano.

Traffic on the Malecón—always thin at night—had as good as disappeared. Even the couples who usually courted on the seawall were gone. If Ofelia was angry with Renko, she was furious with herself. She had removed the picture of him from the crime scene. She had broken the law. For what, so he could accuse her of taking the same picture from Pribluda's? She knew by now his taste for frivolous minutiae and then the diagonal question that cut across the board. As for the documents he pulled from the briefcase she was not surprised by the lengths Russians would go to discredit Cuba. All she needed, Ofelia told herself, was to keep Renko alive until his plane left for Moscow. She wanted a clear conscience.

Determined not to be baited again, she went back in the house. Halfway up the stairs Ofelia heard steps above and a soft knocking at Renko's door. When he opened the door the light of his room fell on an extraordinarily fair woman with braided black hair in a Mexican dress and bare feet. She was a rose on a long stem, a glamorous white flower tinged with blue. Ofelia recognized her from the Santeria ceremony, the friend of George Washington Walls, the dancer.

Ofelia watched Isabel lift her face and kiss Renko. Before they saw her, she retreated down into the dark of the stairs, getting smaller and smaller until she reached the street again.

18.

"You're making a mistake," Arkady told Isabel.

"No mistake."

She guided his hand between her legs so that he could feel her through the cotton of the dress, then kissed him and slipped into the sitting room. Maybe this was a test for signs of life, he thought. The dress was thin to show the slimness of her body and the dark caps of her breasts, and if he were a normal man he would feel healthy lust. The truth was he did feel a first stirring, feeling her breath on his neck, taking in the almond scent of her hair braided like long black silk. Her pale skin made her lips all the more red.

"No mistake," Isabel said. "I asked you to do something for me. Fair trade. Gordo keeps the rum over the sink."

"I thought Gordo was the name for the turtle."

"For both. Sergei, turtle."

"What do you call George Washington Walls?"

"I call him done with. I have a new boyfriend, no?"

"Well, I can't imagine who that is."

Isabel touched the coat hung on the back of the chair, and when he pulled her hand away she said, "Relax. Such a strange man, but I like you." She found the rum herself and rinsed two glasses. "I like strong men."

"That's not me."

"Let me be the judge." She handed him a glass. "I know you've heard about my father."

"I heard there was a conspiracy."

"True. There's always a conspiracy. Everyone complains, and He . . ."—she pointed to her chin—"He lets them, as long as they don't *do* anything. As long as they don't organize. All the same, every year there's a conspiracy, and it's always a mix of conspirators and informers. That's Cuban democracy at work, that's how we will finally vote, when even the informers decide enough is enough and they keep their mouths shut and this country is delivered." She brushed Arkady's cheek. "But not yet, I don't think. This is the first place where time does not exist. People have been born and died, yes, but time has not passed because time demands fresh paint, new cars, new clothes. Or maybe war, one or the other. But not this, which is not dead or alive, which is neither. You're not drinking."

"No." The last thing he needed was Isabel and alcohol.

"Do you mind?" She took a cigarette.

"No."

"The reason my father agreed to the coup in the first place was the assurances from his Russian friends that he would have their complete support. It wasn't his idea."

"He should have known better."

"I think I'm choosing more wisely." She inhaled as if the smoke would travel the length of her body, exhaled and spun, her arms spread, so that the dress clung to her and smoke trailed behind. "I think we're the best. English dancers are too stiff, the Russians are too serious. We have the elevation and technique, but we are also born with music. There is no limit once I'm out, once I have my letter and my ticket."

"The letter hasn't come."

"It will. It has to. I told George we were looking into going back to Moscow together."

"You and I?"

"Yes, wouldn't that be the simplest way?" Isabel came to rest against the coat and an ember from her cigarette spilled on the sleeve. "Are you married?"

Arkady brushed the ember off and took Isabel by the wrist. It was a slim wrist, an elegant wrist, but he led her to the door. "It's late. If something comes for you I promise I'll let you know."

"What are you doing?"

"I'm saying good night."

"I'm not done."

"I'm done."

He pushed her out and only had a glimpse of her in the hallway crushed as a moth before he shut the door.

"You son of a bitch," she shouted through it. "You prick, *coño*. Just like your friend Sergei. All he wanted to do was talk about that stupid plot that got my father killed. You're just the same, another *maricón. El bollo de tu madre*."

Arkady shot the bolt. "I'm sorry. I don't speak Spanish."

His way with women was astonishing, he thought. What a charmer. He wrapped himself in the coat and shivered. Why was everyone in Cuba warm except him?

It was midnight, and dark had overwhelmed the city when Arkady wasn't looking. A power outage arranged by Luna, or was his imagination expanding in the dark? There were no streetlamps on the Malecón, only a couple of faint headlights like the sort on luminescent fish found in an ocean trench. Although he latched the shutters closed and lit a candle, darkness continued to seep into the room with a solid, tarry quality.

A car horn woke him. The horn blared until he opened the balcony doors and saw that the morning had started hours before. The sea was a brilliant mirror to a huge sky, the sun high and shadows reduced to mere spots of ink. Across the Malecón a boy flipped small, silvery bait out of a net up to a partner standing on the seawall with a pole. Another boy gutted his fish on the sidewalk and threw the entrails up to a hovering gull. Directly below the balcony was a streamlined cloud of chrome and white, Hemingway's Chrysler Imperial convertible with George Washington Walls at the wheel and John O'Brien in a golf cap and Hawaiian shirt.

"Remember, we were going to talk about possible employment," Walls called up. "And show you some famous sin spots."

"You can't just tell me?"

"Think of us as your guides," O'Brien said. "Think of it as a Grand Tour."

Arkady looked to Walls for any sign that Isabel had reported her midnight visit and he looked to O'Brien for an indication that word of the AzuPanama papers reached him via Osorio, but all he saw shining up from the car were bright smiles and dark glasses. Employment in Havana? That had to be a joke. But how could he dare to miss learning more about AzuPanama and John O'Brien? Besides, he thought, what could happen in Hemingway's car?

"Give me a minute."

The desk drawer had envelopes. Into one Arkady fit all his worldly evidence: Rufo's house key, Pribluda's car key, AzuPanama documents and the photo of the Havana Yacht Club. Arkady taped the envelope to the small of his back, put on his shirt and coat, a man equipped for all climates and occasions.

The car even rode like a cloud, the warm upholstery adhesive to the touch. Arkady noticed even from the backseat the push-button transmission, how could anyone miss that? They breezed along the Malecón while Walls gossiped about other famous cars, Fidel's penchant for Oldsmobiles and Che's '60 Chevrolet Impala.

Arkady looked around. "Have you seen Luna?"

"The sergeant is no longer associated with us," Walls said.

"I think the man's unhinged," said O'Brien.

Walls said, "Luna is one funky dude." He dipped his glasses from his blue eyes. "When are you going to dump the coat?"

O'Brien said, "It's like driving around with Abe-Fucking-Lincoln. It is."

"When I get warm."

"You read Hemingway in Russia?" Walls asked.

"He's very popular there. Jack London, John Steinbeck and Hemingway."

"When writers were bruisers," said O'Brien. "I'd have to say I think of *The Old Man and the Sea* every time I see the fishing boats go out. I loved the book and the film. Spencer Tracy was magnificent. A better Irishman than Cuban, but magnificent."

"John reads everything," Walls said.

"I love movies too. When I get homesick I put on a video. I have America on videotapes. Capra, Ford, Minelli."

Arkady thought of Vice Consul Bugai and the $5,000 deposit in Bugai's name at O'Brien's Panama bank.

"Do you have any Russian friends here?"

"There aren't that many. But to be honest I have to say I steer clear, as a precautionary measure."

"Pariahs," said Walls.

"The Russian Mafia would love to get in here. They're already in Miami, Antigua, Caymans, they're in the neighborhood, but Russians are such a sore subject with Fidel there's no point in being associated with them. But more than that, they're stupid, Arkady. No offense."

"None taken."

"A Russian wants money, he says, I'll kidnap someone rich, bury him up to his neck and demand a ransom. Maybe his family will pay and maybe they won't. A short-term proposition either way. An American wants money. He says, I'll do a mass mailing and offer an investment with an irresistible rate of return. Maybe the investment pays off or maybe it doesn't, but as long as I have lawyers those people will be paying me for the rest of their lives. After they're dead I'll put a lien on their estate. They'll *wish* I had buried them up to their necks."

"That's what you did?" Arkady said.

"I'm not saying that's what I did, I'm saying what's done in the States." He raised his hand and his biggest grin. "Not lying. I have testified in district court in Florida and Georgia, federal court in New York and Washington and I have never lied."

"That's a lot of courts to tell the truth in," Arkady said.

"The fact is," said O'Brien, "I prefer happy investors. I'm too old to be stalked by unshaven, angry men or have to duck subpoenas from men who can stand outside a door for the rest of *their* miserable lives. Hey, we're here!"

Walls swung across oncoming traffic to the curb of an airy high-rise hotel, an angled tower of blue balconies that nestled at its base the separate dome in mottled colors. Arkady had passed the hotel before without fully registering how its architecture was pure American fifties. And they'd arrived in the perfect car, gliding to a stop under a cantilevered entrance by a statue of, perhaps, a seahorse and siren carved from the largest of all whale bones. John O'Brien had visited before, judging by the doormen's zeal.

"The Riviera," O'Brien explained in a hush to Arkady, as if they were about to enter the Vatican. "The American Mafia built other hotels here, but the jewel was the Riviera."

Arkady asked, "What does this have to do with me?"

"A little patience, please. It all fits."

O'Brien removed his cap as a mark of respect before they climbed the stairs and entered glass doors to a low lobby of white marble under inset ceiling lights spaced as irregularly as stars. Sofas as long as boxcars reached across the floor toward a skylit grotto of elephant-ear ferns. Along one side was the tidal murmur of a bar, at the far end a staircase suspended on wires wound around a stabile of black stone, and a bright haze that was plate glass leading to a pool. O'Brien glided at a reverent pace across the lobby, tassels of his shoes flopping. "Everything deluxe. Kitchen like a cruise ship, beautifully appointed rooms. And the casino?"

One step ahead of O'Brien, Walls opened the brass doors to a convention hall emblazoned with the colorful, forceful logos of Spanish, Venezuelan, Mexican banks. Knockdown displays and charts on easels forecast Caribbean economic trends. Business cards and four-color brochures littered the carpet. O'Brien stopped at a particularly outsized booth with a row of chairs facing a giant monitor.

"It's pathetic," O'Brien said. "Market projections, rates of interest, capital protection, all languages spoken. Look at this." He tried to turn on the monitor at the screen. "Hell, it doesn't even work."

"Maybe this does." Arkady picked up a remote control from the booth counter and pushed ON. At once, images of serious men and women in expensive suits marched across the screen. Dollars, pesetas, deutsche marks flowed from them like lines of electricity.

"Right," O'Brien said. "They know how to put your money to work for your benefit around the world, sure they do. The only trouble, this isn't the world. This is Cuba. You know what Fidel says about capitalists. First, all they want is the tip of your little finger, then the finger, then the hand, then your arm and piece by piece all the rest of you. He's made up his mind. So the banks didn't come all this way to make their presentations to Fidel, think about that. Thank you, Arkady."

Arkady turned the remote off.

"Anyway," O'Brien said, "the banks have it backwards. Nowadays people are not interested in a slow accrual of assets. What they want is a jackpot, the lottery, payday. Look around, you can still see it." He called Arkady's attention to walls of baroque cream and gold, pointing out how the dropped ceiling hid the dome overhead. They were in the painted dome they had seen from outside. If the Riviera was the Vatican, this was the Sistine Chapel. As O'Brien removed his dark glasses and made a slow, complete turn a small miracle happened, the lines on his fine-as-an-eggshell forehead seemed to smooth away and Arkady saw a hint of the redhead O'Brien once had been. "The Gold Leaf Casino. You have to imagine the way it was, Arkady. Four roulette tables, two seven-eleven, one baccarat, four tables for blackjack with mahogany rails, the nap brushed twice a day. Not an ash. Pit manager on a bishop's chair. It was a meeting of two classes, the rich and the mob. The French have a word for it: *frisson*. A little charge and, by God, it sparkled. Chandeliers lit like bubbling champagne glasses. Women wearing diamonds from Harry Winston, I mean rocks. Movie stars, Rockefellers, you name it."

"No Cubans?"

"Cubans *worked* here. They hired Cuban accountants and made them into croupiers and dealers. Taught them grooming, bought them suits, paid them well to keep them honest. Of course, they were still vacuumed for chips at the end of the day."

Arkady had seen casinos. There were casinos in Moscow. The Russian Mafia loved to strap leather jackets over uncomfortable holsters so they could belly up to a table and lose money loud and big.

"Mind, there was always gambling in Havana," O'Brien said. "The Mafia just made it honest, with a fair split for President Batista. Batista and his wife got the machines, the Mafia got the tables and there was no more honest operation in the world. Plus, biggest names in entertainment, Sinatra, Nat King Cole. Beautiful beaches, best deep-sea fishing and the women were unbelievable. Still are."

"It's hard to believe there was a revolution."

"You can't please everyone," O'Brien said. "Let me show you my personal favorite, though. Smaller but more historical. America's last stand."

On the way, as soon as they left the Riviera, they drove by picturesquely rotting houses, the sort Arkady might have expected to find in a mangrove swamp, the pavement rolling over banyan roots.

Arkady asked, "So, what kind of business have you been doing here? Investing?"

"Investing, consulting, whatever," O'Brien said. "We solve problems."

"For example?"

Walls and O'Brien glanced at each other, and Walls said, "For example, Cuban trucks here need spare parts because the Russian factory that used to produce them is turning out Swiss Army knives now instead. What John and I did was find a Russian truck factory in Mexico, and buy the whole thing just for the parts."

"What did you get out of that?"

"Finder's fee, costs. You know, I used to think because I was a Marxist that I understood capitalism. I didn't know anything. John plays it like a game."

O'Brien said, "I have always noticed that people from the socialist camp take money far too seriously. You should have fun."

"It's like a second college education being with John."

"Yes?" Arkady was ready to be educated.

"Like boots," said Walls. "The Cubans ran out of boots. We found out that the U.S. was getting rid of surplus boots at a dollar a pair. We bought all of them, which is why the Cuban army is marching in American combat boots."

"You must be appreciated here."

"I'd like to think that George and I are," said O'Brien.

"But how do you do that from Cuba? I would think you'd need a third party."

"In a third country, of course."

"In Mexico, Panama?"

O'Brien twisted in his seat. "Arkady, you've got to stop being such a cop. Over the years, I have helped a lot of police in your situation, but it's a matter of give and take. You want to know this and you want to know that, but you have yet to give me a believable explanation how you came to stand on the dock of the Havana Yacht Club."

"I was just visiting places where Pribluda might have been."

"What made you think he might have been there?"

"There was a map in his apartment and the club was circled." Which was true, although not as true as the photograph. "It was an old map."

"Just an old map? That's how you heard about the Havana Yacht Club? Amazing."

The Hotel Capri was a pocket version of the Riviera, a high rise but off the Malecón, and no dome or spiral stairs, instead a simple lobby of glassy sounds and chrome furniture. Cubans were not allowed upstairs; they sat and nursed colas as they waited for appointments to materialize, ready to wait all day. The air-conditioning eddied around potted plants.

"I can't get over the coat," Walls told Arkady. "Do you mind if I try it on?"

"Go ahead."

Although Arkady didn't want other people even touching the coat, he helped Walls in. The coat stretched a little over Walls's shoulders. He ran his hands along the cashmere outside, the silk lining in, felt the pockets inside and out.

O'Brien watched the fashion show. "What do you think?"

"I think he's a man with empty pockets." Walls returned the coat. "But nice. You got this on an investigator's pay? Good for you."

"A good sign for us all." O'Brien led the way off the lobby and through the doors into a small, darkened theater. Arkady could barely see the stage, steps, speakers and overhead lights with colored cels. "La Sala Roja. It wasn't a cabaret then. It was a better show. Use your imagination and you can see red drapes, red carpet, red velvet lamps. In the center, four blackjack tables and four roulette. In the corners, seven-eleven and baccarat. Girls selling cigars, and I mean beautiful girls selling Cuban cigars. Perhaps a little cocaine, though who needs it? It's the sound of the ball on the track, the excitement around a craps table. The man says 'Bets, gentlemen' and people bet. Do you gamble, Arkady?"

"No."

"Why?"

"I don't have the money to lose."

"Everyone has the money to lose. Poor people gamble all the time. What you mean is, you don't like to lose."

"I suppose so."

"Well, you're unusual, most people need to. If they happen to win, they keep on playing until they do lose. Right now around the world more people are gambling than ever in the history of man." O'Brien shrugged to show that the phenomenon was beyond him. "Maybe it's the coming millennium. It's as if people want to shed material things, not in a church but in a casino. People are willing to lose everything as long as they have fun. They can't resist. It's human. The worst snub in the world is a casino where they won't take your money."

"Were you here before the Revolution?"

"A dozen times. Jesus, that was a long time ago."

"Did you gamble?"

"I'm like you, I don't like to lose. Mostly, I admired the operation. You know who I pointed out to my wife? I pointed out Jack Kennedy. He had a peroxide blonde on one arm and a sultry *mulata* on the other. During the missile crisis I wondered if Jack ever thought back to that night."

"There were other casinos, too," Walls said.

"Deauville, Sans Souci, Montmartre, Tropicana," said O'Brien. "The Mafia's great plan was to tear down Havana and rebuild it, make it completely modern and create a triangle of tourism between Miami, Havana and the Yucatan, an international zone of prosperity. That's what the revolution stopped, not that the revolution wasn't overdue but, economically, Cuba lost forty years."

"That's your plan, to reopen old casinos?"

"No," O'Brien said, "still too many hard feelings. Anyway, the Havana Yacht Club and Casino can be ten times bigger than any of these."

"You're ambitious."

"Aren't you?" Walls asked. "The Cold War's over. I was a hero in that war and look what it got me. Marooned."

"What kind of life is Moscow?" said O'Brien. "Wake up. You have sailed into paradise and you're about to sail out. Don't do it. Stay here and work for us."

"Work for you? Take Pribluda's place?"

"Like that," said Walls.

"Why is it that I can't take this offer seriously?"

"Because you're suspicious," said O'Brien. "It's the Russian attitude. You have to be positive. Every millionaire I ever met was an optimist. Every down-and-outer expects the worst. It's a new world, Arkady, why not plan big?"

"You would share your Cuban gold mine with a man you'd never met before?"

216

"But I've met your type before. You're the man at the end of the pier, who's either going to jump in the water or change his life." O'Brien's eyes glowed with . . . what? Arkady wondered. The showmanship of a salesman or the zeal of a priest, all his efforts bent to one moment of plausibility for this thoroughly ridiculous proposition. "Change it. Give yourself a chance."

"How?"

"As a partner."

"A partner? This gets better all the time."

"But partnership demands trust," O'Brien said. "You understand what trust is, don't you, Arkady?"

"Yes."

"But you won't show it. For two days I've been waiting for you to be as open with George and me as we have been with you. Please don't piss on my back and tell me it's raining. Don't tell me about an old map. Sergeant Luna told us about the picture of the Havana Yacht Club. We know about it. A picture of a dead Russian at the Havana Yacht Club is exactly what we don't need now."

"John would feel better if he had it," Walls said.

"If I had it I wouldn't have to worry about it. And I'd know that you had extended your trust to us the way we have with you. Can you do that, Arkady, and trust me with that picture?" O'Brien put out his hand.

Arkady felt the envelope with the photograph sticking to his back. "I don't know about business partnerships, I've always worked directly for the state. But what about this? If I accept your proposition and work for a year and have a villa and boat and a satisfying social life, at that point I will give you the photograph. Until then it's safe because we will be, as you say, partners."

"Are you hearing this?" Walls asked. "The mother is bargaining."

"Resisting." John O'Brien let his hand drop. He looked his age, suddenly a little spent, silver hair sticking to temples that were wet like sweat on the edge of greasepaint, like an actor who passionately acted a play for a dull, deaf audience. "Because you're Russian, Arkady, I'll make allowances. This is a new way of thinking for you, being part of a plan."

"Remind me, what part would I be?" Arkady asked.

"Security. George told you, in case any Mafia does show up."

"I'd have to think about this. I'm not sure I'm that tough."

"That's okay," Walls said. "People think you are."

"Appearances go a long way," O'Brien said. "I'll tell you why the Capri is my favorite casino. You know, the Mafia hired an actor, George Raft, to front for the Capri. Raft acted a gangster so many times people thought he was. He thought he was. Comes the night of the Revolution crowds start looting casinos. One mob heads for the Capri. Who goes out on the steps but Raft himself and says in his gangster voice, 'No punks are busting up my casino.' And they went away. He chased them. America's last stand."

19.

The bodega was a warehouse with the dimmest light in Havana, and the fact that the lines were short and Ofelia was going to do the mule's work of carrying a sack of Vietnamese rice and a tin of cooking oil did nothing to improve her mother's mood.

"You either come home late or you don't come home at all. Who is this man?"

"He's not a man," Ofelia said.

"He's not a man?" Her mother amplified her wonderment to include as many people as possible in the conversation.

"Not a man like that."

"Like the musicians? Great husbands. Where is the last one, massaging Swedes in Cayo Largo?"

"I came home last night. Everything is okay."

"Everything is wonderful. Here I am with the world's greatest work of fiction." She slapped her ration book. "What could be better? To know why you come home so late?"

"It's a police matter."

"With a Russian! *Hija,* maybe you haven't heard, the Russian boat has sailed. Gone. How did you even find one? I'd love to see this stranded Lothario."

"Mama," Ofelia begged.

"Oh, you're in your uniform, you're embarrassed to be seen with me. I can wait in line all day so you can run around and make the world safe for. . . ." She indicated a beard.

"We're almost there." Ofelia fixed her eye on the counter.

"We're almost nowhere. This is nowhere, *hija*. Remember that boy you knew in school, the one with the fish tank?"

"Aquarium."

"Fish tank. Nothing but dirty water and two catfish that never moved. Take a look at those clerks."

At a counter with a register and scale were two women with whiskers who looked so much like those catfish that it was difficult for Ofelia to keep a straight face. There were four counters in the gloom of the bodega, each with a chalkboard that listed goods, prices, ration per person or family, and date available, the "date available" clouded from many corrections.

"Tomatoes next week," Ofelia said. "That's good news."

Her mother exploded with a laugh. "My God, I've raised an idiot. There will be no tomatoes, no evaporated milk, no flour and maybe no beans or rice. This is a trap for morons. *Hija*, I know you are a brilliant detective, but thank God you have me to shop for you."

A woman behind them hissed and warned, "I will report this counterrevolutionary propaganda."

"Piss off," Ofelia's mother said. "I fought at Playa Giron. Where were you? Probably waving your tits at American bombers. I assume you had tits."

Her mother was good at shutting people up. Playa Giron was what the rest of the world called the Bay of Pigs. Strangely enough, she actually had been in the army and shot an invader, although now she claimed she should have made him take her to Florida while she had a gun on him.

"I have a question," Ofelia said.

"Please, I'm reading the board. Two cans of green peas per family for the month. They will be delicious, I'm sure. Sugar is available. You will know the end is near when no sugar is available."

"About pickles."

"I don't see pickles."

"Where would I find them?" The Eastern Bloc had tried to unload bottled pickles in Cuba, but Ofelia hadn't seen them for years.

"Not here. In the free market you buy cucumbers and pickle them."

"Different sizes?"

"A cucumber is a cucumber. Why would anyone want a small cucumber?" At the counter her mother made a show of having her book properly marked and announcing, "You know, if you live on your rations you will enjoy a very balanced diet."

"That's true," one of the clerks was stupid enough to agree.

"Because you eat for two weeks and starve for two weeks." Having delivered her torpedo, Ofelia's mother turned and sailed for the exit, leaving Ofelia to follow with the heavy sack and can of oil the length of the bodega while everyone stared.

When they reached the street her mother stumped toward home.

"You are impossible," Ofelia said.

"I hope so. This island is driving me crazy."

"This island is driving you crazy? You've never been off this island."

"And it's driving me crazy. And having a daughter who's one of *them*." Her mother had been stopped by the police for selling homemade cosmetics door to door. They'd let her go, of course, as soon as they learned Detective Osorio was her daughter. "Your uncle Manny wrote to say there is a rocking chair waiting on the porch for me in Miami."

"With a drive-by shooting every night is what he wrote me."

"In his new letter he says he could take Muriel and Marisol. He says they would love South Beach. We could all go and the girls could stay."

"We are not going to talk about this."

"They would knock Miami out. They're beautiful girls and they're light."

That was always the insinuation her mother could twist like a knife, that Ofelia stood apart in the family by the deeper color of her skin, that Ofelia was different from her own daughters and, in reverse, a lifelong and bitter disappointment to her mother. And Ofelia knew her mother could see the red heat in her cheek.

"They're staying with me. If you want to go to Miami, you can go."

"I'm only saying, it's a new world. It probably doesn't involve a Russian."

...

Arkady had Walls and O'Brien drop him off a couple of blocks short of the Malecón. Because he had the sense that Luna could leap over the seawall any second with an ice pick or machete once Arkady reached the boulevard, he stayed in the shadows of building columns until he reached an address with the tricolored banner of the Committee for the Defense of the Revolution, knocked at Abuelita's door and entered.

"Come in."

Light squeezed through with him into the narrow confines of her room, to the statue of the shrouded, dark-skinned Virgin and her shimmering peacock feather. Scents of cigar and sandalwood tickled his nose. Abuelita sat before the Virgin and solemnly laid cards. Tarot? Arkady looked over the old woman's shoulder. Solitaire. Today she sported a pullover that said "New York Stock Exchange." Arkady noticed that the statue also wore something new, a yellow necklace like Osorio's.

"May I?"

"Go ahead." When he touched the necklace beads Abuelita said, "In Santeria this virgin is also the spirit Oshun and her color is yellow, honey, gold. Oshun is a very sexy spirit."

That hardly described Osorio, Arkady thought, but he didn't have time to delve into religious matters.

"I saw you leave this morning in that big white car, that chariot with wings," Abuelita said. "The whole Malecón was looking at that."

"Did you happen to notice any tall, black sergeant from Minint go in the building after I left?"

"No."

"No one fitting that description carrying a machete or a baseball bat?" He added five dollars to the crown at the virgin's feet.

Abuelita sighed and took the money out. "I know the man you mean. The one who arranged the Abakua. I was at my window like I always am, but the truth is, I fell asleep right there standing up. Sometimes my body gets old."

Arkady put the money back. "Then I have another question. I still need a picture of Sergei Pribluda for the police and I'm looking for any close friends of his who might have one. No one here does, but the first time we met you mentioned that Sergei Pribluda was a man who shared his pickles. Yesterday I was at a market that sold vegetables, including cucumbers, but nothing like the homemade pickles in Pribluda's refrigerator. Because you're right, there's nothing like a Russian pickle. Did he have a special visitor?"

Abuelita spread her hand wide as a fan and hid her grin. "Now you're talking. There was one woman, a Russian, who came sometimes with a basket, sometimes not."

"Could you describe her?"

"Oh, like a fat little dove. She came on Thursdays, sometimes alone, sometimes with a girl."

Ofelia climbed a ladder to Hedy Infante's home, a platform built under the ceiling of a rococo foyer. The ten-by-ten loft held her cot, rack of dresses and stretch pants, electric bulb and candles, cosmetics and shoes, window with rope to a pail and view of the chandelier and, far below, a marble floor. The house had been built by a sugar magnate with a taste for froth, and the ceiling's swirls of white plasterwork evoked a sense of nesting in the clouds.

Hedy's interior decoration was just as fantastic, an interior of pictures she had clipped from magazines and taped to her walls, a handmade wallpaper of Los Van Van, Julio Iglesias, Gloria Estefan singing soulfully to a microphone, bathed in strobe lights, reaching out to fans. On one singer she had superimposed her own face, which reminded Ofelia of the real condition of Hedy's neck. The loft wasn't the sort of room a prostitute took a client, it was more her true, private place.

Private but violated by the little touches left by forensic technicians, police tape around the dresses, fingerprint powder on the mirror, the subtle disarray when men rather than women put things away. Hedy had collected hotel soaps, cutlery, coasters, made a seashell frame around a photograph of her *quince*, her fifteenth birthday party—the picture showed off the state-supplied frosted cake, beer and rum. In another photograph Hedy wore the blue ruffles and scarf of a devotee of Yemaya, the goddess of the seas, and, sure enough, on the wall was a statuette of Our Lady of Regla, spirit and saint being one and the same. A cigar box held snapshots of a variety of tourists with Hedy, toasting her with daiquiris or *mojitos* at cafés in the Plaza Vieja, Plaza de Armas, Plaza de la Catedral, the make-believe world of Old Havana. Hedy's favorites, though, seemed to be two photos pinned to a heart-shaped pillow of her and Luna. What had the techs made of that, the dead girl with the officer in charge? The photos had apparently been taken at different times because of a difference in clothes, but both in front of a building that bore in rusty stains the name Centro Russo-Cubano. On the underside of the pillow was pinned a third snapshot, this of Hedy, Luna and the little *jinetera* Teresa in the back of a white Chrysler Imperial. There were no names, telephone numbers or addresses around the bed, in the cigar box or on the wall.

There were no neighbors in the building to talk, and Ofelia went across the street to a *botánica*, where a cardboard listed guava for diarrhea, oregano for congestion, parsley for gas. A Coca-Cola mirror hung on the wall, and taped to it were testimonials, including a postcard from Mexico with the illustration of a dancer with the same sort of ruffled skirt, black hair and fair skin as the woman she had seen kissing Renko. Ofelia personally couldn't care less, but she was annoyed, after all her efforts to ensure the *bolo*'s safety, to see him invite just anyone in. Ofelia remembered how the woman leaned into Renko and brought his face down to hers.

"Hija?" the *herbalista* stirred from a chair.

"Oh, yes." Ofelia bought a bag of mahogany bark for her mother's rheumatism before mentioning Hedy.

"*Yerba buena*," the herbalista remembered Hedy by remedy. "A pretty girl but a nervous stomach. A dancer, too. Such a shame."

The woman knew Hedy from the local group that performed at Carnival. There had been sixty dancers, drummers, men balancing giant tops, all dressed in Yemaya's signature blue and swirling like waves all the way up the Prado where the Comandante himself was in the reviewing stand. And she remembered Hedy's friend, who could burn a hole through wood with his gaze.

"There, that's him."

A Minint Lada stopped outside Hedy's address, and Luna emerged with more haste than usual. Ofelia turned her back to the door, removed her cap and watched the street in the mirror, which meant she had to endure more recommendations from the herbalist and the stupid card from Mexico, but only for a minute before the sergeant came out of Hedy's with the heart-shaped pillow.

But it didn't matter to Ofelia that none of the technicians who visited Hedy Infante's loft had gathered the pillow and its photographs in time. It didn't matter whether or not they dusted Hedy's childish possessions for prints. None of them for all their expertise would understand Hedy as well as she did.

Ofelia lived in two worlds. One was the ordinary level of ration lines and bus lines, of streets of rubble, of the blue trickle of electricity that allowed Fidel to flicker on the television screen, of oppressive heat that made her two daughters spread like butterflies on the cool tiles of the floor. The other was a deeper universe as real as the veins beneath the skin, of the voluptuous Oshun, maternal Yemaya, thundering Chango, spirits good and bad that brought blood to the face, taste to the mouth, color to the eye and dwelled in everyone if they were evoked. Just as drums carried a kola seed that was the soul of the drum, that only spoke when the drum was played, every person carried a spirit that spoke through their own heartbeat if they would only listen. So Ofelia Osorio carried the fire of the sun hidden behind her dark mask and saw with a penetrating light the double worlds of Havana.

This time Arkady found Olga Petrovna in a housedress and her hair up in curlers as she was organizing bags of food in the front room of her apartment. She gave him the pained smile of a pretty woman, an older woman caught by surprise. A fat little dove? Perhaps.

"A side business," she said.

"A healthy side business."

What had been a Russian nook was obscured by rows of white plastic bags stretched to the bursting point by Italian coffee tins, Chinese tableware, toilet paper, cooking oil, soap, towels, frozen chicken and bottles of Spanish wine. Each bag was taped and marked with a different Cuban name.

"I do what I can," she said. "It was so much easier in the old days when there was a real Russian community here. Cubans could depend on us for a decent supply of dollar goods from the diplomatic market. When the embassy shipped everyone home, that put a heavy burden on those of us who were left."

For a percentage, Arkady was sure. Ten percent? Twenty? It would have been vulgar to ask such a perfect Soviet matron.

"I'll be right back," she promised and slipped into a bedroom, which emitted a hint of sachet. She called through the door, "Talk to Sasha, he loves company."

From its perch a canary seemed to examine Arkady for a tail. Arkady peeked into the kitchen. Samovar on an oilcloth, oilcloth on the table. Calendar with a nostalgically snowy scene. Salt in a bowl, paper napkins in a glass. A sparkling shelf of home-bottled jams, pickles and bean salad. He was back in the front room when she returned, ash-blond hair brushed into place, primped in record time.

"I would offer you something, but my Cuban friends will be arriving soon. It makes them nervous to see strangers. I hope this won't take long. You understand."

"Of course. It's about Sergei Pribluda. You said the first time we spoke that some women on the embassy staff speculated because of the improvement of his Spanish that he had become romantically involved with a Cuban."

Olga Petrovna allowed herself a smile. "Sergei Sergeevich's Spanish was never that good."

"I suspect you're right, because he was so Russian. Russian to the core."

226

"As I told you, a 'comrade' in the old sense of the word."

"And the more I investigate, the more it's clear that if he did find a woman to admire that deeply, she only could have been as Russian as he was. Would you agree?"

While Olga Petrovna maintained the same bland smile, something defiant appeared in her eyes.

"I think so."

"The attraction must have been inevitable," Arkady said. "Perhaps with reminiscences of home, a real Russian dinner and then, because an affair within the embassy is always discouraged, the necessity to plan liaisons that were either secret or seemed accidental. Fortunately, he lived well apart from other Russians, and she could always find a reason to be on the Malecón."

"It's possible."

"But she was seen by Cubans."

There was a knock at the door. Olga Petrovna opened it a crack, whispered to someone and shut the door gently, returned to Arkady, asked for a cigarette and, when it was lit, sat and exhaled luxuriously. In a new voice, a voice with body, she said, "We didn't do anything wrong."

"I'm not saying you did. I didn't come to Havana to ruin anyone's life."

"I have no idea what Sergei was up to. He didn't say and I knew better than to ask. We appreciated each other, was all."

"That was enough, I'm sure."

"Then what do you want?"

"I think that someone close to Pribluda, who cared for him, probably has a better photograph than what you showed me the first time."

"That's all?"

"Yes."

She rose, went to her bedroom and returned a moment later with a color photograph of a tanned and happy Colonel Sergei Pribluda in swim shorts. With the warm Caribbean at his back, sand on his shoulders, and a grin as if he'd shed ten years. For Blas's purposes of identification the photograph was perfect.

"I'm sorry, I would have given it to you before, but I was sure you would find another one and this is the only good one I have. Will I get it back?"

"I'll ask." He slipped the picture into his pocket. "Did you ever ask Pribluda what he was doing in Havana? Did he ever mention anyone or anything to you?"

"Men like Sergei perform special tasks. He would never say and it wasn't my place to pry."

Said like a true believer, Arkady thought; he could see what a match Pribluda and Olga Petrovna had been.

"You're the one who sent the message from the embassy to me in Moscow, aren't you? 'Sergei Sergeevich Pribluda is in trouble. You must come at once.' It was unsigned."

"I was worried, and Sergei had spoken so respectfully of you."

"How did you manage to send it? You must need authorization to send messages to Moscow."

"Officially, but we're so understaffed. They rely on me to do more and more, and in some ways it's much easier to get things done. And I was right, wasn't I? He was in trouble."

"Did you tell anyone else?"

"Who would I tell? The only real Russian at the embassy was Sergei." Her eyes brimmed. She took a deep breath and glanced toward the door. "What Cubans don't understand is while we may not sing and dance as much as they do, we love just as passionately, don't we?"

"Yes, we do."

Certainly Osorio would never understand, Arkady thought. It was a relief to be away from the detective's steamy mix of revolutionary zeal and Santeria spirits, to be in a more solid world where post-Soviet romance blossomed over pickles and vodka, and motive could be measured in dollars and bones were left in the ground and murder made logical sense.

The sight of chicken thawing in a plastic bag seemed to bring Olga Petrovna back to earth. She heaved a bosomy sigh, twisted out her cigarette in an ashtray and in a minute became a businesswoman again, checking a mirror for the proper image of a sweetly gray grandmother.

On the way out Arkady passed a file of people waiting on the steps. From the top of the stairs, Olga Petrovna had a second thought.

"Or, maybe I've been here too long," she said, "maybe I'm turning Cuban."

20.

Ofelia parked the DeSoto near the docks for fear of blow- ing a tire. Havana had been the staging area for the treasure fleets of the Spanish empire. Over time silver and gold were replaced by American automobiles, which were replaced by Russian oil. All of this was handled in the warehouses of a barrio called Atares, and when the Soviet Union collapsed parts of Atares, like a half-empty vein, did too. One decrepit warehouse dragged down its neighbor, which destabilized a third and spewed steel and timbers into the street until they looked like a city that had undergone a siege, stone pulverized in heaps, garlands of twisted steel, not to mention the potholes and shit and doorways heady with the reek of urine. Ofe-lia had done invasion training in Atares and remembered how con-vincing it was to carry make-believe wounded across a landscape of collapse. It was no place you'd want to drive into.

The single building standing on its corner was the Centro Russo-Cubano. The center had served as a hotel and social meet-ing place for Soviet ships' officers in port and was designed like a three-story ship's deckhouse in cement with porthole-style win-dows and a red Soviet flag of glass set into the house at bridge height, although at this point the ship seemed to have sailed through bad weather and run aground, rubble piled around the steps, iron railings ripped off. Ofelia was surprised the doors opened as easily as they did.

Inside, faint rays of light fell from the windows into a lobby. A curved reception desk of Cuban mahogany was flanked by a girl in black marble cutting a brass sheaf of cane and, on the other end, a bronze sailor hauling a net. The cane cutter was barefoot, work clothes molded to her body. The sailor bore heroic Slavic features, and his net overflowed with fish. Russo-Cubano, indeed! Cubans had never been allowed in, this had been strictly Russians only. All the signs, RECEPTION, BUFFET, DIRECTOR, were in Russian. Through the dust Ofelia made out a floor mosaic of a hammer and sickle on a barely discernible pattern of blue waves. The only sign of recent life was in the middle of the lobby where a dull red ray of light reached down from the glass flag to a Lada with Russian diplomatic plates.

The sound of clicking drew her eyes up to a lightbulb hanging on a cord, to busts of Martí, Marx and Lenin decorating a mezzanine balcony and finally to a goat moving along the balcony rail. The goat stared down with disdain. Nothing but a goat could have climbed the stairs, blocked as they were by the ripped-out and abandoned cage of the elevator. No great loss, Ofelia thought. Since power outages began, people didn't trust elevators anyway. An extension ladder reached from the lobby to the balcony. More goats appeared.

At the steering wheel of the Lada sat a black man, his head twisted toward her, staring. When he didn't answer her or get out she pulled her gun and opened the door. Out sagged a rag doll, Chango, with a half-formed face and glass eyes, dressed in pants and shirt, a red bandanna around his head. She looked into the car. Red candles were burned down to waxy tears on the dash. From the rearview mirror hung a shell necklace and a rosary. The sound of a bell drew her attention back to the balcony, where a Judas goat pushed its way to the forefront of the other goats and stretched its neck to stare down. As a group they stiffened and, in a clatter of hoofs, scattered not at the sight of her, she realized, but someone else behind her.

Ofelia wasn't so much aware of being hit as plunging to the floor and then waking in a burlap sack, blind as a rabbit bagged for market. She'd lost her gun and a large hand wrapped tight around her throat as a suggestion not to scream. When the fingers relaxed, the sweet, milky scent of coconut burst into her mouth.

Sometimes, not knowing was better than knowing. Isabel's long-awaited E-mail from Moscow glowed on Pribluda's screen.

Dear Sergei Sergeevich, what a pleasure to hear from you and what a surprise! I should have written you long ago and told you how sorry I was to hear of the passing of María Ivanova, who was always so kind to everyone. You were blessed to have such a wife. I remember the day we came in off an assignment and were so cold we couldn't speak. We had to point at the frostbite on each other's noses. She made practically a banya in the bathroom with herbs and birches and steaming water and a cold bottle of vodka. She saved our lives that day. All the best people are gone, it's true. And now there you are in the tropics and I am still here but not much more than a librarian. But busy, every day someone wants to declassify this or that. Last week I had a visit from a lawyer of a Western news organization demanding I open the most sensitive archives of the KGB as if they were nothing more than a family album. Is nothing sacred? I say that with tongue in cheek but also seriously. We can no longer simply say, "Those who know, know." Those days are gone. However, promises made must be promises kept, that is my watch-word. Where society and historical truth are served by disclosure, where traitors will not be lionized or honor-able reputations destroyed, where innocent people who thought they were doing their duty in often hazardous circumstances are not victimized by new standards then, yes!, I am the first man to drag facts to the sunlight.
  Which brings me to this inquiry of yours about a for-mer leader of the Cuban Communist Party, Lazaro Lindo. In

particular, you ask whether Lindo was involved in a so-called Party conspiracy against the Cuban state. As I remember, Castro claimed that a circle within the CCP, feeling that he had led his countrymen down a path of adventurism, was conspiring with the USSR against him. True or not, the consequences were severe: strained relations between the Cuban and Soviet states, arrest and imprisonment of some of the most devoted Cuban party members, Lindo among them. Naturally, this was and remains a most sensitive matter. What you ask for is documentation that no such conspiracy existed or that, if it did, Lindo was not part of it. I understand this might allow his daughter to gain permission to travel. Unfortunately, I cannot satisfy you. But it was a wonderful surprise to hear from an old friend.

By the by, the entire country is a cheese full of maggots these days. You're well out of it.

Roman Petrovich Rozov
Senior Archivist
Federal Intelligence Service
Rozov@RRFISarch.org

Arkady printed the letter out to give Isabel, but it was clear that Rozov, Pribluda's old comrade-in-arms, as good as admitted both the plot and Lindo's part in it, and although Arkady didn't know Isabel well or even like her, he dreaded passing the letter on because he had recognized the desperation in the kiss she had given him the night before. Why kiss him otherwise?

The kiss angered him because it was a parody of real desire, her hard mouth clinging to him until he pushed her away. All the same, he asked himself, would a Cuban have rejected her? Would any warm-blooded man?

The other answer he dreaded was in the photograph he had extracted from Olga Petrovna, the picture that could conclusively identify the body in the morgue as Sergei Pribluda, yes or no. It was revealing how relieved he was that Blas had not been at the laboratory. Arkady had left the photograph rather than wait for the doctor to learn for a certainty that Pribluda was the body in the drawer.

Arkady folded the printout from Moscow to slip under Isabel's door.

How many sorts of coward could a man be?

She was inside a car trunk in a sack, arms tied at elbow level, more burlap sacking piled on top of her. Ofelia threatened and reasoned, but whoever put her in closed the lid and never said a word. A car door shut without the sagging of someone getting in. Steps walked away. White or black, she hadn't seen, but an inner part of her had registered his scent, the sound of his breathing, his speed and size, and she knew it was Luna.

She shouted until her throat was raw, but the sacks stuffed on top muffled her and she doubted she was heard more then ten steps away, let alone from the street. She decided to wait until she heard someone, although she didn't feel even the reverberation of a car passing the Centro Russo-Cubano. Well, who would drive there? She could as well have been at the bottom of the bay.

With every breath, sacking clung to her face, hemp and coconut shag filled her nose and mouth, and she became aware that with all the bags over her she'd already consumed most of the trunk's available oxygen. She'd never thought of herself as having an unusual fear of tight spaces. Now it took all her concentration not to hyperventilate and waste what air was left. She felt her gun under her but outside the sack, a particularly embarrassing tease. At least she didn't yet need to empty her bladder; she thanked God for small favors.

Irrelevant items came to mind. Whether the trunk was clean. What sort of dinner her mother was cooking for Muriel and Marisol. Something with rice. She started tasting tears as well as sweat.

Ofelia thought about the statue of the girl gathering cane. The hair was wrong, long and flowing instead of wiry, but the face was right, especially the eyes anxiously twisting up, surprised.

234

Depend on the Russians. There was no spare tire and the nut and bolt that usually held one down dug painfully into her back. She squirmed, trying to hook the bolt on the rope that pinioned her arms, but it was like twisting in a shroud.

He was more depressed by the possible identification of Pribluda's body than he would have expected. Originally he had refused the body simply to goad the Cubans into some sort of investigation, but now he found there was also part of him that at a more basic level irrationally and against all the evidence refused to accept the colonel's death. How could anyone so tough and ugly die? The man was a brute, and yet Arkady felt like a one-man funeral cortege, perhaps for selfish reasons. Sergei Pribluda was the person on earth he knew best and, in the colonel's way, one of Arkady's last connections to Irina.

When she had been wrapped in white on a gurney, her hair brushed, her eyes meditatively shut, her mouth relaxed into a smile the doctor reassured him it was normal to think that a loved one was still breathing. The cool chilled his sweat. He recalled Pushkin's lines how the lover

> . . . counts the slow hours, vainly trying
> To hurry them: he cannot wait.
> The clock strikes ten: he's off, he's flying,
> And suddenly he's at the gate.

This was the gate that would never open. He would return again and again, race and pant like a schoolboy, strain to see her breathe one more time and the gate would stay barred.

Did people die of love? Arkady knew a man on a factory ship in the Bering Sea, a killer, who had fallen in love with a woman, a whore who died at sea. He erased himself from the face of the earth by stripping off his clothes and plunging through the ice. The shock of the water on bare skin must have been incredible, but the man was immensely strong and kept swimming away,

away, away from the light. For murderers, senators, whores and good wives, love proved to be not the lamp at the ship's bow but the ship itself, and when the light was gone a person had no place to go but down.

Although Arkady was no expert in love he was an expert in death, and he knew the possibility of a relatively painless death for the diver. What killed expert swimmers practicing underwater laps in pools was not a strangling on water but the soft oblivion of oxygen deprivation. At the end they no more than gently stirred, even if in the last lit cell in their brain they were still stroking powerfully ahead.

Ofelia prayed. There was a panoply of spirits and saints that might help her if they only knew. Sweet Yemaya, who saved men from drowning. Meek Santa Bárbara, who changed in an instant to Chango wreathed in lightning. Ofelia's patron, though, had always been Oshun, not that Oshun had particularly helped in the past if husbands were anything to go by. However, the gods picked you more than you picked them, and Oshun was the useless god of love. Ofelia saw herself sometimes as a little dark boulder in the middle of a river of useless love. What she needed was a sharp knife. Unless she got out of the car trunk soon, she would asphyxiate and Blas would be tweezering hemp threads from the depths of her throat for the edification of new admirers. The image of herself naked on a steel table for the doctor's examination was bad enough, but she'd seen other bodies after a day or two in a warm car trunk, and the recollection was enough to make her saw the rope against the tip of the bolt whether it cut her or not.

She tried to think of music that would lend a vigorous rhythm to work to, but all that came to mind was a famous lullaby by Merceditas called "Drume Negrita" that whispered, "Go to sleep, my little black girl. If you sleep I'll bring you a new cradle and for your new cradle I'll bring a new bell. You are my favorite, my pearl, my beloved girl, so don't cry no more," though strangely enough the voice Ofelia heard was her mother's.

Floating in the dark above his bed the halo of the ceiling fixture put Arkady in mind of Rufo's white hat of woven straw, made in Panama with Rufo's gilded initials on the sweatband, which didn't mean anything to Arkady at the time because he hadn't connected it to AzuPanama S.A. Now he had to wonder what else he had seen in Rufo's room and not understood. The fact that neither Luna nor Osorio had come for Rufo's key suggested that they still hadn't tried the key Arkady had surrendered, and it was even possible that no one had been in the room since.

Was Luna waiting? Was Luna coming? Since the odds were even, Arkady slipped on his overcoat, his protective shadow, emptied the envelope of meager evidence into a pocket and went down to the street. He walked a block until he flagged a car. Arkady didn't remember Rufo's address, but he recalled the fading words on the wall next door and asked for the Gimnasio Atares.

"Te gustan los pugilistas?" The driver punched the air.

"Absolutely," Arkady said. Whatever they were.

Fighters. Next door to Rufo's the open-air boxing arena of the Gimnasio Atares had come to life, and Arkady got a glimpse over a line pushing through the gate of a ring illuminated by a hanging rack of lights. Spectators chanted, blasted whistles, rang cowbells under a layered atmosphere of smoke and orbits of insects. It was between rounds, and in opposite corners two black boxers shining with sweat sat on stools while their trainers convened like great minds of science. As the gong rang and every head craned to the center of the ring, Arkady unlocked Rufo's door and slipped inside.

There were some changes from his earlier visit. Bed, table and sink were in place. Rufo's Panama still hung on its hook, the photos of the boxing team still populated the wall and by the sofa was the same curious list of phone numbers for a man without a phone. The TV and VCR hadn't disappeared, nor the boxes of running shoes and cigars, but the minibar had disappeared.

With an eye for other souvenirs from Panama, Arkady once more went through the closet and drawers, shoes and cigar boxes.

The Rogaine came from a Panamanian pharmacy and a cardboard coaster came from a Panama City club, but he didn't find anything significant.

It seemed possible to Arkady that a man who memorialized a visit to the Eiffel Tower might have taped a trip to Panama. He turned on the television, slid a cassette into the player and at once turned down the volume of hyperexcited Spanish as on the screen two fighters pummeled each other around a ring under the auspices of their national flags. The tape had the blotchy color of old East German film and the jerkiness of too few frames per second, but he could make out a young, lithe Rufo hammering an opponent and, a moment later, having his glove raised by a referee. The next fight on the tape featured Mongo, and it occurred to Arkady how boxers were basically drummers, each man trying to establish his rhythm as *the* beat: I am the drummer, you are the drum. A dozen tapes were of other international tournaments, and another half dozen were instructional: proper ways to jump rope, work the bag, move without falling down.

All the other tapes had glossy sleeves with pornographic pictures and titles in different languages. Bringing sex films to Cuba seemed to Arkady like bringing pictures of pearls to an oyster bed. A couple of French videotapes had been shot in Havana and featured couples romping on deserted beaches—no one he recognized. One tape titled *Sucre Noir* had been shot on a rainy day. It featured interracial couples sporting in a living room decorated with cinema posters. Arkady was interested in the decor because he realized that he had been in the same room. Down to the stacks of photo albums, collection of cast-bronze bells, ivory phalluses arrayed by size, he recognized the apartment of Mostovoi, the Russian embassy's photographer. On the wall between the posters were the same framed photographs of friends in Paris, London, waving from a boat. He paused the tape. There was one more photograph that hadn't been up when he'd visited Mostovoi, five men with rifles kneeling around what looked like a dead rhinoceros, too unfocused on the tape for him to make out faces. Big-game hunters in Africa, a Hemingway-style memento given center stage in Mostovoi's collection. Why would Mostovoi hide that?

Someone was trying to unlock the door. Arkady turned off the VCR and listened to a key trying to force its way through the cylinder, followed by a low curse in a voice he recognized. Luna.

Arkady could hear him thinking. The sergeant probably had the key Arkady had given to Osorio, which worked perfectly well on Arkady's apartment in Moscow. Luna wouldn't know that; all he'd know was that keys didn't *stop* working, and either the lock had been changed or this was the wrong key. He'd examine his other keys. No, this was the key the detective had given him. Maybe he hadn't had to use it before. On Arkady's first visit he had closed the door but not set the latch and anyone could have simply turned the knob to open it. Someone had, since some items were gone and the latch had been set by the time Arkady returned, although setting it didn't necessarily require a key, just pushing a button on the lock plate, and this might be the first time Luna actually had to try the key.

For his part, Arkady became aware that the Gimnasio Atares was silent, the riot of whistles and bells over. Luna had been annoyed to see Arkady merely venture to the *santero's*. How unhappy would he be to find Arkady in Rufo's room?

The door jumped as a fist hit it. Arkady could feel Luna stare at the lock. Finally, feet turned away, accompanied by the sound of metal scraping stone. When Arkady cracked the door open, Luna was a block away under a streetlamp that had faded to brown. Two fighters in sweatsuits shuffled painfully out of the arena gate, followed by a trainer mopping his face with a towel. As they reached his door, Arkady slipped out in front of them, close enough to screen himself from Luna and merge his shadow with theirs all the way to the far corner. Focused on their own aches, the trio stumbled on. Arkady stopped and looked back.

Luna was returning. The sound of metal was an empty cart with iron wheels that he pushed to the curb outside Rufo's. The captain was in plain clothes and this time, instead of relying on the niceties of a key, he jammed his ice pick into the latch, applied his shoulder and the door swung open. The captain seemed to know what he was after, carrying out the television, VCR and boxes of running shoes to the cart. He rolled the load away, the wheel's grinding reverberating on either side. Despite the dim lights, with the cart's slow pace and noise Luna was easy to follow.

Somehow the sergeant was able to find more empty and desolate streets as he went, maneuvering the cart around mounds of broken stone, the sort of scene that made Havana appear an earthquake zone. Some warehouses had fallen in so long ago that palm trees leaned out the windows. The two men traveled about ten blocks before Luna stopped at the darkest intersection yet and let the cart stand while he positioned a board on the steps of a corner building, then muscled the cart up the makeshift ramp and through outward-opening double doors. Arkady heard the cart roll on stone and what sounded like the bleat of goats.

He followed up the steps. Somehow power had been fed to the building because in the vaulted dark was the ember of a hanging bulb. Luna had moved out of sight to a deeper interior; Arkady heard the cart progressing through a hallway.

He felt as if he had uncovered a Soviet mausoleum. There were the floor design of a hammer and sickle under the dirt, unlit sconces of red stars, busts of Marx and Lenin along the balcony, the difference being that instead of a sarcophagus in the middle of the floor there was a Lada with plates that read 060 016. Pribluda's car. And some lighter touches: at opposite ends of a counter of dark wood were two statues, black and white. The black figure looked too frail for the sugarcane she had cut, but the white was a Russian superman who had scooped the bounty of the sea—flounder, crab and octopus—in a single net. A tapping led Arkady to look up toward the mezzanine again. Between Marx and Lenin shone the gunslit eyes of goats. Dust stirred around the bulb. Although no one was visible in the car it shifted from side to side and not just as a trick of the feeble light.

The keys to Pribluda's car had been in Arkady's possession since the autopsy. He opened the trunk and felt a mound of burlap sacks. The bottom sack was heavy and tied with a rope. Arkady untied the sack and pulled it off while the goats bleated. Osorio raised her head, too stiff to stand. As he lifted her the front doors of the lobby swung open and a goat bell rang. Luna had returned not from the hall but through the same door Arkady had just used and the sergeant carried not a bat but a machete. He said some-thing in Spanish that pleased himself enormously.

Osorio pressed her mouth to Arkady's ear. "My gun."

He saw the Makarov in the car trunk. As Osorio hung on, he picked up the gun and cocked it. "Get out of the way."

"No." Luna shook his head. "I don't think so." Arkady aimed over the sergeant's head and squeezed the trigger. He needn't have bothered, the hammer snapped on an empty breech. Luna pulled the lobby doors closed. "This is justice."

Arkady put Osorio into the front passenger seat of the car and went around to the driver's side. Ladas were not known for their power, but they did start. In the coldest or warmest weather they started. Arkady turned on the engine and lights and, blinded, Luna stopped for a moment, then crossed the floor in two strides and brought the machete down on the car. Arkady reversed so that the blow landed on the hood, but Luna slapped the blade sideways and split the windshield into two caved-in sheets of safety glass. Unable to see, Arkady drove forward, hoping for a piece of the captain, only to hit the long counter head-on. The rear window crystallized as the machete swung through. Arkady backed up, cutting the wheel to sweep Luna away. The blade came straight down through the car roof, probed and vanished. Just when Arkady thought the Cuban was actually on the car, one headlight exploded. A ladder toppled, crushing Osorio's side of the car.

Arkady peeled off enough windshield to see. The falling ladder had grazed the bulb, and as the light swung, goats, stairs, statues swayed from side to side. He backed into a column hard enough to rock the balcony, shot forward and aimed at Luna, silhouetted by crystals on his shoulders. Missed him, but as the hanging bulb flared to life Arkady saw an electric highway of glass leading to the doors and followed. As the doors burst open, the Lada landed askew on the steps, righted itself and shouldered through debris. The left-front fender was crushed, and left turns seemed to be impossible. He drove toward the streetlamp, and when he was a block beyond he looked back through the gaping rear window to see Luna running after. Arkady pushed the car as fast as it could go until the sergeant was out of sight.

At last the streets ended at docks and the deep black and trailing lights of the harbor. Air blew through the windshield and windows and safety glass sparkled on their laps. The Lada limped over railroad tracks and finally swung into an alley, scaring the spangly green eyes of a cat caught in the headlight, and lurched to a stop.

A black hand swung around Arkady's seat and hit him in the chest. He grabbed its wrist and twisted in his seat to the figure of Chango. The man-sized doll had been riding in the back of the car, still wearing its red bandanna, still holding its walking stick in its other hand, its dark expression the glower of a kidnap victim. Ofelia aimed the Makarov, loaded or not, at the doll.

"*Dios mio.*" She let the gun drop.

"Exactly." Arkady got out of the car on weak legs.

He counted the gashes in the roof and sides of the car. The front was crushed, headlights empty sockets.

"If it were a boat it would sink," he said. "It will get you to a doctor."

"No." Ofelia said.

"To the police."

"To say what? That I've refused orders from the police? That I hid evidence? That I'm helping a Russian instead?"

"It doesn't sound so good when you put it that way. Then what? Luna will only follow us to Pribluda's."

"I know where to go."

Considering that Ofelia made the arrangements in the middle of the night, she didn't do badly. A switch from the Lada, Chango and all, to her DeSoto and then to a room at the Rosita, a love motel on the Playa del Este just fifteen miles outside the city and a block from the beach. All the Rosita's units were free-standing white stucco cottages from the fifties with air-conditioning and kitchenette, television and potted plants, clean sheets and towels at a price only the most successful *jineteras* could afford.

The first thing Ofelia did once they were inside was to shower the burlap and shag off her body. Wrapped in a towel, she asked him to pick nuggets of glass from her hair. He'd expected her curls to be stiffer, but they were as soft as water and his fingers never looked more thick and clumsy. Between the wings of her shoulder blades the skin was rubbed raw and seamed with grains of glass. She didn't flinch. In the bathroom mirror he saw her eyes on him and the natural kohl of their lids.

She said, "You were right about the photograph Pribluda took of you. I found it when I dusted his rooms for prints just as you said. I was the one who gave it to Luna."

"Well, I never told you that what Luna wanted from me was the photograph that Pribluda called the Havana Yacht Club. We're even."

"*Claro*, we're both liars. Look at us."

He saw an unlikely pair, a woman smooth as soapstone with a ragged man.

"What was Luna saying when he came back?" he asked.

"He said Rufo's television was warm, so he knew you were there. Why didn't you think of that?"

"Actually, I did."

"You followed him anyway?"

Arkady wondered, "Are you possible to please?"

She said, "Yes."

21.

She was a dark sprite, except that in bed she was a woman. Her breasts were small, tipped in purple, her stomach sleek down to a triangle of sable. He laid his mouth on hers, and it was so long since he had been with a woman that it was like learning to eat again. Especially when the taste was different, heady and strong, as if she were coated in sugary liqueur.

He was helpless in his own greed, working his way through the exquisite unfolding as Ofelia, his new measure, drew him in. There was something convulsive in this feast for the starving, who had taken the vow of hunger.

He would have said he cared for people, wished them well and did his best by them, but he had been dead. She would raise Lazarus and close her legs around him so as not to let him go. She kissed his forehead, lips, the bruises on the inside of his arm as if each kiss healed. She was hard and lithe and soft and certainly more artful and vocal than he was. This seemed to be allowed in Cuba.

Outside, he heard the ocean say, This is the wave that will sweep away the sand, topple the buildings and flood the streets. This is the wave. This is the wave.

On the bed Arkady arranged Pribluda's photograph of the "Havana Yacht Club," the AzuPanama documents, his chronology

244

of Pribluda's last day, list of dates and phone numbers from Rufo's wall. While Ofelia sorted through them Arkady took in a cement floor painted blue, pink walls with paper cupids, plastic roses in ice buckets and an air conditioner that gasped like an Ilyushin taking off. They had placed Chango in a corner chair, the doll's head resting heavily against a kitchen counter, hand balanced on his stick.

"*If* these documents are real," Ofelia said, "*entonces,* I can see why a Russian would think AzuPanama is more an instrument of the Cuban Ministry of Sugar than a genuine Panamanian corporation."

"It would seem that way."

Arkady told her about O'Brien and the Mexican truck parts, the American boots and the real Havana Yacht Club.

"He's a charmer, an intriguer, he goes from one story to another. It's like being led down a path."

"I'm sure it is."

He was distracted by the fact that all she wore was his coat and a glimpse of yellow beads. He hadn't noticed when she had put on the necklace. The coat was huge on her, and the sight was like finding a photograph of one woman in a frame that had always held a picture of another. Every second that it clung to her, it was exchanging auras of scent and heat and memory.

Ofelia knew. It was not totally true, but the charge could be made that once she had detected his grief she had suspected his loss, and once she had observed the tenderness with which he treated his coat and discovered the faint history of perfume on its sleeve, from that moment on she was determined to wear the coat herself. Why? Because here was a man who had loved a woman so deeply he was willing to follow her right into death.

Or it might be he was just the melancholy sort—in short, a Russian. But it had to be said that when she was in the trunk of the car, trussed, bagged and barely breathing, the one person she thought might save her was this man she hadn't even met a week before. *Muevete!* Ofelia told herself. Get your clothes on and run. Instead, she said, "In Panama almost anything can happen. O'Brien's bank is in the Colón Free Trade Zone of Panama where *everything* happens. Still, he has been a friend to Cuba and I don't see what sugar has to do with the Havana Yacht Club or Hedy or Sergeant Luna."

"Neither do I, but you don't try to kill a man who is leaving in a week unless whatever is going to happen will happen soon. Then, of course, everything will be perfectly clear."

In his disheveled way, in a white shirt, sleeves rolled, long fingers cupping a cigarette, he was Ofelia's picture of a Russian musician. A musician sitting by a bus stalled on the side of the road somewhere in the Urals. "Let me get this right. You're saying that Rufo, Hedy, Luna, everything that has happened so far is to cover up a crime that took place not in the past but hasn't even taken place yet? How are we going to find that?"

"Think of it as a challenge. The biggest advantage a detective usually has is that he knows what the crime is, that's his starting point. But we're two professional investigators. Between the Russian Method and the Cuban Method let's see if we can stop something before it happens."

"Okay. For the sake of argument, somebody's planning something and we don't know what. But you force their hand when you come here with a picture of Pribluda with his friends, the two car mechanics, at the old Havana Yacht Club, which, incidentally, since the Revolution, is the Casa Cultural de Trabajadores de Construcción, but that aside, Rufo tries to kill you for this picture. It would have been much easier to ignore you, so we will give some weight to that. Second, you force someone's hand again when you visit the Havana Yacht Club and Walls and O'Brien come out to take you off the dock and offer you some sort of employment, which, by the way, is too ridiculous to consider. Again it would have been easier to pay you no attention at all. Third, Luna beats you with a bat, but he doesn't try to kill you, maybe because he can't find that picture. Meanwhile, is anyone trying to kill you over AzuPanama? No. Trying to put the smallest hole in you over AzuPanama? No. Forget about AzuPanama, it's all about this picture," she said and stabbed it with her finger.

"That's one way to look at it."

"Good. But what this picture has to do with the future I don't know and neither do you. You just like to play games with time."

She was all too accurate about that, Arkady thought. She was right about a lot. "There are two ways back to whatever happened to Pribluda. One is Mongo and the other, I think, is through O'Brien and Walls."

"Well, your friend O'Brien is nuts if he thinks he's going to start a casino. Not while Fidel is alive. No casinos. That would be complete surrender. And let me tell you something else, two men like O'Brien and Walls are not going to share their fortune with someone who lands in a plane from Russia." Ofelia hesitated to ask, "Do you have a plan?"

"According to a note on Rufo's wall something about Angola is happening at the yacht club tomorrow night." He looked at his watch and corrected himself. "Tonight. We might drop in."

"Angola? What has Angola got to do with this?"

"Rufo wrote 'Vi. HYC 2200 Angola.'"

"This is some plan."

"I'd also like to find Rufo's cell phone."

"He didn't have one. In Havana cellular phones come from CubaCell, which is a joint venture between Mexico and Cuba. Anyone with dollars can get one, but I called CubaCell myself and they have no listing for Rufo Pinero."

"He had a phone, we just haven't found it. I'd like to push that phone's MEMORY and learn who his best friends were."

This was the way he was at the boatyard, Ofelia thought. Absolutely certain about something invisible. The problem was that she agreed. A hustler like Rufo was incomplete without a cell phone.

There was an explosion of laughter outside as a couple walked by to a different unit. Ofelia felt compelled to explain how she knew about the Rosita, the system of *jineteras* and police. From the Ministry of the Interior an officer like Luna could protect Hedy and a whole string of girls at tourist bars, hotels and marinas. The Rosita was safe because it was under the wing of the police in the Playa del Este. She added, "Luna also does things for his own protection. He and Rufo were involved together in political activities, silencing dissidents. Maybe some of those people are anti-Cuban but Luna and Rufo sometimes went too far."

"Did Mongo?"

"No."

"Captain Arcos?"

"I don't think so."

"And were they all involved in Santeria, too, like the ceremony I saw?"

"That was not Santeria." Ofelia touched her necklace. "Leave the spirits to me."

The second time was not as ravenous but just as sweet. Pleasure left alien for so long made the skin a sensual map to be explored in detail from an undercurve of the breast to the pink of the tongue to the fine hairs of her brow.

She had a variety of endearments in Spanish. He simply liked the name Ofelia, the way it filled the mouth and spoke of dreaminess and flowers.

The second time had a slow rhythm that rolled up the spine. He wouldn't know the beat but Ofelia did, the steady rocking of the tall drum, the sideways shake of the shells on the gourd, the quicker pace of hourglass drums and then the mounting acceleration of the *iya*, the biggest drum with the deepest pitch and in the center of its skin a red resinous circle that spread the warmer it grew until she felt herself stretched to the breaking point, breathless while he held on, his heart pounding like a machine that hadn't worked in ages.

"Now I know everything," Ofelia murmured. "I know all about you."

She laid her head on his shoulder. The oddest thing, he thought, was how well she fit. Staring up at the dark, he felt he was free-floating now, as far from Moscow as a man could get.

"What does *peligroso* mean?" he asked.

"Dangerous."

"A man said that at the Hemingway marina. We can start there."

. . .

In the dark Ofelia told him about the priest in Hershey, the town where she grew up.

The priest was not only Spanish but so frail that people said it was his cassock that held him up. He became a scandal, though, when he fell in love with the manager's wife. The manager and his wife were American. Hershey was American. There were two great smokestacks of the mill belching black smoke and the wooden shacks of the workers, but in the center of town was a road of shade trees and cool stone houses with screened windows for Americans, where only Americans or Cubans with work passes were allowed. There was a baseball and basketball team run by the Americans, and American women taught school for Cuban and American children. Both the wife and the priest taught school.

She had angelic blond hair that shone through the mantilla she wore to church. All Ofelia could remember about the husband was that his Oldsmobile always gleamed because it was always being washed. The problem in Hershey was the heavy soot that came from burning bagasse, the sugarcane after the juice had been pressed out. Bagasse burned very hot and produced soot as thick as fur. It was well known among maids who worked in the houses that the manager drank, and when he was drunk he hit his wife. One time when he came to school and began to drag her out, the priest stepped in between and that was probably when all three realized that the priest and the wife were in love. Everyone saw, everyone knew.

Then all three disappeared the same night. Weeks later when men cleaned ash from the furnaces at the mill, they found a crucifix and pieces of bone. They recognized the priest's crucifix from around his neck. Everyone assumed that the manager killed him and threw his body in the oven and took his wife back to the States and that was the end of it, except, a year later, someone came back from a trip to New York and said he had seen the manager's wife walking on the street arm in arm with the priest, who wasn't dressed like a priest anymore but just an ordinary man. Everyone else in Hershey laughed at this account because they remembered the priest, how timid he was. But Ofelia believed because she had seen that very same priest fight a bull.

22.

Ofelia had gone out earlier, and he didn't recognize her at first when she returned in skintight white jeans, white tube top and white-rimmed dark glasses, and carrying bags of coffee, sugar, oranges. She had a blinding new aura, he thought, like a nuclear reactor when control rods were withdrawn, and she had for him a shirt with the embroidered design of a polo player, short-brimmed straw hat, fashionable hip pack, sunglasses.

"Where did you find these?"

"There are hotels in the Playa del Este with dollar boutiques. It's your friend Pribluda's money, but I think he would approve, no?"

He picked up the shirt. "I don't think it's me."

"You have no choice. Luna has a picture of you. In case he circulates it, we have to make you look different."

"I'm never going to look Cuban."

"Not Cuban, no. If people can mistake a tourist for you, maybe they'll mistake you for a tourist."

The truth she admitted only to herself: that she had experienced a shameful thrill walking into boutiques with so much money. She had also added a new comb and brush to her floppy straw bag. Necessities for a certain role. And to dress a man was a pleasure she felt in the marrow of her bones.

She folded his coat over a chair. "We paid for two nights, we can leave your coat here for now."

The Playa del Este offered the overwhelming nothingness of sand and sea and houses wearing a sun-bleached memory of color rather than color itself. A billboard announced the imminent construction of a French hotel by a "Socialist-Leninist Brigade of Workers," and down the beach rose ranks of new hotels already built. Ofelia drove, and Arkady discovered that to ride in Ofelia's DeSoto, a vintage monster with wedge-shaped fins, was to be invisible. A white tourist with an attractive Cuban woman was instantly categorized and dismissed. For the first time, he fit in because there were examples of him and Ofelia everywhere, a tall Dutchman and a nearly miniature black girl sitting at a table under a single Cinzano parasol that constituted a sidewalk café, a Mexican with a blond *jinetera* taking the air in a bicycle cab, a beefy Englishman with a girl tottering on new platform shoes. Ofelia identified their nationality at a glance. What Arkady noticed was that each couple held hands but had no conversation.

"They each have a fantasy," Ofelia said. "He that he can leave his ordinary life and live like a rich man on an island like this. She that he will fall in love with her and take her away to what she thinks is the real world. It's better they can't communicate."

But Ofelia, too, felt a welcome invisibility in her dark glasses and jeans, in the attitude of her chin, and when they passed the plate glass of a gift shop she saw the reflection of a perfectly acceptable *jinetera* and tourist, perhaps slightly more handsome than usual.

At the approach of a Cuban girl the guard at the gate of the Marina Hemingway started from his box, only to step back in when he saw Arkady escort her around the barrier. He led Ofelia by the marina shop and across the grass to the dock where George Washington Walls had left him off after his visit to the Havana Yacht Club. The same loud volleyball game seemed to be in progress. Other Americans trafficked back and forth with bags of laundry. A boy in cutoffs hand-trucked cases of beer to a blue-water yacht the size of an iceberg, yet Ofelia treated the sight of three canals filled with million-dollar power yachts as offhandedly as Cleopatra reviewing her barges. Perhaps she was unimpressed, he thought, because of the Cuban girl suspended in a hammock from a sailboat boom.

"What's so dangerous here?" Ofelia asked.

"I don't know. You've been here before?"

"Once or twice. You go ahead. I'm looking for someone."

Among the sameness of fiberglass boats the *Gavilan* had a dark, distinctive silhouette, and Arkady picked it out at the slip Walls had been heading for when he was waved off by a harbor master yelling *"Peligroso!"* at snorkelers. There were no swimmers in the water now, and Arkady couldn't see any problem. The seaplane tender nudged peacefully against the tire fenders of the dock while lines fed electricity from a shoreside outlet box over the boat's brass rail. No swimmers, no shouts, only the deep throbbing of a motor yacht taxiing down the canal.

He continued along the canal, seeing no obstructions in the water, no flotsam by the dock. A galvanized pipe led water to each slip; a foreign crew was washing down a three-story megayacht, spraying one another, drinking the water, so it was even potable. American boats in Cuba made for an interesting community, grandiose white palaces mixed in with raffish fishing boats mustached with stains, all bending the law by even being where they were. Arkady had no experience on yachts himself, but having spent some time in Vladivostok around factory ships and trawlers, he knew a little about bringing power on board, and what caught his eye about the waist-high electrical distribution boxes spaced along the dock of the Marina Hemingway was how few had ordinary outlets to plug into. Instead, a power line led from the box while another led from the boat, and where they met the lines were spliced and taped together, the connection protected from water by a clear plastic shopping bag taped at the ends. He worked his way to an empty outdoor bar at the far end of the dock. Fully half the hookups he saw on the way went through spliced and bagged electrical lines sitting in water between the hull of the boat and cement wall of the dock.

The transom of the *Alabama Baron* was smeared with fish guts and scales, although the *jinetera* in the sailboat's hammock didn't look like a fisherman to Ofelia. The girl had the Julia Roberts look from the film *Pretty Woman*, very popular in Cuba, tons of hair, myopic eyes, pouty lips, and she was watching a bracelet being sold on a portable television connected to a small satellite dish bolted to the dock. Ofelia recognized the Home Shopping Network, also very popular in Cuba among those with access to dishes. The woman on the television laid the bracelet across her wrist to let the light play on the stones. The sound was off, but the price flashed in the corner of the screen.

"That's beautiful," Ofelia said.

"Isn't it? Good price, too."

"Diamond?"

"Same as. Last week, they had a chain for the ankle with the same stones. You think that's a good price, but wait." The woman on the television spread the bracelet on a bed of velvet and added a pair of earrings. "See, I knew. You order too soon and you don't get the earrings. You have to know to wait and then pick up your phone and give them your credit-card number and the bracelet's yours in two days." Julia Roberts glanced over. "You're new here."

"I'm looking for Teresa."

The television woman brushed back a mantle of hair to model the earrings, left, right, frontal. Another girl in a top and thong came out of the cabin. Her hair was almost as short as Ofelia's but peroxided blond. "You know Teresa?"

"Yes. Luna told me she would be here."

"You know Facundo?" The girl in the hammock sat up.

"I met him."

"Teresa's real upset," the blonde knelt by the rail and whispered. "She was next door when Hedy got her throat slit. They were close."

"She got run in, too," Julia Roberts said. "Some police bitch gave her a tough time. For helping feed her family, you know."

"I know," said Ofelia.

"Teresa's scared," the blonde said. "She went home to the country. I don't think she's going to be here for a while."

"Is she afraid of the sergeant?" Ofelia asked.

"You met the sergeant, what do you think?" Julia Roberts said. "With all due respect, what do you think? I just know him, but Teresa and Hedy were his private girls, understand?"

The blonde checked out Ofelia's vital points. "Aren't you a little old to be doing this? What are you, twenty-four, twenty-five?"

"Twenty-nine."

"Not bad."

"I-am-trying-to-sleep," a deep voice in American came from the bowels of the sailboat, and a form struggled up the galley steps. It had to be the Alabama baron himself, Ofelia thought. He wore a Houston Astros cap, shorts and a Hawaiian shirt that couldn't cover a sunburned belly that he salved by rolling a can of beer over its expanse. He loomed over the two Cuban girls on his boat. "Talk-talk-talk-talk-talk-Jesus-Kayrist-you-women-talk. Whoa," he said as he caught sight of Ofelia, "the talent contest may still be open."

"She's with me," Arkady said. He had worked his way back along the dock to the tender and the sailboat, berthed one behind the other. "We were just admiring the boats."

The baron glanced around at the beer cans on his deck until he noticed that Arkady meant the *Gavilan*.

"Yeah, sure, that's a fucking classic. A genuine rumrunner, everything but the bullet holes."

Rumrunner? Arkady liked that. That smacked of Capone.

"Fast?"

"I'd say so. You're talking a V-12, four hundred horses, sixty knots, faster than a torpedo boat. 'Cept with a woodie you spend all day at the dock sanding, varnishing, polishing."

"That's a drawback," Arkady agreed.

"No time to fish. Of course, *they* do all the upkeep for him here. He gets special treatment. Where you from?"

"Chicago."

"Really?" The Baron digested that. "You fish?"

"I wish I could. I don't have enough time."

"Locals keeping you otherwise occupied?" The baron's eye returned to Ofelia, who kept her face blank of comprehension.

"Busy."

"Well, it's a fish or fuck world, it really is. I'll tell you what, the last thing in the world I want is lift the embargo. Cuba is cheap, beautiful, grateful. Take away the embargo and it'll be 'nother Florida in a year. Hell, I'm a man on a pension, I'd hardly be able to afford Susy here." He pointed with his free hand to the girl in the hammock, whose eyes had returned to the shopping network and a new item, a clock in a crystal elephant. Arkady remembered Rufo's list of names and phone numbers. Susy and Daysi. Did the other girl peroxide her hair for a daisylike effect? Arkady could tell that Ofelia had caught the name too.

"What do you mean, 'special treatment'?" he asked the baron.

"The owner of that boat is George Washington Walls. Their hero. Hey, I was a fireman twenty years, I know about heroes. Heroes don't put a gun to no pilot's head."

"You're not just . . . ?" Arkady raised his eyebrows delicately.

"Racist? Not me." The baron waved his arm toward the *jineteras* and Ofelia as proof.

"For example, then?"

"For example." The baron was hot now. He hung on to a guy wire for balance and pointed to the hookup servicing the tender. "Check out the power lead installed specially for him just yesterday. Now, look at mine." Where the *Alabama Baron*'s lead dipped into the water was the typical splice in a bag that was filthier than the others. "I understand they're clever devils here and they got American boats and European boats with whole different electrical frequencies and they got to jury-rig a new line for every boat that hooks up, but I'm a fireman and I know hot lines and water. Get this lead in the water and spring a little leak and you will fry yourself some very surprised fish. All I'm saying is, how come Señor Walls has himself the only berth in the entire marina with a new power lead?"

"And if a swimmer was in the water?"

"Kill him."

"Heart attack?"

"Stop it cold."

"And there would be burn marks?"

"Only if he touched the line. I've seen bodies in tubs with a hair dryer, same thing. Look at her"—the baron gave Ofelia an approving nod—"like she understands every word."

The very statement that Teresa had gone back to the country made Ofelia believe that the *jinetera* was lying low in Havana in the rooms of her friends. Calling from the DeSoto, Ofelia tried the numbers Rufo had listed for Daysi and Susy, and when neither phone answered, Ofelia called Blas.

"It's not like a bolt of lightning but yes"—the doctor agreed with her—"if a live wire falls into water, there would obviously be a charge."

"How strong?"

"It depends. Submerged in water, power is diffused exponentially depending on the distance from the source. Then there is the size and physical condition of the victim, and the peculiarities of each individual heart."

"A fatal charge?"

"Depending. Alternating current, for example, is more dangerous than direct current. Salt water is a better conductor than fresh."

"Leaving marks?"

"It all depends. If there was contact, there would be a burn. Farther away, a person might only experience a tingle in his extremities. But the heart and the respiratory center of the brain are regulated by electrical impulses and an electrical shock can initiate fibrillations without necessarily causing trauma to tissue."

"Meaning," Ofelia said, "that somewhere between too near and too far to a live wire in water, a victim could suffer a heart attack and there would be no entry or exit mark, no burns, absolutely nothing?"

There was a silence at the doctor's end. Traffic rattled on the Malecón. Arkady seemed to be enjoying his cigarette enormously.

"You could put it that way," Blas finally said.

"Why didn't you say so before?"

"Everything in context. Where would a *neumático* encounter an electrical wire in the middle of the sea?" There was a burst of static and Blas changed the subject. "Have you seen the Russian?"

"No." She met Arkady's eyes with hers.

"Well," Blas said, "I notice that he left a new photograph of Pribluda for me."

"Have you matched it to the body yet?"

"No. There are other murders, you know."

"But you will try? It's important to him. You know, as it turns out he's not a total idiot."

Since they'd skipped breakfast, they stopped at a park table for ice cream. Huge leathery trees overhung a playground and a shooting gallery. Ofelia was going after Teresa and Arkady wanted to see Mostovoi's apartment again, but at the moment the detective looked like a movie star on the Riviera, lips pink with strawberry.

"We can meet here later and have ice cream for dinner," Arkady said. "At six? And if we miss each other, then ten o'clock at the yacht club and we'll see what that has to do with Angola."

Ofelia was suspicious. "What will you do in the meantime?"

"A Russian named Mostovoi has a picture of a dead rhinoceros I want to take a look at."

"Why?"

"Because he didn't show it to me before."

"That's all?"

"A simple visit. And you?"

"You said last night when you followed Luna he was pushing a cart of what looked to you like black-market goods. Well, what goods? Maybe they're still there. Someone has to see."

"You're not going alone?"

"Do I look crazy? No, I'll take plenty of help, believe me," Ofelia said. She looked very composed for a moment and then pulled down her dark glasses in shock.

Arkady turned to face two girls in maroon school jumpers. They had green eyes and hair streaked with amber and held cones of ice cream close enough to drip on his shoulder. An energetic gray-haired woman in a housedress and sneakers followed with a vengeance.

"Mama," Ofelia asked, "why aren't the girls in school?"

"They should be in school but they should see their mother from time to time, too, don't you think?" Ofelia's mother took in Arkady. "Oh my God, it's true. Everyone's meeting a nice Spaniard, a little Englishman, you found a Russian. My God."

"I just asked her to bring some toiletries," Ofelia told Arkady.

"She looks unhappy," Arkady said.

"Don't offer her your chair."

But the deed was done and her mother was settling in where Arkady had been.

"My mother," Ofelia muttered as an introduction.

"My God," her mother said.

"My pleasure," Arkady said.

With a pride Ofelia couldn't suppress, "My daughters Muriel and Marisol. Arkady."

The girls rose on tiptoe for his kiss.

"Where do you even find a Russian?" her mother asked. "I thought they were gone like the dodos."

"He's a senior investigator from Moscow."

"Good. Did he bring food?"

"They look just like you," Arkady told Ofelia.

"You dressed so nice." Muriel looked Ofelia up and down.

"Those are new clothes." Ofelia's mother took a second look.

"*No hablo español*," Arkady said.

"Just as well," Ofelia assured him.

"He bought them?"

"We are working together."

"Then that's different, that's absolutely different. You're colleagues exchanging gifts of esteem. I see possibilities here."

"It's not what you think."

"Please, don't disabuse me when I have hopes. He's not so bad. A little lean. A week or two of rice and beans and he'll be fine."

"Do you like him?" Marisol asked Ofelia.

"He's a nice man."

"Pushkin was a Russian poet," her mother said. "He was part African."

"I'm sure he knows that."

"Pushkin?" Arkady thought he heard something to hang on to.

"Does he have a gun?" Muriel asked.

"He's not carrying a gun."

"But he can shoot?" Marisol asked.

"The best."

"The target gallery!" the girls shouted together.

"They see you so little," Ofelia's mother said. "You shouldn't begrudge them a little fun, and your Russian marksman can show off."

The shooting gallery was a gutted bus on blocks, the back end replaced by a counter of air rifles that faced an array of American jet planes and paratroopers cut from soda cans. Behind them, on a black dropcloth, an artist had added cutout stars and comets and a vista of the Malecón with drivers shooting from convertibles. Sound effects were supplied by a tape of machine-gun fire. The sisters pushed Arkady into an open space at the counter.

"He should feel right at home," her mother said.

"Pump it." Muriel pushed the rifle into his hands.

"You have to pump it," Ofelia said as she paid.

"First the planes, first the planes," Marisol said.

The rifle was a toy with a tiny bead at the tip of the barrel. He fired at a particularly mean-looking bomber, and the paratrooper next to it jumped.

"What are you aiming at?" Ofelia asked.

"I'm aiming at everything."

The wrong target was the best he did. Kids around him made planes hop, spin, dance, but for all the shiny, dangling invaders every other shot of his thudded ignominiously into the backdrop.

"He must be high up in the police," her mother said. "I don't think he ever shot at anything."

The girls pushed a rifle into Ofelia's hands. She gave the lever two quick pumps and aimed at a big bomber from Tropicola.

"I think the bead's a little off," Arkady suggested.

The bomber pinged and spun.

"No, Mama," Marisol complained. "In the center."

Balancing her glasses on her forehead and tucking the stock more firmly against her cheek, Ofelia pumped and fired at a more steady pace. Silvery planes swung and paratroopers sang and danced. A comet, too, for good measure. The glasses dropped down over her eyes, it didn't matter, she had half the targets swaying at once. Arkady thought of the plane that had brought him less than a week ago, which now seemed an age. Here he was out in the open with Luna looking for him, but what better camouflage was there than a Cuban family? What could be more strange and more natural? Twelve hits with twelve shots earned Ofelia the prize of a can of lighter fluid that her mother tucked into a net bag. As she said, "Everything counts."

Appeased, the girls allowed themselves to be kissed by Ofelia and taken in hand by their grandmother, who dipped into her bag to give Ofelia a plastic toiletries bag and something wrapped in greasy newspaper. "Banana bread from Muriel's bananas. You remember the bananas?"

"I can't take this bread."

"Your daughters helped make it. They would feel much better if you did."

Muriel and Marisol made their eyes huge.

"Okay, okay. Thank you, girls."

A farewell round of kisses.

"Feed it to him," her mother advised. "And take care of him."

23.

What Arkady remembered of Mostovoi's accommoda- tions on the sixth floor of the Hotel Sierra Maestra was a runway balcony of parked tricycles and, within, a living room with movie posters, African artifacts, a plush shag rug, leather sofa and a balcony facing the sea. He also recalled a front-door lock and deadbolt, a sensible precaution considering the cameras and equipment inside. And in case he thought of rapelling athletically by rope from the hotel roof down to Mostovoi's oceanview balcony, he had noticed in Rufo's videotape *Sucre Noir* that the sliding glass door was jammed shut by a steel bar. Spetznaz troops knew all about swinging in through glass doors; Arkady did not. Also, the trick was not just getting in, it was getting Mostovoi out and taking another look at the photographs on the wall.

Mostovoi was correct in calling his hotel Central Europe. The café and boutique of the Sierra Maestra was Russian, the graffiti on the elevator door was Polish and the entire lobby was empty. Even the smell of rancid oil from the popcorn machine at the entrance stairs couldn't conceal a standing funk of cabbage.

The last time Arkady had visited, Mostovoi had switched a photograph of a sailboat for the safari picture. Or perhaps he had given away the rhino since filming *Sucre Noir*. Or gotten tired of seeing a dead animal on his wall. The safari picture, however, had looked like the exotic centerpiece of his private gallery, and Arkady wanted to see it on his own before Mostovoi could rearrange the pictures again. The idea was to get Mostovoi out in a rush.

Arkady may not have been a marksman or a commando, but one valuable thing he had learned was that fuel for mayhem was everywhere. Behind a door marked ENTRADA PROHIBIDA filthy drapes lay on a three-legged chair of black leatherette set between plastic bags of corn kernels and potato chips and containers of cooking oil. Arkady made sure the other lobby exits were unlocked before he carried the chair and drapes to the popcorn machine and returned for the chips and oil. He opened the containers and poured the viscous oil down the hotel steps, threw the drapes on the oil, added the bags of chips to the drapes and lit the last bag with his lighter. Rufo's lighter, actually. The plastic bag caught nicely and potato chips, dry and saturated with grease, were by weight about the best kindling on earth. The chair and drapery were polyurethane, a form of solid petroleum. Cooking oil had to get hot enough to vaporize, but when it did it was a hard fire to put out. Then he climbed the stairs to the sixth floor.

Arkady took his time. The alarm, an old-fashioned clapper on a bell, sounded before he was halfway up, and by the time he reached the stairway door on Mostovoi's floor and looked down, the blaze was a brilliant orange accelerated by the grease of the chips while darker flames lapped at the chair and drapes. Residents lined the balconies for the spectacle of motorcycle police leading a red fire-engine pumper and a tank. The hotel was only blocks away from Miramar's embassy row and Arkady had expected a fast response. A bald Mostovoi in shorts peeked out his door, ventured to the balcony rail with the other residents on his floor and jumped back before his door latched behind him. Spectators on the sidewalk scattered as the oil ignited with a orange whoosh all the way from the popcorn machine down to the street. The effect of shore breeze over the hotel created just enough vacuum to draw black smoke toward the building. Plastic silk floated up as a fireman with a bullhorn waved for the gawkers on the balconies to evacuate. Arkady stood aside rather than be stampeded by families rushing down. Mostovoi's flat was nearer the stairs at the other end of the balcony. He hopped out again in pants, shirt, toupee, camera bags slung every which way off his shoulders, shoes in hand, the dapper sort who hated to be hurried. Even as Mostovoi started down the far stairs Arkady walked to the door, pulling Pribluda's wallet from his new hip pack as he went. Burdened with gear, Mostovoi hadn't paused to turn the deadbolt, the door was only on the latch. Arkady selected a credit card; he'd seen this done in movies, but he'd never actually tried it. If it didn't work, he'd just wait for Mostovoi to return. He slipped and wiggled the card in the jamb as he turned the knob and swung his hip into the door. Three hits and he was in.

The apartment looked again like the residence of a middle-level Russian diplomat abroad decorated with souvenirs of a man who had seen much of the world, who cleaned for himself better than most bachelors, with an interest in books and the arts, who kept his own creative efforts under wraps. The photograph Arkady had noticed in the videotape was on the wall, back in its place between the pictures of a colleague at the Tower of London and a circle of friends in Paris.

It was a photograph of five men with assault rifles, one standing and four kneeling around a dead rhinoceros. Now he could see that the poor animal's feet were shredded and its stomach winking with shiny intestine. The men were not hunters but soldiers, one Russian soldier and three Cubans. Mostovoi, twenty years younger and balding even then. Erasmo, his beard mere boyish wisps. A coltish, skinny Luna cradling an AK-47. Tico with the bright, reckless smile of a leader, not the nearsighted focus of a man searching for leaks in an inner tube. And standing behind them in a safari jacket of many pockets, George Washington Walls. On the bottom border was written, "The best demolition team in Angola shows a fellow revolutionary their new mine-sweeping device." The rhinoceros's legs were pulp to the knees. Arkady considered the beast's frenzy of agony and confusion when it had wandered into a minefield, and he also thought of the callousness men develop in the midst of trying to stay alive. Tico and Mostovoi were on the ends of the group. By Tico's knee was the flattened pot of a pressure mine. By Mostovoi's was the convex rectangle of a claymore, an antipersonnel mine with the warning in English "This Side to Enemy." It was a good photograph, considering that Mostovoi had most likely set the camera's timer and run to take his place, considering the sharp African light, considering that mines were probably still all around. Arkady could almost hear the flies.

Arkady moved through the rest of the apartment before Mostovoi returned. On his first visit Arkady hadn't seen the autographed photographs in the hallway of Mostovoi with famous Russian film directors or the erotic boudoir series of Cuban girls that seemed to have been shot in his own bed. Arkady looked in the bureau, night table and under the pillow. A side table held a laptop, scanner, printer. The laptop denied him access as soon as he turned it on. The chances of hitting Mostovoi's password were remote. There was no gun in the drawer or under the bed.

Arkady walked farther down the hall into a small room redone as a darkroom with a black curtain inside the door. A red light was on, as if Mostovoi had been interrupted in the middle of developing. Arkady squeezed between an enlarger and trays of sour-smelling fixer and developer. Red film curlicued from a red clothesline. Held to the light, the film had nothing more than volleyball in the nude, and the developed pictures pinned to a board were embassy fare: Russians visiting a sugar combine, delivering postcards from the children of Moscow, pushing vodka on Cuban editors. The Russians, indeed, looked like *bolos*.

Back in the hall, Arkady had to push past more cabinets of photographs. He riffled through contact sheets of vacations in Italy, Provence. No nudes, no Africa. Finally in the kitchen he opened the refrigerator and found vichyssoise, an open can of olives, Chilean wine, canisters of color film and behind a bag of eggs a 9-mm Astra, a Spanish pistol with a tubular barrel. He emptied the magazine on the side of the sink, replaced the clip, wiped the gun and returned it behind the eggs. An empty ice tray sat in the sink. Arkady filled the tray with bullets and water and put it in the freezer before he sat in the living room and waited for Mostovoi to return.

Going by Rufo's sort of calendar—the urgency, that is, in trying to kill someone who would be in town for only a week—Arkady felt that time was running out. His time was. Tomorrow night he could be boarding his flight for home, he and Pribluda, but he felt he was still before the event, whatever it was that would make sense of the Havana Yacht Club, Rufo and Hedy, and the best demolition team in Africa.

Ofelia didn't bring anyone. Careful not to scuff her new shoes, she walked up the steps of the Centro Russo-Cubano, dropping her dark glasses into her bag with the banana bread as she stepped into the lobby, which had changed from the day before: the statues of the cane cutter and the fisherman had toppled facedown on the tiles, the ladder stretched by a splintered counter and no car sat on the lobby floor. Dust climbed the red ray of light falling from the stained-glass overhead. Centro Russo-Cubano? From what she knew of this place, when the Russians thought they led the way to the glorious future, it was a very rare Cuban who had ever been invited in.

She took a deep breath. Ofelia had come alone to see whatever Luna had carted in the night before because she didn't want to involve anyone else until she knew what evidence she could find. The PNR did not accuse an officer of the Ministry of the Interior lightly. That was her professional reason. The real reason was personal. Nothing humiliated Ofelia more than being afraid, and inside the trunk of the Lada she had been afraid to the point of tears. She took extra target practice at the Guanabo range just so that wouldn't happen. A dusty mirror hung over the counter. She caught sight of herself as she took the gun from her straw bag and swung, body and weapon moving as one dangerous little *jinetera*.

Being back in the lobby made her taste the hemp and coconut milk again. That was the way Luna had picked her up, like a coconut to be thrown into a bag and the bag tossed into a trunk. She'd tried to find the Lada on the way, and it had disappeared, perhaps already being cannibalized in an Atares warehouse. A shiny track showed where the cart's iron wheels had rolled over the floor tiles of a hammer-and-sickle pattern toward a grim corridor of cement walls and doors of Cuban hardwood.

Ofelia kicked the first door open, entered an empty luggage room, scanned with the gun and returned to the hall before anyone could approach behind her. The next door had the title of "Director" and promised to be larger and farther from the dim light of the lobby. She'd reloaded the gun but she should have brought a flashlight. She knew she should have thought of that.

This was the sort of situation where a person had to gauge what they were most likely to encounter. A sergeant of the Ministry of the Interior carried the same firearm she did, but a man from the Oriente might have more confidence in his machete. Also, he knew the layout of the Centro Russo-Cubano, she didn't. He could pop out of any corner like an oversized goblin.

Ofelia shoved the door with her foot, slipped in and crouched against a wall. When her eyes adjusted she saw that the office had been stripped of desk, chairs, rug. All that was left were a bust of Lenin on a pedestal and horizontal red-and-black stripes spray-painted on the walls, windows, across Lenin's face. She heard something move in the hall.

It occurred to Ofelia that perhaps she should have changed into her uniform. If the PNR found her dressed like this, what would they assume? And Blas? He'd think what fun they could have had in Madrid.

She slid out of the office on one knee aiming left, then right. Whatever it was had stopped, although Luna could be coming from either direction. This was a time when target practice paid off just for holding a heavy gun steady for so long. Banana bread was a ludicrous item to be toting and she considered lightening her load. But the girls had helped bake it.

The next office was empty except for corn kernels and feathers underfoot. She heard a step behind her again, tentative, hanging back, and she tried to get low enough to sight on a silhouette. She moved across the hall into what had been a meeting room with no table, no chairs, no windows, just a faint row of framed Russian faces and ships. She thought if there was more than one individual after her this was a perfect opportunity to lock the doors at each end and seal her in as effectively as entombing her.

Slower, she told herself, although she was blinking through sweat, mouth breathing too, not a good sign, and her shoulders ached from the weight of the gun. She was in the dark until she opened a door to a linen room, where the light poured through unbroken windows onto shelves that once held sheets and pillowcases still white, even the dust was white as talc. On the floor a headless white chicken lay in a circle of dried blood. She left the door open to illuminate the hallway and followed a sign that pointed to "Buffet." Checked into a pantry with nothing except lists on the wall in Russian of meat, dairy and starchy goods expected six years before. There was a note to a certain Lena, "Russian potatoes, not Cuban potatoes." Historical documents that faded as the linen-room door shut.

This was the darkest yet. Reentering the hall was like stepping into a pit. Nothing but black behind her, and nothing ahead but faint light tracing a buffet door. She could feel as much as hear the step behind her, it was that close. Her father had cut cane, she knew how cane cutters worked. First slice to the base, second high to lop off the cane head. Arkady had said Luna was right-handed, which meant that, constrained by the dimensions of the hall, a downward swing to the left. She got as small she could on the right side.

She felt breathing on her. A hairy face pressed against hers and she reached out to feel two stubby horns. A goat. She'd forgotten about the goats. The rest were gone or this was the only one that had found a way down to the ground floor. A small goat with a stiff beard, sharp ribs and an inquisitive muzzle that pressed into her bag. The banana bread, of course, Ofelia thought. She laid her gun between her legs, unwrapped the bread and broke off half. She couldn't see the goat but she could hear it devour the bread as if it hadn't been fed for days. The scent of the bread must have been an irresistible trail through the building. She was glad her Russian hadn't seen this.

When the goat tried to tear up the rest of the bread Ofelia gave it a not unkind kick, then scratched its scrawny neck to make amends. Growing up in Hershey, she'd had to deal with goats, chickens, voracious hogs.

Discouraged, the goat backed away with a tremulous baa, and although Ofelia expected it to go the way it had come and return to the herd, something seemed to pull it in the opposite direction. She couldn't see the goat, but she heard its hooves tap closer to the buffet door, to the ghostly smell of food six years past. It was a swinging door. The goat nosed it open, there was a glimpse of dingy light, enough to invite the goat and it trotted through. The door flapped twice, settled, and then flew open to flame and smoke.

Although she was shielded at the moment of detonation Ofelia's ears rang, her face felt scoured. Cement dust filled the dark hall, and devoid of both sight and hearing she swung the gun one way and then the other until the air cleared enough for her to make out again the faint light that traced the buffet door. She crawled forward, felt a cord hanging slack on its lower lip and pushed the door open.

It had only been a fragmentation grenade, Ofelia thought, but in close quarters it accomplished its mission well. Half the goat was close to the door, half well down the hall, like a botched job of being shot from a cannon. One wall was pocked from metal shards. Burn marks on the other showed where the grenade had been placed at floor level, the cord around its ring. Soft clots dripped from the ceiling.

Beyond, the hall opened to the buffet, where Russian sea captains and their officers had once been served cognac and cakes, and farther on she saw a large kitchen with a vent that someone from the outside had once tried to break through, bending a louver enough let a single finger of light pierce the murk.

She waited for the nerve to move forward. It would come any second.

Arkady missed the park rendezvous with Ofelia. He sat in Mostovoi's living room facing the door and flipped through the pages of an address book he had found in the nightstand. Pinero,

Rufo. Luna, Sgt. Facundo. Guzman, Erasmo. Walls. No Tico that Arkady could find, but otherwise the old team was all accounted for. Plus, Vice Consul Bugai, Havana hotels and garages, French film labs, many girls' names with notes on age, color, height.

Eight o'clock. Mostovoi was taking a long time to reappear. The emergency was long over, fire engines gone and residents returned to their apartments. He'd expected Mostovoi to enter, be surprised and affect outrage at the sight of an interloper. Arkady would ask him questions about Luna and Walls and pose them in a manner designed to make Mostovoi resort to the gun in the refrigerator. It was Arkady's experience that people who were upset were much more talkative when they felt they had turned the tables. If Mostovoi actually pulled the trigger, that would be information too. Of course, this scenario depended on Mostovoi's not carrying another gun in one of his camera bags.

Arkady only had to close his eyes for images to appear. Pribluda's Havana Yacht Club. Olga Petrovna's Pribluda and Pribluda's farewell snapshot of him. The best demolition team in Africa. The images we carry. Tribal people seeing photographs for the first time thought they were stolen spirits. Arkady wished that were true. He wished he had taken more photographs of Irina, but he saw her all the time whenever he was alone. Of course, being in Havana was like living in a faded, badly tinted picture.

Nine o'clock. The day had disappeared while he had waited for a man who wasn't coming back. Arkady carefully replaced the address book where he had found it, refiled the photos in their boxes and slipped out the door to the balcony, where tots up late raced tricycles back and forth. From halfway across Miramar the lights of the Russian embassy stared back. He took the elevator down. The popcorn machine was gone and the stairs were charred; otherwise it was as if he hadn't come at all.

Following First Avenue along the water, he put one foot in front of the other in the manner, he thought, of a sailing ship towed by rowboats when the wind had died. Not until he passed Erasmo's family house did he realize his legs were taking him to the rendezvous with Ofelia at the Havana Yacht Club. "Vi. HYC 2200 Angola." Tonight was the night.

Or maybe not. He was late when the royal palms of the yacht club's driveway came into view and Ofelia's DeSoto wasn't in sight at all. The club was black, the only lights two flashlight beams patrolling the long driveway. No sound except cars circling the rotary and the laugh of a bird nesting in a palm. This had been his brilliant idea, his chance to jump ahead of events. Whatever this event was, it was on a different Friday night. He looked for Ofelia on the other streets feeding the rotary. Although half an hour didn't seem very late in Cuba, she wasn't there.

A taxi stopped for him and Arkady dropped into the seat beside the driver, an old man with a cold cigar.

"A donde?"

A good question, Arkady thought. He had gone everywhere he could think. Back to Mostovoi's? To the Playa del Este and Ofelia? See, this was exactly the way he'd lost Irina, he reminded himself. Inattention. How else could a man miss not one but two rendezvous? In English he said, "I'm looking for someone. Maybe we can just drive around."

"A donde?"

"If we could drive around here, around the yacht club?"

"Where?" the old man took the cigar from his mouth, blew the word as if it were a ring of smoke.

"Is there an event nearby for Angola?"

"Angola? Quieres Angola?"

"I don't want to go to the embassy for Angola."

"No, no. Entiendo perfectamente." He motioned for Arkady to be patient while he pulled a stack of business cards from his shirt pocket, found one and showed Arkady a well-thumbed pasteboard card with an embossed tropical sun over the words "Angola, Un Paladar Africano en Miramar."

"Muy cerca."

"It's near?"

"Claro." The driver stuffed the card back in his shirt.

Arkady understood the routine. In Moscow when a taxi driver delivered a tourist to a restaurant, he had an arrangement by which he collected a little extra from the establishment. The same

270

in Havana, apparently. Arkady thought they'd just drive by in case the DeSoto was there.

The Angola was on a dark street of large Spanish colonial homes only a minute away. Over a tall iron gate hung a neon sign of a sun so golden it seemed to drip. The taxi driver took one look and kept on going.

"*Lo siento, no puedes. Está reservado esta noche.*"

"Go by again."

"*No podemos. Es que digo, completemente reservado. Cualquier otro día, sí?*"

Arkady didn't speak Spanish but he understood *completemente reservado*. All the same he said, "Just drive by."

"No."

Arkady got out at the corner, paid the driver enough for a good cigar and walked back under a dramatic canopy of ragged cedar branches. Along both curbs were new Nissans and Range Rovers, some with drivers sitting almost at attention behind the wheel. Along the sidewalk were shadows within shadows and the orange swirls of cigarettes used in conversation, voices hushing as Arkady slowed to admire a white Imperial convertible reflecting the neon sun. When he pushed the gate open, a figure materialized from the dark to stop him. Captain Arcos in civilian clothes, like an armadillo out of his shell.

"It's all right." Arkady pointed to a table inside the gate. "I'm with them."

The Angola was an outdoor restaurant set in a garden of under-lit tree ferns and tall African statues. Two men in white aprons worked an open-air grill and although Arkady had been told that a *paladar* could serve no more than twelve diners at a time there were, at tables arranged around the grill, easily twenty customers, all men, in their forties and fifties, most white, all with a bearing of command, prosperity, success and all Cuban except for John O'Brien and George Washington Walls.

"I knew it"—O'Brien waved Arkady in. "I told George that you'd show up."

"He did." Walls shook his head in wonder more at O'Brien than at Arkady.

"When I heard Rufo was so stupid as to write the place and time on a wall I knew you couldn't fail." O'Brien had another chair brought. Even the developer was in a Cuban guayabera; the evening's uniform seemed to be guayaberas. The two Cubans at the table looked to O'Brien for a lead; although they were hard, mature men, O'Brien seemed to have for them the status of a priest among boys. The entire restaurant had gone quiet, including Erasmo in a wheelchair two tables away with Tico and Mostovoi, their old comrade-in-arms, the only other non-Cuban. It was strange to see the mechanics so spruced. "It's perfect that you're here." O'Brien seemed genuinely pleased. "Everything's falling into place."

Walls said to the Cuban next to him, "*El nuevo bolo.*"

Relief spread to every face except Erasmo's. He telegraphed Arkady a glum look from across the garden. Mostovoi saluted.

"I'm the new Russian?" Arkady asked.

"It makes you part of the club," O'Brien said.

"What club is that?"

"The Havana Yacht Club, what else?"

Waiters poured water and rum, although coffee seemed as popular at the tables, an odd choice for the hour, Arkady thought. "How do you know I visited Rufo's?"

"You know George is a big fight fan. He went to see some sparring today at the Gimnasio Atares, and a trainer told him about a white man in a black coat he saw come out of Rufo's last night. George went in and there it was right on the wall, a clue no one as sharp as you was going to miss. Maybe you would, maybe you wouldn't. We have to be careful. Remember, I have been the target of more police stings and entrapment than you could dream of. By the way, keep in mind that all our friends here tonight still remember the Russian language. Watch what you say."

Walls ran his eyes over Arkady's new clothes. "Big improvement."

The chefs lifted lobsters from a huge sack to a cutting board, where they sliced and cleaned the underside of the tails before setting the lobsters alive onto the grill, poking them with wooden sticks when they tried to crawl from the flames. Arkady saw no menus, no African food. The two Cubans at Arkady's table shook his hand but offered no names. One was white, the other mulatto, but they shared the musculature, direct gaze and obsessionally trimmed fingernails and hair of military men.

"What does this club do?" Arkady asked.

"They can do anything," O'Brien said. "People wonder, what will happen to Cuba when Fidel dies? As a Caribbean North Korea? Will the gang in Miami march in and take back their houses and sugarcane fields? Will the mafia swoop in? Or will there just be anarchy, another Haiti? Americans wonder how without a managerial infrastructure full of MBAs Cuba can even hope to survive."

The lobsters were monsters, the largest Arkady had ever seen. They reddened among flares and sparks.

"But the wonderful thing about evolution," O'Brien said, "is that it can't be stopped. Eliminate business. Make the army the preferred career route for idealistic young men. Send them to foreign wars, but don't give them enough money to fight. Make them earn it. Make them trade in ivory and diamonds so they have enough ammunition to defend themselves, and you end up with an interesting group of entrepreneurs. Then, because it works cheap, when the army comes home make it go into farming, hotels, sugar. Reassign heroes to run the tourism and citrus and nickel industries. Let me tell you, negotiating a contract with a construction company from Milan is as good as two years at Harvard Business School. The ones here tonight are the crème de la crème."

"The Havana Yacht Club?"

"They like the name," Walls said. "It's just a social thing."

When the first lobsters were done, a chef stirred a glass bowl full of twists of paper, picked four twists, unrolled and read them before sending the lobsters to a table. It seemed to Arkady a better system for a lottery than a restaurant. How did the chef know who ordered what? Why were there only two choices, lobster or nothing?

"I thought private restaurants weren't allowed to serve lobster," Arkady said.

"Maybe tonight is an exception," O'Brien said.

Arkady caught sight of Mostovoi again. "Why am I the new Russian? Why can't Mostovoi be?"

"This is an enterprise that needs more than a pornographer. You've replaced Pribluda. Everyone can accept that." O'Brien adopted a forgiving tone. "And you can keep the photograph Pribluda sent to you. It would have been nice if you'd offered it as a sign of trust at some point, but you're on the team now."

"Rufo died for that picture."

"Thank God, I much prefer you. I mean, it's worked out wonderfully."

"Do some of these people work in the Ministry of Sugar? Are some of them involved with AzuPanama?"

"We met some that way, yes. These are the men who make decisions, as much as anyone can make decisions besides Fidel. Some are deputy ministers, some are still generals and colonels, men who have known each other all their lives and now in their prime. Naturally, they're making plans. It is a normal human aspiration, the need to better themselves and leave something for their families. The same as Fidel. He has one legitimate son and a dozen illegitimate children salted away in the government. These men are no different."

"The casino fits somewhere in here?"

"I hope so."

"Why are you telling me all this?"

"John always tells the truth," Walls said. "Just that there are a lot of layers to the truth."

"Casino, combat boots, AzuPanama. Which is real and which is fake?"

"In Cuba," O'Brien said, "there is a fine line between the real and the ridiculous. As a boy, Fidel wrote Franklin Roosevelt and asked for an American dollar. Later Fidel was scouted as a pitcher by the major leagues. Here was a man who could have been a model American, an inch away. Instead, he becomes Fidel. Incidentally, the scouting report was 'Fair fastball, no control.' At heart, my dear Arkady, it's all ridiculous."

The body in the bay was dead, Rufo was dead, Hedy and her Italian had been slashed to death, Arkady thought. That was real. The Cubans at the table listened with half an ear as they watched lobsters continue to march off the grill and the curious ceremony of reading papers at random from a bowl. It didn't seem to matter who had lobster so much as that they all did. Arkady had the sense that if one anonymous twist of paper was blank, if one diner hadn't ordered lobster, the group to a man would have stood and left at once.

"Do you mind . . . ?" Arkady nodded toward Erasmo's table.

"Please." O'Brien gave his blessing.

Tico was happily dismembering his crustacean and Mostovoi was caught sucking on a claw.

"You can't get lobster this succulent anywhere else in the world." Mostovoi wiped his mouth as Arkady dropped into a chair. There was no sign from the photographer that he had connected the fire at the Sierra Maestra to Arkady.

Erasmo didn't say a word or touch his lobster. Arkady remembered him drinking *ron peleo* and swaying in his wheelchair to Mongo's drum at the *santero's*, leaning out the Jeep like a bearded buccaneer as they cruised the Malecón. This was a more subdued Erasmo.

"So, this is the real Havana Yacht Club," Arkady said to him. "No Mongo, no fish."

"It's a different club."

"Apparently."

"You don't understand. These are all men who fought together in Angola and Ethiopia, who fought side by side with Russians, who shared a common experience."

"Except for O'Brien."

"And you."

"Me?" Arkady didn't remember the initiation. "How did that happen?"

Erasmo's head lolled as if he'd been trying unsuccessfully to drink himself into a stupor. "How does it happen? By accident. It's like you're in the middle of a play, say, Act II, and someone wanders onto the stage. Somebody new, never in the script. What do you do? First, try to get him off, drop a sandbag on him or lure him behind the scenery so you can hit him over the head with a minimum of fuss because there is an audience watching. If you can't get the son of a bitch off the stage what do you do then? You start incorporating him into the play, find him a role of someone who is missing, feed him some lines as smoothly as you can so that the Third Act goes virtually unchanged, just like you always planned."

The last lobster was delivered. Every plate was covered by a lobster or a well-picked carapace, although Arkady had noticed that many guests had shown no interest in their dinner once it had been served. A tall man with aviator glasses rose with a glass of rum. He was the same army officer Arkady had seen in a picture with Erasmo and the Comandante. The man proposed a toast to "The Havana Yacht Club."

Everyone but Arkady and Erasmo stood, although Erasmo raised his glass.

"Now what?" Arkady asked. "A meeting's going to begin?"

"The meeting's over." Erasmo added in a whisper, "Good luck."

In fact, men were leaving as soon as they set down their glass, not pouring out as a crowd but slipping under the neon sun to the dark of the street in twos and threes. Arkady heard a muffled sound of car doors opening and engines starting. Mostovoi vanished like a shadow. Tico pushed Erasmo, who leaned his brow on his hand like Hamlet considering his options. Soon the only ones left in the *paladar* were the staff, Walls, O'Brien and Arkady.

"You're part of the club now," O'Brien said. "How does it feel?"

"A little mysterious."

"Well, you've only been here six days. Cuba takes a lifetime to understand. Wouldn't you say, George?"

"Absolutely."

O'Brien pushed himself to his feet. "Anyway, we have to run. It's almost the witching hour and, frankly, I'm bushed."

Arkady said, "Pribluda was involved in this?"

"If you really want to know, come by the boat tomorrow evening."

"I'm flying to Moscow tomorrow night."

276

"It's up to you," Walls said and opened the gate. The Imperial glowed at the curb.

"What is the Havana Yacht Club?" Arkady asked.

"What do you want it to be?" John O'Brien said. "A few guys goofing off with a fishing line. A dump of a building waiting to be touched by a magic wand and be turned into a hundred million dollars. A group of patriots, veterans of their country's wars, having a social evening. Whatever you want, that's what it is."

24.

The DeSoto was parked outside the Rosita. Ofelia was inside on the bed, curled up tightly in the sheets. Arkady undressed in the dark, slid beside her and knew by her heartbeat that she was awake. He ran his hand over her breast and up her arm to the gun in her hand.

"You went back to Luna's place."

"I wanted to see what he had there."

"You went alone?" he asked and read her silence. "You said you would take someone with you. I would have gone."

"I can't be afraid to go into a house alone."

"I am, often. What did you find?"

She described the condition of the Centro Russo-Cubano, the lobby and each room as she had investigated them, the goat, the buffet door and the grenade that was wired to it. Also how she had picked her way through the aftermath of the blast into a buffet and kitchen without ovens, freezers or refrigerators, then retraced her route back to the lobby, set the ladder on the balcony rail and climbed to the mezzanine to search the rooms on that level, opening every door with the tip of a broom. There were no more booby traps, no goats, nothing but their droppings and open jars of Russian hair pomade that they had licked clean. By then their meeting time at the park had come and gone, and when she went to the Havana Yacht Club he never showed. She let go of the gun and kissed his mouth and released him slowly. "I thought you weren't coming."

"We just missed each other, that's all."

He gathered her in his arms and felt her slide down him. In a moment, he was in her and she wrapped herself around him. Her tongue was sweet, her back hard, and where he joined her she was endlessly deep.

They ate banana bread with beer while Arkady told Ofelia about his trip to Mostovoi's apartment, everything except the fire. Arson she might be a stickler about. He had to smile. She had sneaked through his defenses, a small bird on barbed wire. There was also pleasure—morbid or professional—in talking with a colleague. She was a colleague even though her point of view was not so much from a different world as from a different universe. She was a colleague even though she sat naked, cross-legged, in the haze of light produced by a power brownout.

"There are parts of Havana that haven't had electricity for weeks, although you won't read that in there." She pointed to the newspaper the bread had come in. On the front page was a blotchy picture of revolutionaries celebrating victory and a red banner that said *Granma*. "It's the official Party newspaper."

Arkady looked at the date. "It's two weeks old."

"My mother doesn't read it, she only gets it for wrapping food. Anyway, whatever Luna had to move—TV, VCR, shoes—he moved. It was gone."

"He tried to kill us in the car. He killed Hedy and her Italian friend if the combination of ice pick and machete is anything to go by; I don't think that's an everyday technique. And if he cleared mines in Angola he can rig a grenade. I think the least of his crimes is taking Rufo's VCR."

"He really only hit your side of the car," Ofelia said.

"What?" This was a new tack, Arkady thought.

"He only put me in the car trunk."

"He left you to suffocate."

"Maybe. You got me out."

"And then he tried to chop up the car."

"You mostly." This seemed like splitting hairs to Arkady, but Ofelia went on. "So, you went to the yacht club and didn't find me. What then?"

"I don't know exactly." He told her about the lobster dinner at the Angola *paladar*. "They were military types and they called themselves the Havana Yacht Club. How unusual is it for army officers to take over a private restaurant like that?"

"It's not unknown."

"Or have lobster there?"

"Maybe it was their own lobster. A lot of officers spearfish. The navy sells lobster, too. The officers don't eat so bad."

"They seemed unhappy."

"This is the Special Period—except for you and me, everyone is unhappy. What were they driving?"

"Sport utility vehicles."

"See!"

"But at least half of them didn't eat the lobster."

"That," Ofelia granted, "is strange."

"No speeches."

"Very strange."

"I thought so from what I know of the Cuban character. Also, Walls, O'Brien and Mostovoi were there. O'Brien described me to them as the 'new Russian' as if I was taking Pribluda's place. I feel something happened in front of me that I just didn't see. O'Brien is always ahead of me."

"He hasn't committed any crime."

"Yet." Arkady didn't quibble over the arrest warrant from America or the $20 million sugar scam of Russia. "Why would twenty highly placed Cubans call themselves the Havana Yacht Club?"

"A joke?"

"That was the answer for Pribluda's photograph."

"You think this is different?"

"No, I think it's the same. I don't think it was ever a joke."

"Did the officers at this dinner have names?"

"No names that I heard. All I can say is that they all wore guayaberas and ordered lobster on pieces of paper that had to be unfolded to be read. Some, like Erasmo, didn't touch their lobster at all, just watched, counting the lobsters, and as soon as the last one was delivered to a table dinner was over, as if they'd reached a unanimous vote. Maybe I'll find out tomorrow. I'll see Walls and O'Brien before I go."

"As long as you don't miss your plane," Ofelia said.

He knew she was studying him for a reaction about leaving. He didn't know what his reaction was. They were both so far out on a limb that the slightest shift made for dizzying sways. His eye fell on the newspaper her mother had wrapped banana bread in.

"What is Chango up to?"

"What do you mean?" Ofelia was not ready to change subjects.

He picked up the newspaper. It was a greasy broadsheet folded to a photo of a black doll with a red bandanna. Under the photograph a news caption read, NOCHE FOLKLÓRICA APLAZADA. *Debido a condiciones inclementes fue necesario aplazar el Festival Folklórico Cubano hasta dos Sábados más, a la Casa Cultural de Trabajadores de Construcción.*

"Inclement weather I understand and *Sábado* is Saturday and the *Casa Cultural* is the Havana Yacht Club."

" 'Because of rain a folkloric festival is postponed for two weeks,' that's all."

Arkady checked the newspaper's date. "Until tomorrow." He got up to look at the Chango sitting in the corner, the doll's left arm lank on a cane, feet sprawled, half-formed features and glass eyes returning Arkady's gaze. The more Arkady studied the doll the more convinced he was that it was the one that had disappeared from Pribluda's flat on the Malecón. Same red bandanna, same Reebok shoes, same baleful glare. "He reminds me of Luna."

"Of course," Ofelia said. "Luna is a son of Chango."

"A son of Chango?" Once again Arkady had the sense that any conversation with Ofelia had trapdoors that could open and drop a person into an alternative universe. "How do you know this?"

"It's obvious. Sexual, violent, passionate. Chango all over."

"Really?" He leaned to better see the yellow beads around her neck. "And . . ."

"Oshun," she said stiffly.

"I've heard of that one."

"You are a son of Oggun."

Arkady felt he was about halfway through the trapdoor.

"Go ahead, who is Oggun?"

"Oggun is Chango's greatest enemy. They often fight because Chango is so violent and Oggun guards against crime."

"A policeman? Doesn't sound like fun to me."

"He can be very sad. Once, he was so angry at the way of people, their crimes and lies, that he went into the deep woods, so deep no one could find him, and he was so silent no one could talk to him or could coax him out. Finally, Oshun went after him and walked through the woods and walked through the woods until she came to a clearing by a stream. She could feel Oggun carefully watching from behind the trees. She didn't make the mistake of calling out to him. Instead she began to dance slowly with her arms out like this. Oshun has her own dance, very sexual. When she felt that he was curious and moving closer she still didn't call his name. Instead she danced a little faster, a little slower, and when he came out of hiding she danced until he was close enough to her to dip her fingers into a gourd of honey hanging from her waist and she smeared the honey on his lips. He had never tasted anything so sweet in his life. She danced and filled her hand with honey and put more honey in his mouth and more honey while she tied him to her with a rope of yellow silk and led him back into the world."

"That could work."

Not honey but the sweet salt of her skin. No silken rope but her arms. No words but hands and lips, and Arkady was pulling her closer when Chango's cane scraped across the linoleum. The doll sagged forward, head askew, tipped in the slow fashion of a drunk releasing himself from the obligations of respectability, slumped off the chair and landed with a thud on its face.

"Some spell," Arkady said. It had been working on him. He swung out of bed, picked up the doll and set it in the chair again. Here was a figure that had followed him all over Havana, his shadow companion, and how he'd ever managed to get Chango to stay in the chair Arkady didn't know because the cane slid one way and the doll perversely slumped the other. "The head is just too heavy, it won't sit up."

Ofelia motioned Arkady back. "Leave it. It's just papier-mâché."

"I don't think so." The spell was broken. He lifted Chango and brought him to the bed, the better to see how the head was sewn to the shirt. "Are there scissors in your toiletry kit?"

Arkady pulled on pants and Ofelia slipped into his coat. Because the nail scissors were small, Arkady had to cut the threads one at a time to slide the head off a wooden stake that was the doll's backbone. He let the headless body roll onto the floor.

Ofelia asked, "What are you doing?"

"Looking into Chango."

He cut off the bandanna, leaving a red ring of cloth still glued. The head was papier-mâché coated with a lacquer-hard paint like a lumpish skull daubed black. Ofelia found a serrated knife in a drawer of the kitchenette. Arkady sawed through the head from ear, over the crown, to ear, until he pulled the doll's face like a mask off a layer of cheesecloth that had been formed on someone's face to lend the effigy its rough features. Under the cloth were crumpled newspapers, and under the newspapers was a flat oval of slick silver tape. In tiny snips Arkady cut around the edges and peeled the tape off five thick brown waxy sticks that said in English "Hi-Drive Dynamite." The sticks had been warmed and molded to pack tightly together with a Plexiglas backing in the oval space of the head. On the middle stick was a printed circuit board of a radio receiver the size of a credit card with a built-in kopeck-sized battery and antenna. Arkady prodded the board up. Its wires were crimped around the leg wires of a blasting cap inserted deep into the dynamite itself. In spite of the air-conditioning he felt a bloom of sweat. He and Ofelia had been around the doll on and off for almost a week. Someone could have pressed a remote transmitter and brought his Havana trip to an end at any time.

He put the scissors and knife aside. "Something nonsparking?"

Ofelia cradled the doll's head in her lap and delicately dug the cap out with her fingernails.

You had to admire a woman like that, Arkady thought.

25.

Enough daybreak sifted through the window shade for Arkady to see Chango lying on the table, the front and back of the head resting separately on the doll's chest. Disconnected, the face seemed more animated and malevolent than ever.

Ofelia was under Arkady's coat, asleep. He dressed in his old clothes, strapped on the hip pack and stole his coat as quietly as he could. This was the point where they went their different ways. As she said, it would be difficult enough to explain how she had come into possession of the doll. Having a Russian along wouldn't help.

"Arkady?"

"Yes?" He had already opened the door.

Ofelia sat up against the headboard. "Where will I see you again?"

They'd gone over this the night before. "At least at the airport. The flight's at midnight. It's a Russian plane and a Cuban airport, we should have lots of time."

"You're going to see Walls and O'Brien? I don't want you to go. To their boat? I don't trust them."

"I don't either."

"I'll be watching. If that boat leaves the dock with you on it, I will send a police boat out after you."

"Good idea." They had decided all of this already, but he returned to burrow for a moment in her neck and kiss her mouth. Love's exaction for forward motion.

"What about Blas and the photograph?" she asked. "I'll be see-ing him."

"Leave the photograph to me."

"And after?"

"After? We will shop on the Arbat, ski among the birches, go to the Bolshoi, whatever you want."

"You'll be careful?"

"We will both be careful."

Her eyes let go. Arkady slipped out into a morning with a dull pewterish light rimming the water, streetlights fading, on his way, appropriately enough, to see Sergei Pribluda's lover.

A block on, he encountered another SOCIALISMO O MUERTE! billboard with a giant Comandante in fatigues, shambling again in mid-stride, keeping pace.

Ofelia took a little longer to dress, tape the doll's head back together and take it in her straw bag to her car. It was eight by the time she reached the Instituto de Medicina Legal, found Blas in the autopsy theater and sent a message that she would be waiting for him at the anthropology room. No one was ever completely alone in that room, there were too many skulls and skeletons, pre-served beetles and snakes huddled in the light. On the desk a newly scrubbed skull was positioned under a video camera. She turned on the monitor, and a picture of a robust Pribluda at a beach emerged on the screen.

"Not yet," Blas said as he came in drying his hands with a paper towel. "No show until we have our other Russian. Detective, I under-stand you're dressed for a certain kind of duty, but I must congratu-late you for how convincing you are." She was in the white *jinetera* outfit. Blas threw the towel into a waste basket and ran his hands up and down her arms as if performing an inspection. "Irresistible."

"I have something for you," she said.

After all, who else could Ofelia go to? He was sympathetic and sophisticated, with connections at Minint, the army, the PNR well above the level of Captain Arcos and Sergeant Luna.

"A gift?"

"Not quite." She took the head wrapped in newspapers out of her bag and placed it in front of the screen.

"Well, I'm always interested." Blas pulled the paper off and revealed Chango's obsidian stare. The doctor's anticipation disappeared. "What is this about? You should know by now that my interest in Santeria is strictly scientific."

"But this head was on a doll that was in Pribluda's apartment. Later it was found with black-market goods in a building near the docks."

"So? I've seen hundreds of these dolls across the country."

Ofelia peeled off the tape that held the front and back of the head together. "Go ahead."

As Blas lifted the doll's face his own went whiter than usual. *"Coño."*

"Five charges of eighty percent dynamite. American-made, but we get it through Panama all the time for construction and making roads. There was a receiver and blasting cap that I removed. This is a bomb."

"That was at Pribluda's?"

"That was removed from there, I believe, by Sergeant Luna, who had also taken Pribluda's car and put it in an abandoned building in Atares, where this doll was recovered."

There was much Ofelia didn't have to say. In recent years incendiary devices had been set off at different hotels and discos by reactionaries from Miami. Just for the sake of terror. Then there was The Target whose name Ofelia was afraid to invoke, the leader who for forty years had dodged bombs, bullets, cyanide pills.

"This is a very grave matter. Does the sergeant know you have it?"

"Yes, he tried to stop me. This was two nights ago. I only learned it was a bomb last night. There don't seem to be any fingerprints on the outside of the head, but I think there are latent prints on the dynamite."

"Leave it to me. You should have come to me right away. When I think about that poor Hedy and you." Blas put down the mask to wipe his hands on his lab coat. "You're so cool about all this. Do you have the receiver and cap?"

"Yes." She brought them wrapped in newspaper from her bag.

"Better that I have all of the device. Who else knows?"

"No one." She was going to omit Arkady as long as possible. A Russian and a bomb, how would that look? Especially with those assassination files he had found on Pribluda's computer, it would muddle everything. The reason the doll's head was clear of prints was that she had wiped Arkady's off. "Except that we have to assume there are more people involved on Luna's side."

"A conspiracy in the Ministry of the Interior? Sergeant Luna is a nobody, this could go much higher. It's no wonder he and Captain Arcos refused to investigate. They're reporting to someone. The question is who? Who assigned them? Who do I call?"

"You will help?"

"Thank God you came to me. Detective, I have always said it, you are a marvel. Were you going someplace from here?"

"To the apartment where Rufo died." She didn't want to say where Arkady killed him, even if it was in self-defense. "It seems to me a hustler like Rufo must have had a mobile phone. Cuba-Cell has no listing for Rufo but—"

"No, no, no. Stay off the street. We must find someplace safe for you. You must sit and write a complete statement of all the facts while I cogitate how to approach this problem. The first call is the most important. Since we have the means of destruction, thanks to you, we have a minute to think. The safest place is right here. There's paper and pencil in the desk. You have to put down everything and everyone involved."

"I've written statements before, no?"

"You're right. The main thing is, don't move from here until I come back. Don't let anyone else in. Promise?" Blas eased the two halves of the head together, wrapped the head in newspaper and carried it under his arm to the door. "Just be patient."

Ofelia was surprised that her anxiety did not dissipate even when the doll was in competent hands. She found writing materials in a drawer as Blas had said, but discovered that she had become overly used to typing reports on PNR forms. Also, beyond the simplest statements of Luna's involvement with the doll it was difficult not to drag Arkady in. Questioning would even be worse. Who had identified the doll as being at Pribluda's? If Luna had attacked her, how had she escaped? Better a brief statement than either the complete truth or a lie. Once Arkady's name surfaced she knew that suspicion, hard earned by Russians in Cuba over so many years, would swing right to him.

Pribluda, proud of his tan, grinned from the monitor. The skull lay under the video camera. Chango and Russians, a terrible combination. Ofelia flicked the screen off and on. Why was she waiting? How would she get to the marina if she was kept in a room? She admitted she would feel easier once Luna was arrested. At the same time she had a niggling memory of the sergeant standing over Hedy at the Casa de Amor and how his entire body seemed to turn to stone. Which reminded Ofelia of Teresa, Luna's other special girl.

Between two jars of pickled snakes was a telephone. Ofelia opened her notebook and dialed Daysi's number. This time there was an answer.

"Yes."

"Hello, is Daysi there?" Ofelia asked.

"No."

"When will she be back?"

"I don't know."

"You don't know? I have this swimsuit of hers she keeps asking for. It's the suit with the Wonder Bra like she saw on QVC. She wanted it today. She's not there?"

"No."

"Where is she?"

"She's out."

"With Susy?"

"Yes." A little more relaxed. "You know both of them?"

"They're still at the marina?"

"Yes. Who is this?"

Ofelia said, "This is the friend with the swimsuit. I drop it off today or it's mine. Frankly, it looks better on me."

"Can you call tomorrow?"

"I'm not calling tomorrow. I'll be gone tomorrow and the suit will go with me and you explain to Daysi why she doesn't have the suit."

During the silence Ofelia could see Teresa Guiteras, hair tangled, knees up to her chin, chewing on her fingernails.

"Bring it over."

"I don't know where you are," Ofelia said. "You come here and get it."

"I thought you were a friend of Daysi."

"Okay, since you're a better friend, you explain to Daysi how she lost her QVC swimsuit. It's fine with me. I tried."

"Wait. I can't come."

"You can't come? Some friend."

"I'm on Chavez between Zanya and Salud, next to the beauty shop, in back and up the stairs to the roof and the pink *casita*. Are you near?"

"Maybe. Look, I have to get off the phone."

"Are you coming?"

"Well . . ." Ofelia drew the moment out. "You're going to be there?"

"I'm here."

"Not going to leave?"

"No."

Ofelia hung up. She signed her statement and tucked it under the monitor. She hated waiting. Besides, Ofelia still wanted to know why the homicidal Luna, rather than putting her in the car trunk, hadn't simply killed her, and to that question Teresa conceivably had the answer.

Vice Consul Bugai arrived at his office at a casual eleven o'clock, removed his jacket and shoes, replaced them with a silk Chinese robe and sandals. He poured himself tea from a thermos and stood, cup in hand, at his window, which was twelve stories up, waist level in the tower that was the Russian embassy. The green palms of Miramar spread to the sea. Satellite dishes lifted their faces to the sky. Outside, the city baked. Inside, the air-conditioning throbbed.

"So you do come to work on Saturdays," Arkady said from a corner chair.

"My God." Bugai spilled his tea and stepped back from the cup. "What are you doing here? How did you get in?"

"We have to talk."

"This is outrageous." Bugai set the cup on a stack of papers and picked up his telephone. In his robe the vice consul was the picture of an affronted mandarin. "You're out of bounds. You can't just break into people's offices. I'm calling the guards. They will sit on you until they put you the plane."

"I think they'll sit on both of us and put us both on the plane because I may be out of bounds, but you, my dear Bugai, have far too much money in the Bank for Creative Investment in Panama."

Arkady had once seen a militiaman, shot, take ten slow jerky steps before he sat and rolled over. That was the way Bugai moved as he set down the phone, bumped against the desk and dropped into his chair. He clutched his heart.

"Don't die on me yet," Arkady said.

"There's a good explanation."

"But you don't have it." Arkady moved the chair so that he was within arm's reach of Bugai. He said more softly, "Please don't make things worse by trying to lie. Right now I'm more interested in information than your hide, but that can change."

"They told me there would be bank security."

"You're a Russian and you thought there would be security in a bank?"

"But this was Panama."

"Bugai, concentrate. At this moment the affair is between you and me. Where it goes from here depends on your cooperation. I'm going to ask a few basic questions just to see how honest you're going to be."

"That you already know the answers to?"

"That doesn't matter. It's your cooperation that counts."

"It could have been a loan."

"Would pain help you concentrate?"

"No."

"We don't want to resort to that. Who wrote the checks deposited in your account?"

"John O'Brien."

"In return for?"

"For what we knew about AzuPanama."

"For what Sergei Pribluda knew about AzuPanama."

"That's correct."

"Which was?"

"All I know was that he was getting closer."

"To finding out AzuPanama was a fraudulent sugar broker created by the Cubans to renegotiate their contract with Russia?"

"In so many words."

"They were concerned."

"Yes."

"O'Brien and . . ."

"The Ministry of Sugar, AzuPanama, Walls."

"So Pribluda had to be stopped."

"Yes. But there were many ways to stop him. Include him, pay him, get him working on something else. I said I would have nothing to do with violence. O'Brien agreed, he said violence only attracts more attention."

"Except Pribluda's dead."

"He had a heart attack. Anyone can have a heart attack, not just me. O'Brien swears no one touched him."

Arkady walked around Bugai and the desk, viewing the vice consul from different angles. Despite the air-conditioning Bugai sweat through his robe at the armpits and lapels.

"Have you ever been to Angola?"

"No."

"Africa?"

"No. No one wants those postings, believe me."

"Worse than Cuba?"

"No comparison."

"Tell me about the Havana Yacht Club."

"What?"

"Just tell me what you know."

Bugai frowned. "In Miramar there's a building that used to be the Havana Yacht Club." He relaxed enough to dab his face with a handkerchief. "Quite a place."

"That's all you know?"

"That's all I can think of. One story."

"What's that?"

"Well, before the Revolution the old dictator Batista applied for membership in the club. He was complete ruler of Cuba, held the power of life or death and all that entails. It didn't matter, the Havana Yacht Club turned him down. That was the beginning of the end for Batista, they say. The end of his power. The Havana Yacht Club."

"Who told you that story?"

"John O'Brien." Bugai had a chance to look around his desk. "Why is my intercom on? I thought this was just between you and me."

Arkady motioned Bugai to follow. They walked out of his office and across a floor of empty desks to Olga Petrovna, who sat in a small workstation that she had tried to make pleasant with decals and pictures of her granddaughter. A voice-activated tape recorder sat by her intercom, and behind her stood a thickset man with the sort of face a person could grind knives on. Olga Petrovna, as it turned out, had missed Pribluda more rather than less as days went by, and the mere suggestion from Arkady when he had found her at a breakfast that another Russian had betrayed Pribluda's work was reason enough for her to introduce Arkady to the chief of embassy guards and set up her tape recorder.

"We were talking in private," Bugai said.

Arkady admitted, "I wasn't being entirely truthful. If I made any other mistakes, Olga Petrovna was making notes."

She had been. Pribluda's plump pigeon finished with a flourish and lifted to Bugai a gaze that would have done Stalin proud.

There were black angels bearing wreaths above the Teatro García Lorca. A black bat that roosted on the Bacardi Building.

Then there was the little black *jinetera* sitting on top of Daysi's pink *casita,* which was not much more than a water tower with a coat of paint.

For hiding out it wasn't such a bad place, nothing but chimney pots and pigeons all around. Since the water tank had been removed, water had to be hauled up by pail, but what Ofelia saw of the tower interior was surprisingly roomy, tiles on the floor, a bed adorned with paper flowers. Teresa had carried a chair and an illustrated romance up a ladder to the roof. Her knees looked scuffed and her curly mass of hair was misshapen, lumped to one side.

As Ofelia came up the ladder Teresa squinted down. "You have the swimsuit?"

"I'll show you."

"Don't I know you from the marina? The Malecón?"

Ofelia waited until she reached the roof before she lifted her glasses. "The Casa de Amor."

The scales fell from Teresa's eyes. She looked Ofelia up and down and tabulated the slim shoes, white rubbery pants, white top, wide Armani dark glasses. She herself was in the same bedraggled outfit she had been wearing when Ofelia arrested her. "*Puta,* look at you. I don't think you dress like that on a detective's salary, no, no, no. I'm not blind. I know competition when I see it. *That's* why you're always after me."

Ofelia's first impulse was to say, "*Stupida,* there are a thousand girls just like you in Havana." She looked down to roofs that spread to the sea, clotheslines bright as paper cutouts. Sparrows scattered by a peregrine. The pursuit swirled around the capital dome and to the trees of the Prado. Winter was hawk season in Havana. Instead she said, "Sorry."

"Fuck your 'sorry.' There's no QVC swimsuit, is there?"

"No."

"This is funny. I lost my German. I lost my money. You put me on a list of whores. I can't go back to Ciego de Avila because my family is depending on me to stay here and send them money, otherwise I would be in a fucking school, like you say. And now that you have fucked with my life you're a *jinetera,* too? That's funny."

"You're not on the list."

"I'm not on the list?"

"Not on the list. I only said that to scare you."

"Because we're competition."

"You're a smart girl."

"Fuck off." Teresa's nose ran, making a wet smear of her upper lip.

"Teresa—"

"Leave me alone. Go the fuck away."

Ofelia couldn't go away. Luna had gone insane at the sight of Arkady at the Centro Russo-Cubano, but the sergeant had only stuffed her in the car trunk when cutting her throat would have been as easy. Why?

"Sit down."

"Fuck away."

"Sit *down*." Ofelia pressed down onto the chair and moved behind her. "Stay there."

Teresa's eyes rolled back to follow. "What are you doing?"

"Be still." Ofelia reached into her bag for her new brush and comb and pulled back the black excelsior of Teresa's hair. "Just sit."

Waves, curls and spit curls close to the scalp and tight as springs would have daunted Ofelia if Muriel's hair weren't almost as thick. One pull wouldn't do, she had to firmly feather the hair out, work it loose, put some shape back into it.

"You have to take care of yourself, *chica.*"

To begin with, Teresa submitted with silent grimness, but after a minute her neck started to roll with the strokes. Hair like this warmed up with brushing, especially on a hot day, polished up like silver with a little attention. As Ofelia lifted the hair from the nape of the neck she could feel Teresa soften to the touch. Fourteen years old? Alone for two days? Frightened for her life? Even a stray cat needed to be petted.

"I wish I had hair like this. I wouldn't need a pillow."

"Everyone says that," Teresa murmured.

"That's looking better."

As Teresa relaxed, though, her shoulders began to shake. She turned to Ofelia and revealed her whole face wet with tears.

"Now my face is a mess."

"I'll cheer you up." Ofelia put the brush into her bag. "Let me show you what else I have."

"The stupid swimsuit?"

"Better than a swimsuit."

"A condom?"

"No, better than that." Ofelia brought out the Makarov 9-mm pistol and let Teresa hold it.

"Heavy."

"Yes." Ofelia took the Makarov back. "I think all women should be issued guns. No men, just women."

"I bet Hedy wished she had something like this. You know my friend Hedy?"

"I'm the one who found her."

"*Coño*," Teresa said more in awe.

When Ofelia put the gun away, she stayed kneeling and lowered her voice as if they didn't have the whole skyline of Havana to themselves. "I know you're afraid the same thing is going to happen to you, but I can stop them. You have an idea who did it or you wouldn't be hiding, no? The question is, who are you hiding from?"

"You really are police?"

"Yes. And I don't want to find you like I found Hedy." Ofelia let the girl contemplate that for a moment. "What happened to her protection?"

"I don't know."

"The man who protects you and Hedy, what's his name?"

"I can't say."

"You can't because he's in Minint and you think this will get back to him. If I get to him first, then you'd be able to leave this roof."

Teresa folded her arms and shivered in spite of the heat. "I didn't really think some *turista* was going to come here and marry me. Why would he want to take home some ignorant black girl? Everyone would make fun of him. 'Hey, Herman, you didn't have to marry your whore.' I'm not stupid."

"I know."

"Hedy was really nice."

"You know, I think I can still help you. You don't have to say his name. I'll say his name."

"I don't know."

"Luna. Sergeant Facundo Luna."

"I didn't say that."

"You didn't, I did."

Teresa looked away, as far as the angels that balanced on the theater. A breeze lifted her hair the same as it seemed to do to the angels'.

"He gets so mad."

"He has a temper, I know. But maybe I can tell you something that can help. Did you sleep with him?" When Teresa hesitated Ofelia said, "Look me in the eyes."

"Okay, once. But Hedy was his girl."

"When you slept with him—"

"No details."

"One detail. Did he keep his drawers on?"

Teresa giggled, the first light moment since Ofelia had found her. "Yes."

"Did he say why?"

"He said he just did."

"All the way through?"

"The whole time."

"Never took them off?"

"Not around me."

"Did you ask Hedy about it."

"Well." Teresa bobbed her head from side to side. "Yes. We were really good friends. He never did with her either."

"You know, *chica*, it wouldn't be a bad idea to stay here for another day, but actually I think you're probably pretty safe."

"What about Hedy?"

"I'm going to have to rethink that." As Ofelia gathered her bag and stood she kissed Teresa on the cheek. "You helped."

"It was nice to talk."

"It was." Ofelia started down the ladder and paused midway. "By the way, did you know Rufo Pinero?"

"A friend of Facundo's? I met him once. I didn't like him."

"Why not?"

"He had one of those mobile phones? Mr. Big-Time Jinetero, always on it. No time for me. So you really think I'll be okay?"

"I think so."

Because the question for Ofelia ever since Sergeant Facundo Luna hadn't killed her right off at the Russian Center was whether he was Abakua. It was hard to say about a member of a secret society. The PNR had tried to infiltrate the Abakua and the result was the opposite: the Abakua had penetrated the police, recruiting the most macho officers, white as well as black. Identifying them had become an art. An Abakua might hijack a truck from a ministry yard, but he would not steal even a peso from a friend. Never allowed an insult to go unanswered. Might murder but never informed. Wore nothing feminine, no earrings, tight belts or long hair. There was one conclusive identification: an Abakua never showed his bare behind to anyone. He never pulled his drawers down even for making love. Ofelia thought of it as a kind of Achilles' ass.

One more thing an Abakua never did.

He never hurt a woman.

26.

Arkady returned to Mongo's room in the back of what had been Erasmo's boyhood house. An empty house today, enervated by heat. After a courtesy knock on the door Arkady reached to the upper lip of the frame and found the key.

Not much had changed in the bedroom since Arkady's first visit. Shutters opened wide enough to take in the curve of the sea, fishing boats trolling against the current, *neumáticos* wallowing in their wake. Not a cloud in the sky or a wave in the water. Dead still. The coconuts, plastic saints and photographs of Mongo's favorite fighters were just as Arkady had seen before, and whether a sheet was tucked in the same manner he couldn't tell, but a different disc topped the CD stack, and the swim flippers that had hung from a hook on the wall and the truck inner tube that had been suspended above the bed were both gone. Arkady returned to the window to see three different groups of *neumáticos* listlessly paddling, each group at least five hundred yards apart from the other.

Arkady went down to the street and walked a block west to a café of cement tables set in the shade of a wall with the sign SIEMPRE—. *Siempre* something because bougainvillea had taken root and smeared the rest of the slogan with magenta. Arkady was not surprised that Mongo would venture out on the water. Mongo was a fisherman. He had probably been warned away from Erasmo's repair shop while a Russian investigator occupied the apartment above. Where better to hide than on the water? If he was out on his tube, sooner or later he would have to come in, somewhere along Miramar's First Avenue or the Malecón, too much ground for Arkady to watch. But it seemed to him that he could lower the odds by remembering that what a man with an inner tube needed most of all was air. From his table he had a view of a gas station with two pumps under a canopy styled with a modernistic fin, blue once, now the off-white found on the lip of a clamshell. It was a station on his Texaco map. By the office was a faucet and an air hose.

Cars came and went all afternoon, some struggling like lungfish up to the pump and then crawling away. *Neumáticos* had to deal with a garage dog that accepted some and chased away others. Arkady sipped his way through three Tropicolas and three *café cubanos*, his heart tapping its fingers while he sat, invisible in the shadow of his coat. Finally a skinny asphalt-black man approached the station office with an inner tube that was going limp in his arms. He threw the dog a fish, went into the office and came out a minute later with a patch he applied to the tube. When he felt the adhesive had set, he added air to check the repair. His clothes were a green cap, loose running shoes and the sort of rags a sensible man would choose for floating in the bay. Balancing the tube with its net and sticks and reels on his head, he lay his flippers over one shoulder and a string of rainbow-sided fish over the other. When he saw Arkady cross the intersection, the *neumático*'s red, salt-stung eyes looked for an avenue of escape, and but for his inner tube and the day's catch, he no doubt could have easily outrun someone in an overcoat.

"Ramón 'Mongo' Bartelemy?" Arkady asked. He thought he was starting to get a grip on Spanish.

"No."

"I think so." Arkady showed Mongo the picture of himself proudly displaying a fish to Luna, Erasmo and Pribluda. "I also know you speak Russian." It was worth a stab.

"A little."

"You're not an easy man to find. Join me for a coffee?"

The Elusive Mongo had a beer. Crystal beads of sweat covered his face and chest. His mesh sack of fish lay on the bench beside him.

"I saw a tape of you fighting," Arkady said.

"Did I win?"

"You made it look easy."

"I could move, you know? I could move with anyone, I just didn't like to get hit," Mongo said, although his nose was splayed enough to suggest he had been caught a few times. "Then when they dropped me from the team I was eligible for the army. *Oye*, suddenly I was in Africa with Russians. Russians don't know the difference between an African and a Cuban. You learn Russian fast." Mongo grinned. "You learn 'Don't shoot, you assholes!' "

"Angola?"

"Ethiopia."

"Demolition?"

"No, I drove an armored personnel carrier. That's how I became a mechanic, keeping that *puta* APC alive."

"Is that where you met Erasmo?"

"In the army."

"Luna?"

Mongo regarded his large capable hands, callused from drumming and scarred from barbs. "Facundo I know from way back when he first came from Baracoa to join the boxing team. He could have been a fighter or he could have been a baseball player, but he had no discipline with women or drinking, so he wasn't on any team for long."

"Baracoa?"

"In the Oriente. He could hit."

"He and Rufo Pinero were friends?"

"*Claro*. But what they did I didn't know." Mongo shook his head so emphatically his sweat sprayed. "I didn't want to know."

"And you were Sergei Pribluda's friend?"

"Yes."

"You went fishing together?"

"*Verdad.*"

"You taught him how to fish with a kite?"

"I tried."

"And how to be a *neumático*?"

"Yes."

"And what is the most important rule a *neumático* has to follow? Never go out alone at night. I don't think Pribluda went out alone on that Friday two weeks ago. I think he went out on the water with his good friend Mongo."

Mongo rested his chin on his chest. Sweat poured off the man as if he were a fountain, not the sweat of fear like Bugai's but sweat that came from the heavy work of guilt. It was late in the day. Arkady got more beers so Mongo could sweat some more.

"He said it was like ice fishing for sharks," Mongo said. "He used to tell me all about ice fishing. He said I should come to Russia and he would take me ice fishing. I said 'No, thanks, comrade.'"

"What time did you go into the water?"

"Maybe seven. After dark, because he knew how that would draw attention if people saw a Russian in a tube. Voices travel on water, so even when we were out there he would whisper."

"What was the weather like?"

"Raining. He still kept his voice low."

"Is that a good time to fish, when it's raining?"

"If the fish are biting."

Arkady considered that fisherman's truth and asked, "Where did you go in?"

"West of Miramar."

"Near the Marina Hemingway?"

"Yes."

"Whose idea was that?"

"I always said where we were going to go, except that time. Sergei said he was tired of Miramar and the Malecón. Sergei wanted to try somewhere new."

"Once you were in the water you stayed there. Or did you go west? North? East?"

"Drifted like."

"East because that's the way the current runs, by Miramar and the Malecón and towards Havana Bay."

"Yes."

"And, on the way, the marina? Whose idea was it to go in there?"

Mongo slumped against the wall. "So, you already know."

"I think I do."

"We really fucked up, huh?" Mongo beat nervously on the bench, stilled his hands and let the rhythm drop. "I said, Sergei, why would we want to fish in the marina with the *guardia* to chase us and maybe a boat moving through? That's an active channel, and it's night and the boats won't see us, I said, it's crazy. But I couldn't stop him. The *guardia* was in their office out of the rain. If you come in close they can't see you anyway, not at night in a tube. I followed Sergei up the channel, that's all I could do. He seemed to know where he was going. They have lights there, but they don't reach down to the water so well. No one was fueling. The disco was shut down because of the rain. We could hear people at the bar, that's all, and then we were in a canal where boats were docked one after the other and Sergei headed for this one I couldn't even see at first, it was so low and dark. Very sleek, an old boat but fast, you could tell. There were lights in the cabin and Americans on board, we could hear them but we couldn't see who. Right away, I knew that this was some kind of business of Sergei's he was getting me into. I told him I was going, but he wanted to climb up and see who was in the boat, which is difficult because there is an overhang on the dock. I was leaving when the lights on the boat went out. My whole body vibrated. Sergei was about five meters away between the boat and the dock and he was shaking, shaking, shaking. They let those fucking power leads lie in the water. I couldn't get any closer. Then I saw flashlights come up on deck and I hid." Mongo nodded in doleful self-judgment. "I hid. They came up to see if it was just their boat or everyone and while they talked back and forth to the person in the cabin Sergei drifted out. He wasn't shaking anymore. They didn't see him and they didn't see me because I stayed in the dark.

"As soon as his tube's clear, I told myself, I'd pull Sergei over, but before I could get to Sergei another boat came up the canal. There's not a lot of room. The boat went by and then Sergei went by. Sometimes, you know, boats trail tackle in the water, they shouldn't but they do, and Sergei was hooked by the net of his tube. He went by faster than I could keep up. I knew he was dead by the way he sat. They went out the canal together, the boat and tube. I knew once they cleared the *guardia* dock and opened the throttle they would feel the line and find Sergei or the hook would cut the net.

"Or maybe they would find Sergei and just cut him loose, because who needs to get involved with a dead *neumático*, no? That would be a story they could tell in a bar in Key West about a crazy Cuban they caught one time. I don't know, I just saw my friend being towed in the dark until I couldn't see him anymore. By the time I got past the *guardia* I couldn't even see the boat."

"Did you see its name?"

"No." Mongo drank the last of his beer and stared at the pail of fish. "I didn't even do that."

"Who did you tell about this?"

"No one until you showed up. Then I told Erasmo and Facundo because they're my *compays*, my good friends."

The water was flat and glassy enough for pelicans to skim their reflection. Despite the accumulated heat of the day Arkady felt oddly comfortable, balanced by beer and overcoat.

"The men who came on deck of the boat that lost its power, did you recognize them?"

"No, I was looking for Sergei or trying to hide."

"Did they have guns?"

"You know," Mongo said, "it doesn't matter. Sergei was dead by then and it was an accident. He killed himself, I'm sorry." Mongo looked at the fish. "I have to go keep these fresh. Thanks for the beer."

An accident? After all this? But it made sense, Arkady thought. Not only the heart attack but the general confusion. Murders had much better cover-ups. Then he had arrived from Moscow the same time the body was found in the bay. Small wonder why Rufo had rushed to be his interpreter, and why Luna had been so badly surprised by the photograph of the Havana Yacht Club. No one had known what happened to Pribluda.

As Mongo resettled his cap and inner tube on his head, and picked up his flippers and fish, Arkady thought of Pribluda's tow in his rubbery sleigh out of the marina to deeper water—the Gulf Stream, O'Brien had said—where he either tore loose or was cut free by a no doubt exasperated fisherman. "Cubans are biting tonight!" Would that have been the joke? Then the long journey in the rain, drifting past Miramar, along the Malecón to the mouth of the bay, a "bag bay," as Captain Andrés of the good ship *Pingüino* had said. Under the beam of the lighthouse on Moro Castle and then a swing toward the village of Casablanca to gently snag among the nest of plastics, mattresses and worm-riddled piers, all sheeted by petroleum scum, where a body could comfortably rest in the rain for weeks.

Arkady took Pribluda's photograph from under his coat and asked, "Who took this picture?"

"Elmar."

"Elmar who?"

"Mostovoi," Mongo said as if there had been only one photographer in the group.

Confession was always short-lived and always conditional, and both men knew it wasn't as if Arkady had the authority to question anyone. Just for the sake of a reaction, though, Arkady read the reverse of the picture. " 'The Havana Yacht Club.' Does that mean anything to you?"

"No."

"A joke?"

"No."

"A social club?"

"No."

"Do you know what's happening there tonight?"

That was pressing too hard. The Elusive Mongo backed into the street and broke into a gliding sort of trot, a one-man caravan, his headgear undulating with every step. He slid by a blue wall, pink wall, peach and the shadow of an alley seemed to reach out and swallow him up.

Ofelia had not been at the embassy apartment since she had seen Rufo spread out on its floor. She remembered the building's blue walls and Egyptian decoration of lotuses and ankhs, that hint of the Nile. In the dusk even the car sitting on the porch had some of the silent grandeur of a sphinx in residence. Flecks of paint made a red skirt around the car. Salt pitted once proud chrome, windows were open to the elements, upholstery cracked and split and the hood ornament was missing, but hadn't the sphinx itself lost a nose? And although they sat on wooden blocks the wheels were caked in grease, a promise that someday this beast would cough and rise again.

Ofelia was looking for Rufo's phone. Arkady had said that in Moscow a hustler like Rufo would have as likely stepped out of his house without a leg as without a cell phone. If this were a real investigation she could have taken a laundry list of names associated with Rufo to CubaCell and worked backward from their calls. Instead, she'd have to find the phone itself. It was somewhere. For killing someone with a knife, work that could get messy, Rufo had taken the precaution of changing shoes and wearing over his clothes a one-piece silvery running suit; Goretex let in the air, kept out the blood. Likewise, cell phones were delicate, dollars-only items, not something a careful man placed in harm's way. Rufo thought ahead, the trick was to think like him.

The door knocker to the ground-floor apartment was answered by a white woman in a drab housedress and flamboyantly coiffed and hennaed hair. Half the women in Havana, it seemed to Ofelia, spent their lives getting ready for a party that never happened. In turn, the woman made a sour study of Ofelia's *jinetera* gear until presented with a PNR badge.

"Figures," the woman said.

"I'm here to see the murder scene upstairs. Do you have a key?"

"No. You can't go in there anyway. That's Russian property, no one can go in. Who knows what they're doing?"

"Show me."

The woman led the way in slippers that snapped against the stairs. The lock on the apartment door was shiny and new even in the poor light of the hall. Ofelia remembered making a search of the sitting room, pulling out *Fidel y Arte* and other books, a sofa and sideboard, performing a more hurried look into the other rooms for fear that the confrontation between Luna and the Russian would get out of hand. There was a chance the phone was inside the embassy apartment, but not likely. She reached on tip-toe to the dark underside of the stairs above for any ledge that Rufo could have set the phone on. No.

"You didn't find anything here?" Ofelia asked.

"There's nothing to find. The Russians don't put anyone there for weeks at a time. Good riddance."

As Ofelia went back down the stairs she let her hand trail on the risers above. She stepped out onto the porch with nothing but a dirty hand.

"I told you," the woman said.

"You were right." The woman was starting to remind Ofelia of her mother.

"You're the second one."

"Oh? Who else?"

"A big *negro* from the Ministry of Interior. Really black. He looked everywhere. He had a phone, too. He called on it and didn't speak and just listened, but not to the phone, understand?"

Naturally, Ofelia thought, because Luna was calling Rufo's number and was trying to hear it ring. That was the trouble with trying to hide a phone, sooner or later someone would call the number and the phone would announce itself.

"Did he find anything?"

"No. Don't you people work together? You're like everything else in this country. Everything has to be done twice, no?"

Ofelia walked out to the middle of the street. It was a block of old town houses transformed by revolution, idealism followed by fatigue and lack of paint and plaster. One front yard a parking lot for bicycles, another an open-air beauty salon. Collapsing build-ings but busy as a hive.

She tried to imagine a reconstruction of the facts. The same street late at night. Arkady upstairs, Rufo outside in his freshly donned running suit, improvising on the run because no one had expected the arrival of a Russian investigator. Perhaps even plac-ing one last call before he went into the house and up the steps to what he assumed would be the Russian's doom. Between the two corners of the block, where was the most likely place for Rufo to put, just for a few minutes, his precious phone?

Ofelia remembered María, the police car and Rufo's cigars. She returned to the porch.

"Whose car is this?"

"My husband's. He went to get some windows for the car, and the next thing I know I got a letter from Miami. I'm keeping the car till he gets back."

"Chevrolet?"

"'57, the best year. I used to get in and pretend Ruperto and I were driving to Playa del Este, a nice cruise to the beach. I haven't done that for a long time."

"Car windows are hard to find."

"Car windows are impossible to find."

The upholstery was more a rat's nest than seats. From her bag Ofelia took a pair of surgical gloves. "Do you mind?"

"Mind what?"

With gloves on, Ofelia reached through the open window and opened the glove compartment. Within was a wooden cigar box with a broken Montecristo seal of crossed swords. Inside the box were ten aluminum cigar tubes and an Ericson cell phone set on VIBRATE instead of RING.

Ofelia heard a *click* and looked through the car at a man taking her picture from the sidewalk. He was a large, middle-aged man with a camera bag over a shoulder and the sort of vest with many pockets that photographers wore, all topped by an artistic beret.

"I'm sorry," he said, "you just looked beautiful in that old wreck of a car. Do you mind? Most women don't mind if I photograph them—in fact, they rather like it. The light is awful but you looked so perfect. Do you think we could talk?"

Ofelia put the phone in the cigar box and the box and gloves in her bag before she straightened out. "What about?"

"About life, about romance, about everything." Despite his size he made a show of coming shyly through the gate. His Spanish was fluent, with a Russian accent. "Arkady sent me. Even so, I'm a great admirer of Cuban women."

. . .

Arkady didn't set anything on fire at the Sierra Maestra and didn't knock on Mostovoi's door. Instead he inserted the credit card into the jamb the moment he arrived and hit the door with a grunt that took the breath out of a watching toddler. Inside, Arkady looked to see whether the "greatest demolition team in Africa" was still the centerpiece of the wall. It was.

On his first visit he had gone to pains to make sure Mostovoi wouldn't notice that he'd had any guests. This time Arkady didn't care. Where there was one photograph of the Havana Yacht Club there were bound to be more, because a man who documented his greatest moments didn't destroy his pictures when the wrong company came—he just put them out of sight.

Arkady took off his coat to work. He emptied shoe boxes and suitcases, spilled book and kitchen shelves, upended files and drawers, pulled the refrigerator from the wall and tipped over chairs until he had discovered more photographs, pornography that was not so sporty and not so sweet, and videotapes of sex and leather. But everybody had a side business, everyone had a second job. All Arkady really produced was the sweat on his face.

He visited the bathroom to wash up. The walls were tiled and the medicine-cabinet mirror was half silvered, half black. Inside the cabinet were a couple of nostrums, hair elixirs and recreational amounts of amyl nitrate and amphetamines. As he dried his hands he noticed that the shower curtain was closed. People with small bathrooms usually kept their curtains drawn for the illusion of space or a childish fear of what was on the other side. Since that was an anxiety Arkady freely admitted to, he pulled the curtain wide.

Floating in the tub in ten centimeters of water were four black-and-white photographs not of nubile sports or foreign travels but of the dead Italian and Hedy. Blood showed as black and the carpet and sheets were soaked and striped. The Italian looked almost gilled from machete wounds. Arkady didn't know him, but he did recognize Hedy even if her head balanced precariously on her

308

shoulders. At first Arkady thought that Mostovoi had gotten hold of police photographs, but of course these pictures had just been developed and none of the usual evidence markers had been laid, no shoe tips of detectives trying to stay out of the camera's way, and the darkness of the shadows themselves suggested that no other source of illumination had been on. The photographer had worked alone in a dark room the night before Ofelia arrived, and real skill must have been required just to estimate the focus. He'd only chanced four shots or only developed four from a roll. A single shot of the Italian as he dragged himself, still alive, toward the door. More thought had gone into the pictures of Hedy. A low shot from between her legs up to her head. A second that framed her head between deflated breasts. A third just of Hedy's face, surprise still fresh in her eyes. The man with the camera had been unable to resist marking the moment, thrusting his tubular white wrist and hand into the sheen of her curls to improve the pose.

27.

By eight o'clock the Marina Hemingway had the social
hum of a small village at night. Younger crew, an international set
with stringy blond hair, spread out in front of the market or carried bags from the ice bunker. From the far end came the amplified pulse of a disco, glitter and sound reflected in the canals.
Overhead an edge of the moon burned through the electric haze
of the marina. He didn't see Ofelia but she tended to be fanati-
cally good to her word.

The *Alabama Baron* was gone, replaced by a launch so new it
smelled of plastic. Already ensconced in its cabin was a *jinetera*
mixing rum and Coke. Ahead, George Washington Walls and John
O'Brien were having beers in the cockpit of the *Gavilan*, firebrand
and financier at their ease. The new lead from the power box
snaked smoothly down to the water and up the dark flank of the
seaplane tender.

"You're here." Walls looked up at Arkady.

"Right on time, too," O'Brien said. "Wonderful. Back into your
cashmere coat, I see. Join us."

"I have a plane to catch. You said we were going to talk about
Pribluda."

"A plane to catch?" O'Brien said. "That is sad. This means you
are turning down the chance to be part of our endeavor? I have
always counted myself as fairly persuasive. Apparently with you
I've failed."

"The man is a disappointment," Walls said. "That's what Isabel says."

"Arkady, I was hoping to persuade you because I sincerely thought it was for your own good. I had looked forward to working with you. Come on, have a drink for God's sake. We'll have an Irish good-bye. Your plane's at midnight?"

"Yes."

Walls said, "You've got hours."

Arkady stepped out of the light and down into the boat, settling against a cockpit cushion. Instantly a cold can of beer was in his hand. At night the boat seemed to ride even lower, the polished mahogany dark as the water.

O'Brien said, "You're taking back the body of your friend Pribluda? That means you've positively identified him?"

"No."

"Because you don't need to anymore, you already know."

"I think so."

"Well, that's a comfort. Your decision to go is final? What we can do"—O'Brien tapped Arkady's knee—"is give you a return ticket. Take a week in Moscow, in that miserable ice chest you call home, and if you change your mind come back. Is that fair?"

"More than fair, but I think I've made up my mind."

"Why?" Walls asked.

O'Brien said, "Because he found what he came for, I suppose. Is that it, Arkady?"

"Pretty much."

"To a single-minded man." O'Brien raised his beer. "To the man in the coat."

The beer was good, far better than Russian. On the dock a line of *jiniteras* slipped quietly as mice toward the disco, lamplight haloing their hair. It was Saturday night, after all. The salsa accelerated. Walls balanced on the captain's chair in a black pullover that reminded Arkady of the sleek young radical who had stepped out of a plane with a gun and a burning flag. O'Brien wore his black jumpsuit. Pirate colors. He unwrapped a cigar and turned its tip over a flame, drawing it in. The boats in their slips sighed as a ripple of water lifted them.

O'Brien said, "You know what happened to Pribluda, but you don't know why? And I'm the only one who hasn't had a say?"

"You say a lot, but it's different every time."

"Then I won't tell you, I'll show you. See that seabag?"

Although the cabin was dark, Arkady saw one end of a canvas bag in the light at the bottom of the steps.

"Sergei's," Walls said.

Arkady was nearest. He put down the beer and went down the cabin stairs. As he picked up the bag the door shut and locked behind him. The inboard engine started in the space ahead, producing a reverberation like being inside a double bass. Overhead, feet nimbly stepped fore and aft, releasing lines and gathering fenders. The *Gavilan* backed, swung and eased forward. As the boat passed the disco, laughter and strobe lights flickered on the curtains. Canal echo dropped behind, and Arkady heard Walls talking on the radio. Arkady beat on the door more for form than conviction; a boat as classic as this was built of hardwood. He moved around a galley table to an engine-room door that was locked as well. He pulled aside a porthole curtain just in time to see the *guardia* dock slide by with no sign yet that Ofelia had raised an alarm. Past the dock the brass bow of the *Gavilan* sliced its way so smoothly Arkady felt no more than the faintest rise and fall, headed directly to sea by the evenness of wave slap.

Along Fifth Avenue were the first signs of a major event: *brigada* trucks of huddled Interior troops parked in the night dark of side streets, motorcycle policemen in white helmets and spurred boots straddling their bikes, K9 units sniffing the crowd that filed up the driveway of the Construction Union House, the former Havana Yacht Club. Ofelia's PNR badge didn't work, but Mostovoi somehow produced a pass that let them through.

There were telltale signs that the Noche Folklórica was a more important event than she had expected. A feature of national security was that no one ever knew which of his residences the Comandante would sleep in, let alone what functions he would attend. However, when he did appear certain precautions were always taken. Tracks led on the lawn to seven armored Mercedes, an ambulance, a radio command truck, a media van, two dog vans, a circle of soldiers and a cordon of men in shirts and windbreakers holding newspapers folded over cell phones and radios and standing around for no apparent purpose until a guest deviated from the driveway. The house's two grand stairways met at a central porch. From there, under the molding of a ship's wheel on a pennant, soldiers scanned the crowd, although this was not, to Ofelia, a group that was likely to get out of hand. Some officially approved Santeria priests were on hand, but mostly she saw stiff ministry and military types and their spouses following the designated route around the mansion to the oceanfront side. The occasional man was patted down or a woman stopped to have her purse searched, but Mostovoi and Ofelia were waved through, and despite his camera bag the photographer pushed so quickly through the crowd she could barely keep up.

"Why would Arkady want to meet here?" Ofelia demanded. "How would he even get in?"

"He's been here before," Mostovoi said. "He gets around."

The Noche Folklórica was an event Arkady had asked about, Ofelia knew. If he had changed his mind about talking to O'Brien and Walls, that was just as well. She saw the colors of dancers sequestered behind spiky palms: blue for Yemaya, yellow for Oshun. Spaced along the beach were soldiers. Tied to the end of the dock was a black patrol boat. All the light and all the sound was concentrated on an outdoor stage facing the water. The Noche Folklórica had already begun, and from the clubhouse balconies men in plain clothes scanned the crowd. Most people stood on the patio around the stage, but there was also a reviewing stand with five tiers of special guests. She knew only the figure in the middle of the front row, a man with a flat, nearly Greek profile set in wiry gray hair and beard, the face that was the second sun of her lifetime. Beside him was an empty chair.

· · ·

The doors opened and O'Brien peeked through to say, "Come on. It's too lovely a night to miss."

Arkady marched up. This far out the cockpit sat under a canopy of stars. Walls steered parallel to the shore, running at dead slow. Besides his cigar O'Brien also held, casually but not negligently, a pistol with a barrel extended by a silencer. The marina had passed from sight, but approaching on the Miramar shore was a far brighter nexus of excitement and music. Arkady recognized the Havana Yacht Club brilliant in floodlights. On the patio leading down to the beach a crowd surrounded a stage and reviewing stand.

Along with floodlights the yacht club displayed the colored lights of carnival, although the club's twin docks were empty and only a black patrol boat had tied up to enjoy the spectacle. As the *Gavilan* drew closer Walls slipped forward to snap covers over the running lights and John O'Brien dropped his cigar into the water.

"Quite a show." He handed Arkady a set of heavy binoculars. "Now your trip to Cuba is complete."

The glasses were 20x Zeiss with a matte metal body, and through them the scene at the yacht club meters leaped into view. Spectators filled two levels of the patio. A troupe of women in yellow scarves and skirts ascended the stage while a band filled the time with a percussive rhythm, whistles, bells clearly audible even from the *Gavilan*. Arkady zoomed in on the reviewing stand, on a tall man with aviator glasses, Erasmo's friend, the same man who had raised a toast to the Havana Yacht Club at the Angola *paladar* the night before. Arkady ran the glasses along the other seated guests. In the front row's places of honor were an empty chair and a man with a gray beard who looked as if he had been big once but had since shrunk into a stiff green shell of ironed fatigues. He had the abstracted expression of an old man regarding a thousand grandchildren whose names he could no longer keep track of.

Arkady went back to the patrol boat. By now, Ofelia ought to have communicated with someone, and although the *Gavilan* ran low in the water Arkady assumed it appeared on the patrol boat's radar. Whether or not Ofelia had made contact, the *Gavilan* was within four hundred meters of the stage. Either the patrol boat at the dock would come out to inspect the *Gavilan* or another patrol boat was closing from a different direction. Arkady was surprised that the *Gavilan* hadn't been challenged already by radio.

O'Brien said, "The marvelous thing about you, Arkady, is that you're both suicidal and insatiably curious. 'What' isn't good enough for you, you have to know the 'why.' When you came out to the boat you had to know something like this was going to happen, but you had to see."

"And then maybe fuck us up," Walls said. "Go out in a blaze of glory."

"Or leave a message behind," O'Brien said. "Look on the beach to the left of the stage."

Arkady swung his glasses and saw Ofelia work her way from the spectators. He'd missed her when she was in the crowd. A PNR shield was pinned to her white halter. He waited for her to move toward the patrol boat or the stage. Instead, she moved in the opposite direction. At her side, being helpful, was Mostovoi, a camera bag swinging from his shoulder.

"What do you want?" Arkady asked.

"I have what I want," O'Brien said.

Walls nudged Arkady. "You're missing the show."

Arkady swung his glasses to the reviewing stand and saw the man in aviator glasses carry a man-sized doll with a cane and a red bandanna down to the chair in the front row, where a drummer helped make the doll sit up, its face turned toward the man on its right. Chango and the Comandante. Arkady focused on the doll's bandanna and walking stick, different from the ones he had left on a doll's body at the Rosita. The Comandante returned the doll's gaze at first, then looked up and joked with his friend in the aviator glasses, who laughed and retreated from the stage to the side of the stands, where he was joined in the crowd by Dr. Blas, too energetic to stay in the shadows any longer. Arkady refocused on Chango, on the doll's roughly molded head, patched and repainted, with the same glittering eyes.

"This is murder," Arkady said.

"Not just murder, please," O'Brien begged, "This is the elimination of an individual who has survived more assassination attempts than anyone else in history."

"That demands respect right there," said Walls.

"And let's admit it," O'Brien said, "the death of this man is the only crime down here of any interest. You can steal five dollars or a million, it's still petty crime while he's alive. Because you can't leave with it and essentially it's all his."

"You can stop," Arkady said. "You haven't done anything violent with your own hands yet. I know Pribluda's death was an accident."

"See, we told you we never touched him," Walls said. "We had no idea where Sergei disappeared to."

"But we couldn't stop now," said O'Brien. "In the last forty years only one generation of Cubans has tasted independent thought, one group has experienced command on the battlefield and operated in the greater world. There are two hundred forty generals in the Cuban army, and the army is getting smaller and smaller. Where do you think they're going to go, what do you think they're going to do? This is their prime, their window of opportunity."

"Their time to throw the dice?"

"Yes."

"And they all ordered lobster."

O'Brien gave Arkady an appreciative smile and lifted his own pair of binoculars. "That's right, very good. That was the vote. They all wanted in."

The pageant had begun again. Golden skirts and brown legs obscured the guest of honor in his front-row seat. His green cap seemed to weigh as heavily on him as a bishop's miter. Chango's roughly molded face was slightly cocked, glass eyes bright in the lights. At the side of the stage the man in aviator glasses reached down to shake someone's hand. Erasmo. Appearing gravely pale and weary, the mechanic lifted his eyes toward the *Gavilan*, although Arkady knew the boat had to be invisible from shore.

More figures slipped out of the back rows of the reviewing stand; Arkady recognized them all from the *paladar* Angola. The front rows appeared mesmerized by swirling skirts, the insinuating pace of the drums booming from speakers, echoing off the clubhouse. Chango's head listed heavily to the bearded man on his right. "This Side to Enemy," Arkady thought. No doubt the man's uniform fit as badly as it did in part because of an armored vest, which would stop a small-caliber bullet but not a shaped charge of dynamite. No shards or ball bearings, Arkady guessed. They didn't want a general slaughter, just an effective circle of impact, and who more expert with explosions than Erasmo?

He swung the glasses and found Ofelia and Mostovoi going in a completely different direction, working their way far from the stage and along the sand to a white wall that separated the grounds of the Havana Yacht Club from the neighboring beach. Arkady saw Mostovoi check his watch.

"It's La Concha, the old casino," Mostovoi said. "I consider it one of the most romantic settings in Havana. I've shot here daytime, nighttime, it's got that exotic feel that women love."

He ran his hand up a column. For all the police and military presence on the other side of the beach wall, Ofelia and Mostovoi had this area entirely to themselves. It was now the social center for a catering union, but she remembered that before the Revolution it had been not only a casino but a Moorish fantasy, with a minaret, date palms and orange trees, tiled roof. Ofelia and the Russian stood in the long shadow of a colonnade of horseshoe arches. The fact that she had followed Mostovoi didn't mean she trusted him. For all his assurances there was a shiftiness about him. His beret shifted, his hair shifted and his eyes seemed to be over everything, especially her. She wouldn't have spent a minute with him except for the fact that he claimed to know where Arkady wanted to meet her.

"First one place, then another? Why would he come here?"

"You'll have to ask him that. Do you mind if I take a picture of you?"

"Now?"

"While we're waiting. I think that Cuban women are nature's children. The eyes, the warm color, a lushness that can be almost too overripe at times. Not you, though."

"Where and when exactly is Arkady coming?"

"Right here. Who can say exactly when with Renko?" Mostovoi unzipped his bag for a camera and a flash unit that he tightened into the camera shoe. The unit made a warm-up whine.

"No pictures." Ofelia wanted to keep eyes adjusted to the night sky, the arc of sand, the dark of the water. The last thing she needed was a flash. "You keep looking at your watch."

"For Arkady."

The white light blinded her. She was unprepared because Mostovoi shot without raising the camera and she saw nothing but a fixed image of flash unit's faceted lens and the photographer's smirk until she blinked her way back to normal.

"If you do that again," she said, "I will break your camera."

"Sorry, I couldn't resist."

"Was that a signal?" Arkady noticed that with the flash from the casino Walls eased the throttle forward, bringing the *Gavilan* even closer to the beach. Why wasn't the patrol boat at the dock responding?

Walls said, "When my friend John O'Brien plans something the *i*'s are dotted and the *t*'s are crossed."

"Thank you, George. The devil, as they say, is in the details. Speaking of whom . . ."

Ahead in the water was a *neumático* with a hand shielding a candle. As Walls slowed the boat to idle again, the *neumático* snuffed the flame with his fingers, spun his tube and paddled backward to the stern of the *Gavilan,* where Walls helped him on board and tied the tube to a transom cleat. Luna stood dripping in the cockpit. Wet, he had the dank look of a body disinterred and he stared at Arkady with anticipation.

"Now you'll know what it feels like," Luna promised.

"What feels like?"

"I'm sorry, Arkady," O'Brien said. "It's time to give up the coat now. In fact, everything. You can do it yourself or we can do it for you."

318

While Walls took the coat and the rest of Arkady's clothing, too, Luna went below to change clothes, a modesty that surprised Arkady. The sergeant reappeared in uniform swollen with a menace kept in thin control, and Arkady wondered how he had ever managed to throw Luna into a wall. He was, himself, past lifting weights or fattening up. Then it was Arkady's turn to put on Luna's sodden shorts and shirt. Up to the point of pulling on flippers Arkady considered himself relatively safe because they were so difficult to put on the feet of a dead man. With the flippers on he felt both unsafe and ridiculous. Still, a patrol boat had to be coming.

Holding the binoculars by the strap, O'Brien returned them to Arkady. "See how it ends."

Onstage, a melee of golden dancers moved to a quickening pace. Daughters of Oshun, Arkady thought. Well, he'd learned that much. It wouldn't be a detonation set by a timer, he thought, because there were too many variables in public events. The back two rows of the stands had thinned out. Erasmo backed his wheelchair from the stage. An ecstasy in rays of sweat flew from the dancers. Chango leaned. By the side of the stage a dozen men looked at their watches. In the front row, the leader himself and Chango seemed to look straight through the frenzy of the dancers. How the dancers could turn faster Arkady didn't know, but they did, their golden skirts spread and spinning at the runaway pace of the congas. He braced for the flare of explosion.

Instead, plainclothes men started to appear. They came in pairs, quietly taking away the man in aviator glasses, Blas and, one by one, the other men Arkady recognized from the *paladar*. Each man reacted with the same sequence of surprise, bafflement and resignation. Their military training showed. No one ran or called out at the moment of his arrest. Arkady looked for Erasmo being wheeled away. Instead, Erasmo seemed to be in charge of this new phase. Hardly anyone else in the audience seemed to notice, fixed as they were on blurred hands on drums and the golden skirts of sensuous Yemayas, every eye transfixed except for the old man in too much uniform in the front row. He dropped his head by small degrees until Arkady realized that under the bill of his cap the nation's leader was checking his own watch.

"He knew," Arkady said. "He knew about the plot."

"Much better," O'Brien said. "He helped start it. He does it every few years to weed out malcontents. The same as he did with Isabel's father. The Comandante didn't last this long by waiting for a conspiracy to come for him."

"Erasmo helped, too?"

"In spite of himself, Erasmo is a Cuban patriot."

"You took care of the details?"

"More than mere details."

"The talk about the Havana Yacht Club?"

"All true to a degree. The fact is, Arkady, revolutions are chancy things, you never know how they're going to turn out. I prefer to bet with the house, whoever the house is. The glasses?" He took the binoculars from Arkady by the strap and lowered them into a plastic Ziploc bag, which he placed in the seabag that was supposedly Pribluda's. "There's nothing trickier than an assassination, especially an assassination that's not supposed to succeed. You have to keep the means and trigger of destruction in your own hands. And you have to undermine the conspirators in the public eye. These are highly regarded men, military heroes. It helps paint them black if the man who actually tries to set off the blast isn't Cuban at all but a generally unpopular figure as, say, a Russian. A dead Russian, to be precise."

Walls and O'Brien weren't just waiting to explain how brilliant they were, Arkady knew. There was more to come. Luna opened a cockpit bench to take out a speargun. He placed the butt against his hip, cocked the power bands and slid into the muzzle a shaft with a spearhead with folded wings for barbs. No patrol boat, Arkady understood, was on the way.

"Why would anyone connect me to the blast?"

Walls held up another Ziploc bag so that Arkady could see inside a television remote control. "Remember the monitor you turned on for John at the Riviera? We modified the remote, it's a radio transmitter now, but it still has your fingerprints. Then, people saw the doll in Pribluda's apartment while you were there. We may have lost Sergei, but John said you were so bright you'd serve even better."

O'Brien answered his cell phone. Arkady hadn't heard a ring. After a word of satisfaction, O'Brien folded the phone up.

Luna fished in the pockets of Arkady's coat and found the snapshot of Pribluda, Mongo and Erasmo. "Fuck your Havana Yacht Club." He tore the picture into pieces that he threw onto the water. He kicked the inner tube off the transom after the bits of paper. "Get in."

Standing at the carved doors of the old gambling hall, Ofelia caught the button tones and soft fluorescence of Mostovoi's cell phone. The call was over in a second.

"Who did you call?"

"Friends. Have you ever posed?"

"What friends?"

"At the embassy. I explained that I was helping somebody, which I certainly am trying to do. I meant it about posing."

"For what?"

"Something different."

Her attention was half on Mostovoi talking to her in the dark interior of the hall and half on the pale strand of the beach. Music played on the other side of the beach wall. A rumba for Yemaya.

"How different?"

"I mean very different."

She couldn't tell what was in the room, but its large space magnified sound, and she heard Mostovoi swallow in a way she found unpleasant. All she could see of him was the oily eye of his camera and she talked mainly to keep track of him.

"What was in this room?"

He slipped sideways from the moonlight at the door.

"What was here? It was the main casino. Chandeliers from Italy, tiles from Spain. Roulette tables, craps, blackjack. It was a different world."

"Well, no one's here now."

"I know what you mean. You think maybe Renko went to the plane?"

Would Arkady do that? she wondered. Slip away without a word? It was one of the things men did best. They didn't need planes, they just disappeared. Her mother could count them: Primero, Segundo and now Tercero. Blas would deliver Pribluda's body to the airport. Arkady still might wander in like a beachcomber or stroll down the portal of arches that framed the sea, but it was more likely with every minute that he had accomplished the classic retreat, the exit with no good-bye. She felt profoundly stupid.

"I could see you in any number of poses," Mostovoi said.

But she thought about Arkady's black coat and decided, no, his problem was that he abandoned no one. One way or another, he was going to come.

"There in the moonlight," Mostovoi said, "is perfect."

Ofelia heard the shutter of his camera click, although the flash failed. She heard two more rapid clicks before she realized they weren't from a shutter but from a hammer on the empty breech of a gun. She tried to dig her own gun out of her straw bag, but it was under Rufo's phone. The hammer clicked again. When Ofelia found her own gun, it was tangled with straw. She fired one wild round that exploded the bottom of the bag. Something crushed the plaster wall by her ear. She dropped to her back and held her gun with both hands more deliberately. Her second shot through the bag lit Mostovoi, a flash of him swinging his gun down like a club. The third tunneled into his mouth.

Arkady floated in the tube on a short rope from the stern of the *Gavilan*. The Caribbean was warm, the net a hammock, the rubber tube actually cushy, but he felt as if he were looking up from the bottom of a well at O'Brien, Walls with the gun and Luna with the speargun. They blocked the stars. Arkady would have liked to think at least he was stalling. No, they were only waiting, having outthought and outmuscled him all the way. One stunning accomplishment: he not only found out how Pribluda was duped but got to be the dupe too. Finally a *neumático* himself.

Their heads lifted at the sound of gunshots.

Walls said, "The son of a bitch was supposed to use a silencer."

"And why three shots?" asked O'Brien.

A cell-phone tone came from Luna's shirt pocket. He flipped the phone open and answered. As he listened he turned toward the beach.

"Who is it?" Walls said.

"It's her, the detective." O'Brien followed Luna's eyes turn to the casino; it really was wonderful to see how quickly the man calculated, Arkady thought. "She got Mostovoi's phone. Or Rufo's, and she's using the memory." O'Brien told Luna, "Hang up."

Luna raised the speargun for quiet and pressed the phone tight against his ear.

"Take the phone from him," O'Brien told Walls.

Luna pointed the spear at Arkady. "She says he never harmed Hedy. You told me he came looking for me. What she says is he wasn't after me at all."

"How does she know?" Walls said.

"The night someone killed Hedy, she says he was with her."

"She's lying," Walls said. "They sleep together."

"That's why I believe her. I know her and she knows me. Who hurt my Hedy?"

"Do you believe this?" O'Brien appealed to Arkady as one sane man to another. "George, will you please take his fucking phone away?"

"Your stupid Hedy," Walls told Luna, "was a whore."

The speargun jumped and a steel shaft with a line of white nylon stuck out of Wall's stomach. When he looked down blood under pressure sprayed his face.

"George," O'Brien said.

Walls sat down on the gunwale, raised his gun and shot Luna, who took a single backward step before moving forward. As Walls tried for another clear shot the two men fell over the side.

Arkady began climbing out of the tube. On deck O'Brien had pulled the second speargun from the cockpit bench and was trying to insert the spear and pull back the two stiff elastic power bands, not an easy task at the best of times, worse standing amid loose spear cable and blood on the deck. But as Arkady came up over the transom O'Brien managed to notch one band and pull the gun's trigger, and Arkady found himself on his back in the water, a spear through his forearm and the spearhead lodged shallowly in his chest, the spear's force spent on his arm. Spear cable led back to O'Brien, who had one tasseled shoe on the transom and was already, Arkady could tell, calculating ten or eleven moves ahead. With his free hand Arkady yanked the cable. O'Brien dropped the speargun overboard, but the line that tangled around his ankle stretched him over the polished mahogany. Arkady pulled with both hands and O'Brien slid all the way over the stern and in.

O'Brien shouted, "I can't swim!"

The *Gavilan* was low-slung enough for O'Brien to try to claw his way back on, but Arkady towed him by the line away from the boat. O'Brien turned to the inner tube, but his splashing chased the tube more than it closed the distance. The speargun floated, but not enough to hold up a man.

The spear tip's wings had spread outside the muscle of Arkady's chest. He closed them under the spear's sliding collar and drew the shaft from the arm while it was numb. With his good arm he swam underwater. The sea was a cave around a quarter-moon with glints of fish. On the other side of the boat Walls and Luna still struggled, trying to climb over each other to the surface. Bubbles streaked from Wall's gun. Luna had wrapped the spear line around the other man's neck. Arkady came up for air and made his way back around the stern of the *Gavilan*. No more than a meter away the top of O'Brien's head bobbed in the water.

The patrol boat hadn't moved, although Arkady saw lights along the casino beach. The yacht club was still bright.

He could haul himself onto the *Gavilan*, but at this point Arkady was happy to rest, watch the stars swarm overhead and float on a blackness that held him up.

28.

Snow fell again in April, enough to dust the streets and spiral in confusion around the intersections. Trucks hunched along the embankment road with lights on, a winter habit dying as hard as winter itself.

Arkady had left the prosecutor's office and walked down to the embankment hoping to find fresher air along the river, but there really was no escaping the pollution, the usual pall mixed with snow into a sharp, urban brew. Streetlamps were on and pools of light swayed overhead, tugged this way and that by the wind. Buildings along this stretch of Frunzenskaya were an institutional yellow, etchings of themselves behind lines of snow. The river, choked with water and ice, ground against stone walls.

He'd gone a block before he realized that a man in a wheelchair was catching up with him at a determined pace. Not an easy task in such weather, he thought, with the wheels of the chair slipping on the slick pavement and detouring around the bodies in bedrolls who had taken up residence along the embankment. Arkady had stepped aside for the chair to pass when he saw who it was.

"Spring in the Arctic." Erasmo was packed into a parka, ski cap, damp leather gloves. He brushed snow off his beard and watched his breath with disgust. "How can you stand it?"

"You keep moving."

Erasmo looked massive in the parka and vibrantly healthy as only Cubans could in Moscow. When he offered his hand, Arkady waited until it dropped.

"What are you doing here?" Arkady asked.

"Renegotiating the sugar contract."

"Of course."

"Don't be that way," Erasmo said. "I'm in Moscow for one day. I called your office, and they said this was the route you were most likely to take. Please."

"Come on, then, I'll give you the Russian perspective." Arkady went at a slower pace while Erasmo rolled at his side. "'98 Jaguar, a banker who flies dollars out of Moscow in a Gulfstream jet. '91 Mercedes, a deputy minister or lesser mafioso. That homeless man under the streetlamp, well, he may be harmless or he might be an intelligence officer, you never know."

"Of course I was," Erasmo said. "Where else would we let a Russian spy live except over a spy of our own? It's elemental. I tried to warn you off at the graveyard. At the restaurant I told you to drop it. After you found Mongo you could have stopped."

"No."

"There's never any reasoning with you, no middle ground. How is the arm?"

"Nothing broken, thank you. It's my Cuban tattoo."

"I almost didn't recognize you. Here you are in a parka like me. What happened to the wonderful coat?"

"It is a wonderful coat, but I decided I was wearing it out. I still wear it on special occasions."

"Well, you're still alive, that's the main thing."

"No thanks to you. Why did you do it, Erasmo? Why lead your friends into a trap? What happened to my intrepid hero of Angola?"

"I had no choice. After all, the officers were already plotting. When the threat is from men I served with and loved, I mitigate the damage, channel them and do as little harm as possible. At least no one was killed."

"No one?"

"Very few. O'Brien and Mostovoi did some things I knew nothing about."

"But you tossed me to them like bait."

"Well, you proved to be more than just bait. Poor Bugai."

"He's still alive."

"For God's sake, do you have a cigarette?"

The snow was thicker. Arkady put his back to the wind, lit a couple of cigarettes and gave one to Erasmo, who inhaled and coughed at the insult to his lungs. He took in a wider scope of the street to include figures stirring the flakes with brooms. "Russian women. Remember that day we drove the Jeep down the Malecón?"

"Of course."

"How long do you think that's going to last? Not very. You know, sometime we're going to look back at the Special Period and say, well, it was a ridiculous mess but it was Cuban. It was the sunset, the last Cuban age. Miss it?"

They had come to a halt under a lamp. Flakes sparkled on Erasmo's beard and brows.

"How is Ofelia?" Arkady said. "I tried to reach her through the PNR and there was no reply. I don't have a home address for her. That night they just wrapped up my arm, threw some clothes on me and put me on the plane with Pribluda. I never saw her."

"And you won't. Keep in mind, Arkady, you left a lot of confusion behind you. Detective Osorio will be kept busy for quite a while. But she sent this." Erasmo removed his gloves and felt inside his parka until he pulled out a color snapshot of Ofelia. She was in an orange two-piece on a beach with her two girls and a tall, light-brown, handsome man. The girls looked up at him with adoration and clung proudly to his hands. A conga drum was slung over his shoulder as if music might be called for at any moment, and on his face was a smirk somewhere between penitence and self-satisfaction. Behind this domestic tableau, planted on a towel by the weight of her horror, was Ofelia's mother.

"Which father?" Arkady asked.

"The smaller girl's."

Arkady couldn't see anything coerced about the photograph, no ominous shadows on the sand or signs of anxiety besides the family tension. Ofelia, however, seemed to be totally apart from the others. Her hair was damp, combed into ink-black waves. Her lips open, on the point of speaking. Her expression said, yes, this is the situation, but the intentness of her eyes had nothing do with anyone else in the picture, as if she were looking not from the photograph but through it.

Nothing was written on the back.

"You don't seem particularly moved," Erasmo said.

"Should I be?"

"Yes, I would think so. I wanted to reassure you that all in all, things came out pretty well for the detective."

"Yes, they look happy."

"I wouldn't go that far. Anyway, you can keep the picture. That's the reason I came out in this blizzard looking for you just to give it to you."

"Thank you." Arkady unzipped his parka so he could put the photograph safely away without bending it.

Erasmo blew on his hands before pulling his gloves back on. Suddenly he looked miserable. "Cold people for a cold climate, that's all I can say." Snow started to clump on his brows and under his nose. He swung his chair and gave Arkady half a wave. "I know my way back."

"Just follow the river."

Going back, the wind was against Erasmo. He leaned into it, bucking the oncoming current of headlights, his wheels losing a little friction on the melting snow but maintaining the speed of a man who knows where a warm room waits.

Arkady's apartment was in the opposite direction. Headlights fanned his shadow ahead of him. Like pachyderms, trucks stepped in and out of potholes. In true winter the reflection of lights off river ice made an illuminated path through the city, but a late snowfall merely dissolved in sheets into black water. Traffic police waded between cars, pulling aside that luckless soul whose lights were deemed malfunctioning until dollars, not rubles, passed hands. It was the sort of evening, Arkady thought, when each individual apartment window looked like a craft tossing in a dangerous sea. The Kremlin was out of sight but not its bonfire glow. Snow outlined lampposts, gutters, sills; packed against truck tarps and wing mirrors and on the collars people clutched up to their eyes; melted at the wrist and neck, trickled down the arm and chest; flew down one flagstone wall of the river and up the other like sparks from a chute; turned the trees of the park into whitecaps; made each step a visible memory and then covered it over.

ABOUT THE AUTHOR

MARTIN CRUZ SMITH is the author of *Gorky Park,* as well as *Stallion Gate, Polar Star,* and *Rose,* among other novels. He lives in California with his wife and three children.

A NOTE ON THE TYPE

This book was set in Fairfield, the first typeface from the
hand of the distinguished American artist and engraver
Rudolph Ruzicka (1883–1978). In its structure Fairfield
displays the sober and sane qualities of the master craftsman
whose talent has long been dedicated to clarity. It is this
trait that accounts for the trim grace and vigor,
the spirited design and sensitive balance, of this
original typeface.

Rudolph Ruzicka was born in Bohemia and came to America
in 1894. He set up his own shop, devoted to wood engraving
and printing, in New York in 1913 after a varied career
working as a wood engraver, in photoengraving and banknote
printing plants, and as an art director and freelance artist. He
designed and illustrated many books, and was the creator of a
considerable list of individual prints—wood engravings, line
engravings on copper, and aquatints.